· The Werewolf

Library of World Fiction

Kallocain
Karin Boye
Translated from the Swedish by Gustaf Lannestock

The Werewolf
Aksel Sandemose
Translated from the Norwegian by Gustaf Lannestock

The Werewolf

By AKSEL SANDEMOSE

VARULVEN

TRANSLATED FROM THE NORWEGIAN BY
GUSTAV LANNESTOCK
WITH AN INTRODUCTION BY
HARALD S. NÆSS

THE UNIVERSITY OF WISCONSIN PRESS

The University of Wisconsin Press
1930 Monroe Street
Madison, Wisconsin 53711

www.wisc.edu/wisconsinpress/

3 Henrietta Street
London WC2E 8LU, England

3   4   5

Printed in the United States of America

Library of Congress Cataloging-in-Publication Data
Sandemose, Aksel, 1899–1965
[Varulven. English]
The Werewolf / Aksel Sandemose ;
translated by Gustaf Lannestock; with an introduction by Harald S. Næss.
(Library of world fiction.)
Originally published by H. Aschehoug & Co. (W. Nygaard)
ISBN 0-299-03744-4 (pbk.: alk. paper)
Library of Congress Catalog Card Number 65-24188

Introduction

When the Danish-born writer, Aksel Sandemose, settled in Norway in
1929 it was because his temperament was rather more Norwegian than
Danish. He had strong things to say, and he wanted to be outspoken; he
was less concerned with artistry and composition than with a shocking
message. Critics received his first major book with enthusiasm, though in
some conservative quarters labels like "confused" and "hysterical" were
used, as they have been since of Sandemose's work. But the confusion
referred to has given Sandemose his place in Norway's literary history;
he is one of the few experimenters in recent Norwegian literature, and
his attempts to change the conventional form of the novel have been
hailed in all Scandinavian countries. Sandemose's other great asset is his
social indignation—his so-called hysteria. The "Jante law," a list of
proscriptions by which modern society cudgels each of its members into
conformity, became famous with the publication of *A Fugitive Crosses
His Tracks*. Alfred Kazin read this work by the angry young Norwegian
and found "the average novel perfunctory by comparison."

At sixty-six,* Sandemose still shocks readers, but his dreams are less
distant than in his earlier works. For all along Sandemose has had
dreams, and in spite of his seemingly somber outlook they have been
constructive dreams of how enlightenment will lead mankind toward a
state of freedom and harmony where actions are determined by reason
rather than by passion.

* Sandemose died August 5, 1965, while this book was in press.

Aksel Sandemose was born in Nykøbing Mors, Denmark, on March 19, 1899. His father, Jørgen Nielsen, was a blacksmith; his mother, Amalie Jacobsdatter Sandemose, was a Norwegian who had come to Denmark in the 1870's to work as a housemaid. After leaving school, Sandemose attended a one-year seminary, 1914–15, then went to sea and later stayed for shorter periods in Newfoundland and the Canadian prairies. During the 1920's he held a variety of positions, working for some time as a journalist with the Copenhagen papers *København* and *Berlingske Tidende,* besides traveling (Canada, West Indies), and writing six books.

The characters in Sandemose's first stories are settlers in Labrador or sailors on the North Atlantic. Critics were eager to show that older patterns, especially the style of Johannes V. Jensen, had influenced the young writer more than was good for him, though they did admit that his refreshing descriptions of life at sea had brought something new to Danish literature. And in the way their people thought and acted these early tales already struck a note of Sandemose's main theme—the outcast. His first success in this new field was *Klabavtermanden* (*The Klabauter Man*, 1927), a strange story of a captain who, for violating a young girl, is doomed to sail the seas forever. *Ross Dane* (1928), a more conventional novel of Scandinavian immigrants in Canada, was also well received, and Sandemose was given a Danish stipend. But during the following year he settled in Norway, where he has lived ever since.

Sandemose's next book, *En sjømann går iland* (*A Sailor Disembarks,* 1931), was in Norwegian, and was the first of four books about Espen Arnakke. It consists of two rather loosely connected parts, of which the first treats a crucial event in Espen's life: his slaying of a hated but admired companion, in Misery Harbor, Newfoundland. The second part of the book, in which Espen finds himself among settlers on the Canadian prairies, is rather low-keyed and uneventful by comparison. Espen Arnakke's childhood milieu, the town of Jante where the murderer grew up, is the subject of the important novel, *En flyktning krysser sit spor* (*A Fugitive Crosses His Tracks,* 1933). Espen's life is further traced in the books *Der stod en benk i haven* (*A Bench Stood in the Garden,* 1937) and *Brudulje* (*Hullabaloo,* 1938). The Canadian setting in the second part of *A Sailor Disembarks* is repeated in the novel *September* (1939) and in some of the stories of the two collections *Sandemose forteller* (*Sandemose Tells Stories,* 1937) and *Fortellinger fra andre tider* (*Stories from Other Days,* 1940).

Typical of Sandemose's work habits is the revision and republishing of earlier works. In 1932 *The Klabauter Man* appeared in a new (Norwegian) edition; and the author has claimed that even *Vi pynter oss med horn* (*Horns for Our Adornment*, 1936) is nothing but a third, greatly revised edition of the old Klabauter Man story. This novel was so harshly criticized for "immoral" language that Sandemose brought suit against the reviewer. He lost, but many prominent people, among them the Christian writer Sigrid Undset, supported the book against its severe critic. In 1955, *A Fugitive Crosses His Tracks* was republished, and in the text of this new revised edition the author had incorporated *A Bench Stood in the Garden*. Sandemose's revising was even applied to the work of other writers. A strange book, Ole C. Hansen's *Reisen til New Zealand* (*Journey to New Zealand*, 1935), is a Sandemose adaptation of the chaotic manuscript of a nearly illiterate Norwegian sailor.

After the German invasion of Norway Sandemose was active in the resistance movement and in 1941 had to flee to Sweden. Here, in 1944, he published a book in Swedish, *Det gångna är en dröm* (*The Past Is a Dream*), which did not appear in Norwegian until 1946. By that time Sandemose had moved back to Norway and written another novel, *Tjærehandleren* (*The Tar Dealer*, 1945), the story of a marriage swindler. World War II, forming part of the background of this and the previous novel, is the setting of Sandemose's next book, *Alice Atkinson og hennes elskere* (*Alice Atkinson and Her Lovers*, 1949), which takes place in England and Germany; while a following novel, *En palmegrønn øy* (*Island of Green Palms*, 1950), is a humorous fantasy of seventeenth-century treasure hunters. After his return to Norway Sandemose settled with his family on a small farm, Kjørkelvik near Risør. From here he sent out a quarterly journal, *Årstidene* (*The Seasons*, 1951–55), written entirely by himself. In 1954 a volume of memoirs, *Rejsen til Kjørkelvik* (*Journey to Kjørkelvik*), was published in Denmark. More recently Sandemose letters have appeared regularly in the popular weekly *Aktuell* (Oslo). Since 1952, Sandemose has received a yearly stipend from the Norwegian state.

In 1958 Sandemose published his great novel *Varulven* (*The Werewolf*), which was followed in 1961 by a second part, *Felicias bryllup* (*Felicia's Wedding*). Between the two novels appeared *Murene rundt Jeriko* (*The Walls Around Jericho*, 1960), which is a volume of essays and stories in memory of his son Espen, who died in 1955, and his wife Eva, who died in 1959. Another novel, *Mytteriet på barken Zuidersee* (*Mutiny on the Ship Zuidersee*), was published in 1963.

Sandemose does not write plays or poetry. His forms have always been either the essay or the story; and the alternating narrative and essayical digression which make up the curious plotless course of the typical Sandemose novel cohere only through focus on a chief character or set of characters. *Alice Atkinson and Her Lovers* consists of three letters, of which one occupies nine-tenths of the book; *The Past Is a Dream* is a diary of sorts, with four prefaces; *Felicia's Wedding* is supposed to take place in the narrator's mind during a plane ride from Stockholm to Oslo in April 1959, but there are reports in this book of things happening in 1961. Deliberate disruption of chronology is perhaps the most typical feature of a Sandemose novel. Some have used the term "archaeological" of his method; i.e., a careful unearthing of different layers at different levels. In a Freudian manner, relics of the past are dug up and sorted out so as to produce in the end some meaningful torso of a personality. The novels are often written in the first person and have the form of a confession addressed to a friend or close relative. Their subject is love and murder.

Sandemose's books are also autobiographical to a greater degree than is normally the case. With certain natural reservations, dates and place names as well as many incidents correspond to the circumstances of Sandemose's own life, and the result is an intensification of suspense: "Is he really a murderer?" In this respect there is little difference between Sandemose's fiction and his memoirs; they are both, to use Goethe's title, *Dichtung und Wahrheit*. Sandemose is a *Dichter* of his own life in the sense that he adapts, abridges, and arranges; but also in the sense that when he speaks, the world recognizes itself. By his own account, what he writes "is no novel, and if the result is a work of literature, it is unpremeditated. It is not my intention that what I tell you should be a cosmos. It is a tool in my hand to complete my own cosmos. As I write I look deeper into myself." Regarding his subject matter Sandemose says: "I believe I have never had any other goal than finding out what man is. Wherefrom? Wherefore?" And he adds, "I feel deep contempt for people who sit scribbling together words, sentences, chapters and do not move on the outermost edge of consciousness where you hear the screams from the inferno."

In Sandemose's production three works stand out: *A Fugitive Crosses His Tracks, The Past Is a Dream,* and *The Werewolf.* These are the canonical books of his religion, and Sandemose enthusiasts will read and reread its myths for the beauty and intensity of their message. The three works are from different stages in the author's development, and yet they belong together in some dialectic scheme whereby the themes of the first two blend and reach a resolution in the third.

A Fugitive Crosses His Tracks is the story of Espen Arnakke, who once killed a friend when this friend took his girl away from him. At that moment all his past defeats were gathered as in one focus and resulted in the murder. The book is a panorama of the boy's past, seen like glimpses of night landscape illuminated by lightning. A few situations are sweet with happy memories, several are full of boisterous humor, but for the most part Espen is possessed with hatred as he recalls life in his home town of Jante. Jante is the symbol of all his tormentors, as well as of John Wakefield, whom he killed in Misery Harbor. Jante has only one desire—to force all men down to its own low level of happiness and intelligence. Jante holds Jante down by means of a cruel decalogue which runs monotonously as follows:

> Thou shalt not believe thou *art* something.
> Thou shalt not believe thou art as good as *we*.
> Thou shalt not believe thou art more wise than *we*.
> Thou shalt not fancy thyself better than *we*.
> Thou shalt not believe thou knowest more than *we*.
> Thou shalt not believe thou art greater than *we*.
> Thou shalt not believe *thou* amountest to anything.
> Thou shalt not laugh at *us*.
> Thou shalt not believe that anyone is concerned with *thee*.
> Thou shalt not believe thou canst teach *us* anything.

Espen, unlike other Jante dwellers, does not forget his defeats. His good memory becomes his weapon: "Journeying back to the past for the purpose of seeing how the whole thing had really been I eventually found myself standing with my bloody knife in hand before the law of Jante." When *A Fugitive Crosses His Tracks* appeared, critics pointed out that while it did give a painful and powerful picture of a tormented youth, it broke down as a gospel of salvation, as a contribution to a better social order. But how can Espen point to a successful therapy when he is not free? He is still a fugitive; in spite of his apparent emancipation he still lives in the shadow of the Jante law. He is obsessed with hatred like an animal thirsting for revenge.

In his bitter review of the past, Espen's honesty will not permit him to overlook the days of happiness when the children played in Adamsen's barn (Adamsen's barn being the wondrous land which adults may view from afar, but never enter). In *The Past Is a Dream* Sandemose's diarist, the middle-aged John Torson, is overcome by an urge to see this lost paradise. Torson is a well-to-do San Francisco businessman visiting his home parish in Norway before and during the early parts of World War II. Immediately upon his arrival he is involved in a murder case, which by his account remains an unsolved mystery, but in which the reader is given to understand that he is the murderer. Later he sees an impoverished, shapeless woman of fifty—the mother of eleven children—and dimly recognizes her as the Agnes for whom he would once have given his life, before she took other lovers and turned him into a fugitive. Now, in desperation, he relives their distant love affair, with another woman. He believes Agnes has come back to him as Susanne, wife of his only good friend, the great author Gunder Gundersen, whose downfall from drink and jealousy he watches with perverse joy.

John Torson is a kind of demon-magician. With his money he buys friends and makes them play over again the sweet play of his childhood. Still, the astounding events of his cool confession are only an attempt to talk himself out of the truth: as he relives the dream of the past he cannot avoid an agonizing identification with all its characters. He is at one time the murderer and the slain, the lover and the cuckold, the poet and his mad twin brother. And even at that he must confess: "I have not told you of the unifying power behind it all, Satan's eye which was upon me all the time." John Torson's actions appear consistently irrational; he seems at all times in the hands of powers outside himself which lead and protect him. But he is led in accordance with a certain pattern. Though he had no reason to kill a man he did not know, the murder does make sense as a symbol. Through it John Torson avenges himself on a society which has struck him with blindness so that he cannot look upon love as a free man: his sight will always be dimmed by jealousy and by the primitive man's vision of his *virgo immaculata*. As a novel *The Past Is a Dream* appears structureless; the "plot" moves back and forth in a manner typical of Sandemose's "archaeological" approach. The book has less force, but more tragic beauty than *A Fugitive Crosses His Path*; it affirms faith in a "distant dream," a faith reflected in its portrayal of Norway's stubborn resistance to Nazi force and Nazi ideas: "We thought that every man would be for sale, if only the price were right. Now we know it is not so."

The Werewolf is an answer to questions posed in Sandemose's two other great novels. Can there be no harmony in society? Is there only the choice of being crushed into conformity or else driven out as a fugitive? Also, is there no way out of jealousy, no true equality between the sexes, so that woman is neither a holy virgin nor a prostitute, but another human being? In *The Werewolf* three people, two men and a woman, succeed in arresting their fugitive selves and realizing their dreams in the present. In the midst of Jante they build an Adamsen's barn for adults and live in it until the forces symbolized by the werewolf (in the person of Gulnare) destroy their quiet happiness. These characters are marked in some way by the past; to use Sandemose's language, they have all met the werewolf—a complex symbol into which the author has worked all the destructive pettiness and negation that the Jante law voices. Essentially the werewolf symbolizes a perverted lust for power, the desire to force one's will on others, to possess others and control their thoughts and feelings, and in the end to press all society into a mirthless monotony. In this book, as in *The Past Is a Dream*, the demon or werewolf is manifested most clearly in the feeling known as jealousy. To fight jealousy, therefore, is the main concern of the book's three heroes—Jan Venhaug, his wife Felicia, and her lover Erling Vik. "Hero" is not an inappropriate term, for their lives are heroic, their stature is out of the ordinary, they practice what to others is yet only a dream. But they are modern heroes with all the marks of lost battles. The author Erling Vik cannot free himself from a feeling of social inferiority; his small-town background and his working-class upbringing mark his relationship to middle-class Gulnare and to upper-class Felicia. His relationship to Gustav is also important and shows that though he has at last outgrown his fear of the older brother, he is still left with a kind of perverse respect for this stubborn, simple-minded Jante man. Serious consequences of their struggles against the werewolf are Erling Vik's alcoholism and Felicia's "séances" in the greenhouse. When she exposes her naked body to the passionate peeping of a local werewolf—stupid, "innocent" Tor Anderssen—it is a symbolic revenge on the meanness of male sexual brutality, and more especially on the ugly memory of her humiliation as an eighteen-year-old girl, when Erling Vik made love to her and casually went on his way, like a working-class boy defiling his princess.

The Werewolf is a conglomeration of thoughts and theories, of strange situations and striking personalities. In some parts, as in the story of the young Gulnare, all Sandemose's gifts combine to produce episodes of great beauty. But what makes this book different from his two other main works is the creation of an outstanding woman character, something more in the Ibsen than in the Strindberg tradition. Sandemose admires Strindberg above other writers, and it is natural that it should be that way; their temperaments seem so alike. But Strindberg's idea that jealousy is "a man's sense of cleanliness which prevents his thoughts from entering, through his wife, the sexual sphere of another man" (*Black Banners*) is now seen by Sandemose as by the fictional Jan Venhaug to be an idea of the past. "How strange," Jan remarks, "to see jealousy elevated to a first-class virtue, this feeling which is always combined with self-contempt and invariably ends in a complete feeling of shame." Sandemose does not encourage "immorality," but he defends his characters' right to live their lives as they see fit, and he condemns a person's or society's wish to regulate the life of others, if this wish is based on envy. In most cases, he concludes, it is: the werewolf is everywhere.

In *The Walls Around Jericho* Sandemose tells how *The Werewolf* grew out of an experience he once had on the west coast of Jutland. He lived in a small cabin among the sand dunes. It was out of season, and his only company was the constant roar of the North Sea waves. One day he saw in the far distance a girl who walked along the beach to the south. He stared at her until she disappeared from sight. Later he followed her footprints and tried to read her personality in the sand until the incoming tide washed it away. In recollection this simple incident became the source of "a never completed story of how love can grow out of a deep humiliation." "I have used this material often," Sandemose writes, "and at times I feel that after the experience on the beach I have written nothing that doesn't somehow center upon it." Perhaps this is the finest achievement of *The Werewolf*, that in Felicia the mysterious girl on the sand has come to life without losing any of the beauty, pride, and courage which are part of the vision.

Harald S. Næss

Madison, Wisconsin
May 1965

· Bibliography

WORKS BY AKSEL SANDEMOSE

In the Original Language (Norwegian, if
Not Otherwise Stated)

Fortællinger fra Labrador (Stories from Labrador). Copenhagen, 1923.
  Danish.
Storme ved Jævndøgn (Storms at Equinox). Copenhagen, 1924. Danish.
Ungdomssynd (Sins of Youth). Copenhagen, 1924. Danish.
Mænd fra Atlanten (Men from the Atlantic). Copenhagen, 1924.
  Danish.
Klabavtermanden (The Klabauter Man). Copenhagen, 1927. Danish.
  Norwegian edition: *Klabautermannen.* Oslo, 1932.
Ross Dane. Copenhagen, 1928. Danish.
En sjømann går iland (A Sailor Disembarks). Oslo, 1931.
En flyktning krysser sit spor (A Fugitive Crosses His Tracks). Oslo,
  1933. New edition, 1955.
Vi pynter oss med horn (Horns for Our Adornment). Oslo, 1936.
Sandemose forteller (Sandemose Tells Stories). Oslo, 1937.
Der stod en benk i haven (A Bench Stood in the Garden). Oslo, 1937.
Brudulje (Hullabaloo). Oslo, 1938.
Fortellinger fra andre tider (Stories from Other Days). Oslo, 1940.
Det gångna är en dröm (The Past Is a Dream). Stockholm, 1944. Swed-
  ish. Norwegian edition: *Det svundne er en drøm.* Oslo, 1946.
Tjærehandleren (The Tar Dealer). Oslo, 1945.

Alice Atkinson og hennes elskere (*Alice Atkinson and Her Lovers*). Oslo, 1949.

En palmegrønn øy (abbreviated title) (*Island of Green Palms*). Oslo, 1950.

Årstidene (*The Seasons*). A quarterly magazine. Oslo, 1951–55.

Rejsen til Kjørkelvik (*Journey to Kjørkelvik*). Copenhagen, 1954.

Varulven (*The Werewolf*). Oslo, 1958.

Murene rundt Jeriko (*The Walls Around Jericho*). Oslo, 1960.

Felicias bryllup (*Felicia's Wedding*). Oslo, 1961.

Mytteriet på barken Zuidersee (*Mutiny on the Ship Zuidersee*). Oslo, 1963.

In English Translation

A Fugitive Crosses His Tracks, trans. Eugene Gay-Tifft (from *En flyktning krysser sit spor*). New York, 1936.

Horns for Our Adornment, trans. Eugene Gay-Tifft (from *Vi pynter oss med horn*). New York, 1938.

"Murder in Gayeysgayey," trans. Lida Siboni Hansen, in *American-Scandinavian Review*, 26:63–66. New York, 1938.

"Stupidity Rampant," trans. Gerda Andersen, in *American-Scandinavian Review*, 32:254–57. New York, 1944.

"Journey to Kjørkelvik," in *The Norseman*, 14:54–59. London, 1956.

LITERATURE ON AKSEL SANDEMOSE

Braatøy, Trygve. "Kjærlighet og hat," in *Edda*, 32:153–78. Oslo, 1933.

Brochmann, Georg. "Sandemose-saken," in *Den norske forfatterforening*, pp. 418–36. Oslo, 1952.

Brøgger, Niels Christian. "En norsk Damaskusreise," in *Den nye moral og andre essays*, pp. 17–26. Oslo, 1934.

———. "Aksel Sandemose," in *Norsk Biografisk Leksikon*, 12:218–22. Oslo, 1954.

Groth, Helge. *Hovedlinjer i mellomkrigstidens norske litteratur*, pp. 257–59. Bergen, 1947.

Guterman, Norbert. Review of *A Fugitive Crosses His Tracks*, in *The New Republic*, 88:80. August 26, 1936.

Haaland, Arild. " 'Varulven'–'Flyktningen'–Tur-retur," in *Vinduet*, 19:22–31. Oslo, 1965.

Hoel, Sigurd. "Aksel Sandemose," in *Tanker om norsk diktning*, pp. 258–63. Oslo, 1955.

Houm, Philip. "Aksel Sandemose," in Bull, Paasche, *et al.*, *Norsk litteraturhistorie*, 6:420–38. Oslo, 1955.

Jarrett, Cora. Review of *A Fugitive Crosses His Tracks*, in *Saturday Review of Literature*, 14:11. July 18, 1936.

Johansen, F., and Johannes Væth. *Aksel Sandemose og Danmark: En bibliografi.* Copenhagen and Oslo, 1963.

Kazin, Alfred. Review of *A Fugitive Crosses His Tracks*, in *New York Herald Tribune Books*, July 12, 1936, p. 3.

Krog, Helge. "Aksel Sandemose," in *Meninger*, pp. 69–72. Oslo, 1947.

Kronenberger, Louis. Review of *A Fugitive Crosses His Tracks*, in *New York Times Book Review*, July 12, 1936, p. 1.

————. Review of *Horns for Our Adornment*, in *New York Times Book Review*, September 25, 1938, p. 26.

Larsen, Petter. "En morders barndom," in *Vinduet*, 16:93–101. Oslo, 1962.

Lindegren, Erik. "Flyktningen som emigrant," in *Bonniers Litterära Magasin*, 14:145–47. Stockholm, 1945.

Nordberg, Carl-Erik. "Sandemose, den obesegrade," in *Ord och Bild*, 69:457–72. Stockholm, 1960.

Popperwell, Ronald. "Aksel Sandemose: *Det svundne er en drøm*," in *Den 2. internasjonale studiekonferanse om nordisk litteratur*, pp. 10–18. Oslo, 1958.

Rugoff, Milton. Review of *Horns for Our Adornment*, in *New York Herald Tribune Books*, September 11, 1938, p. 13.

Schjelderup, Alv. G. "Aksel Sandemose," in *Samtiden*, 48:266–79. Oslo, 1937.

Storstein, Olav. "Aksel Sandemose," in *Fra Jæger til Falk*, pp. 142–48. Oslo, 1950.

Thesen, Rolv. "Perspektivets stil," in *Mennesket i oss*, pp. 117–31. Oslo, 1951.

Væth, Johannes. "En torpedo under arken," in *Vinduet*, 17:29–34. Oslo, 1963.

· Contents

· The Werewolf

HE BECAME AN UNCONQUERABLE LEGEND, EVEN TO HIMSELF.

Felicia Venhaug, one morning early in August, 1957, received a telephone call from Erling Vik; he was coming to Venhaug that same day.

When she hung up she tossed her head as a colt would do, making her mane of white hair fall back in order. She walked quickly in her flat shoes through the rooms, calling Julie, Erling's daughter; but there was no one else in the house. She stopped at a window and looked down into the garden, where Tor Anderssen, the gardener, was busy cutting some withered roses which he gathered in his old, badly worn hat.

Felicia knit her brows; the flower garden was none of Tor Anderssen's business, and least of all her rose garden. He had his definite domain—the kitchen garden, the fruit garden, and two of the three greenhouses. There, he was his own master as long as he met his obligations; he should keep away from her roses.

Her anger died down. She knew that if Erling hadn't called she wouldn't have cared whether the gardener tended her roses or not. But as she watched the man her expression grew more threatening; she clenched her fist around the key in her skirt pocket, the key to the third greenhouse, *her* greenhouse, and her lips parted in a smile that was difficult to interpret; perhaps scorn, with a touch of hate, or fear.

She took a step backward so as not to be seen by Tor Anderssen as he straightened his abnormally long back and scanned the windows of the manor house. Just then, in that very motion, he resembled a sea-animal that breaks through the surface and looks about, wet and repulsive, like a nightmare phantom, gray and depressing, the heavy-lidded eyes glancing past the windows. Tor Anderssen Haukas was his name, according to his papers, but if anyone called him "Haukas" you could see the anger smouldering in his eyes. What could be wrong with a fine name like Haukas? A good, euphonious name no one should be angry over. She had taken the trouble to investigate whether the name Haukas was listed in the criminal register, but it wasn't. Though she would have been glad to find some definite reason, it annoyed her that she had gone to the trouble. But no, he was angry only because his name was Haukas; he wanted to be called Anderssen. A good name, Anderssen, but Haukas wasn't despicable. She stared at him, wondering what other faults she could discover in him. His gray coat was too long, in spite of his great height, and then the pockets were so low that his arms hung perpendicular when he stood in his usual position with his hands in his deep pockets not reaching the bottom. Where could he have got hold of that ridiculous coat? The question irritated her; no one would ever order such a garment, and no tailor would originate it, except possibly Erling Vik's late, blessed father, the village tailor at Rjukan. And that walrus-mustache! Everything *hung* from that man as if he himself hung— which should have happened long ago, and which so easily could have, during the war; not a few would have enjoyed doing it, would have gladly stoned him and hanged him, she thought bitterly. But neither the Germans nor the native traitors had as long legs as Tor Anderssen, and no one was a better shot than he—that stupid fool Tor Anderssen who had been too dumb and unimaginative to believe that he might lose his life, and too cunning to be caught in a trap. People like him had survived, while her brothers . . .

Again Felicia sheeted in her sails; why bother about Tor Anderssen? But she clenched the hothouse key and thought: You should know who has telephoned! You should only know how he called at the right moment to let you slobber in vain!

She went down into the garden and pretended not to see the gardener. This was rather easy since one never knew exactly where he lurked. As she arrived at the greenhouse and pushed the key in the door she glanced around the garden; Tor Anderssen had vanished. She smiled. That demon would find no satisfaction today.

She walked the length of the hothouse, small birds fluttering about her, until she reached the ventilator at the far wall. She closed it and picked up a sackcloth towel from the floor and hung it over the ventilator. Then she walked back, still followed by the birds, turned the tap above the big barrel and let the water run. It was lukewarm; now in the summer it came from pipes that lay in the sun on the ground.

Felicia began to water the plants. Walking back and forth with the hose she now and then raised her free hand to remove a finch from her hair, all the while a smile playing over her lips, an absent look in her eyes.

Erling Vik lived at Lier and took the train from Drammen to Kongsberg when he came to visit at Venhaug, which was at Numedalslagen, west of the river, about fifteen miles north of the town of Kongsberg. He had been her lover for thirteen years, yet each time she was to see him she was seized with the same warm joy. She relived again *something* of what she had felt that day in spring of 1950, when he returned after sixteen months in the Canary Islands.

Then—1950, more than seven years ago—that demon Tor Anderssen had not yet taken her into his power, and today she would not enter into his mountain-hold. She had felt early in the morning that it would be today, but now Erling had called. Her knight Erling had, through a mere telephone call, saved her from the demon.

She felt that the reunion with Erling that time in 1950 had been their first great meeting as lovers, in spite of the fact that their affair had begun during their refugee days in Stockholm. That time in 1950 had been a reunion to dream about, glorious moments very few are destined to enjoy. In the beginning so much had been wrong—the war that had hurt her so profoundly, and all the conflicts arising when she was unwilling to choose between two men she loved.

Later, a shadow had come over her at Venhaug. She said to herself that Erling was to blame, but she said it with a feeling of pain that perhaps was a bad conscience. We have guilty thoughts, she whispered to her birds.

· *Alone in her lover's house*

It was on the ninth of May, 1950, and during the two following days that it had happened. She had slowed down the car in good time before she approached Erling's house. She breathed heavily and her hands trembled. She carefully drove the car well off the road to the right and stopped; she had better collect herself a little, she thought. Erling was not home as yet, but someone else might see her emotion, one could never be sure. And now she was trembling as violently as she had done the first few minutes, eight years earlier, after she had revenged her brothers, with the informer lying dead at her feet. Now she was afraid she might lose control of the car; she felt her heart swell and press her lungs against the sides of her breast, she felt she was choking with joy and about to faint, she groaned in futile anger as she bent forward over the steering wheel and fought her emotion. She thought wildly and blindly that it must stop when the shaking of the motor was stilled and no longer could affect her, although it never had affected her before. She bent over the wheel, kicked with her feet, bit her lips until she tasted blood. Then it died down. She remained slumped over the wheel, her eyes empty, until she heard another car approaching. She started the motor again, afraid the driver might stop and ask if she needed assistance. When he had passed, she backed her car up the narrow road to the house, since it would be impossible to turn in the small yard when she was ready to leave. She maneuvered the car behind the house and turned off the motor. She sat a few minutes and looked in front of her. There stood the house, as before, and it was spring. A wagtail showed off in front of the car. Sixteen months it was since she had seen Erling. What had he been up to in Las Palmas? she wondered. She hoped he had been tempted by the cheap wine. Every day. Night and day. His letters had been neither so many nor so long as when he was at home. For a moment it struck her that they had seemed unusually sober, written by a completely sober person. His newspaper articles had been warmer, and suddenly her eyes were wet, and she saw the wagtail in front of her as if it were walking on the bottom of a clear, vernal woodland lake, below a surface stirred by a light breeze. She dried her eyes, and the wagtail walked there again as a wagtail should.

When Felicia had unlocked the door of the house she walked from window to window and opened them up, sending the blinds heavenwards with a bang. The dust rose and tickled her nose. Then she wound the clock and set it: a quarter to two. Erling would arrive by plane in Fornebu about five and he had promised to take a taxi from the airport directly home to Lier. He ought to be here by seven at the latest, she thought, even counting minor delays. What his house needed first and foremost was a thorough cleaning. Strange how a house could stand unoccupied and still accumulate dirt and dust.

She had had the electricity turned on and made sure the telephone was connected. Now she must fix herself something to eat, brew coffee. She carried in food from the car—bread, butter, bacon. Soon the smell of steaming coffee came from the kitchen.

Felicia had regained her good humor again; it was half past two when she threw the cigarette butt into the fireplace and cleared the table. First she went after the window frames and sashes with soap and water, then the panes; they were as dirty as those in a storage room. Then she scrubbed the hopelessly worn floor. This was really a job for a laborer. While working in the corner farthest to the right, she happened to push the brush hard against the wall and had a feeling that the lowest log moved a little. Just then she didn't think much about it, but a few minutes later she went back and pushed it hard with the brush again. Yes, it did move a little, but how could that be? She fell down on her knees to inspect it and discovered that the two lowest logs were sawed through, a yard and a half or so from the corner. Felicia was known always to have her eyes open and to draw conclusions from what she saw. It took her less than a minute to discover the mechanism and open the secret safe. One by one she pulled out eight bottles of whisky and stood them in a row. She straightened up as she knelt there and looked sadly at the bottles. Erling had arranged to have a supply ready—that drunkard had looked ahead almost two years!

She bent down again and pulled out some packages. "The Story of Gulnare" was written on one of them. On another, "Letters from Felicia." She pulled out all the packages, but no more had writing on them to indicate they contained letters from women. Probably literary works, all of them, even "The Story of Gulnare." She found again the bundle with her own letters and started to cry.

Then she put everything back where it had been and closed the door. The rest of the scrubbing seemed much harder but at last she was finished. She sat down to rest with a glass of vermouth. It was now four o'clock. The house smelled clean. Whistling gaily she went after the kitchen utensils, scrubbed and washed and put them in place, polished all the glasses and inspected each one against the light. Erling was no model of tidiness but he was one to observe and was always deeply grateful. It was ten to five, now he would soon land at Fornebu and have thoughts for her only. She hoped he hadn't taken too much on the plane. She wasn't afraid he would be drunk, that wasn't it, but it was never good for him to drink when they were to meet, and now when it had been sixteen months since . . . . The mattress was spread over the car hood, in the sun; she had beaten it soundly. Now she carried it in. She made the bed, with sheets she had warmed over chair-backs in front of the fire, found blankets and pillows and arranged them with quick movements. Felicia was efficient and it suited her body to be—she knew her value. She followed meticulously the order of Holy Writ not to put your light under a bushel.

Soon she had the table laid—she had brought most of the food prepared—and she looked at the result of her handiwork; now for a few violets, they were just what was needed, with the sun glittering over plates and dishes. She sniffed the air, everything smelled clean. It was twenty minutes after five. From that moment her heart was in her throat, for Erling had promised to call from Fornebu. How often had this telephone rung during these last sixteen months, rung in a silent and empty room with no Erling? Faithful, in this word's common meaning, she had never felt he was. The telephone had rung and rung, but no Erling had answered, and when it stopped the room had been more silent than before.

Felicia put her hand in the tub of water on the edge of the stove; it was no longer ice-cold. She locked the door, pulled down the blinds, and doffed garment after garment. She wouldn't risk smelling of cleaning-woman or kitchen-frau. She lifted the tub to the floor, but then she hesitated; she wouldn't wish to be standing dripping from cold water when Erling called.

In that very moment the telephone rang, a shrill, longed-for sound that startled her. Her hand trembled violently and felt clammy when she lifted the receiver. His voice sounded as though he were in the room. She didn't recognize her own, it reminded her suddenly of the screech-ing wild doves in the forest at Venhaug early in the morning. She continued to call hello a few times after he had hung up.

She wanted to *see* her own happiness and walked slowly across the floor to the tall mirror she had once given him (for her own vanity's sake). He had insisted on a curtain for it. This she pulled aside now, and looked at herself with eyes that appeared black. Her cheeks were rosy; she knew that only a minute ago they had been pale. She looked for signs of age—will he think I still look young? Her breasts stood out, big and firm; it was only a week since she had stopped nursing. Slim as ever around the waist . . . . She was thirty-three and sighed in gratitude at the thought that civilization had granted women perhaps twenty years more than their mothers.

Felicia washed and put on a change of clothes, a flower-patterned short skirt, a jersey, sport socks, and flat shoes. She glanced at the clock from time to time as she meticulously attended to her hair and face. The sun was falling in streaks across the floor but it was beginning to grow chilly; she threw a few pieces of kindling and wood on the embers in the fireplace; she listened for cars passing by on the road. At last one of them slowed down and came to a stop. She remained standing, completely immobile, in the middle of the room, and waited.

• The occupation of Gotland

The following day they had been sitting out-of-doors on the sunny side of the house against the wall, talking a little but mostly dozing in the sunshine, lost in their own thoughts. The sun was high, there was a smell of earth and growth. The telephone rang a few times; Erling let it ring.

He was thinking of Gotland where he had never been, but where Felicia had. She and Jan had gone there with their daughter last year about midsummer, and she had written him four long letters while they were there. Jan had suggested the trip after the spring work was over, she had written. Erling knew she was expecting a child at that time and surmised there was some connection. It wasn't like Jan to suggest journeys anywhere; only reluctantly would he leave Venhaug. Happiness, reward, or what? he had thought, as he sat under the awning with the letter in his hand.

Those four letters had given him an impression of a fairyland Gotland which he wouldn't wish to destroy by going to see for himself how it really was. Only now was he beginning to realize this. It was something he had experienced this one single time only; any other time he had needed to see a country to gain an impression of it, even of its most elementary geographical features. Perhaps it is so with everything, he thought. My eyes must absorb it before it is mine. I will have no God until I stand before his throne, but due to one of God's most important edicts, I will never be permitted near him. Why this difference between our senses? "He that hath ears to hear, let him hear," it is written, but we who instead have eyes to see have no chance. No wonder I have always been afraid of losing my sight. It's strange that only teachers and preachers are created in God's image, and then they demand that we must believe in them too, apparently for no sensible reason. The world I *see*, in that same moment it is mine until my light is forever extinguished. Until that happens no one can rob me of anything in this world. As far as I understand not even in hell. I must be one of the world's richest men, one of the few who owns all he has seen. There is very little of Norway that isn't my personal belonging, I own forests and fields and whole cities, besides half of the West Indies, great parts of America, a bit of Morocco, places in Portugal, Spain, Italy, all of Copenhagen, Stockholm and three royal palaces, all of the wine-monopoly's shops, the Norwegian Folkmuseum, the Vatican, the whole heaven, the University Library, the sun and the moon and all the stars, and something of Felicia.

On top of everything, Felicia, most generously, had presented him with a Gotland, a Visby, and other fairyland objects. How had this been possible? She never formed her sentences particularly well when she wrote, and most of all it annoyed him when she put a full stop in the middle of a sentence and kept on writing about something else, which entirely pushed out the beginning of the sentence. Truly, she expressed herself in writing like a child in the third grade—when she wasn't angry. When angry she expressed herself with the most uncomfortable logic. He glanced at her legs, so Nordic May-white, and felt for a moment he was even with Felicia for at least some of her angry letters. Then his eyes came to rest on her hand—and the memory was still with him, now and always like a birching across his face: a peevish, dirty old man, without hands, except for the two last fingers on his right hand which uselessly reached out for nothing. How often hadn't he thought, figuratively speaking, to hurl this man, with his stinking clothes and stinking beard, in Felicia's face!

During the war he had been to the other big Swedish island in the Baltic—Öland—and that island had become his in the same way as he annexed all geographic entities when he had seen them long enough. Gotland he had seen only as a blue shadow far out at sea more than forty years ago; yet perhaps no other place had become his so deeply and intimately as Gotland. He would tell this to Felicia sometime. Not now. Some other time.

He had mused that she was the goddess who created Gotland through her four heavenly decrees. When he sobered up he soon realized this could not be so—Gotland had been there before Felicia's visit. Then it must be that her four letters were inspired by some secret power who had decided that now the truth must out. The Inscrutable One had chosen as his herald a woman of mature age, superior in every way to any other woman on Gotland. Unsuspecting, she had written it all down, in the four letters, like four original creations, and at the High One's bidding she had sent them to Las Palmas to make it easier for the sceptical recipient. Obviously they must be sent to a man who considered it nothing less than a miracle that an actual piece of geography could be created within him in spite of the fact that he had not seen it.

Already after the first letter Gotland had assumed vivid contours, and after the second he had recognized this island he had never seen. But after the fourth letter Gotland had been created for a second time—and Felicia had not described it, only mentioned casually some facts about the house where they were staying, the view over the sea, and such. Most of what she had written had been illuminations about himself, with the final confession that in spite of all she loved him.

· Felicia Venhaug

Erling had known her for many years but was still on a journey of discovery into her world and knew he would continue so for the rest of his life. He had found the woman for whom the light within him never would burn out. There were not many who knew her well, but the opinions a great many people had about her were most definite. Concerning worth-while persons, opinions are always definite and conflicting, and the truth is to be found neither in the middle nor at the fringes. Perhaps the conflicting impressions constituted the truth.

Felicia insisted, to an especially high degree and as far as humanly possible, on being her own master, and on planning for the future as long as there was some sense in doing so. She did not want a commuter's life, broken up by the daily round trip; she wanted a definite world in *one* place—even if in a submarine, she had once said. As a child—a rich little girl—she had read about "ladies of the world" and had become rather frightened. She herself did not doubt that she was vain, but she did not care to put on airs for just anyone. Her family background was such that she knew a great many people, but she accepted no invitations and invited no one. Guests very seldom came to Venhaug. As a young girl at home in Slemdal she had found it almost painful when her father had to give a party. She had been greatly pleased one time long ago to read about the drop of water mirroring the whole world, and she had always, almost automatically, limited her outside world, but felt she had received the whole world in the bargain. She might still pick up some needlework and withdraw to her room, sit down with it on the bed, a book on the table beside her, and be quite happy. Not long ago she had received a letter from a schoolgirl friend who when quite young had married an Englishman and later made a name for herself in the theater over there, a ball of energy like herself, but to Felicia she was a stranger. It was pleasant to read what Lydia wrote, pleasant to answer her, nice perhaps to visit her some time, or have her come to Venhaug, but that was all. A career was nothing for Felicia, and when she married Jan she had clearly realized what this would mean to her: that he wasn't torn by an ambition which expresses itself in search for publicity, in restlessness, much journeying, and perhaps a few drops of poisonous envy. On the other hand, she must not have realized how hated she was, or why her friends were so few. To outsiders she seemed the conceited, scheming Felicia Venhaug, who always buttered her own bread, and took with force what wasn't given her freely. Perhaps there was this ounce of truth in it, that she never had pretended to be humble or self-effacing, and that she wasn't at all blind to her own position; but they were completely wrong on the point where most were sure they were right; as the women expressed it: every male in Østlandet between fifteen and sixty had been in her bed. Some men, worse gossipmongers than their wives, often said the same, because they either didn't know her or were silly enough to believe the stories. Felicia herself seemed entirely uninterested in the talk. She never cared what was said about her, wouldn't listen to it even, and proved her lack of interest in the only way such things can be proved: she had never bothered to say she was not interested in what others thought and said.

A common device for probing into other people's private lives is to express discreet warnings under a cloak of morality and thus provoke a defense. It was a long time since Felicia had been exposed to this, and those who had tried were not happy with the result. They would never forget her frozen smile and waiting silence while they themselves began to stammer, look in other directions, finally giggle in embarrassment, not knowing what to do with themselves—until at last Felicia mercifully would ask how things were at home, with the children, or whatever one asks girl friends for no reason whatsoever. Afterwards Felicia did not immediately forget such an experience, but she suppressed it completely and didn't worry about it, and when something similar was repeated she quite automatically turned on the old reaction. The result was inevitably the same.

Erling knew she was a hated and feared "desire-dream," and the most miserable imitations of her roamed the bars. She herself did not seem to know this, and to her the likeness would hardly have been striking. One of them had casually said to him across the table, while putting on her lipstick: "Is it true that I look exactly like Felicia Venhaug?" He might otherwise have considered spending the night with her, since as usual he had left Lier without getting a hotel reservation.

All Felicia knew and learned was bound up in her own world at Venhaug. She might listen to a political discussion but would rather not enter into it. She voted at the elections, but no one knew how. Once her tongue slipped and after that Erling suspected she voted with the conservatives, because in principle she was against any party in majority. It might be just as good a political prejudice as are all the others by which the country is ruled. Actually, she spoke very seldom about anything not related to Venhaug and the people there; even the sun and the moon seemed to have been placed in the firmament in order to serve Venhaug, and it might sound as if she thought meteorologists exceeded their competence when they spoke of the weather in other places.

• The cock under the wash tub

"Sixteen months is a long time," said Erling, "but with you time seems to have stood still; you haven't looked so young since the war ended."

She felt her heart beat faster; she leaned back and stole a glance at him, where he sat stooped with his arms round his knees. Erling had a deep tan. She looked for gray hairs but didn't see any. "You have been away two birthdays," she said. "I hope you'll stay home a while now."

He kept on inspecting his hands as he replied: "No need to walk around the hot porridge, Felicia. It was quite natural we didn't speak of this yesterday or last night, but I have been away on only this one long journey since before the war, and I feel no need to repeat it. For me there will be no more journeys except in Scandinavia."

A long silence ensued. Felicia felt uneasy and wondered if she should break the ice, but wasn't quite clear where she had him now. He could be unpredictable. Perhaps she had hoped the subject now brought up might never have been mentioned. And then she herself had happened to say something silly that might drag everything out into daylight.

When Erling spoke it was obvious he was trying to weigh his words and wanted to arrive at some agreement without exaggeration: "You know very well I didn't leave Norway of my own free will, but most unwillingly when the journey had to be in the direction of the equator. I was caught up by all your nonsense-talk that I must once more get out and see the world, and then, half-committed, I had this extremely advantageous stay in Las Palmas suggested to me. What business had I there? Of myself I would never have dreamed of going. If you had told me honestly what it was all about I would willingly have gone, and, not being entirely ignorant or almost in the dark, I would have agreed to be sent to Las Palmas. You said yourself you got the idea because I had once been there, but only when I was a boy, and I can't see it was a particularly brilliant idea to send a grown man to some place just because he had been there before. I was nearing fifty when I left and I'm past fifty-one on my return. It might have seemed less of an exile to me if I myself had chosen the place in which to spend my time while you got yourself another child. The farmers are said to put a brooding hen under a wash tub, but this must be something new to put the rooster there when he isn't wanted. Things were enjoyable enough in the Canary Islands, but I would rather have seen the pyramids or Mexico."

"Don't be unfair," whispered Felicia. "You mustn't exaggerate."

"Your strong need to arrange things for others probably played a part; and I must say you usually do it sensibly and effectively—sometimes too sensibly and effectively; this puts matters in a somewhat better light. You were born to be self-willed in matters concerning other people, even when there is nothing to be gained for yourself. But you must realize how I feel—a victim of white slave trade in reverse at the age of fifty!"

Felicia squirmed, her eyes flashing; she half opened her mouth but said nothing.

Erling kept staring at the ground before him and continued in a low voice, "I wish I hadn't said that. I don't mean it."

She didn't reply. Erling went on, calmly, "I have had plenty of time to think this over. And now I'm back. I am terribly happy to be with you again. And I look forward to being at Venhaug soon. I also know why you acted as you did. You couldn't make yourself tell me in advance why I couldn't be closer to you than near the equator. Shall we make fun of the whole thing and express it this way: Caesar's wife must be above suspicion? You've always been drastic in your rules of conduct."

"And who taught me that, Erling? It was you first—and then the Germans!"

"Felicia! Now it's your turn to be just and not to exaggerate. Can you never free yourself of things that happened—well, many years ago. It's 1950 now, no longer 1934."

"Yes, Erling, I did promise to forget, but now—"

"Fine, Felicia! May I go on? You know what happened to me once, something I am not happy to be reminded of. You weren't responsible for that, but when you poke into other people's lives you never know what you might turn up. I was once madly in love with a girl who didn't want me around while she was pregnant. She didn't want me to see her that way, she said, and she meant it. It was pretty hard on me but I felt it was right for her to decide what she wanted. I went on a journey. Much later, when she and I were arguing bitterly, it was not pleasant to have it hurled at me that I had left her in the lurch because I didn't enjoy the way she looked while pregnant!"

"But, Erling, that was something entirely different!"

"The one situation must of necessity remind me of the other. If I can't tell you how I have felt and still feel, it'll always stand between us."

He noticed her right hand, on the bench beside her. It was clenched and the knuckles white.

"You have succeeded in all you had in mind, Felicia. You wished to have one more child. Like the first one it must have Jan for the father, and there must be no doubts; neither in your mind, nor in his, nor in anyone else's. Your second daughter was born, as God and everyone knows, one whole year after I had left for Las Palmas."

She said, in a low, hard voice, "And when the village tailor's son discovered that no one would suspect *him* of being the father to my child—then he felt he had been made a cuckold of!"

Erling rose and took a few steps away from the bench. She remained sitting, looking at his hair, so sun-bleached, the sinews in his neck, his shoulders, almost black tanned, his brown, solid back. He wore white shorts, held up by a belt she had lent him. She was furious with him for making her lose her temper. Now he had her!

He turned slowly toward her, his eyes narrow slits. When he spoke there was a vibration in his voice she had heard before: "Is that *all* you have to say? I was frank. I told you exactly how it was. We must get this cleared up if possible. Is there nothing else *you* have to say?"

He repeated what he had said, and this time she thought his voice was different, milder, even though he added a word that made it sound coarse: "Is that all you have to say—society-bitch!"

"Erling—come and sit down."

He would rather not, because he was so anxious to. Always a woman used weapons not available to a man. It was unfair. He sat down.

Felicia was using, at least this time, regular weapons. "Listen, Erling, you're right in saying I wasn't fair with you before you left. Can't you write it off as a regrettable mistake—if it *was* unjust? It is true I wanted a child, and perhaps laid some unfortunate plans—but no one sent you to Las Palmas under guard, and I did nothing, I believe, except use some old connections of my father's to make your journey and stay inexpensive. And you've paid with your own money. You say I lured you away, or however you expressed it, but in such cases it's never just black or white. I was playing with the thought of having another child; then one evening at Venhaug you were saying it was time you had a long journey abroad. Possibly you weren't very serious about it. But it *would* have been a problem for me, this with Jan and you; it couldn't have been anything else if I had another child. As a consequence I never thought of another child very seriously. Of course there must be no doubt as to who the father was. Then you got to talking about a foreign journey. Silly, silly Erling! At first I was suspicious—did you perhaps want to get away from me? Then I took hold of myself and realized that that wasn't it; probably there was nothing more to your plans than you would forget in the morning; in fact, you had been drinking. Suddenly it struck me that here was the solution—and I took your loose talk seriously, because it suited me. I spun out your plans; your objections—which seemed less and less important—I wouldn't listen to because I was beginning to realize how immensely I wanted this child. As far as your trip was concerned, well, I believe I fooled even myself—for a while I thought I was working for you only. I learned you could live cheaply in Las Palmas, and—God forgive me—I felt sure you had no greater wish than to go to Las Palmas. It was all stupid, but it was you yourself who had started it from the beginning."

Erling wanted to interrupt her, but she held his arm firmly and continued: "And you must realize, Erling, that—that *there must be some balance in what people do*—we must arrange life's weights and measures sensibly: no one except Jan must be the father of the child, if there was to be one. You two are friends; the way you have come and gone at Venhaug for years—don't you see, Erling, the balance would have come to an end."

She rushed on: "And then the fact that you already *have* a daughter at Venhaug, even though everybody knows the truth that I couldn't possibly be her mother. Am I not right in what I have done with what I call the *balance?* You fooled me when I was seventeen, and then, so to speak, walked round the corner and had a child with another woman. This you must admit! You mustn't try to make out *I* am the one to do everything wrong; that time you came with the charm of a grown man, and your name, and made an impression on a schoolgirl—"

Erling rose; he pulled her up from the bench and said, "Enough, Felicia. Let's go inside."

• *The shadow of the Werewolf*

The sun was streaming across the floor when Erling was awakened by sounds in the kitchen. He had been sleeping so heavily he wasn't at first quite clear as to where he was; before he opened his eyes he felt apprehensive lest he be somewhere he didn't want to be, seeing a strange room or, still worse, encountering some person he must talk himself away from, while still thirsty, unwashed, disgusted, empty.

He was in his own room, he was at home, and Felicia was there once more at long last! How he had missed her, longed for her! He stretched himself, arching his body, sensuously conscious of muscles and sinews, stretched himself blissfully once more and yawned like a dog. It was like stretching oneself after being born.

A fragrance of coffee reached him. Outside, the birds were singing, and through the window he could see the virginal glitter of budding birches, ready to burst. It was a calm morning; the sun across the floor boards made him feel good; he must have slept late for the sun already to have reached the windows, and now he wanted to get hold of Felicia.

But he decided against it; first one must get up, and then go to bed again. Shake off the sleep. And one thing and another. He had, remarkably often, read about people being awakened with a kiss to a lovely day, and then immediately beginning to make love—how else to interpret the most endearing words and dashes?—there was no talk about coffee, and a beer would have been in horribly bad taste; then talk and talk about the sweet things in life, while the imaginative reader suffered with the one who had been awakened with kisses and who undoubtedly was lying there thinking hopefully about something else.

Such aside, it was one of his physical imperfections that he would awaken in the most cheerful spirits when he had been drinking in the evening; conversely, he was in an abnormally bad humor when he hadn't had anything to drink; indeed, the awakening seemed like a horrible accident. In his younger days he had often wished he might get some small (not too big) stomach ulcers to dampen his thirst, since he wasn't lucky enough to turn green after a bout, or be kept in line some other way. When drunk he also lost all sense of shame, was apt to laugh at the wrong time, and felt embarrassed when others were highly entertained. Once he had felt—as did all his friends—that he wasn't quite normal; with the years, however, there was much he had taken up for further evaluation. His children had once, long ago, suggested that he get drunk every evening when it had such a pleasant result in the morning. Ellen had been unable to suppress her smile, even though she strongly clung to morals and thought it was completely out of line to be happy, when it was God's will that one should feel rotten and remorseful after being drunk.

He stole out silently. Felicia caught sight of him through the window, as he was pouring a bucket of water over his head and jumping about after the shock; she came running out with a towel which he grabbed from her on his way inside—he noticed in passing her slender waist under the belt, the yellow, tight skirt which allowed more than a suggestion of the play of muscles in thighs and hips, her straight legs, and her feet in the low gray suede shoes—and he rubbed himself, shivering and only half dry, before he pantingly disappeared under the blanket. "Something to drink!" his teeth clattered. "I'm thirsty, terribly thirsty!"

Only then did he discover that she already had an opened beer bottle in her hand. "Here you are, drunkard!" she said, but her voice was almost devout.

He drank eagerly from the bottle and lay down with happy sighs and groans. Felicia went back to the kitchen. A pleasant warmth spread through Erling, he was conscious of every particle of his body and seemed to breathe through every pore, even sucking in air through his outstretched toes.

Out in the kitchen Felicia was singing in a low voice, while preparing something that undoubtedly would be good. She sang pensively and with interruptions one of the old werewolf ballads he had once taught her. With the song he could almost discern her actions in the kitchen—it was louder, or lower, or there was a pause, depending on what occupied her:

> I had been told as a tiny maid,
>   So falls the dew and gathers the frost,
> The wild werewolf would be my death,
>   So please it God wherever I be.
>
> My dearest wolf, please don't bite me!
>   So falls the dew and gathers the frost,
> My silken shift I give to thee,
>   So please it God wherever I be.
>
> Little Kirsten she cried so hard,
>   So falls the dew and gathers the frost,

Herr Peder heard from his farmyard,
So please it God wherever I be.

But when he came to the rosy grove,
So falls the dew and gathers the frost,
There met he the wolf with bloody mouth,
So please it God wherever we be.

Herr Peder straightway drew his sword,
So falls the dew and gathers the frost,
And cut to pieces the wild werewolf,
So please it God wherever we be.

He leaned the sword against the earth,
So falls the dew and gathers the frost,
The point it cut into his very heart,
So please it God wherever we be.

His ideas about Man's fall Erling had gathered from the Werewolf.

In his youth he had known people who were considered religious and who occupied themselves with problems related to theology, but they had squirmed uncomfortably when he had asked them if they believed in any of it. He could never get an answer. He must then assume that they didn't believe, only played with an empty shell, toyed with senseless problems that they had picked up in religious homes as children, or whatever the circumstances.

He realized now he hadn't been mature enough to understand the context, and perhaps they also had not been too convinced. Or, if they were, perhaps they felt he was unable to understand because they clothed their life problems in the old rags they had inherited, and in *that* sense one could be as sincere as a believing person. It was barely a hundred and fifty years since poets and others had expressed themselves through Greek mythology—just because they didn't believe in it, weren't bound by it, and didn't commit any sacrilege when they filled it with their own thoughts and used the symbolism as they wished. Then Greek mythology became obsolete, too narrow and too distant, and by that time it was fairly safe to annex the Christian mythology instead, with its universally familiar symbols and expressions. A weakened Christianity had opened the Bible to the unbelievers and the profane; they had been able to gather treasures there in the same way as one takes from classical literature in general, once the memory of school and its daily grind and platitudinous explanations have been safely forgotten. Similarly, one could hardly be expected to understand a figure like Lucifer, until one had studied him closely and grown familiar with this bearer of light, who had become the great hater and had supplied people with the darkness they eagerly desired when frightened by the light.

Erling felt he had many times seen the Werewolf. It mattered little whether sometimes it appeared in the shape of an ordinary tiger or a saber-toothed tiger. Some Africans had chosen to drape themselves in leopard or tiger skins when they gathered for ritual blood-drinking. He believed in the Werewolf as one believes in mythological figures, but also somewhat further: the old Werewolf had become the modern Satan-god, the Destroyer, and the priests and worshipers of the earlier god could not get over to the new god fast enough. The good god had only too late discovered that his camp was full of deserters and quislings; in his heaven he must have been wondering if there was anybody left outside of collaborators and cowards. But Erling had learned that truth is never new:

> Und wie des Teufels einziges Ziel und Streben Verderben ist, so treten nun auch beim Werwolf alle anderen Interessen vor dem Drang nach Mord und Zerstörung zurück. Er nimmt die Thiergestalt an, einzig und allein um Schaden zu stiften.

There wasn't a deviltry people hadn't figured out and perpetrated against each other, and would continue to do:

> In der christlichen Zeit, wo man die Existenz der heidnischen Götter zugab, um sie zum Teufel erklären zu können, wurde der heidnische Cultus zum Greuel der Teufelsanbetung, die Diener der Götter zu Teufelsdienern (I Corinther 10:20–21), und hier entstand mit dem Hexenglauben die Vorstellung von Menschen, die sich mit Hilfe des Satans aus reiner Mordlust zu Wölfen verwandelen. So wurde der Werwolf in düster poetischer Symbolik das Bild des thierisch Dämonischen in der Menschennatur, der unersättlichen gesammtfeindlichen Selbstsucht, welche alten und modernen Pessimisten den harten Spruch in den Mund legte: *Homo homini lupus.**

The Werewolf is a child-killer and scents his way to the foetus in the woman's womb; he always unerringly finds his way to the source of life. Through all ages he has represented what man prefers not to see but to put outside himself—and it becomes more real than man himself.

---

* This passage, equating the Werewolf symbolically with what is animalistic, demonic, and insatiably egoistical in human nature, is from Wilhelm Hertz, *Der Werwolf: Beiträge zur Sagengeschichte* (Stuttgart, 1862).

But it is also true that man's dream of atonement never fades, whatever shape it might assume: There were once a farmer and his wife who labored in the field. When it was dinner time they sat down in the shade of the wood to eat their bread. Then a wolf came out of the forest. There was something peculiar about that wolf; they were not frightened by it. It didn't seem dangerous to them; rather, it looked very sad. "It seems unhappy," said the wife. "Don't you think we should offer it a piece of bread?"

The husband gave the wolf a piece of bread, and it walked some distance to eat it. Then it turned into an old man with a tired, sad face. He knelt before them and thanked them. He had been promised he would not have to die as a werewolf if some person unasked, purely from the kindness of his heart, offered him a piece of bread.

Felicia came in with the tray; there were coffee and boiled eggs and marmalade and toast. She let him hold the tray while she doffed her kimono and arranged the pillows so they could sit comfortably. Then she too crept under the blanket and sat beside him. "Eat now, drunkard! Aren't we playing the good children who are being rewarded with coffee in bed!"

When they had eaten, Erling carried out the tray and, returning, picked up a book and brought it back to bed with him. "Do you intend to lie and read in bed?" asked Felicia, in consternation. "And I thought you had got all the cognac out of your system by now!"

"I shall read aloud," said Erling. "Listen well, this is Holberg. He always has some well-chosen words for every occasion: 'One might in some degree control one's passions. One might also know the rules to follow for this purpose. But if the blood is hot, and the fluids in the body stirred up, then there is little use in following the rules. When fire reaches the powder there is an explosion, and when the fluids for one reason or another begin to ferment they continue until they are released. I know there are persons who will not agree with me in this. There are also certain persons who will bear witness through their own experience that by following rules they have, so to speak, conquered themselves and become different persons. It is possible there are such warriors; it is also possible that many boast of victory without fight. Generally speaking I believe if someone has fought his desires so long that he has conquered them, then his passion might not have been very ardent in the first place.'"

"The fluids are fermenting, Felicia!" he added, tossing Holberg on the floor, and after it the many pillows. "You are most desirable in pearls and wrist watch."

• *The past is a dream*

Felicia dozed off for a moment but awoke with a start at the sight of some devilish figure which might be the gardener at Venhaug, Tor Anderssen. He was stooping over her as if ready to sink his sharp claws into her breast. She pulled up the blanket and shuddered.

"Did you fall out of a tree?" asked Erling. "It's supposed to be race-memory—the ape-child dropping from the tree."

"Perhaps a still older memory," thought Felicia. "Our fall from the Tree of Knowledge."

"Or a dream of being caught while stealing apples?"

"Well, it's the same thing, isn't it?"

The gardener had been that wolf with iron claws one sees in old church paintings. Felicia had not been the first to see the semblance of a wolf in Tor Anderssen; Aunt Gustava had said as much when she visited Felicia once and the gardener happened to walk by: "Down in Kongsberg I saw a wolf once in a four-wheeled cage, a sort of circus wagon, and when Anderssen came here it was exactly like looking through the bars again."

Felicia had great respect for Aunt Gustava's gift of *seeing*. Tor Anderssen had the head of a wolf and he snooped about the farm with the same lurking, restless movements as a wolf. She had told Jan how she felt but he had smiled and said, "Tor is from Østerdalen; they walk that way there. Observe his long, stealthy steps. He comes from an old hunting-people who can scour for miles. An Østerdal man is as much at home in a mountain as a Nordlander is in his boat on the Lofoten Sea, the same indefatigable self-assurance. And, Felicia dear, wolves do not have mustaches."

The gardener had a walrus-mustache. For some reason it looked like a false one, but whether or not wolves have mustaches, Anderssen's made him look even more like a wolf. And when he shouldered a gun at Venhaug, he *was* a wolf. Sometimes he could look like a ragged, unsuccessful Nansen, a sort of Nansen who would never have dreamed of crossing the Polar Ice when there was no moose to kill, a Nansen without fire, envious-looking, a nitwit Nansen, a parody of the real Nansen, a miserable, doomed-to-failure attempt by a devil to pretend he was Nansen. "The Østerdal men walk like moose," said Jan. "Don't you recognize that shuffling, from the moose you've seen?"

Well, as a moose, then, she had thought, what's the difference. He is like a forest animal. But he shed the forest-animal when you came close to him and looked into his narrow, rather miserable eyes, and when his mushy, common voice spoke of carrots and beets. Anderssen was quite orderly, as one might expect of a good gardener, but not one ever to offer any suggestions; what he had learned he knew by rote. His mental capacities were limited, his imagination meager, and one had better not be ironic or ambiguous in conversation with him: Anderssen did not understand such, and his face would assume the stiff mask of a wholly humorless person, promising no good. Then his hands might begin to tremble; he could never forget what his wooden head once had understood to be an insult; in May 1940, some German soldiers, quite humanly, had happened to laugh at Tor Anderssen when he skidded on something on the sidewalk in Kongsberg and had to dance about and flail his arms grotesquely to regain his balance. This he had never forgiven the Germans; Tor Anderssen became an avenging angel, completely heartless, strong as a pile-driver, and with the courage of a pile-driver. A little mess on a sidewalk, a few thoughtless German boys laughing, and Tor Anderssen was at the throat of anything German as long as the war lasted. It probably never entered his head that the Germans had put him in a perfect wish-situation: to gain praise and honor for acts of vengeance. Perhaps he was the only one in the whole resistance movement who felt no relief when peace came; but then, strictly speaking, he had been on the wrong side. Neither Jan nor Felicia—Erling was somewhere else—had had the slightest doubt during the war that Tor Anderssen was the born Nazi; through a ridiculous incident he had become furious with his brothers under the skin. Tor Anderssen had *not* crossed the border into Sweden when he no longer could show himself anywhere, as other resistance people did; he became a forest-runner and his own private army for more than two years. He tramped into Hamar in a rather tight and lumpy German uniform, most certainly taken from a dead Nazi, when he saw that the Norwegian flags had gone up at the farms in the neighborhood. His revenge didn't seem to have been sweet enough. At least he was as sour and sulky as before and glared suspiciously when the crowd greeted him as a hero. He was and remained an uninteresting lone wolf, and one who never in his wanderings had had a mate, but looked at all females with belligerent suspicion. What were they giggling at? Him?

It was not without reason that Erling, when he met Tor Anderssen at Venhaug, began to compare him with his brother Gustav. They were both men who were sufficient unto themselves. Gustav had indeed married, but actually he had swallowed his wife and digested her. It was obvious that Gustav did not miss his son who had run away to America.

He was only mentioned as some vague figure who had refused to become absorbed.

The sun streamed into the room where Felicia and Erling lolled in bed. She turned on her side and put her arms round his neck. "Erling, I'm thinking about that business, falling down from the Tree of Knowledge. I played with you in my daydreams, Erling, from my seventeenth year until Norway came into the war. Especially the first two years after I had met you. I imagined you would roam the roads in the neighborhood, hoping I might pass by. As this gradually seemed less and less probable I grew more courageous in my dream; I made up that you must have hid in the garden to get a glimpse of your princess. Perhaps you remember—no, I'm sure you don't—but my room was on the second floor, opposite a little hill in the garden, maybe fifty yards away. From this knoll one could see into my room when the light was on. I went up on the hill myself to make sure."

Her voice grew unsteady; even though it had been so long ago she relived the shame she would have felt then had her love-play been discovered. "Sometimes I almost persuaded myself you were there; then I would pretend I had forgotten to pull the blind; I took an extra long time at undressing, and then I walked about in the nude, picking up things, straightening up, until, very deliberately, I would put on my pyjamas and go to bed. A moment later I would appear really shocked at discovering someone might have seen me, and I would jump out of bed and pull the blind. Those were the things I was remembering when we were together our first night in Stockholm."

She was lying with her head in his armpit while her thoughts wandered home to Venhaug where she enjoyed the pleasure of playing with a man, conscious of his presence in the garden, watching him wait expectantly, or seeing him look out of his window hopefully. Or, best of all, letting him sneak up to the ventilator-opening from the outside only to discover that she had closed it from the inside; then his disappointment and his fear that she might open it again and discover that he was trying to peek in. That must never happen; she had no intention of unmasking him and ruining the whole set-up, but Tor Anderssen couldn't know that. She was always careful and made sure that he had stepped aside before she opened the ventilator. Many a time she had stood there, listening, conscious of his apprehension which reminded her of an animal's—afraid someone might come and catch him there. She enjoyed the game passionately with this impotent Cartesian devil whom she could make jump up and down at her bidding. She visualized him standing in line outside the ventilator, eager to peek when she was undressed, a whole long parade of Tor Anderssens, from the greenhouse all the way back to the grove of silver spruce, and still far, far back through the land of Norway, an endless line for the whorehouse. Let them stand there and shiver in the cold; this was not the day the courtesan Felicia received. Until she began this game she had never derived any pleasure from playing with anyone. Practical jokes had always seemed pure stupidity to her; but she liked to torture and degrade Tor Anderssen and watch him play the fool. Her blood would throb, she would smile enchanted, and her eyes would glitter from something akin to hot, selfish evil, while standing there only a foot from him, on her side of the wall.

Such was one of her games. Another one happened at longer intervals. Like a few days ago. Tor Anderssen had appeared among the silver spruce and stopped still. No one could see him from the main house standing there so immobile, scanning about. No one except her, who was watching him through the greenhouse ventilator, dressed in nothing but her flat shoes. She had just been on the point of closing the ventilator, for he must not spy on her except when she was aware of it.

As he began to move and cautiously approach, she pulled back her lips like a snarling dog, but only for a moment; then her face froze to a mask as she watched him moving closer step by step, soundlessly, his eyes riveted on the ventilator.

Strangely enough, Felicia had never seen the connection between the young girl waiting for an Erling Vik who never came, and the black game with the gardener at Venhaug. It wasn't that she didn't try to find an explanation, but the completely obvious she did not see. Not even though the one game always reminded her of the other.

As a wise and experienced person she knew well enough that the ghost of one's painful past will appear on dark paths, cloaked in black joy-dreams. But not even Felicia remembered this when it was vital to her. For her, as for everyone: always much later, some other time, too late, or never.

• The story of Gulnare

They had one more day, spent mostly outside in the sun against the wall, before they said good-by and Felicia drove home to Venhaug. It was warmer than the day before; the sun, so high, and the good wine put them beyond time and place as they sat side by side, exchanging a word now and then. Cars would approach, rush by and disappear, but they couldn't see the road from where they sat. Erling experienced that day something that was mostly in the dim past but at times reappeared with amazing vividness: a great love that once had left deep scars and driven him hither and yon over the globe. It had also sent him to Las Palmas, just as Felicia had done now. He smiled as he thought of it; it must not happen a third time.

She had been the first woman to come into his life, and she had had a rather unusual name, Gulnare. After she had receded several years into his past he would often use her name for girls he knew only casually, as a sort of secret caress. He had at that time just undertaken his first job away from Rjukan, in sprawling Christiania, where his brother Gustav also lived. Gustav had been greatly upset when Erling arrived. "Must I look after you too?" he had complained, and they had argued. "A pup like you ought to stay at home!" Pup yourself, thought Erling, but of course he said nothing. In the main he had taken care of himself since he was eleven, been entirely on his own since fourteen, as Gustav also and his other brothers and sisters had done. But there was something self-righteous and almighty about Gustav, and at the same time one had to admit that he was the most capable and keenest of the brood that the invalided, philosophizing village tailor had sired. Indeed, Gustav had acted like a grown man at the age of seven—at least Erling had thought so in those days, when his brother obtained a job as helper to the horse-butcher; it was there also he had joined the temperance movement and learned manners. Gustav had talked like a grown man before he was eight; Erling remembered his own admiration when Gustav one day had said to the butcher who was returning home with an old nag he had bought: "Good morning, Olsen, what have you paid for this beast?" The butcher chewed on his cud, spat, and said he wouldn't tell while an outsider listened. He glared at Erling, five or six by then, and added wisely: "People go around telling tales."

Gustav took the rebuke like a man: he stood with his hands in his pants pockets and looked in derision at Erling who had been stricken with the suspicion of carrying tales about prices and such. "Well, you are so right, Olsen," he said.

Already then Erling had been aware of Gustav's courage; he dared do things without being told. He acted as if the butcher business was his and always occupied himself with something. He learned to sharpen knives, an art Erling never could acquire, regardless of how long he lived. He would push Erling aside in utter disdain, but did not object when this lowly being admired from a distance his great sharpener-brother. Gustav never played with other children—it would have been beneath his dignity—and later he never became intimate with anyone except Elfride, whom he married. Really not with her either, she was just another piece of furniture in his house.

When the butcher clubbed a horse in the head, back in the narrow yard, and its joints folded and it fell, then Gustav was right there fast, yet with a man's calm, sure movements. The knife sparkled, the blood spurted, but Gustav was not touched, either by the squirting blood or the kicking hoofs. Erling was hiding behind the fence, pale with admiration. Whatever Gustav did he did as if he had never done anything else. Erling did not learn until much later how this was possible: secretly Gustav would lure people to teach him their tricks, and with equal secrecy he practiced on dead and living objects until, with the self-assurance of a grown-up, he would step forth and perform his feat. Gustav did not accept praise; no one was worthy of praising him. If someone tried, he would turn an imaginary tobacco cud, spit, and move on. He was a man after the butcher's heart, and together they carried on wise conversations about innards.

Gustav was fifteen when he became a handy man in a blasting gang. Since then dynamite and blasting had been his life. He had an inclination toward the violent, and violent he was, rebuffing and brutal, but as he grew older he would avoid fights. In later years, when he thought no one could see or hear him, he might frighten a child or a dog merely by muttering something he considered endearing. His other brothers and sisters Erling didn't bother to think of; they seemed only pale, skinny ghosts. To Gustav he was tied by evil, and an unmistakable blood-bond. Erling thought of him as always ready to spring, always tense, always ready to hit, spit or spew abuse, filled with an ever-consuming belief that his almost unfathomable egotism was nothing but hunger and thirst after righteousness. Gustav was a worker worthy of his pay, and strikingly stupid. He mastered *everything* within a certain limit, but that limit was indeed his ceiling, a solid, yard-thick ceiling of reinforced concrete—his low, gray, flat heaven. Above it, according to his honest, irrevocable conviction, nothing existed except nonsense and damned rubbish on which Erling and similar parasites made a living. He was a repulsive person, lacking imagination, cruel from principle. Erling wondered if Gustav, perhaps already as a small boy, might have been fed up with their father's gibberish; for many years Erling too would grow hot when he recalled it. Their childhood and early youth had been a ghost-world, no less so in retrospect; semidark, damp, *unreal,* a sort of small community of mentally defective demons, reminding one of jackals in a cemetery at night, digging for corpses, brother Gustav rising between desecrated graves like an absurd wrought-iron monument, surrounded by an impregnable wall with broken pieces of glass on top, in case anyone might try to climb over—God knows why—when the monument slept.

When Erling arrived in Christiania, his working clothes in a neat bundle of gray paper for which he had paid ten øre right off the storekeeper's roll, he went to live with Uncle Oddvar. Welcome he was not but neither was he thrown out, for where should he have lived if not with relatives. This was something taken for granted, but with Uncle Oddvar and Aunt Ingfrid there was also this, that they were too passive to throw out anyone at all. The misfortune was that Gustav already lived there and made life miserable for his relatives. The first evening when he came home and saw Erling he stood mute a few seconds before he exploded as only Gustav could explode. He raved like a dangerous beast in a trap. As an unwitting compensation he didn't speak for three days. Then he came home, after work-hours—no one in the world must be in doubt about the fact that Gustav had a permanent job—dragging an old leather trunk with many straps. It was worn but strong and solid; it was meant for lifetime and so it turned out to be; there was something invincible about Gustav, and Erling observed with admiration that for the first time a trunk had come into the family. Still threateningly silent after the storm, Gustav opened the trunk in the small bit of unoccupied floor space and methodically placed his belongings in it, there being room for ten times as much; Gustav had looked to the future in buying his trunk. When he had gone out, Uncle Oddvar said, still shaken and cautious, that he had believed, sure as hell, Gustav was going to live in the trunk. This was long ago when Uncle Oddvar still was capable of a thought. When Gustav had closed the trunk, as a noisy farewell gesture, and fastened the straps well and locked it, he pulled this piece of property out through the door, which he kicked shut as a "Thank you! Good-by!" Hiding behind Aunt Ingfrid's long-deceased aspidistra plant they watched him cross the street with the trunk on his head, and they could plainly read in his back that never had he free-loaded on a sorrier crowd. Erling could still feel vaguely the pangs of guilt he had had because he, the troublemaker and the useless one, had caused Gustav inconvenience; nor did Gustav ever let him forget it. Even now, sitting there in the sun against the wall, Felicia at his side, Erling realized he was arguing with his brother—now more than forty years later: Didn't I have as much right as he to go to Christiania? And we would never have thought of living with anyone except Uncle Oddvar; that was what relatives were for. Oddvar and Ingfrid had, uninvited and as a matter of course, dragged their brood to Skien and later to Rjukan. We were a rat-family; if eight lived in one room and four more arrived for a visit, what difference did it make? If there was heart-room there was house-room, said the dismayed hosts, sure of a similar reception themselves another time. Rooms for transients they had heard of, but did not consider these as places to stay in; they were considered temporary abodes for high-falutin society folk. Yet Gustav and Elfride had been forced to stay at a hotel for one night shortly after they were married. This led to another tenet in Gustav's creed: decent people did not stay at hotels. It had been expensive, and Gustav had refused to pay until threatened with the police, and they had got vermin. Gustav still took pleasure in relating the circumstances of the vermin: the host had dared insinuate that Gustav and Elfride had brought the vermin, because the night before a very refined gentleman, a sea captain, no less, had slept in the bed. This only caused Gustav to harbor a lifelong disdain for all sea captains; his generalizations and his inexorable stupidity made the world foursquare and secure. The way past Gustav was over his dead body. Thirty-five years later Elfride would still blush when recalling the hotel manager's saying she was lousy, and she was unable to sleep when she thought of it. Gustav ought to have spared her this, thought Erling, but no, outrage must be kept alive. "Lice?" Gustav might say, and add with unassailable inconsequence, "Never seen a louse in my life!" This would make Erling think of the family fine-tooth comb at home in Rjukan—Gustav himself had named it the Lice-Chaser. Yes, thought Erling, Gustav had in all respects torn himself free. So had Elfride too, who had come from a similar family. She and Gustav did not raise vermin; not even the most bashfully unobtrusive louse would have escaped them.

It had been early one evening near Midsummer when Erling first saw Gulnare. He had strolled along the silent streets, almost empty now between dinner and promenade-time. He had come from Aker Street through City Passage down to a corner where he stood for a while and looked at the Church of Our Saviour, it too deserted, staring with its single clock-dial eye. Then he crossed the square and looked at shoes in a window. It had struck him that life actually was very depressing, still more depressing when one was looking at shoes in a window; nor would it be better looking at something else. He heard slow, light steps and turned around. It was a girl. She glanced at him, and he thought how nice it would be if people wore a sign indicating willingness to talk. His shoulders straightened as he saw her stop to look at shoes, she also. "Aren't those nice," said Erling, and pointed toward a pair of ladies' shoes, so shocked at his own temerity that he almost took off around the corner.

She looked at him quickly and blushed: "But too expensive," she whispered, and stared at the shoes.

Erling had nothing more to say. Was this accosting a lady in the street? He began to perspire profusely and his hands felt clammy. What was it one should say now to appear casual and experienced? He remembered something about the weather but this she could see for herself; if only it were raining and he were carrying an umbrella; he had read about such situations. She was a beautiful girl. Two heavy braids hung down her back, but there were some short, fluffy locks on her forehead that she had been unable to tuck in; the sun played on these. He had often remembered those sun-kissed locks, and now he turned to look at Felicia. She was leaning far back in her chair, her head to one side, and was looking at him inquisitively. "You must be thinking of some old flame," she said. "Out with it!"

But he turned away and did not reply; it was another Gulnare Felicia knew about.

Blood, sweat, and tears.

She had been so young, only a schoolgirl, the one he had stood beside in the pleasant sunshine. So young that his courage had come back to him. He had asked if they couldn't go for a walk down to the pier, the weather was so nice. He had purposely suggested the pier because he knew where it was; he couldn't appear to be a country bumpkin who didn't know Christiania as well as she. Then she had turned crimson red. Probably no one had asked her to go for a walk before, but now it had happened. "Why do you want to walk with *me*?" she had asked, and sitting here now, next to Felicia, his remembrance of the emphasis on "me" made his heart tender.

Confronted with an unsure, dubious child, all airs had fallen from Erling, who wasn't much older himself. "Because I'm alone," he had answered. "I am from Rjukan, please don't be so formal with me, I'm only sixteen."

"I'll be fourteen in August. My name is Gulnare Svare."

"How wonderful to have a name that rhymes!"

"Yes, everybody says that. What's your name?"

"Erling Vik. I am—"

He stopped, but honesty got the upper hand: "I'm an errand boy." But he must embroider it a little: "I couldn't get anything better just now, and one has to live." He had been looking at her nice clothes and his courage rose. He added, "I have to earn my own living."

But Gulnare, without hesitation, went him one better; she looked admiringly at him and said, "How lucky! I don't think I ever will be allowed to earn my own living."

Erling was astonished and thought she must be rich. He had some vague recollection of reading about "gilded drawing rooms" and "Her Grace." And here he had been bragging to her that he was an errand boy. But so it went with a great many things in life.

He had always measured everything in victories or defeats, in spite of the fact that life was neither the one nor the other.

"Why would you never be allowed to earn your own living?"

"I must only go to school—all the time 'til I'm eighteen. It's disgusting to think of it. And then I must go to school again—home economics. You're always chaperoned there too. When people go to school they're always watched over, even if they're grown. Does anyone tell you when to come home at night?"

"Tell me? Who would that be? I live with my aunt and uncle; I think they would rather I never came home."

"How funny! I must be home before nine, and in the wintertime I can't go out at all because it gets dark so early."

They had started to walk. Gulnare was still scanning him shyly out of the corner of her eyes while they talked about one thing and another. Suddenly she blurted out, "Suppose someone should see us!"

He had been thinking the same but hadn't said so. That they might meet anyone who knew *him* was almost unthinkable, but if it should happen he would be very proud. He was apprehensive about the humiliation if they should meet someone from her family, her father, an older brother.

"What would your parents say?" he asked.

She explained they would be upset. Terribly upset. They would tell her to come home at once.

He noticed a few people on the street and wasn't happy about it.

Now out in the bright sunshine he felt ashamed of his clothes; for a moment he comforted himself with the thought she was only looking at his face, until he remembered the two front teeth with great cavities; he kept his mouth closed as much as he could.

Gulnare had worn flat children's shoes. Lying here in his chair now he recalled how Felicia had walked across the floor toward him that time in the restaurant in Stockholm, wearing flat shoes. Gulnare wore a blue dress with a gray belt. When she wasn't looking at him he became quite excited about her profile; he was immensely taken by this serious, wistful face, longing for something in the distance. How wonderful it would be to tell a girl to her face how he felt while looking at her. There was so much one couldn't say and had to keep to oneself. He must learn how to say it, and say it to Gulnare. Why wasn't she his sister? He thought of his own three sisters with their red-rimmed eyes. Better tell Gulnare he didn't have any. If she asked.

Gulnare was trying to make conversation. She said, "When do errand boys take their vacations?"

Erling was immediately on guard. Was she after all trying to make fun of him? But her eyes looked open and querying. Well, so that's all they know about us, he thought. And he flirted with the idea he might say, casually: A littler later in the summer. About the middle of July. But the thought of a vacation—he connected it with long journeys abroad, murders on the night-express, coral reefs—was too ridiculous, and he found it easy to be honest: "You're mistaken. Errand boys never get any vacations." And since his imagination couldn't grasp that one might receive pay without working, he added. "What would one have to live on? And someone else might take the job. Then what would happen?"

Gulnare knitted her brows a little; she had come up against one of life's realities. But for the moment she only registered that errand boys did not take vacations.

"Father isn't taking a real vacation this summer," she said. "Someone asked him to do something and he agreed. He says the money will come in handy. Then Mother also wants to stay in the city, even though he nagged and told her she needed a vacation. Then I too must stay at home and do a lot of chores."

Erling felt secretly he had nothing against the father's money difficulties.

Early evenings with sun in Upper Castle Street, summer of 1915. It always amazed him in later years how little the First World War had occupied him and his contemporaries. The shock in August 1914 had been violent and would never be forgotten, but afterward—well, that was the war business and that was that, but they were growing youths in puberty and had more serious things to think of than a war far away. He could only smile as he recalled that the Swedish police, when he escaped across the border, had in detail recorded his membership in a socialist club for a few weeks when he was fourteen.

He wondered for a moment how old Gulnare would be by now. It was easy enough to figure out but he brushed it aside; she was and remained for eternity the fourteen-year-old with her healthy, beautiful hair in virtuous braids. Only once had he seen that hair tucked up as an attractive crown on her head—to keep it from getting wet—so that for that short moment she wasn't dressed even in her braids. No, they had not gone swimming together, the fourteen-year-old and the sixteen-year-old, that summer of 1915, when the world was so gropingly new and unbelievable and displayed visions of bliss, and let him see that Gulnare was grown, and made him feel that then he must also be the same. Everything was permissible, everything must take place, down there among the pines at the shore!

But it didn't happen. It never happened. Yet the "great" had happened anyway when he saw her down there on the rocks in the glittering sun and the world caved in to recreate itself from the beginning. Until then there had been a dissonance in him, a sickly melody in all the continuous joy. He had thought he could silence it if they could go to a place where they were entirely alone, with no possibility of anyone pointing him out as a grown criminal, pursuing a young girl.

He smelled the fragrance from Felicia's hair and smiled in his chair in the sun. He need only reach out to touch her hand. He might have tried to tell himself that there was no difference in age between him and Gulnare, but it didn't hold—she the schoolgirl with braids, while he sported the clothes of a grown man, with a high, stiff, painful collar, and a lacquered straw hat. The impossibility of it all had also given ripeness to his years: he had felt like a paternal protector for the child Gulnare. A great wave, like one of those long, heavy ones in the Atlantic, had in a short moment swept away all the exalted nonsense from his mind, as he sat there crouching behind the bushes that summer day of 1915 and for the first time saw a naked woman—not an indifferent schoolgirl unlike the boys in only one respect, but a young woman, fullfledged from nature's own workshop, a miracle that in a moment dissolved something in the chafed boy-soul and at last released natural, good tears for once, a miracle that would always remain his. O Lord! he thought, sitting there at the side of Felicia, O Lord! that youth of the summer of 1915 had gained insight from such a revelation only to suppress it shortly and forget he had cried in joy. *Insight* and *insight*— he could not possibly have realized that everything that day was true and right and good, but had long ago been forbidden because it did not fit in with offices and schools and factories. Long ago it had been banished by morality's smooth words and by the law's bombastic edicts: Love as much as you wish once you have passed the crest and have been registered in Love's black-book, but not at other times, places, or ways than those decided on.

They reached the pier, Gulnare and he, and he was pleased that it was quite calm. Otherwise he might have had trouble with his straw hat. He had bought it with much solemnity for Whitsun, because one bought a straw hat for Whitsun if one wanted to be up to date for the summer; one did not argue about customs. He had never wasted a thought about how idiotic the hat was, stiff, impossible to keep on one's head, carried away by the least breath of wind. Admittedly, it came with a black string, wound around the crown, the storm-line, which could be unwound and attached to a coat button; but custom prescribed that the line must be used by old men and farmers only. Anyway, it wouldn't be nice to have the stiff, sharp-edged thing fluttering round one's head like a kite. Consequently, one must hold on to it in a sort of continuous salute, rewarded by a kind of slimy paint on one's fingers. Or one might make murderous attempts to press it down over the skull, and then hold one's head at the right angle so the wind didn't catch the brim of this jewel, or tilt one's head backward if the wind came from behind. This would cause a red streak across the forehead, with sores and eczema, but this had to be endured. Some men learned a trick, though never with perfect success: they pressed a layer of skin under the front of the hellish hat, making the head thicker above than below the edge and giving the wearer a stiff, military look, since he couldn't blink. This arrangement demanded excruciating concentration and discipline on the part of the wearer, and if he wanted to turn around he had to do it slowly. The original thought with this hat must have been that it would shade against the sun—thus in some magic way persuading the sun to shine in Norway—and offer an airy comfort. God knows the hat was worn from Whitsun to October in all kinds of weather. The most elegant type came with a multicolored band, but the price of this elegance might prove ill-spent when the colors failed to withstand the rain and trickled down the face of the dandy. As soon as this summer hat had been purchased every young man went to the photographer to have his picture taken in it, against a background of snow-covered mountains.

Erling was one of the many who never needed a hat at any time of year, but like others in the same situation he never questioned why he should bother with so much unnecessary trouble; it was understood that a grown man wore a hat.

It was Gulnare who for the first time, perhaps unconsciously, made him feel that one could have conversations with those awe-inspiring people who lived in a rarified atmosphere, that perhaps they were indeed the only ones he could talk with. He had a dawning, feeble suspicion that talk might not be a good word for the quarrel, bragging, and treachery he was familiar with. He was so terribly willing to believe that this other place existed in the world, willing like a dog with teeth bared, ready to jump on anyone daring to deny it. But his dream of this other humanity was turned into snobbishness; Gulnare had been saying that her father was superintendent of schools, and Erling already prided himself that in spirit he associated with so high a person; soon he let it slip out that he knew the daughter of a superintendent. He let it slip out quite frequently, but felt himself that it sounded flat, empty; after all, it could only be repeated to other little snobs who believed everyone bragged as they did.

Suddenly Gulnare had to catch the streetcar; she dared not wait for the next one. He hadn't got up courage enough to ask if they might meet again. She waved to him from the tram and he waved back and was almost run over by a brewery truck loaded with old furniture. The driver started to give him hell, but Erling got even with him, for he was not backward when it came to using foul language: "You must have stolen that brewery truck to move your dirty belongings, you old drunkard!" The driver laughed until he almost fell off the seat when he recognized that Erling came from the same background as himself. This made Erling still madder, for he had scratched his knee; he put his hands to his mouth and howled, "Beer-truck thief!"

He kept roaming the streets until the sun was going down. Perhaps there was another world for him too. Gulnare had been so happy—was she always like that? Down on the pier they had been all alone for several minutes, walking among the lumber piles, with no one in sight, but Gulnare had not been the least bit afraid. He thought this a mark of honor. Not that he had intended to attack her; however, that seemed to be what they always expected, those upper-class people.

He recalled Olga at home in Rjukan and shut his eyes tight for a second, a reflex that had stayed with him through the years when he encountered something that smelled bad. Olga, the girl of his own kind, Olga whom he had meant to seduce, but instead managed to rouse the whole town with.

A dream of something he didn't as yet have words for, which had been with him from early childhood, but had been so badly mauled—this dream rose great and golden from its imprisonment that June evening in the year 1915 and throve for long in his heart, the dream he dared not believe in or profess until many years later, the dream of a better humanity, forgiveness, good will, talks about world situations, without a knife in the sleeve, the dim dream of peace and thaw in the heart, the dream that made him long and weep.

He stole in silently at Uncle Oddvar and Aunt Ingfrid's, with its familiar smell of beds, beer, and brandy. Those happy drunkards were sleeping deeply and noisily in the same bed, as they often did even though they had their own beds; they were like an insoluble knot of two short snakes. "Sure as hell!" groaned Uncle Oddvar in his strained sleep. He never closed his eyes while sleeping, but turned them inward as if searching his soul. The children slept silently on their bunks along the walls; it was like a storeroom of brats, for future use. Erling undressed quickly, hung up his good suit in the communal closet, donned his working clothes and stretched out on the floor, happy and tired, with a roll of toilet paper under his head; he had never seen one until he came to Uncle Oddvar and Aunt Ingfrid; they bought a few rolls every Saturday night for the children, who liked to play with them, especially on windy days when they could let the paper flutter from the window, if it was dark enough outside. Their parents each raised a bottle to the mouth and laughed loud and long. While the children were still small they were a happy family.

One time in 1940, during the Occupation, Erling had figured out he would tell the Gestapo if they picked him up that he had a bad back that caused him great pain during the night; then they might put him in a cell without a mattress and consider that punishment enough; he felt at home on a floor.

But it was not easy to sleep during those early morning hours after he had met Gulnare in the evening. Every detail assumed great importance and he felt that finally he had experienced a miracle, as a result of stopping to look in a silly window at some silly shoes. He lay on the floor, happy and warm, filled with the warmth of early youth, and when he went to sleep he swam naked and with easy strokes down a river of warm blood and refreshed himself with it when he grew thirsty. He would never give up until he found Gulnare again.

After work he went immediately to the place where he had met her, but he hid in an entranceway. His heart beat with joy when he caught sight of her across the street and he stepped out from his hiding place as soon as she had passed. He followed her a few paces and then they stood again face to face, both equally embarrassed to admit why they had come, but it was Erling, naturally, who spoke: "I thought you might come by here again." He was too proud to say he had just happened by. Gulnare looked away and replied, "I too thought you might come. I am terribly embarrassed," she added, and blushed until her whole face was rosy.

This time she decided the direction of their walk but she pretended it only happened so. Erling noticed a sign which read Willow Street but soon he didn't know where they were and didn't look for signs. They came to a suburb with gardens and trees. When they had gone that far

Gulnare said, innocently honest: "In this direction I'm not afraid of meeting anyone. I'm not supposed to go out—like this." "I don't know the city too well," said Erling. "I'm glad you decide where to go. I've had some trouble finding my way but I'm improving. I really should've worked overtime tonight but I asked to get off."

Gulnare looked at her shoes and said, "That's nice of you. I would have felt terribly silly—"

And then she had to tell what she had done: "I told Mother a story so I don't need to be home so early tonight."

Tensely, Erling asked how late she could be out. She said, her voice trembling, "About half past ten or so, but I can go home earlier if you're busy."

They followed a country road with a hawthorn hedge alongside. Through it they could see a low, wooden building with a large door in the center; on the whole door was painted a green pedestal surmounted by a dove, a nice, fat dove about half a yard high. In its beak it held an olive branch and there was a nest of palm fronds on the socle below with a few plucked quail in it; they were gaping at the olive branch. On either side of the painted monument and of equal height, probably for symmetry, or perhaps to emphasize the stonecutter's importance, one could read in the same color: "Paul H. Thoresen Wiig, Master Stonecutter."

They inspected the art work on the door and accepted it automatically, the way things are accepted by youth without argument and often buried inside without question. Erling was occupied with a practical thought: some place where they could sit down and talk and perhaps hold hands. There were many such places in there on the other side of the hedge; half-finished tombstones were strewn all over. The house seemed locked up and no one around. Erling was born with at least one prerequisite for becoming a fairly capable burglar; if he wasn't too absent-minded he could always tell if there were people in a house he passed. But he had never had any particular desire to steal. Here he realized easily that no one was around: it was only a workshop. One highly polished black granite stone reflected the sun so sharply it hurt the eyes to look at it. On the top of the roof sat a wagtail, and in the field a starling waddled about. The strong colors stood out blatantly on the door's inscrutable symbolism. They heard a finch in a tree, otherwise silence. The remnants of a rotted gate, like a decaying skeleton, were strewn in the grass at the entrance road. "Shall we go in and select our tombstones?" suggested Erling. He tried to be humorous.

Gulnare was hesitant. Were trespassers allowed? But here Erling felt on safe ground: "We can't steal a big stone like that, and anyway there's no gate. If the owner should come I'm sure he would only say 'Good evening!' The worst would be if he told us to leave and I'm sure he won't. After all, he must think of his future customers; he hasn't any others," Erling said finally, but his joke was not appreciated. He became a little unsure of himself; either Gulnare did not understand a joke, or she must have heard it before. This was disappointing since it actually was his own great joke, created in this very inspired moment.

One of the polished stones lay on two smaller blocks; it made an excellent bench. Gulnare sat down, with hesitation which gave way suddenly to the surprised look of a person who has been burnt. She jumped up, with both hands at her behind. The stone had sucked up sun into its black soul all day long. Gulnare dropped her hands as if they too were burnt. She blushed. "It's warm," she said. "The stone is warm," she added, and turned still redder.

Erling pretended, a little too convincingly, that he had seen no double meaning in her words—he who a moment before had tried to use a double meaning. He felt the stone and fetched a planed board which stood leaning against the house, placed it on the stone, and tried it: "Now you won't burn yourself!" She smiled, and they had grown a little more intimate because she had burned her behind. She felt the plank. "How strange," she said, "the sun has been shining on this plank as much as on the stone."

"It is that way with so many things," said Erling, profoundly. As an experienced person he refrained from any attempt to explain nature's mysteries to a woman. He was conscious of his heartbeat now, sitting there beside Gulnare. He accidentally touched her hand and felt waves rush through him. They looked at each other and grew dizzy.

"We should have a snack to eat now," Gulnare managed to say.

Erling felt poor and miserable. It was just such a moment he had dreaded. And here it was. He had no money.

"I can see through the hedge back there," said Gulnare, and inclined her head. "That made me think of it. They have soft drinks and cookies there."

Erling did not reply; he wondered if it was a request. People were apt to think about things just to be talking. Perhaps her thoughts weren't on drinks and cookies at all. But one should have piles of money. Then life would be easier. Here he was without any at all. Suddenly he felt it unendurable, he became a hopelessly lost child. But he didn't say anything. One couldn't say to one's beloved that his pockets were empty, that he had no money for cookies and soft drinks. Only a few nails and junk. That wouldn't get him far.

"What's the matter with you, Erling?"

It was the first time she had used his name and in the midst of all his shame it knocked him over. What a wonderfully beautiful name he had, and he hadn't known it before! He looked down on his plain clothes and said in a hard voice: "It's the middle of the week. Where would I get money from?"

Gulnare breathed heavily, looked at him in fear, suddenly pale. What had she done? Money? Money in the middle of the week? Then she understood in a second: in the middle of the week was the same as the middle of the month, and now she was on sure ground. In the middle of the month she was always told, when she wanted something, that there was no money, and now Erling had thought . . .

Suddenly her tears started falling. "I have money—I wasn't thinking of that at all, I was only talking—"

She jumped up from the tombstone, dug up a little purse from her skirt pocket. "Let's see what I have—" She poked among the coins with her index finger. "I've lots of money! Enough for drinks and cookies! I'll run over and get some!"

She was already on her way. Forgetting she was a lady, she ran like a boy.

"Gulnare!"

She stopped still in the middle of a jump and looked at him: "Can't I?"

He didn't know what to say, so she started running again. He looked after her between the branches of the old, thin hedge. Here he sat on a tombstone, perhaps it would be his own one day—"Here Rests Erling Vik, Beloved, Missed"—and waited for drinks and cookies.

Erling turned in his chair and looked at Felicia. This time she hadn't noticed it; how long ago that had been! All that had taken place before Felicia was born. Next to him now sat the one he loved, the woman who had killed—not in cold blood, but the way the werewolf kills. Step by step one night, through back yards, up staircases, the knife in her clothing, only the point still safe in a bottle cork . . .

At one time people had contrived to distinguish between assassination and war. Which one when Rotterdam was leveled?

Something had held him back; Felicia had not known the connection, she had not known that the informer's widow was the Gulnare of his youth. He himself had known it for a long time now. Strange, how little interest one now had in such matters. Friends were not particularly interested in what friends had done during the war. Erling had by chance, long after the war was over, happened to learn who his potential murderers had been, but he hardly remembered their names. Nor had he cared to report them.

And it was a summer day so long ago:

Gulnare returned with the cookies and the drinks and spread them attractively on the stone. She was greatly amused by popping the corks. In those days the sound was so innocent. "I've had champagne once— have you?"

No, Erling had never tasted champagne; horrible how honest he was: "Is it good?"

"I had only this little, but I think soda pop is much better."

Erling drank his pop from the bottle and felt he was superior because Gulnare's tongue stuck in the bottle throat. The cookies were delicious. He thought of the liquor at Uncle Oddvar's and felt soda pop was much better, but this he couldn't say. To a man liquor must be better than soft drinks. "You are more of a man than your brother!" Uncle Oddvar had said. "While Gustav was here I couldn't take a drink in my own house, sure as hell! Putting on airs to me, his uncle!"—"He was a turd, that's all I can say!" added Aunt Ingfrid, and poured herself an extra drink to Gustav's dishonor. "Oddvar who is as kind as the day is long, and I too, and the only time we could get a drink was when Gustav went down to the privy. It was a dog's life!"

Gulnare kept wondering every now and then what the time might be. He quieted her by assuring her he could see from the sun what time it was; this made an impression on her at least a dozen times that evening. They held hands as they left the premises belonging to Paul H. Thoresen Wiig, Master Stonecutter. It was hard to come away from the peaceful road, and they walked slowly. The finch was still singing. Erling let go of her hand and took hold of one of her braids. It gave him a trembling sense of power, he wished he could walk behind her, one braid in each hand—"Ride, ride to church!"

She looked frightened but let him hold the braid; he saw that something was happening to her too. She said, lips trembling, "If somebody comes you mustn't hold my braid."

It was a Sunday morning in July that they had taken the same boat to Nesoddlandet. They went aboard separately and pretended they didn't know each other. When they landed Erling walked a little behind her until she sat down on the edge of a ditch and waited. He would never forget the way she sat there in the grass and flowers, in a flowery dress, and smiled her happy, embarrassed smile. They walked into the forest along narrow paths she knew and arrived at a flat rock to the east, a place where she apparently felt no one would disturb them. They sat in the sun for a while and looked at the water, but when they were ready to eat they went in among the pines. Gulnare had brought a lunch basket. Again she had told a story about a girl friend. "One day I'll be discovered," she said, "I don't dare think of it even, but I think I'll die if I can't see you any more."

Erling opened his eyes and looked out over the fields at Lier. He felt Felicia's presence more intensely than before just when, in his thoughts, he repeated Gulnare's words: "I'll die if I can't see you any more!"

She had been right. They had killed Gulnare, they had beaten to death that Gulnare when she was fourteen.

Gulnare asked, her mouth full of eggs, "Don't you ever get tired of me, Erling?"

She knew very well she was asking the impossible. That was why she asked. He had never lived before. Many years later—and Gulnare living deep in memory's vague mist—he had thought the same, but was able to add: I had never lived before, and for many years there was no reason to believe I would live again; I know better now, but didn't then.

They sat for a while virtuously apart and looked out over the fjord and the white sailboats. He leaned on his elbow and looked up at her. She must have been reading his thoughts, or her own. She too leaned on her elbow, but a little away from him so that the next move was up to him. Most important were the excuses and the crooked paths around the hot porridge. During the month they had known each other they had only held hands, or he had held her braids; otherwise it had only been the electricity in their nerves when they happened to touch each other, and also one Sunday morning when they had stood pressed against each other on the tramcar and couldn't help it. Erling had all the time been afraid, as afraid as one is to frighten a bird, or a child; how could he know, she might desert him and leave him forever. She did not come from his kind of people, she was no Olga whom he had attempted to make love to in the wash house at Rjukan. That was why his love was so great and strange and profound and all his nights and days so rosy. Now he moved apprehensively closer and soon her head rested on his arm. They were very conscious of each other's bodies, through all the clothes of 1915, for people loved in those days too, and so strong was his emotion that it might happen for years afterward that Gulnare, who was never his, robbed him of his power when he was with some other woman.

There was a line in one of the books Erling had devoured at Rjukan: "She blushed like a young girl at her first kiss." He had often tried to visualize the duke strolling across the floor to kiss some young girl. Kisses had seemed something a lord graciously strewed around him. Erling was nervous about this, for it must come, he must one day kiss Gulnare for the first time. Perhaps it was not unlike being without money when a girl asked for a soft drink; he didn't know how it was to kiss, only that it could be heard at some distance, and this was rather annoying, but he was willing to make any sacrifice, except to look like a fool.

Gulnare cautiously freed herself from his arm, took his face shyly between her hands, and began to kiss him lightly. He chose to lie completely still and passive and he immediately benefited by it. She kissed him lightly and fleetingly—eyes, forehead, nose, and ears, and her lips touched his mouth like a breath of wind. His heart had stopped pounding, he lay with his eyes closed, and now he was lying on her arm, passive, in bottomless bliss. He felt her face was warm and moist, her skin seemed to have taken on a different smell; for a moment he opened his eyes and looked into hers, they were big and clear, and gradually he dozed off.

Erling had gone to sleep in his chair next to Felicia, perhaps only for a few minutes but he was always a little unclear for a moment when waking up, he might confuse an old situation with the present. He came to and recognized with joy that he had gone to sleep with the sheer memory of Gulnare's bewitching of him so many years ago. He wasn't sure Felicia would be pleased to learn that she had been a sort of medium for Gulnare. Or had the fourteen-year-old herself been here?

He had awakened that Sunday at Nesodden with Gulnare sitting and watching him. A new expression had come over her face, almost frolicsome, a touch of wise irony. She reminded him of a cat who sits and purrs and is expectantly happy with her whole body. He had felt so strangely weak and happy, in some inexplicable way older than when he went to sleep. He remained still and looked at her. She had pulled her legs under her and was chewing on a blade of grass without moving her mischievous eyes from his face. "You *are* the one!" she said at last. "Going to sleep!"

She kept chewing the blade and looked out over the fjord. She said clearly and as a matter of fact, without looking at him, in a sure voice, "I love you, Erling. I am in love with you, Erling, and it won't change if I live to be a hundred."

Erling sat up but did not reply. He couldn't; he didn't know what there was to say. Greater than this nothing could ever be.

Gulnare turned to him and said, "But this is terrible. I've been thinking—you are sixteen and I am only thirteen. I won't be fourteen until August. Something terrible is going to happen to us, but I don't care a bit now."

She pulled the blade from her mouth and pointed toward the water. "I would rather go down there and drown myself than give you up. They can do what they want!"

Erling kept fumbling with a parcel he had, some candy he had bought; he felt it was silly with candy just now but didn't know exactly what to do. And it turned out to be a good move; Gulnare quickly bacame the child again, she cried out in joy at the sight of the candy, and they shared a bottle of pop with it. "Candy and pop are awfully good!" she said, her mouth full.

"Wonder if I dare take a swim!" she exclaimed impulsively, still the child.

He had of course had this crazy thought in his mind, too. As soon as he felt able to control his voice he replied, "You could swim at the little beach where we first sat, below the cliff. I'll wait for you here."

Did he really think it would be all right? Yes, of course he thought so. "Please, go and have a dip!"

She moved nervously and pulled the grass beside her. "Well, I will then, if you don't think . . . ?"

"There couldn't be anything wrong in you swimming all by yourself."

She sat yet for a while before she rose, full of apprehension, and left.

When Gulnare returned, Erling had first thought he would pretend to be asleep, but in his confusion he sat down exactly where he had been sitting when she left. She sat down without looking at him, and neither one spoke. At last she asked, as naturally as she could manage, if he didn't want to take a dip too. Yes, he said, he was just thinking about it.

He walked over the cliffs down to the little beach, took off his clothes slowly and laid them on a stone, the same stone where hers had just been lying. The whole time she was in his thoughts. He walked about naked in the warm sand for a little while, stretched himself in the sun. Then he waded out and swam a short distance. This was the first time he had swum in salt water; he observed it was true what he had heard, it was so much easier to stay afloat in salt water. Here he could lie on his back and keep his toes up, something he had not managed before.

The water was tepid; a light wind made it splash over his body. He paddled a little with his hands to keep floating. Even here in the water he felt his desire for Gulnare, and he idly watched his erection and the black hair around it which lifted with the waves and sank again like seaweed. At the same moment he caught a glimpse of her there at the big pine—he had thought that only boys would do a thing like that. He had learned that only boys peeked, street-boys, and they were spanked for it in school. He had never heard of girls peeking. Much later, having become rather cynical, he tried to accuse himself of expecting it and wishing it, but that was not true.

Surprised, ashamed and frightened, his first impulse was to drown himself at once. Then it would be over. He couldn't live when Gulnare had seen him like that, he would never get over the embarrassment. But he felt differently even before he waded ashore. She had done the same as he. At this moment also she was looking at him from somewhere. That was all right and not his fault, like that time in the tramcar. There wasn't, then, such a great difference between him and those others in high society. He was more in love with her now than before. If that could be possible, he added cautiously, as if she might hear him where she sat and looked at him. She had wanted to see a naked man; it was good it had been he and not someone else. She had wanted to see a person of the opposite sex. So had he, and he was glad it was Gulnare he had seen.

While he was dressing, a great assurance took hold of him: he would have Gulnare now, at once, up there among the pines; and if she refused it would be too late, he would have her anyway.

But when he returned and found her in the same place where he had left her, and in the same position, they were not alone—Sin had joined them, for they were so young. They had seen that they were naked and now they sat there in their fig leaves. Even she knew, at least by now, that each had seen the other. It was too overwhelming, and when Erling had time to think he was wise enough to understand; her voice was within him, there was no mistaking it: Wait till we meet again. At last he met Gulnare's look, it was the look of a friend, and they confessed mutely to each other.

• Until we meet again

Thirty-one years had passed—it was in 1946—before he saw Gulnare again. A joyous meeting it could not be. For good reasons one meeting was sufficient. Now—1950—four more years had elapsed, and Felicia had said: *Did she know it was I who liquidated her husband?* On this May day in Lier it was thirty-five years since he and Gulnare said good-by to each other below the wall of Akershus fortress where they were standing, clasping each other's hands after a Sunday at Nesodden, promising to meet on the following Tuesday. He had not been able to refrain from asking her if she realized what he wanted from her when they met next time; there must be no misunderstanding. She had looked up in his eyes and said, "Yes, I know quite well, Erling, dearest."

Some things were unthinkable, yet they happened. Suppose Felicia were to vanish in thin air the same way? He smiled; Felicia looked a little too real.

But so had Gulnare.

It was strange how retribution could strike quite blindly; had *he* felt remorse when he once left Felicia and let her get along as best she could?

Gulnare had not come. He waited evening after evening. She never came. The fact that he had failed to ask for her address was part of the misery; it would have been meaningless to use it while their happiness lasted. There was no Superintendent Svare listed in the telephone book. Not that he would have called, but at least he could have learned in what neighborhood he might hope to run across her. For a few months he often hung around the school he thought she would attend. He never saw her, but the girls began to notice *him*. And one day a man approached him in an alley and asked if he lived in the vicinity. The man had looked severely at him, and from then on Erling stayed away. He never caught sight of her. He read obituaries, but not hers.

Erling was sixteen. He knew this much, that if he talked to the other boys about what he ought to do, they wouldn't know any more than he, but rather mannishly would inform him that when a girl didn't show up it was because she didn't care to. Moreover, he wasn't yet at home in the city and this added to his confusion. He was more anonymous than most of the nobodies. Where could he go to inquire about a thirteen-year-old schoolgirl, the daughter of a man high up on the slippery social ladder? Living as he did in the lower depths of the city, shaped as he was by his background, and having an inexplicable misfortune as his only company, he was fast approaching the explosive running-amuck stage.

It has been pointed out by Europeans that running amuck is a special Malayan trait, a lust to murder, developing in the distorted minds of lovers who have been exposed to ridicule. Mark well that the lover is a Malayan! Perhaps in reality an unusual symptom was interpreted as the expression of a local psychosis, without recognizing behind the disease a universal mental disturbance, not at all unusual anywhere among people experiencing the tragedies of love. Erling was rather inclined to believe this was one more of those common, false excuses people invent when refusing to face reality. Perhaps it suited "advanced Europe" to proclaim that—thank Heaven!—here we behaved more sensibly. The fact was they didn't. It was only that craziness also has its local superstitions, customs, and conventions. Erling had recently seen suggestions that the high percentage of suicides in Denmark perhaps was connected with some such convention, some sort of suicide-convention. He himself had for years considered it a fact that in Scandinavia there was another widely accepted convention, that unhappy lovers should go to America. Now it was said that the Malayan running-amuck had definitely declined during the last century; although no one had bothered to investigate why, it seemed that the Europeans gradually had managed to make the Malayans accept European ideas as to how sexual craziness should express itself. Craziness has its own ideas as to what is considered a conventional craziness. It isn't as crazy as it seems.

Erling at sixteen might invent many a detective story and solve it himself; it became another matter to solve a real mystery. In his narrow circle he knew most of what one needed to know, but nothing of how to go about finding an upper-class schoolgirl. He lived in a confusion of hope and fear, an unmanageable longing, and an impotent hate that stimulated his destructive urge. If he saw something he could destroy he would make sure no one was watching him and then crush it. He had small opportunity to pursue such impulses, but made up for this in his imagination, until one day he almost got into trouble. He had just come into the entranceway of an apartment house to deliver a yard-long parcel, a lamp-stand or something like it. There was a girl walking ahead of him. He had a sudden cramp in his stomach, like a kick, which prevented him from hitting her on the back of her head with the package. He leaned against the package so as not to fall, and someone came and asked if he was sick. This caused him to burst into a fury of foul language and run away. He managed to hold on to the package, and half an hour later paid a boy ten øre to deliver it, while he stood at the corner, waiting for the receipt. Returning, the little imp took advantage of his opportunity and demanded twenty-five øre before he would surrender the receipt. When it dawned on Erling that the boy actually meant it he was too distraught to take matters into his own hands and deal with the blackmailer. And someone was coming along on the sidewalk. Almost ready for tears Erling bargained with the crook and managed to get off for fifteen øre. In the office they complained because he had been gone so long. The boss took the receipt, turned it over a few times, and started to swear and fume. Erling dug in his pockets but found nothing there; he knew this was the paper he had paid the boy fifteen øre for. After a severe scolding the boss telephoned the recipient, but all was in order; the parcel had been delivered and the receipt given. Erling could not understand why the boy had played this trick on him, but apparently everybody was like that in the big cities. A girl named Gulnare probably hid among her friends and laughed when the stupid boy from Rjukan walked by. And a boy demanded an extra five øre for a useless paper considered to be of value. Erling's mind stood still, but he learned that shame and injury go hand in hand.

Gulnare probably wasn't her name at all. Hadn't he actually suspected as much at once? Hadn't he clearly told her one couldn't have a name like Gulnare Svare? He straightened his shoulders proudly as he walked along the sidewalk, and suddenly he began to cry. He was so terribly in love with Gulnare and wanted to be with her. And then she had disappeared. Disappeared as if she had never existed. Had she been put in a dungeon on bread and water? No, one mustn't believe in those upper-class people. He would never do so again. They had had enough fun with that simpleton who was the son of someone everybody laughed at, at home in Rjukan. He was frightened about what might have happened in the entranceway. Better keep away from everyone, never see a soul; but this he had to do. At the same time that he started to bring home liquor he had a relapse into infantilism; he made up a long and self-degrading story that the girl he had been tempted to hit was a friend of Gulnare, and the boy was in on the silly plot—we'll get some money out of that stupid Erling and give him a piece of paper with a dirty word, but then they hadn't had any pencil and then. . . . But one day they would unexpectedly meet on the street, Gulnare and he, and she would be in despair, and he would be disdainful. But the one to cry was Erling, and he did it alone. He looked through tear-dimmed eyes as he cycled along the streets, delivering the hated junk people sent to each other and which he always wished he could throw into the sea. Wasn't there a single soul among all the thousands of people in Christiania whom he could go and talk with and who perhaps might help him? He pedaled a little slower and thought of Gustav—he was eighteen and perhaps for once. . . . But then he clenched his teeth—he could hear his brother: "Eh? You think you could ever get yourself a girl? Eh? The likes of you? Get back to Rjukan! Hah!"

He finally ended up by confessing to Uncle Oddvar and Aunt Ingfrid when they were drunk, and Aunt Ingfrid shook her head: "Have you ever heard the like of such a girl!" And Uncle Oddvar said, sure as hell, his wife was right, and the following day they had forgotten all about it, fortunately. By and by he started to contribute his share of the liquor supply; he had to fall for the nearest temptation, the only possibility of not being alone, he thought. With the two he drank himself away from everything each evening, listening to the children's bawling, talking nonsense—"sure as hell the truth"—and helped the brats unroll their Saturday presents of toilet paper and let it flutter through the windows. In October he learned that a ship in Drammen needed a crew. He went there after he had signed on at the office in Christiania. He no longer had his passport picture from that time, of course; he would have liked to see it, he was sure he hadn't looked like a human being. The ship first went up the coast, then north of the Faeroe Islands, far outside the German mine zone. His first knife wound he received in the Azores.

· Woe unto him who falls into the hands of the Almighty

Shortly before Midsummer, 1946, Erling was in Oslo when he received a telephone call from Felicia, saying that she and Jan would arrive by train from Kongsberg that evening. He invited them for dinner and said he would wait for them at the Bristol, where he called and made a reservation. Then in the evening he walked over rather early, ordered some wine, and sat down at their table to wait for them. Like the guards at the Holy Sepulcher he thought all was in good order, if he thought anything at all. He began to read the evening paper.

Presently someone stopped at his table, and he looked up to see a lady he didn't recognize—or did he after all? In a moment she might feel offended if he didn't. She might be forty-five, perhaps fifty; it wasn't easy to tell, for when a woman becomes masculine she seems to lose her age, and this lady unmistakably wore the pants. Sometimes he would have a painful dream about a woman called Midwife, a composite of all the women he had known who looked stern. Now he was actually experiencing the dream in reverse as it were: this lady reminded him of the apocryphal Midwife in his dreams and made him squirm. There wasn't the slightest doubt but that this woman knew what she wanted, and insisted on getting it; strong and authoritative, dependable when she got her way, accustomed to issuing orders. Yet he was not sure why she made him think of the head laundress in a resort hotel.

"You don't recognize me, Erling Vik?"

He rose. "I'm sorry—I'm unable to place you."

But something stirred within him. Who could she be?

"Then I must inform you that you are speaking to Mrs. Superintendent Kortsen."

"Oh?" he replied, waiting.

Each person has his own secret taboo-words; to Erling, one of them was "superintendent," had been ever since he was sixteen; but this Mrs. Kortsen couldn't know, for no one knew it. School superintendent to him was not only a word evoking memories of senseless humiliation and senseless punishment, it also covered shame, disappointment, defeat, sorrow, and it might recall that he once had imagined he could become intimate with superintendents, for he had never doubted who it was that had come up to him in the alley-way at the girls' school and asked if he lived in the neighborhood: it had been Gulnare's fearsome father, the man to this day frightening him in his dreams.

She smiled stiffly. "My name perhaps doesn't tell you something?"

Erling was slightly irritated. "No, Mrs. Kortsen," he said, "I am sorry to say, your name doesn't tell me a thing."

His irritation grew as he vaguely recalled others who had pursued this infantile sport of asking him what their names were, at last divulging some impossible name he could never have heard of. "You don't recognize me, Erling Vik? Well, I think you might, if you try!" The sort of people one runs into in the men's room, extending a hand in greeting and insisting on old-time friendship at a moment when one is unable to extend one's own hand because one is busy buttoning one's trousers— amazing the number that pursue one in there. Also sweet voices over the telephone: "Please, do try to guess!"

Mrs. Kortsen didn't seem to be hurt but her look was sharp and suspicious. Something not easy to interpret smouldered in her eyes. She thought for a moment before she asked, "Do you really mean to say you never knew that Gulnare Svare was married to Superintendent Kortsen, later Translator Kortsen, and that you don't know *me*?"

Erling stood glued to the floor and stared at her, overwhelmed. Was that Gulnare standing there, she who once could have demanded anything of him and who had changed his whole life? How long ago was that actually?

His confusion was so obvious that she couldn't misunderstand it, and this did not make her any more lovely. She said, sharply, "I see you're expecting guests and I won't disturb you for long; I'm expecting company myself. But I would like to sit down just for a moment."

He did not reply, but she sat down quickly. Nothing had happened according to her expectations, that was obvious, but what had she expected? Apparently she had taken for granted that he must have known who she was as soon as he saw her. He remained standing, looking at her, and now there was no doubt in his mind: this must be something that once had *been* Gulnare, no, something that had attached itself to the dream of his youth, some being who knew it as well as he

did, but had no right to know that dream. This female brute had never
been Gulnare, because then all must be a lie, all that had happened once.
She had no right whatsoever to say that she was Gulnare, that was a
conceited, repugnant fraud. There should be a paragraph in the criminal
code against this. Nor has she the slightest reason, he mused, to believe
that she is confronting the person who, more than thirty years ago, was
Erling Vik. I have never seen her before, nor she me—this is an outrage!
What is it to me that we once shared a holy mystery when she now is
preaching sacrilege? It isn't hers, it isn't mine . . . .

"Sit *down*, if you please! People are looking at us," she said.

Yes, people were beginning to stare. He remembered the girl he had
almost hit in the entranceway. Well, so people were looking; he
remembered his first visit to a whorehouse with a crushed dream of
Gulnare. Let people look at them!

He sat down and kept staring at her, still sure he had been right that
time, right in his supposition that the upper-class girl had only wanted to
play with the errand boy, one of the lowest class, only a slave to practice
on, who could never openly accuse her—but he had felt it couldn't be so.
And it was so long ago. He was beginning to wonder if she would stay
there when Jan and Felicia arrived; perhaps cause trouble, she looked
capable of it. But what did she want of him? He was more curious than
he seemed, and immensely relieved that this Gulnare had gone out of his
life long ago. He recalled everything, as if in a film, the summer evening
they had met, in 1915. Their walks. A Sunday at Nesodden, glittering
sunshine, buzzing bees. And those months following, while he still lived
with Uncle Oddvar and, with trembling heart read the obituaries in the
paper.

Mrs. Kortsen looked at him and said nothing for some time. One
couldn't discern a spark of sympathy in her hard, domineering eyes. She
had come to attack, in one way or another, but had so far only suffered
defeat through a stupid disclosure and had not been able to discover the
weak points in the armor of the one she hoped to crush. Instead, she had
warned him so that he wisely kept silent. He thought: What is happening now could just as well have been an episode in our marriage.

It seemed she must further pursue her theme: "I have kept track of
you. Since 1925 or so. I had naturally thought that you were settled
where you belonged, with a wife and children. Then I happened to read
a book by someone called Erling Vik. Norway is full of people with that
name, and it never dawned on me it was you, until I saw a picture—"

She was watching him steadily with her cold eyes, and in a moment
she added, "I couldn't believe my eyes."

Erling did not answer; how could he get rid of her before Felicia arrived?

"I have seen you often. With girls."

He was ready for anything; not a muscle moved in his face.

"Ridiculous playboy! I just happened to read one of your books. It was as could be expected."

He turned to look at the clock. *What did she want of him?*

"My husband didn't know of our episode. Of course not. But as you undoubtedly know, a few times he felt duty bound to go after you. He despised you."

Erling had no memory of pro-Nazi Kortsen; there had been too many of those, and all had despised him.

Except for the time of his feverish activity, when he became generally known, Erling had never kept what he himself had written, much less what others wrote. And once he had answered another writer in the newspaper he might forget him as completely as if he had never heard his name. Nowadays there was much talk about suppression and repression, but he was quite sure many people had a sounder and better mechanism for dismissing irrelevancies from the consciousness, in the same way as a splinter works itself out from a finger and is forgotten for ever.

Since this lady now was using the past tense for her Kortsen, was she divorced from him, or was he dead? Her stress on what Kortsen had despised probably meant he was a beloved departed with opinions agreeable to her own. Erling noticed that something was near the breaking point in her. No, this had in no respect turned out the way she had thought it would; she was getting closer and closer to a breakdown. Then she might drop her whole arsenal on the floor. Well, never mind, as long as she didn't make too much noise.

"Imagine, dragging me into a thing like that!" she hissed. "And then pretending you didn't know anything! Perhaps you didn't know anything when you took off to Sweden either?"

It must have been something that happened in 1941 then, before he escaped to Sweden in the beginning of October. Well, there had been so much in those days that one had neither time nor opportunity to look into; and afterward one was tired and fed up with anything pertaining to war. There was also something else here, something he recognized; he had come up against it time and again: there were people who believed one knew everything about them. At this very moment he had a letter in his pocket, from a farmer in Minnesota, who wrote as if they had parted the day before yesterday, but it must have been many years ago, for

Erling had not the slightest recollection of the man; yet he wrote as if Erling would be interested in the most inconsequential happenings right up to the last few weeks. This Gulnare must be one of those who never doubted that all watched every step she took and were more interested in her than in anyone else; one who never wondered how others might have obtained such information, or why they might wish to have it, but was convinced that the whole city as well as the country in general followed all her activities, and received revelations about matters they didn't wish to know. He did not suspect the reason for Gulnare Kortsen's anger, and he acted as if he didn't care. Felicia and Jan might come any moment; how to get rid of her?

"Have you lost your power of speech?"

He replied, shortly, "What do you want of me, Mrs. Kortsen?"

She was a little less sure of herself again and a little flustered. She said, "It may be you didn't know what happened that other time either, although I consider it quite unlikely. That time in 1915. Even a child-defiler must have some curiosity. Well, it is probably correct that you didn't care what happened to me."

He would so have liked to have a talk with Gulnare, if she hadn't come *like that*. Hadn't he always dreamed of it: at last to have an explanation, and to tell her how he had felt. But he could understand now that she had no desire in that direction. He had dreamed to find Gulnare as she still lived in his heart, and he had thought: It will be mawkishly sentimental but I don't care.

But *that person there!*

When she now started to talk he felt convinced she wasn't saying what she had intended to say, but got onto it because she had lost control of herself:

"Many a time I've thanked God for my good parents. I didn't wish to confess what I had been up to when Mother took me to her room that Sunday evening when I came home. They had discovered all my lies and were crushed in sorrow, but I was saucy and stubborn. So they took me into Father's den and there they beat me."

Erling felt his face turn white. *Had they beaten Gulnare?* The inexplicable was that the person sitting opposite him agreed that they had been right; she had said so with as pleased and proud an emphasis as if she had won a luxury car in the Good Lord's lottery.

"I can thank them that none of *my* children have strayed."

Quickly, he looked away; how did she know *that?* Indeed, her children must be astray in the worst way.

"At last I had to confess the whole thing. First our meetings. Then that I had to pay for you, when you saw how much money I had—"

"Pay for me?"

"Well—didn't I? Didn't I pay many times? From my own savings. They wanted to get to the bottom of the whole matter and kept beating me, again and again, and so all must out—those indecent swims of ours, and everything—"

"Everything?"

"They got more out of me than actually had happened—well, so it is when one is beaten—but they had first tried in kindness. And I'll tell you one thing—you, with all your sweet talk—I would soon have skidded deep down with your help if I hadn't had my parents; and I had already gone quite far, as you well know, and when it was over I realized how just they had been in beating me until the blood ran, and me dirtying my pants—and I felt it wasn't important if I had exaggerated a little. Well, as far as *that* goes, it was cleared up when they sent for a doctor to examine me, for naturally they feared I might be pregnant. Any little girl who acts the way I did has no right to complain, and— God be praised—my parents put an end to my evil ways."

She rushed on, cold, fanatical: "I've always felt ashamed, for all these years, that I didn't see through you at once, for what you are. A dog-whip might have been good for you too, but I doubt it. Someone ought to have tried, though."

The possibility that perhaps someone *had* tried must not have entered her thoughts. Beatings on different objects, or individuals, do not have the same result. Some break, some hold, some harden, some crack, some die, and the devil is right in one point only—that his medicine is nothing but evil.

Her eyes filled with tears. "Mother was as good as the day is long while they kept me in bed, and we found each other again. We had gotten so far apart while that business with you went on. And you can sit here and have no idea what trouble you got me into—or pretend you don't—oh!"

Again she boiled over in anger: "To be lured by your kind of people, and only fourteen, and parents who had done more than their duty—a lowly errand boy!"

Parents who have done more than their duty, thought Erling, and looked down again. I would have liked to meet them; they think it is a question of duty above all. In love there is no duty, there is nothing except love, and the moment duty enters one is lost. But when it is a question of love we have only thick and vulgar law books about duty.

"Mamma took me to Haugesund where her sister lived. I stayed there a year, and was watched carefully, thank the Lord! Having children myself now I understand."

They had done more than their duty: they had crushed Gulnare. He felt he was beginning to understand what she wanted of him, but she knew so little about it herself that she had difficulty in expressing it. She had been tortured to the point where the victim hangs on to the tormentor; Erling himself appeared as Sin personified to her, but also as one of the tormentors. A wise man had once said to him, "Children will love their parents more if they are treated roughly, and if such children are away from their parents for some time, they miss them more than other children would." Erling had for years known the truth in this: homesickness more persistently plagues those children who have un-solved conflicts at home.

"Skipping over to Sweden when you should have faced it! What kind of man are you? And return when there was peace and no danger, and orate loudly against us who stayed behind and saw to it that our people got food, and little thanks did we get and—"

Deep in his consciousness something was beginning to stir about the name Kortsen.

"And my wonderful husband—gone, without a trace."

Erling had caught a glimpse of Felicia and Jan at the door. He rose: "I'm sorry, Mrs. Kortsen, but—"

"Yes, I noticed her, I too," spluttered Gulnare Kortsen. "That—"

Erling cut her short: "Your side killed both her brothers."

"Well, then they must have done something they shouldn't," she replied in a low, furious voice, "While my husband—while she and you—a gigolo—"

She hit at him but struck his hand which he had quickly raised. Then she rushed off. The headwaiter came running, but Felicia stopped him, smiling and joking, pretending she hadn't seen anything. The head-waiter looked quickly about, realized that it was perhaps only one of those situations which solve themselves, thank God, and everything would be all right now that Mrs. Venhaug had arrived.

Felicia sat down and adjusted her hair. "Who was that person, Erling? Imagine, trying to hit our dear little boy!"

Jan too sat down and said, "Sshh, Felicia, she is looking at us with murder in her eyes. What have you got yourself into now, Erling?"

"She's a Mrs. Kortsen—I'll tell you about her later."

Felicia lowered her mirror and powder puff. "Kortsen?" she asked. "Was she married to Superintendent Kortsen?"

Jan quickly took hold of her arm but she pushed him aside; there was no one within hearing. She studied her face in the mirror and flipped away some speck from her cheek: "Had she discovered that it was I who liquidated her husband?"

• *The myth about Erlingvik*

Erling Vik, sitting at home in Lier, August 1957, was thinking how fateful a name might be. Even as a child he had identified himself with an imaginary spot called Erlingvik. Wherever in the world he had happened to be—and he had been in many and far-away places—he had never been far from Erlingvik. It was a narrow shore on a lake somewhere in Norway. He knew it better than any other shore he had seen or was ever to see. About Erlingvik no one else had ever been given a hint, until he once had said a little about it to Felicia when he was in his fifty-fifth year. He had regretted it, for there are secret places that must be just one's own and no one else's. In no other place in heaven or on earth can one develop, no other place can one populate in one's imagination. If you feel you must say something, tell then about a secret forest if you have a shore in mind, but don't disclose your shore to the profane. Felicia had indeed asked where Erlingvik was located, for women are so earth-bound, and he had been forced to reply: east of the sun and west of the moon. And he had felt uneasy lest he had said too much. The following night he dreamt that he was trying to lead Felicia astray—Erlingvik was not at all where he had said it was; then he felt safe. Again Erlingvik lay in some unknown place in Norway. No people had ever been there except those who were in his heart. Yet Erlingvik had seen much.

An outlaw had come to the shore one time, with longbow and spear; a few hundred years earlier a group of Stone Age people had camped on the hillside where they could look down on Erlingvik, but the men gruffly called the children back when they tried to run on the beach, and told them they mustn't go near it. And the children ran uphill again like fleet animal-babies at their mothers' cries of warning. They stood beside the grownups and imitated their faces as they looked at the shore. The men stood a bit below the place where the women had made a fire, scanning the narrow shores, spitting, making water, and the little boys did the same, their legs apart. The men twisted their beards with one finger, picking out bits of trash and inspecting them; they rubbed themselves contentedly against an oak trunk, shook themselves like dogs, and agreed silently to leave the shore alone. One of them looked up

among the tree tops and expressed his belief that it might rain. A second
man also took a peek and said there wouldn't be any. The rest of them
looked up, scratched their matted heads, caught a louse or two and said
perhaps and perhaps not. They ate at the fire and went to sleep there.
Next morning they left, they had been in the picture and were out of it,
and were never seen again.

Another time, about sunset some time in October, a wounded moose
bull swam ashore, the arrow still quivering askew up into his left side.
His legs struck bottom, his body heaved in a violent splash; he walked
from the water but stumbled to his knees on the shore, rolled over on his
side, and tried to lift his heavy head, blood oozing at the mouth. He
made a few kicks and lay still. Four bearded and hairy men, clad in
skins, had lost track of the moose; they paddled across the bay in two
hollowed-out oaks and searched the shore; but in the dusk they took the
dead moose to be a moss-grown boulder among many others.

Very long ago an old roaming cat had come to Erlingvik, a giant cat
with silent steps and cuspids hanging down like sabers. The other
animals happening by at Erlingvik did not see the saber-toothed tiger
whose ferocious head was bent over the water while it drank, scanning
the bay meanwhile. They did not see it go to rest on the beach,
dangerous, unpredictable, like a mine washed ashore. The saber-toothed
tiger was the dangerous, the alien, the eternal; it only opened its eyelids
ever so little, letting a swimmer pass by undisturbed, a youth on the edge
of manhood, still hairless on chin and body. Wet, his head bent low, he
walked close by the saber-cat, by the skeleton of a human being, its sun-
bleached neck turned up, with the spine-hole gaping like a searching
eye, past boulders hollowed out for fertility rites no longer in use, and
farther on into the mountain which closed behind him, and it was as if
nothing had ever happened.

Fish played in the summer evening, beavers swam out and in as night
darkened. The marten sat half entwined on its branch and waited. The
wagtail tripped on the shore, proudly, flipped aside as the sparrow-hawk
came after it—confine yourself to finches and robins, my friend, I'm too
quick for you. Ducks sailed down in an arc before hitting the water; they
listened, spied cautiously about, and paddled along the foot of the cliff to
the shore to see if they could find something good today.

Erlingvik was not broad; one might throw a stone across it at its widest
place if one was in shape. Yet it was a miniature Norway; there was a
beach of a few yards, a few underwater reefs; a steep cliff, a piece of flat
land like a field. Birches grew there, alders, aspen, maple; there were pine
and spruce, heather and wildflowers. In a corner which the sun never

reached there was a cave into the mountain; the waves gurgled hollowly and forbiddingly in there, even in calm weather. Otherwise a great silence most often reigned at Erlingvik, and it was as if neither animals nor people had ever been there, nor birds flown over it—nothing had been there except what his wishes had sent to Erlingvik, and this God only knew, but perhaps again some time a man might swim ashore at Erlingvik, make sure he had solid ground underfoot before he walked out of the water in his wet, heavy clothing.

Who might you have been, Felicia, if you had had another name, Hansigne, or Lene? How could I without this name of mine have lived in Erlingvik? A person mentions his name and it strikes us—of course, such must be the name of this one. Then we suppress the ridiculous thought, for the person must have been before the name; the name had come as a final addition; one can't imagine a person without a name, or one unable to live up to his name. If someone is killed in an accident it makes a great difference to you whether he is nameless, or if you have heard who he is, even though in either case it doesn't concern you. If a girl is called Olava she is denied personality and identity. Erling knew it was a pure happenstance that Felicia had not been called Maria, and he Valdemar. He grew silent and preoccupied when, as a grown man, he heard of this Valdemar who had disappeared in thin air—who would Valdemar Vik have become? In any case, he wouldn't have been sitting in this chair as Erling Vik; he would have been at most like a relative of the Erling who had almost taken form.

Felicia—Maria? Jan—or for example Petter? Maria and Petter. Very possible that this Petter never would have married this Maria who might have been Felicia. Erling himself and she who didn't happen to be called Felicia, would never have had their nights together at Old Venhaug; this he knew in a cheating sort of way, because he had been attracted to the name before he noticed the girl. He and Jan with other names could not have come to experience a friendship that had been so durable for so many years. This imagined Maria could never have been the Felicia Ormsund whom Jan (formal Jan!) so solemnly proposed to in Stockholm and who the following day had answered him: "Yes, I'll marry you, because I like you, and you are kind, but not stupid-kind. As long as you understand that I am also in love with Erling, and sometimes wonder if I don't love Steingrim most of all."

They could be peculiar, these strongly conservative people like Jan, when fate willed them a name which guaranteed its owner ability to meet any situation. "He did sit down on a chair," Felicia had related, "when I gave him the answer, but that was all." He had looked at her like a faithful dog and said: "I've already thought of that, and if you will just let me know always what I'm up against, in other things as well as this—for I can't handle something that sneaks up on me. It's the same way with informers and anybody who attacks from behind. They make me marvelously angry."

They were with him in Erlingvik and did not know it. So was also— forever now—the late Steingrim.

• A man without a face

Erling could hear the night wind beginning to stir. He raised his head from his papers and listened. It was August 10, 1957; it was two o'clock in the morning and the weather report had indicated rain, much rain during the night. It was balmy. The rustle of leaves against the window made the silence in the room more noticeable. He rose and walked about. The room was thirty-six feet long and fourteen feet wide; the ceiling so low that Erling, who was of medium height, could barely walk without hitting his head against the beams. The walls were of horizontal logs, about a foot in diameter; not long ago he had scraped them and oiled them; a fragrance of oil and pitch pine hung in the air. The floor boards were of pine, too; until last spring they had been worn and knottily uneven. People might stumble and the floor was difficult to keep clean, Felicia had complained during her visits. He had once asked her to forget about cleaning and floor-scrubbing, but who could tell Felicia what to do or not to do? He was thinking of that May day seven years ago—how she had discovered his secret hiding place in the floor and examined its contents. They had never mentioned it but he knew it was she. Anyone else discovering it would have stolen his whisky, probably his papers as well, examined them in some other, more secure place, and thrown them away. Probably Felicia, even in her most distracted moments, realized he undoubtedly had had signs which would indicate to him if the safe had been opened. After she had left the following morning he had discovered at once that someone had opened it, but one does not willingly expose one's friends.

He had inquired the price of such floor boards, planks one would call them, and they were expensive, indeed, perhaps unobtainable; such boards were no longer produced. Then one evening this last spring, a thought had struck him: might the planks be flat on the underside also, or were they split logs with the round side down? He worked the whole night through getting one board loose. It was a plank, in good condition, but unplaned. During the following week he busied himself taking up plank after plank. Every one in perfect condition. He had engaged a carpenter to plane them and lay them down again. Since then he had liked his house even better than before.

It had started to rain. He sat listening to the pleasant sound, while an old problem rose anew: the thought of a person's identity. He recalled, still disturbed, his experience in Stockholm with the saber-toothed tiger. . . .

And he recalled also what had happened earlier this evening. Between seven and eight someone had knocked on the door, and he had called out "Come in!" thinking it was the little girl with the milk; she would step in so sure of herself and so difficult to get rid of. She would ask in her precocious way about his life and mode of living. But it had not been she, it had been a man he didn't know who acted hurt when he wasn't recognized. It never occurred to Erling not to mention his own name when he looked up someone who might have met him only fleetingly, perhaps long ago, and he was always irritated by people who played a sort of hide-and-seek, or who seemed waiting the moment to produce a *curriculum vitae*. Facing the man at the door Erling had said rather roughly, "I have not the slightest idea who you are and I'm not interested in playing guessing games."

The man stared at him like a dog with much suppressed hatred in him—and this must have been easy enough for he looked like a dog. "Oh yes, you recognize me, you do—"

Erling took a threatening step toward his guest, who shied away and suddenly became fawning. "I thought you might recognize an old acquaintance—Torvald Ørje."

Torvald Ørje? Erling recalled him in an instant. And probably he would have recognized the man if it hadn't seemed beyond all reason that Torvald Ørje should want to call on *him*. How long had it been? In September it would be sixteen years. He looked at this person whom life had treated roughly, this repulsive figure with a thin neck and a head like a dog. He had not been particularly interested in the man, but felt a great anger rise against him—a sort of primitive anger at being disturbed by a simpleton, here in his peaceful house.

Yes, he remembered everything about Torvald Ørje—not in a logical sequence, rather as one remembers a landscape, with no particular time involved. Twenty years ago he had insulted Ørje, perhaps simply by existing; anyway he couldn't clearly recall now. The lazy good-for-nothing was a lawyer who had never had a practice; he had some screwy conception that he was a born journalist. He could always be found in some newspaper waiting room, hoping for an appointment that never materialized; he could see no other way to become a journalist; there he would sit, pulling at his left ear lobe—the way he was standing here and acting this very moment—and allow himself to be pushed, overlooked, and insulted. He only winked and pulled at his ear. The very day after the Germans had arrived he was teasing his ear in their waiting rooms and was insulted there too. In the beginning the people in *Nasjonal Samling** were rather haughty when new converts applied for membership (the day would come when they persuaded, pleaded, and threatened). Finally he was accepted; they made him chief of police in various places, for he was of no use as a writer, but they moved him about from place to place until he finally landed as chief of police at Os. There, far up in the North, he was soon forgotten. Not even Erling had known that this confused and always half-drunk deputy-Goebbels in Os was identical with Torvald Ørje; he was said to be harmless because he was too stupid to be allowed a free hand. Erling learned differently; Ørje had sent a couple of NS-men to Oslo to shoot him, but the Germans had already sent their own men. He had to make his escape before any of them had time to strike. The Gestapo was out on honest business, one might say, while Torvald Ørje was only an underling out to revenge someone who once had slighted him.

So strange, so long ago.

The otherwise skinny man had a fat stomach. He used a belt which sat like a furrow across his middle, and Erling found himself thinking of different kinds of fish, the ones called fat and the ones called lean; the fat ones had their fat equally distributed over the body, like halibut, herring, and mackerel; the lean ones had an enormous liver, like codfish and shark. Perhaps it was his liver that made the skinny Torvald Ørje swell so much around his stomach. Erling recalled one of the victims of this revenge-hungry informer, a man who had returned home from Sachsenhausen after the war and said, "You know, you can get hungry enough to eat human liver—but only when it's well peppered." Erling saw only what was vile about Ørje; it made him sick to his stomach to look at the worn belt across this man's swollen belly. And it evoked a memory of the belt in which the informer Jan Husted had been hung.

So unreal and so long ago! For a moment he almost forgot the man Torvald Ørje, as he stood absent-mindedly and evaluated him. It was often said one could see on a person what he was. People looked at pictures of criminals and stated at once: You can see from a mile away

* The Norwegian Nazi party; members were referred to as NS-men.

what sort of man he is! Yes—because it was printed below the picture; they would have had a different opinion if the print had said that the man had saved four small children from drowning.

Everything about Torvald Ørje was disorderly. He had no command of his body, and his face was distorted as if big bubbles were rising and sinking in it. His look might in the space of a few seconds change from fawning, urging, pleading, to arrogance—all the time alert as to how far he dared go. He created an impression of deceit, fear, and a never-resting urge to dominate and hurt. He might fall on his knees and cry if he thought that was suitable—he had indeed done so—and in the next moment turn brutal if he were given a friendly word that to his mind suggested surrender and weakness; a monster, sick with joy when someone fell into his hands.

Erling did not recall how many years Torvald Ørje was sentenced to when brought to justice after the war, nor had Erling been the one to point him out; during the war there might have been some sense in destroying him but now it didn't matter. On the contrary, when he was let out he was a good man to have: he had so thoroughly discredited the traitors' fight for restitution that it looked as if he had been bribed even then.

Erling looked at the man for a moment before he asked, almost reluctantly, "What has got into you to come to *me?*"

Torvald Ørje made a motion as if to sneak by Erling into the room, but Erling did not move. "There could be nothing to say between us that can't be said in the doorway. I won't ask you to come in."

"If I could talk to you for a few moments I would explain—"

"I have no desire to listen to your opinions about the war, and what happened in Norway, if that's what you mean. What do you want?"

"Well—you call it during the *war*—you must mean during the *occupation*—"

"Shut up! What do you want?"

Torvald Ørje stared and now Erling saw that he actually looked like Goebbels, and that Goebbels also had resembled a dog. Ørje changed his tactics and spoke rapidly: he had some paintings, left behind when Erling fled to Sweden. Now he wanted to sell them, for a price; he had bought them when the Germans confiscated Erling's belongings. But Erling could have them back, might even get them as a gift—the fact was, Ørje had written a book about the occupation, and if Erling could find the time to look over the manuscript—he had it with him in his briefcase—

Just then he caught sight of Erling's eyes and realized there was danger brewing. When Erling took a step toward him he stumbled out backwards.

Erling closed the door after him. The worst thing that the Germans had done was to let stupidity loose in the land, all those jackasses who were harmless enough in peacetime. He went to the kitchen and poured himself a drink, which he swallowed before he picked up the telephone and called a lawyer he knew and asked him to start proceedings about the theft. Then he became depressed and nervous. He regretted it almost as he called, although he could see no clear reason why it should distress him. Were his pictures to hang in the house of that person? Then he realized that what bothered him was the fact that he had dirtied himself with that man by turning to someone because of him. Now there would be trouble; Torvald Ørje would never understand that the pictures weren't his; he had obtained them from the Germans who lawfully had confiscated them, and Ørje himself had paid his debt through his prison term; the books were balanced. Erling had met some of that sort, people who tried to pretend that nothing had happened. But to Erling the curtain had gone down once and for all; such people indicated only too clearly through their action that they were nostalgic for the time of great darkness when the Germans wielded the whip over the country; then all of them had acted like people who had been permitted for a short time to return to their babyhood and dirty themselves as much as they pleased; their happy days in the diaper had come to an end when the Germans left.

He was unable to regain his equilibrium after the visit, and he thought of taking to the bottle—but not tonight, no, not tonight; he was afraid of the saber-toothed tiger, that symbol of his identity problem.

He went to bed but sleep did not come. Something labored confusingly in his head, something about the distinction between war and occupation. Then he knew what it was. He went to a drawer, opened it, and found what he was looking for; it was a sort of letter-to-the-editor from a one-time NS-man, signed with a pseudonym, suggesting that it was Erling and his kind who had been the traitors because of their inability to distinguish between war and occupation.

Erling had read similar opinions written by other criminals; formality of procedure characterizes the criminal's argument: one who had plundered and murdered in his own land while it was occupied could make much over the choice of terms for describing the situation in the country, in order to get around the fact that a crook is a crook.

There was no doubt but that the letter was written by Torvald Ørje, the man who had called this evening, the man who in the fall of 1941 had plotted against the lives of Erling and others he didn't like.

Erling recalled that somebody else had published a bloodthirsty article —*The Guilt of the Masses*—defending murders of fishermen up in the North, deportation, torture, and starvation for the rest of the village population, because there had been a British raid in the neighborhood where these people were unfortunate enough to live.

Such people had paid their penalty, it was said, but they hadn't done so formally, and there might perhaps be some sense in not insisting on punishment for actions which could not be expiated. The Italians had been clearer in their thinking when they apprehended Mussolini: when he wanted to defend himself he was told that if he was Benito Mussolini he would be killed: what they were discussing was only his identification. The Quisling case was a comedy and it is difficult to believe anyone acted in good faith; a united people wanted Quisling's head, therefore the people should have taken that head, without hiding their own heads in the bushes. We the people let ourselves become irresponsible children when Quisling was brought to trial and sentenced; we were so tired we did not even hate Quisling any longer, it was said. We had become tired of him, we wished to get rid of him, but I believe it was a common daydream he would die of himself—simply not be there any more; we would have preferred to learn that he had vanished into thin air. But the habits from five years of occupation inclined us to demand his life, mainly because we didn't know what else to do with him. Erling had suggested, privately, that he be put in a glass cage, somewhere along the road between Oslo and Drammen; in winter, he might be allowed to sell Christmas trees, or be given a place down at the docks where he could sit in peace and fish. Not many had actually anticipated criminal proceedings, once the war was over.

The situation created by the Germans and the traitors themselves was so wrong that *they* at any rate had no business complaining about wrongness. To Erling it seemed obvious that people had managed as best they could from day to day, but it was disgusting that some should brag about it. Now some of the worst traitors were free again, simply because they had happened to be brought to justice later than those who were shot, and there was a growing party in the country now who clamored for redress, and received support from the most surprising quarters.

Erling forced himself to think more calmly, mostly because he wanted to go to sleep.

• *Our own genocide*

Oh, all the poison that had been pumped into us, thought Erling, as he turned and tossed in his bed, listening to the rain pouring down. One day at Venhaug—it had been in July some years ago—they had been sitting and talking about the genocide Hitler had planned and in some degree carried out. Then Felicia left to attend to something, saying, "Speaking of genocide, why don't you, Erling, go out and destroy a Babylon for me?" She pointed through the window with her hand, a cigarette between two of her fingers: "You see that little hill behind my workbench—it's an anthill; they're all over me when I sit down there."

Jan had started to fumble with a bunch of keys. "Don't burn the grass there," he said. "It'll leave a spot; there are all kinds of poisons in the closet out in the cottage; here are the keys—this is the one to the outside closet door, this one for the inner door. Double doors for poison," he added proudly. "DDT should do it but use what you want."

In the big closet Erling found enough poison to kill a small army—disinfectant pills, sprays, hormone mixtures, small and large packages and bottles, everything carefully labeled and marked with skull and crossbones the way Jan was able to draw them—precise, careful Jan!

Erling espied a thin wire far back on a shelf. He didn't quite know why he picked it up and weighed it in his hand; it was twisted together in a roll and could easily be carried in a pocket. He unrolled it—it was a pig-snare.

His hand jerked and involuntarily went to his throat. Something dark was taking shape in his thoughts, but at first there was only a touch of wonder: why was this snare *here?* Then he thought of the wild ideas children and thoughtless youths might get into their heads. Eternally careful Jan! And then the dark connection stood clear for him suddenly: it was the object Jan Venhaug had used a few days before Christmas in 1942, when he liquidated another Jan, the informer Jan Husted. He brushed his hand across his forehead: Jan, Jan—here you have locked it up so no one else can use *it* when slaughtering pigs. You incorrigible Jan Venhaug, never able to forget that Jan Husted in spite of all was a human being. Erling still recalled the stammering words in Stockholm: "You understand I couldn't let him cry out, and I couldn't shoot him just there, and so I brought along something to choke him with."

The sequel Jan had not related, but Erling knew that after he had strangled Jan Husted he had taken down a large picture, leaned it against the wall, and hung the victim on the strong hook to make sure. Jan Venhaug was a thorough man, and thoroughly the deed had been done. No one doubted that if Jan returned from a job, it had been well done. Jan had waited there for a quarter of an hour and then let the body down; when Husted was found it was as a suicide hanging by his own belt.

Erling looked over the poisons and felt an impulse to mix everything together to destroy the ants. He suppressed the thought because he knew so little about such matters and was afraid the mixture might explode. He would manage with DDT.

He walked over to the anthill, stirred in it with a stick, and watched the swarm of ants before he dusted on a thick layer of the soapy white powder, which left a repulsively sweetish smell in his nose and mouth. Surely, twenty, thirty times too much, he thought, but at least no ant can come out without getting some of the poison on its body, or return without spreading it down inside the hill.

A week later he had remembered the hill and returned; now there was only a little of the white powder left, but it had rained one night. A few ants, at most about fifty, were still wandering over the hill, but there were none on the ant paths leading to the nest. He bent down and observed something peculiar; every time two ants met they started to fight. Some didn't give up, others stopped after a while. Most of them seemed so confused that they only fought for a few seconds, then took off to encounter a new enemy in a moment.

Erling had started an all-out war of each against each. The odor of their comrades-in-misfortune was not the odor of the hill—that their own odor also had changed they apparently did not realize. All were enemies, they had lost their tribal instinct. Survivors were still busy killing each other.

Toward evening the following day he walked out again and looked. There were still a few ants chasing each other but fewer than the day before. As he was about to leave he discovered something alive moving somewhere near the center of the hill, about as big as a half-crown. He stooped and stared; it was a clump of ants, ants so small it was almost impossible to recognize the individual bodies. He had never seen such small ants, each one no bigger than a pinprick. He went to fetch a jar, in order to look at them with a magnifying glass, but he was interrupted and then the sun went down. When he returned they were gone; he looked for them the following day also but could not find a single one, not even when he dug down into the hill. A few of the forest ants were still fighting, for none must survive. Where had they come from, those dwarfs, surely many hundreds of them, in the middle of the poisoned hill?

Not long ago he had read something he thought might explain the dwarf-ant puzzle; at last he remembered the book and located it on a shelf in Felicia's room. It was an adventure novel titled *The Jester of Bokhara,* by Leonid Solovjev. He found the place:

> From time immemorial the potters of Bokhara have lived outside the east gate of the city on a large clay hill and they could never have found a better place. Here is clay in abundance and they get water from the ditch which runs outside the city wall. The potters' grandfathers, great-grandfathers and great-great-grandfathers had dug out half of the hill; they built their houses of clay, they made pots of clay, and were buried in clay while relatives wailed. Through the centuries it had happened, and probably not so seldom either, that a potter made a vessel, dried it in the sun, hardened it in fire, and marveled at the strength and resonant purity of the vessel. He did not suspect that one of his distant forefathers was contributing to the welfare and success of his descendants in blessing the clay with part of his dust, making it ring like silver.

Then into a closed community like this came foreigners, with overpowering weapons or as thieves in the night, or else brimstone stolen from the sacred hearth rained down from the heavens. Then all attacked all, and at the same time a pygmy race sprang up. Missionaries incited brother against brother, as they were told to do, slave-hunters forced the Africans to sell each other, bombs falling on the cities drove the inhabitants to assassinations among their own ruins. Negroes in South Africa became the most reliable policemen for the whites, India and Polynesia were kept down by soldiers who were the very children of those countries, and by overlords who were allowed to keep their hoarded possessions. In China, the country's own merchants became the trusted allies of the Europeans. One could also send natives money and weapons, assuring them solemnly that these were purely friendly gifts without obligations, thus letting the people themselves handle the situation without outside control; the weapons were used in deep gratitude for the purpose intended.

When a people has been suppressed, by force or by so-called peaceful means, they declare war against themselves, a secret civil war that brings them to their own destruction. The movement by the suppressor to take over the suppression begins at once. During these latter years the great powers apparently have been a little too eager: they can't wait to let the poison run its murderous course, perhaps they are afraid there won't be time enough, and they interfere to hasten the process. In so doing they lay bare their own tactics, with their too obvious quislings. The poison must be given time and not shown up too soon. This mistake is perhaps our only grounds for hope of *not* drifting into slavery for centuries: their great urgency exposes them, and keeps resistance awake. The suppression ought to take place through well planned and patient flattery of those sheep who are always in the majority. Vidkun Quisling was a born loser, and the resistance movement could not itself have concocted him better. The executioner's ax should be kept hidden behind the back (those who understand these things say rightly people should know that the rod is behind the cupboard). One must inch along toward the goal where the suppressed believe they are living under a law they themselves have passed and are allowed to enforce in their free junta.

Erling wished Felicia would stop bothering him about moving to Venhaug for good. Each time it was equally annoying and unsuitable. It seemed that this question disturbed their being together even when it was not mentioned. Their mutual telepathy was something they undoubtedly had to take into account—they knew each other so infinitely well. Erling might meet her eyes when she looked up from a book and know she was planning a new attack on the subject; then he prepared himself silently and could be quite caustic before she had time to begin.

She knew quite well that the problem wasn't the same for both of them. Perhaps she had solved it, as far as it concerned her. It was possible she didn't even see it as a problem. To him it was great and had many facets. He thought of the nights when he sat here at his table for hours, or paced back and forth on the floor, deep in his own thoughts. Or the very early mornings, at any season of the year, when he decided that he had worked long enough; spring mornings with the song of the woodcock; still, daylight-light summer mornings when no one was out on the roads in flat Lier which spread before him in the distance; winter mornings, black and glitteringly white, the frost and the heat working at the walls from either side until one heard it like cautious, stealthy steps. Most of all perhaps the late fall mornings! A morning when he would open the door to the raw darkness where the leaves clung to the flagstones; a piece of wood against the door would keep the wind from closing it. There he would stand and listen to the soughing in the trees, alone and happy, thinking of nothing in particular, just ordinary thoughts: that all the tobacco smoke would escape; that the air in the room was renewed with an abundance of oxygen; that the water would soon come to a boil on the stove; that people round and about were just getting up; that he must bake a couple of loaves today; that he needn't eat the monotonous store-bread; that he would write to Copenhagen for a piece of real cheese; that it was odd of people to ruin their coffee with sugar and cream.

Here I stand alone, darkness facing me. No one knows I am standing here. Now we'll have another shower. Listen to the rain beat against the walls, splash against the threshold!

And then close the door again, make coffee, fry an egg or two, or exactly as many as he desired, or none at all, cut a slice of his delicious bread and spread butter on it. Listen to the fire crackling when he added new wood, and think sweet thoughts of a woman now that he had shed all responsibility.

Such a morning, satisfied and happy, before he stretched out on his bed to sleep, away from all respectable people's workday—wasn't this the very symbol of all he had gained? He was far from a misanthrope indeed, but you do better by others when you follow your own course. He had seen enough of depressing friends who ought to have gone home and to bed.

It was here that his thought-world at last had taken root. This room was his brain, like the box-frames the beekeeper puts in the hive where the honey is collected. Here his thoughts fought their fights, continued while he went for a walk. How often hadn't the result hung ready here when he returned. It was to his thought-world he returned from Oslo, from Venhaug, from Las Palmas. Only a little of it could he take with him. Like a sample in a briefcase.

Steingrim Hagen in *his* day had written much about how to avoid war, Steingrim who besides all his other attainments had the brain of a politician. He dealt only with economy and power when he dreamt of a better humanity. The concept of politics had come to him as a sort of contagion from other politicians; after all, it could only come through mental contamination. Political ideas never absorbed anything new nor gave up anything old. There were only so many false coins in Beelzebub's Bank that the Devil had managed to put into circulation before Hell was closed and the director was sent into political asylum in Stavanger. Even with Steingrim the concept of politics had not developed beyond the eternally same, differing from original sin only in that it had to be learned. He might shake his head leniently and say, "Politics you do not understand, Erling."

Erling had never replied, and now he knew why. It was because of the politicians' solemn seriousness, which is part of the Devil's pontification.

Politicians always began by clearing the throat, and as a rule this was enough to silence the ironic. For political questions are holy and are posed by serious, grown people, who early have been given the impulse to look for a more or less actual revolver if anyone ridicules them. For the sake of their own self-importance politicians consider themselves great individualists, but mostly they are nothing but mediums mouthing established opinions. It would create a sensation if a newspaper printed that a politician had said something he himself had thought up. As a rule he only ogled his Moloch and listened: What might one of the big boys say about this just now? Should one telephone to ask? And it might happen that one of the big boys gave a gracious nod—in order that he himself might not be responsible for such nonsense; if nonsense must be spoken, let someone else speak it.

No newspaperman had as yet proclaimed: "Now foreign minister so and so has again said something only in order to say something, and it has no apparent meaning. When I called to inquire what it meant, a secretary replied that His Excellency had nothing to add. As I do not wish to visit an oracle with less information than any street urchin has, I only want to state that the paper I write for does not pay me to play the Fool to His Excellency, and his statement is pure nonsense, without meaning, and he would have done better by keeping his mouth shut."

But the newspaperman does not do this. He takes the speech seriously, knits his thoughtful brow, he too. And His Excellency is told—in the bathroom, or wherever he might be—that the man must be a climber, or possibly an ass. It was pleasing to remember that Steingrim Hagen had not spared his irony on such political gentlemen.

Erling pulled up the blind and looked out at the dawn over the countryside spreading before him. In a month it would be autumn. A few crows sailed over the landscape, flying low now before people were up. In early morning they would alight in his yard, spy cautiously about with shrewd and impudent eyes, before they approached the garbage, waddling like old women, unable to realize it had been thrown there for them to pick up. It had been bred into them long ago that people were the wisest of all animals in the world and did not like crows because they stole chickens and eggs. Especially during early summer mornings Erling liked to stand at the window and peek at them in the yard through a hole in the blind. The crows knew that people only seldom were up at three in the morning, but they could never feel sure. When Erling watched them through the hole and thought he fooled them, he wasn't quite sure either. The ironic glances those wily garbage thieves cast at the window might well indicate they knew he was standing there peeking. Erling had a weakness for crows.

Now the light summer mornings would soon be over. In foggy weather they could be pitch dark. He picked up his glass but moved it only a bit farther in on the table, trying to fool himself that that was all he had in mind. But he wasn't even sure he could fool a crow.

• Destruction

The recollection of Steingrim and of a fleeting summer brought his thoughts to a farm in Telemark where, Steingrim had said, it might be nice to live for a while. There Erling had seen a love story but not the end of it. He sat down in his easy chair and thought: It is true, my thought-world lives in this house.

The little story led up to the very center of the problem that had occupied him above all during these years after the war: reflections on how people isolated themselves through isolating others, and what their purpose might be in so acting. He thought that the shock the war had brought had at last opened his eyes to the possible reason why people, contrary to their own interests, caused each other loneliness. He had come to the conclusion that in the enforced isolation and uncommunicativeness of the individual lay the most dangerous seed of violence and war. Not the apparent reasons for war—in this Steingrim might well have been right—but the underlying reasons which made war possible and which choked the impulse to avoid war. The consensus was that the individual had no influence in making war, and consequently was not responsible for it either. This was obviously wrong, because a war was started by individuals who at first stirred up their own people, who again were made up of individuals; realistically, war was and remained your business and mine, if for no other reason than because we had failed to show resistance. The individual lacked influence only if he had in advance resigned his will, and thus had become the most profound and actual cause of war. The last ounce of individuality was crushed in military training, after the schools had created the prerequisites. From birth one was taught to believe that all real individual thought was the business of others: Let him to whom our Lord has given the head to think, handle such matters! They did not add—because this also calls for a thought—that a people not under foreign domination owns the government and only the people themselves can prepare the soil for the government they have. They might say: Well, that's progress, evolution.

And they might feel that now everything had definitely been said, and that was that. If this watery nonsense was all that had survived of that genius Charles Darwin, then one could understand people who contrarily believed that apes were descended from men, and perhaps Darwin himself might have shaken his head and begun to suspect it.

It was a few years before the war that Erling one summer had lived on the farm in Telemark. He had had little to do with the people in the house, a family by the name of Larsen and some servants. As a rule he only came in for his dinner; he lived in a cottage at a lake about a mile away. It was a rather fallen-down place and it was said it had been a shed in which to dry fish. Now there was no fishing, except when some small boys occasionally got a few perch on the hook; they would sit out on a little cliff toward dusk and eat something good they had brought along, and fight the mosquitoes while they waited for a bite. From time to time they would yell, and the volume of their voices indicated to Erling how much of a catch they had made.

He did not stay at the farm as long as he had intended, even though, as Steingrim had said, it was a nice place. He felt compelled to leave by happenings that did not concern him and in which he played no part. But he had never been able to keep other people's lives outside his consciousness when gross behavior was involved. What happened was that someone else's brutality opened up scars of old pain-centers from a time when his own life was one long ugly squabble. He could not brush aside other people's troubles by saying they didn't concern him, because they did concern him in the same way as an unpleasant odor must concern him.

What drove him from the farm appeared in bolder relief for having begun with the attractive sight of two human beings falling in love; it put him in a pleasant mood without involving him, in the same way as a beautiful morning might do, or very rarely some letter, or a bottle of cool wine on a summer veranda. Then a third person broke in with her disgusting lust for destruction. He could not take it, he had to leave the following day. Mrs. Larsen stared in disbelief: "But you said yesterday you felt at home here?" "Yes," said Erling, "that was yesterday—but today I must leave." He noticed by her look that a complicated problem had been raised—he had paid for another week, did he really expect to get his money back?

And she had remained disturbed until the very moment he had left with the bus. Probably though, she had been most upset because he had not given her the opportunity to use all the arguments which had kept her awake through the night: that she was not to be blamed because he was leaving; because, because, because. She was standing there bursting with all this. Erling felt it was good for her that he had caused her so much worry; he would not have accepted a refund anyway, and to him it was cheapest to leave at once when his peace was gone. Yet, sitting in the bus it had annoyed him that he had been interested in the fact that he had had a right to demand a refund.

Infamous lust for destruction, he had thought, summed up what had happened, but he was always more interested in what an act was, and what had caused it, than in the name it had. To say that a man's name was Lauris Berg did not describe him; it was the content within him that must be examined. From early youth Erling had gathered striking examples of what was hidden beneath words—words that had been heaped over him like burning tar, and might explain the one who had heaped them, and also something about the victim. Erling's mind was busy with this fifty-year-old farmwife, wondering where her lust for destruction had had its source.

On the farm there was a girl named Mary, a charming creature about seventeen, whom Erling barely had noticed in the beginning. If anyone had asked him what she looked like he could only have said that she was a girl with freckles. He had often read that girls with freckles were supposed to be particularly desirable, but he thought this must be a literary convention akin to the old "damask cheek." He could see nothing exceptionally attractive in freckles, but he knew also that when a young man fell in love, everything about the girl was first class, and he could well imagine the discoverer's exclamations of joy over the freckles. He had also heard about the attraction of a cross-eyed girl, but as far as he knew the time had not yet come to sing about the girl with warts.

He paid little attention to Mary, or indeed, to anyone. But then one day the electrician came. Erling happened to be out in the yard when he drove up in a dilapidated old car; it squeaked like an angry bird and stank of gasoline. Alm was a young electrician, very energetic, and started at once to pull out wires and tools from his car while he whistled and talked to himself. He looked to be about twenty and wasn't still for a moment.

Things didn't start too well; Mrs. Larsen came out and said it wasn't convenient for him to work just then because her husband had gone to bed for his midday rest. Young Alm sat down on the stoop and said he didn't care, he was paid by the hour. Mrs. Larsen gave the young man one quick look and decided Mr. Larsen must get out of bed. But her cheeks had colored a little.

While Mrs. Larsen went to fetch her husband, young Alm discovered Mary in the kitchen window and started to make eyes at her. She laughed, and clattered with her dishes, and he saw that she was good-looking.

Alm was to stay at the farm until his work was finished. Already that same evening he took off into the countryside in his rattling car, Mary at his side; he was a man of action. During the day Erling had seen him string wires across the yard, hanging like a fly on the outside wall, using more arms and hands than a person has and not letting them get in the way of each other. There was something stimulating in watching a young man, in action as lively and agile as an otter. With the same resolution he had put Mary in his car and driven off, for now action was called for.

During the following day the electrician again whistled while he worked, and Mary walked about with that introspective smile which indicates a young woman has withdrawn into herself to meditate over an electrician. In the evening Erling saw them near his cottage. They were sitting close together on a stone, looking out over the lake.

Mrs. Larsen had not retired from the world. Nor did she even manage to appear polite while Erling was present; she shoved the china at him as if they were married. The day after he had seen the young couple on the stone, Mrs. Larsen picked up a dirty wash rag and hit Mary with it across the face. It came without warning; not a word had been said. The girl stumbled backward against the wall and stared in consternation at Mrs. Larsen who was spewing a salvo of abuse. Erling was alone with them in the kitchen and could think of nothing better to do than to go. He could work no more in that place and he decided to leave. He never learned what happened to Mary and her electrician.

· The fear of ecstasy

An ecstasy in which you have no part separates you from the person involved, who slips out of your sphere of domination more thoroughly than in any other way, except possibly in the case of schizophrenia. One becomes totally without influence. Then one tries a reconquest with force. That such a method is not very successful ought to be obvious, and when success fails, one is likely to explode in desperate actions defended on moral grounds. Mrs. Larsen made an issue of morality in her heretofore blameless house. The result was disastrous; her actions did not make Mrs. Larsen happy, and certainly not Mary, nor her electrician. What Mrs. Larsen had in mind, if she hadn't been completely distracted at the moment of action, was difficult to see. She ought to have realized that one must never let morality dominate if one wants to make use of it.

She had carried on about the morals of youth, but whether or not Mary and the electrician had broken any moral code, she did not know; she only scented something alien.

It is amazing that humanity has been able to survive with a vice that has been in ascendance since the time of Adam and Eve. Every new generation practices it and then rages because the following youthful generation does the same. One needn't bother to describe how the old look at the young; one may merely seize upon a quotation in passing: "The youths of today think only of themselves and have no respect for their parents or older people in general. The young take a dim view of having their actions and freedom curtailed, and they talk as if only they understood all things that to us are wisdom and which they consider stupidity. As to young girls—they are foolish and immodest, unladylike in speech, behavior, and dress."

These timeworn words have been used, day in and day out, since they were written in the year of Our Lord 1247, and undoubtedly youth had heard them long before that. There has always been something wrong with youth—God knows where they got it from. Erling wondered if one couldn't turn the irritation about, and direct the blame against the older generation, since they were so eager to harp on it. Then youth might be left in peace for a time, having so long been the scapegoat for a thing so universally human.

An instantaneous turn-about would be unjust, however, for the present older generation has already been lambasted for its sins. Therefore it should be arranged so, that the old ones of today would be let off without further chastising, provided they keep their hands off the youth of today, who in turn would get their planing-down from their descendants in the following ten years or so. Youth would then, in coming generations, entirely assume the monopoly of morals, and could undoubtedly add fresh approaches and invent new and painful experiences. Erling had recently read a thesis by the Danish Doctor Svend G. Johnsen about "fat boys" and their later fate. In it he had come across the following: "The male between twenty and thirty with pronounced *dystrophia adiposogenitales* usually still lives with his parents and declares on questioning that he is fully satisfied with this. Opposition against the preceding generation is totally lacking in these cases, and the patient enjoys being looked after by the mother."

Opposition against the preceding generation was lacking; a medical scientist had labeled it as a deficiency disease if youth isn't rebellious.

Erling had never felt grown-up enough to assume command of youths' morals, as he was still dubious about his own. The moralizing he had been exposed to during his early years had, to no purpose, made him feel a vast disgust which had slackened his work-desire and dampened his lust for life—something which he suspected had been the very purpose. It had also tempted him to sin to the utmost of his ability—which perhaps *also* had been the hidden purpose. Perhaps this in turn had contributed to the view of his mature years that youth should sail its own course and personally get stuck on the rocks, without threatening clouds from above, in the end to realize that after all it had been a wonderful sailing.

Among the causes that made another person escape our sphere of influence, falling in love with someone else was probably first on the list, thought Erling. A classical example is housewives' nosiness about their maids' sexual activities. In its heyday this pursuit had almost been justified for its own sake, requiring only the thinnest excuse on moral grounds to cover up fundamental lust to dominate, brutal sadism, vicarious eroticism, or plain gossipy curiosity. When a maid decided to leave and asked her boy-friend to carry down her belongings to a taxi, it created a vacuum which was felt long and bitterly. Love, long ago, had been proclaimed the enemy, unless one was one of the participants. A person in ecstasy, caught in another's circle, is outside one's power to dominate. We have arrived at a point where fear, automatically and as an entity itself, seizes us when someone is happy. A person who once has lost power—and this usually happens early in life—is consumed by that foolish lust to dominate that is called jealousy; which never can compensate for the original loss, even if it conquered the whole world. Indeed, the search for other conquests starts quickly; the fear of losing influence is the fear of being left alone—in the last analysis the fear of death. It shows up in any number of details of everyday life, from the annoyance against someone who forgot to send us a birthday greeting, or failed to invite us when Fredrik was invited, to the poorly hidden sullenness toward Kristian, whom we are unable to communicate with fully because he is still thinking of his dead brother. Why should he keep mourning about that for months? you say to yourself, and perhaps also to him. It bothers you that friends have friends that are not yours also. You are on the verge of wanting to forbid them to meet people you don't like. The suspicion of not being the most favored makes you sick. Friends of husband or son are viewed with suspicion as being unsuitable company and ridiculed to death. You must be chaste, you must be pure, you must keep to yourself, for I would rather see you dead than know you are with someone else.

• The boy in the field

A friend had once told Erling about an incident during a summer day in his childhood, how he had hid in the tall grass out in a field and was very happy. He had felt he could lie there forever and look up at the clouds, listen to the wind playing in the grass, and watch butterflies fluttering about. It had been with some embarrassment that he had confessed to Erling his memory of that day, but he was also pleased to talk to someone who might understand and wouldn't repeat his childhood secret.

But this had not prevented the man, a few years later, from scaring the daylights out of his son when he had discovered him in the same situation. Apparently his action was a pure reflex; no memories of his own enjoyable experience could have been present just then. Erling had happened to see the boy as he returned from the field, fear in his eyes, embarrassed and confused. "How stupid to lie there and dream!" the father had said.

The boy was fully aware that he was being suspected of something he didn't even understand. But I don't think this was the fundamental reason for the father's scolding; it was only that the boy must not withdraw from the circle of inspection. If the father had had anything else in mind, then this had only been in order to have a rational explanation handy. It was obvious that the boy had been given a most unpleasant shock, the consequences of which no one could foretell. If one called it a kind of vandalism, one might receive the absurd reply that the boy probably wouldn't suffer from it, and anyway he must learn that life wasn't simple and easy like that. Erling felt he might have learned this without his parents' suffering a blemish on their reputation. The prospect for the future was dark; the father had been conscious of his own so-called sin when he had withdrawn to the summer field and stayed alone with the grass and the clouds, beyond the domination of others.

• Out on the marshes

A life might run its course like a river that flows to the sea, according to the parable so often used, but perhaps we shouldn't use images as much as we do, for they sometimes give the impression that images are explanations, while in reality they remove us from the inexplicable which the image was meant to convey.

For many, the comparison of life with a river does not fit. There was once a man who early in his life made a decision to get away from his fate, and being young he could see no deeper nor further than that he must get away in a purely geographic sense—a misconception which has helped distribute people across the face of the earth, and in recent historical times has populated a new continent.

He pursued this misconception for a few years but ended up in darkest confusion and returned to his homeland. He settled down and again ended up in confusion. This was repeated many times. To portray his life one might imagine a man going on a long journey without any means of transportation; he must walk, and the distance is many thousand miles without a road. One morning in his early youth he had left his parental home without saying good-by to anyone. He carried neither compass nor map; he took his bearings from some paling stars and walked. He wandered for thirty-five years and lived many lives in that time, lives in out-of-the-way valleys, or on marshes he had never intended to visit but came onto during the journey, because he was tempted by short-cuts and sometimes gave up following the path according to the stars. Thus it happened that he might leave a place he had thought as good as any and start out again some early morning, without saying good-by to anyone. When he met people who asked where he was headed for he could not answer. He would have liked to answer if he had been able to, but he did not know. And after a short time he had forgotten all the people he had known there, and they seemed as unreal to him as if he had never known them, and so it was with all his experiences; he never wished to return. And it might happen that people from different places where he had lived and intended to stay forever, would meet. And they might say: "Well, it would have been better not to count on him—we weren't good enough for him." He himself recalled his attempts to stay put and would then wonder: How did I get there in the first place?

When at last he had reached his goal he wanted to review and understand what it had all been about, but he pushed it aside as long as he could and thought: Well, some other time; I'm busy now.

One day it dawned on him that he was fooling himself, as most people do in saying they don't have time, because in reality time and events rule us, and our own decisions have little to do with it. And he realized that life had taken him up many blind alleys and out on many swamp lands where he had had no business being, but had experienced an ever increasing confusion, and each time he had been forced to return to his old path to see if the stars were still shining there—and they were, even the last time when he went to look for them and discovered them bright and large above his head.

He walked inside and stared for some time at the embers on the hearth. Long ago others made too many decisions for me, he thought, but later I was alone and no one decided for me any longer. This I could not manage for many years, for my will had been broken, and I strayed into the lone valleys and out in the marshes where I was hoping to find someone who needed me and would make decisions for me. Being homesick for evil I went into the remote valleys and out in the sinister marshes where stupidity and intellectual confusion made their home, and each time I left these places, flayed and unhappy, always sick and despondent, asking again for those years when others decided for me and took from me.

He remained standing and watched the embers fade, and felt as if all sin, also his own, had been obliterated once and for all.

The greatest pitfall on the road to mental health and balance is the struggle to discredit reason. This is attempted in good faith by sick visionaries, and in evil faith by religious demagogues whose interest is to neutralize the minds of others. It is a war that never can be won in the long run, because they cannot attack reason without proving that they themselves are using it also; but as in all war it spreads its pestilence. This war against reason assumes its dirtiest aspects in times of political campaigning, when members of the various party machines spit on each other and degrade themselves to make contact with those vapors that the masses call reason; during the last days before election they become positively vulgar. If this is the road to the majority of the votes, then the politicians must be right in their evaluation of the voters, but at the same time they provide an ominous indication that democracy is a swindle. It isn't the people's voice that is heard, rather the echo of the demagogues' voice. They themselves have elected themselves.

Erling suspected that no one through the years could deal in distortions, misrepresentations, and lies—in defiance of one's own good sense —and still remain uncontaminated. Confronting such a person privately, in his shabbiness and with his smirk, one realized he had indeed been deeply damaged.

Long ago, at home in Rjukan, in a home of sick people, tyrannized over by his strong brother Gustav, who now was a mountain-blaster, Erling had never relinquished during his childhood the belief that the grownups knew all. Especially his helpless parents and the handless grandfather: these knew *all*. They did not wish to let on they knew, yet they surely did and could settle everything with a single sentence, nay, in a single word, but they just wouldn't say that word. They were little gods who begrudged him the light of this single word; the word that contained the whole explanation as to why life *was,* everything, but more important why people were evil, and slew and slew—with a look, or a smirk, or with the fists, spitting on and destroying others—the explanation as to why there wasn't a kind word in the world. Why life *was,* this he had long ago given up the answer to. There was no answer. Surprisingly many explained it by saying only that life would continue when one was dead, and never end. He could not deny that life in one form or another was indestructible, but how could they call this an explanation of something that never would end? He had thought, even before school days, that they either were simple-minded or suppressed a secret when they said such things. Were they wily liars, or were they talking nonsense?

But the key word for all the calamity human beings themselves have chosen, he thought he had now at last discovered. As he had believed long ago in childhood, the explanation for everything could indeed be put into a single word, but with a lifetime of sad discovery behind it—the *Werewolf.*

That morning, when he received a long-distance call that Steingrim was ill—well, seriously ill . . .

Erling realized that the caller had read a little too much about "the most considerate way." He said: "With all that talk—are you trying to tell me that Steingrim Hagen is dead?"

The lady answered with a less graceful "Yes."

"What did he die from?"

There was another attempt at "considerate delay," this time rather confused, which Erling interrupted brusquely with—he was looking for a chair and couldn't find one—"Was it suicide?"

Now there was life in the lady caller: "Well, well! I must say you are—"

Erling had carefully replaced the receiver and walked over to a chair at the table. His joints felt stiff, and it seemed some fluid was floating inside his head.

During the following days and nights he walked a great many miles across the floor. Once he went to sleep in his chair, perhaps for an hour, perhaps for ten, he didn't know, he only woke up and continued to walk. Time stood still, it was night and it was day without his noticing it.

Felicia called. When she heard that Erling had been notified she started to cry and hung up. They had no words for each other.

The day Steingrim's corpse was being cremated in Oslo he began to write something he called "Letter to a heap of ashes."

Erling had never since read the letter; he had only locked it up when he couldn't manage any more; and that was when, after many roads, after many sidetracks and interruptions, tortured with doubts, sometimes almost in desperation, he had arrived at the point he had known for many years he must arrive at: at the single word he used to think they kept from him in childhood.

• Put a chastity belt around your thoughts

One time—it had been thirty-four years ago—he was asked to call on a publisher who had one of his manuscripts. It could mean only one thing.

Erling sat paralyzed in a chair facing this One-of-the-World's-Mighty, who was leafing through the manuscript which had cost him sixty kroner for a final typing but had an abundance of the most amazing mistakes which Erling had corrected in ink, leaving the end product as much in handwriting as in typed script. The man was turning the pages, coughing. "Look!" he said, and turned his eyes on Erling. He coughed again: "Look here!"

Erling leaned over and looked.

"It must be a somewhat misguided radicalism, Mr. Vik, to *write* a word you would never dream of *saying?*"

Erling had turned red, flustered. The publisher had found a substitute for the ugly word Erling had used many times a day for as long as he could remember. He realized fully that he was uneducated, but not that he had *so* far to go on the road of true learning. He did not protest. The man was looking over a list from his catch of words and obliterated the rest of the vermin without further comment. Erling thought he had been careful, had indeed himself used the fly-swatter before he had sent in the work.

The publisher arranged the sheets in a neat pile and folded his hands on top of the manuscript as if he intended to pray. The story lacked feeling, he said. "The author's heart is missing."

Erling listened, but the words were at the moment completely without meaning; would he publish the book, or wouldn't he?

When it became clear that he would publish the book, Erling did not hear another word. He could not remember to this day whether or not he had said anything.

He had never thought of smiling at the publisher's remark that his heart was missing. It only filled him with shame and fury, when he calmed down again after the publication-announcement and was able to think—and this had taken time. The happy fact remained that his book would come out. No world war, no love affair, no joy or misfortune had stirred him so deeply as this announcement; for this they could keep all the world's riches, and the earth might blow up for all he cared.

Until then his existence had been miserable, a sort of balance-arm with weights that could not be controlled.

As to that remark about the heart—the author's heart! It had struck at his deep fear that he might remain eternally in stupidity and lack of knowledge; it had been an exhortation to throw himself to the dogs. He had quite well understood it wasn't *his* particular heart that was in question—the publisher didn't give a damn about that—no, this was a collective heart they were fishing for, a feeling heart, well, you know what kind of heart.

And then the heart was not referred to again. More emphasis was given to what was more important, to that improper word he hadn't thought of as improper, a word used daily, which might even be seen in a newspaper. Erling turned the ridiculous remark into a symbol—not from some taboo word which by the way he never found opportunity to use, rather for what he later expressed by saying, "A distinguished author must put a chastity belt around his thoughts."

"It must be a somewhat misguided radicalism, Mr. Vik, to *write* a word you would never dream of *saying?*"

Every time he had felt himself weaken, those words rose before his inner eye in tall, black letters.

What did the publisher mean?

He could not have referred to foul words, of which there were none in his manuscript.

It was a warning against the use of words in general.

• *The game with Dummy*

Erling strode across the floor toward a shelf but hesitated a time or two in his walk. Then he shook off his indecision and took down a flat wooden box about a foot square. He blew the dust off the lid and placed the box on a table near the fire. Then he placed chairs opposite one another at the table, set out two wine glasses which he filled with whisky. Finally, he slid back the lid of the box and set up the contents for a game of checkers.

The circular wooden pieces were almost half an inch thick. Long ago they had been in two colors but after many years of use they were now difficult to tell apart; to make matters easier he had pushed thumb tacks into half of them. He picked up a Swiss franc from the box, threw it against the ceiling and watched it land on the table. "I start today," he said.

Dummy lost the game; he always did. Once more absolute honesty had been defeated. Erling leaned back in his chair and, as he had done many times before, thought it over. As he must every time he also emptied Dummy's glass (Dummy's defeat was always overwhelming). It makes no difference how you play or how much you think you act impartially and decently toward Dummy, you must win. It is, and remains, under any imaginable circumstances, impossible to lose a game to Dummy without cheating; as impossible as it is to jump leapfrog over oneself, or thumb one's nose at God and not consider oneself almighty. The right and duty to win is always on one's side. In spite of your good intentions, your good will (speak of freedom of the will!), your honesty —you still win the game. It might take a few moments to realize where one cheated or made the one move for Dummy he shouldn't have made; but whether you think it or not, one never doubts deep inside that one did cheat him. To find the formula for squaring the circle, to construct a perpetual motion machine, to see ghosts at high noon, to frighten one's great-grandfather, to tell all to one's beloved, to lose against Dummy— these things are all impossible. The founder of the Oxford Movement played in a quiet moment with Dummy and discovered in him a clever trader who at the last minute advised him to get rid of some dubious holdings. Dear God, where can we find a humble heart when you never punish blasphemers except between the covers of the Bible, but instead let them get by on the advice of a shrewd counselor? Teach me to lose against Dummy, so that perhaps once in the distant future, just once, I might have the experience of behaving justly to another creature.

• The woman you gave me

After a few hours of fitful sleep Erling put in a long-distance call to Venhaug. It was Felicia who answered; yes, he could come. He said he would take a train that left Drammen about two o'clock, and she rattled on about this and that. It was wonderful to hear her voice. She thought Jan might be the one to meet him at the station, and Welcome!

He called Kristiansen's taxi and made ready. The weather was depressing, raining; there should have been sun today, with light in abundance. How fortunate that people like Torvald Ørje didn't know how much unhappiness they could cause by their mere appearance. Thank heaven! they were too stupid to know or they might encircle the house day and night. Anyway, now I'll have a few days with Felicia and Jan.

He made sure that everything was well locked up before he left, but only when he sat in the taxi did it strike him that in giving the door an extra tug to test the lock, he had again been thinking of that vermin Torvald Ørje. He felt relaxed as the car turned onto the highway to Drammen and increased its speed. The rain splashed against the windows. This gave him a thought—why not take the taxi all the way to Venhaug? Then he could be alone with his thoughts, escaped being jostled on a probably crowded train—

He leaned forward: "Mr. Kristiansen—could you drive me all the way to Venhaug? You know the road—"

"Yes, indeed," but then they must stop somewhere and call his wife so she would know in case someone else called for the taxi.

"Good enough! Will you at the same time call Venhaug, then they'll know—"

He wrote down the number and the message on a leaf in his notebook: Erling Vik has asked me to call and say he will take the taxi all the way to Venhaug.

He tore out the page and handed it to Kristiansen. The taxi stopped at a country store and Kristiansen took care of the matter. Erling felt a relief so great he must smile. He pulled out a book he had intended to read, but fell into thought and watched the rain. Once again he noted that he was content. Financially he wasn't well to do but he managed; he had never had any desire either to splash money around or to save a pile. He was satisfied if he could keep his house, and dress fairly decently so no one noticed him either for elegance or shabbiness. His children were not close by but he had a nice relationship with them. Ellen had found another husband while he was in Sweden; now she lived somewhere on Vestlandet but he never heard from her. She had been twenty-six and he forty-one when they separated. Now she is forty-one, he thought, the same age as Felicia, seventeen years younger than I. A woman must always be thought of as young if she was so much younger than oneself. The only thing that remains of that business, he mused, and smiled at the thought, is that I almost daily compare these figures, God knows why. What a misery it had been. The time spent in Sweden had been hard on marriages; couples separated, unable to handle the fact that Norway was at war; but then, perhaps those marriages didn't deserve to last either.

His thoughts raced ahead to Venhaug; he would rather they didn't. For many years it had seemed to him that all expectation was evil. For when anticipations were fulfilled, the real experience was already pale and tarnished, lived-up, drawn out in advance. One might make plans for the future, that was something else, but anticipation ought to be suppressed, or pruned as far as possible. Expectation distorted reality. In spite of his fifty-eight years he still hoped to squelch this parasite of joy-to-come. And to a degree he had managed. It was seldom that he looked forward to a possible experience; he felt that was adolescent, and he directed his thoughts to avoid such speculations. However, it didn't prevent him from thinking of Felicia, but mostly of memories concerning her. Thus the past was being widened, not the immediate future misused. In his youth it had been mostly erotic fantasies that had driven him, their slave, astray in an exotic jungle where the loved one was transformed into a hundred willing girls whom it was his greatest desire to make love to, and with the least effort, perpetually. He managed always to remember this form of youthful dreaming, because it evoked the most grotesque picture of anticipation's ruined reality which each time was turned into a futile repetition of the same dream.

He did not wish to think of the impending meeting with Felicia, because it was wisest not to put too great demands on himself; he might allow himself to think of her, but not in connection with their meeting today. Almost at once he was filled with this ever-returning secret wonder that he could meet the one-time Felicia Ormsund as an equal, and had done so for many years. He made himself comfortable in his corner and mused contentedly over this fact which couldn't be voiced aloud, because then he would sound like a snob. But snob or whatever name, it remained equally remarkable. How about attempting to classify the snobs? Or, for the time being, push aside the degrading implication of the word while investigating snobs in general and the problem of snobbery? No, that was too much trouble now; he just wanted to enjoy himself. Snobbery couldn't be viewed objectively, except by non-snobs, and they wouldn't know what they were talking about. We cannot solve psychological problems of others, only our own.

I am thinking along the wrong lines, he said to himself. One mustn't start a trend of thought as if it were a school composition—*describe a snob*—in which case the subject of the composition is assumed to be well known to anyone able to write. I don't give a damn about behavior as such, I only want to see what lies under it. It seems the others, the ones I know among the so-called upper classes, do consider me their equal. Indeed, frequently I hear it said that I am their superior. Not that this makes me any happier. Having sown my wild oats, I have at least gained a sort of insecure balance, and do not feel at home except among equals—and by equals I mean those who have the same insecure balance as I myself, who are not stupid, who recognize the integrity of others, but who may otherwise possess any qualities or lack of qualities whatever, with age mattering not at all. They must be just as little disposed to feel inferior as to feel superior.

I am proud of Felicia, but most of myself who have her, and I can imagine, aside from the love, there is much that could be called snobbery. I'll try to draw a picture of her, as I see and feel it within me and impressed on the underside of my eyelids—a picture drawn in combat-desire but also blind admiration, drawn by a boy standing below on the street, his head thrown back, ready to tell of the golden girl between the towers of Oslo Town Hall—drawn by Erling Vik, sprung from the last generation of big broods, fifth child of the limping village tailor at Rjukan and his deaf wife Pauline, both long ago laid to rest in the churchyard with some of their children. I don't remember if it is four or five of the thirteen we were when most numerous.

I again met Felicia Ormsund in Sweden, early in December 1942, about a year after I had escaped from Norway. It was on her first day in Stockholm, and she had been met there that morning by Steingrim Hagen with whom she lived for exactly one year. The city girl apparently had a taste for the farm-born. My connection with her dates from the time she was with Steingrim and has never ceased. Before that I had met her only once; that was in 1934, when she was seventeen. Then she was dark-haired but as can happen with coal-black hair, there were already streaks of silver; now she has for long worn her silver crown, without a touch of black in it.

When my thoughts are with her, this fanfare of hair always plays a part. Everyone recognizes her from a great distance because of this silver halo, which she never seems to worry much about. She probably does though.

Of Felicia I can't offer a description that could be used to identify a missing person. I only know the reflection of a reflection a lover feels.

Felicia can take the long view; during the war she often spoke of the seven-hundred-year suppression of the Czechs and anticipated we might have something similar; or a genocide. She acted accordingly. Now, during these recent years, there are countless people who are wise after the fact and who insist they were not traitors, on the contrary, they anticipated a Russian danger. Anyone expressing such a thought then, she sent packing with the statement that Norway had only one kind of suppressors, the Germans, and one must face events in the order in which they appear. She knew something of immediate demands.

• The sneer

Like any sensible person, Erling of course pretended to be ignorant of all the gossip that had blossomed around him. His position was strengthened by the fact that actually he didn't care. To him it was indisputably evident that all this curiosity was nothing but a form of legalized perversion—in other words exactly as much of the "peeker's" form of sex as men had dared let loose on the legal market as virtue, because it was so prevalent. It did not change the fact that it was and remained vicarious eroticism. Sex is too old and too familiar to be sensationalized beyond the degree to which it is your own sensation. Disgust is a protective coloring with a tendency to turn red. Indifference is the token of those who pursue quite different practices. No one is interested in people with inclinations one doesn't understand, and the criminal code is the law-makers' confessional.

Neither Erling nor the Venhaug people could say they had anything to complain about; they had come off easily if one considers the way "peekers" are wont to classify their targets. On the one hand the situation had not been kept sufficiently covered up by the sinners, and this took away a good deal of the glamor. On the other hand, Erling was independent; perhaps less from a financial point of view than due to the fact that he had learned, in younger days, to fight his private wars of survival, many of which he had won. At Venhaug there was money, and a human superiority that was confounding. Sinning was not imagined thus. When people were well dressed, could handle a large estate, and had money in the bank, sin seemed surprisingly attractive. One could almost believe it was justified. People in the neighborhood had at length chosen a middle road: probably there was no truth in the stories.

And there was so much else. Jan was dangerous, although no one was exactly clear about how or why, but it was a fact. Felicia had won because she felt that good neighbors are essential in the country. She would always show up when something was wrong, sickness or the like, and then she would actually do something. The farmers' sure instinct for such things had recognized that, whatever else, Jan Venhaug's rich wife was not pretentious or phony. That writing man who visited with them had been lucky, too. One of the first times he was at Venhaug, he and Aunt Gustava had had a drinking bout in her little cottage; they had sung and carried on till late into the night, and in the morning there had been a man's hat hanging on the top of her little flagpole. That wasn't too good, no, it wasn't, but people would laugh to themselves when they happened to remember the sight of old Aunt Gustava hugging Erling at sunrise while they were taking a morning walk on wobbly legs down the village road.

Erling was, in fact, more exposed than they were at Venhaug, but he had never let anyone see through his coat of mail. Many attempts had been made to get him to reveal himself, all in vain, and by now people knew they had better be careful. As is usual in such cases, only his real friends refrained from making any reference to the situation. Oddly enough, the most stupid incident he remembered best of all. A few years ago, about Christmas time, he had been in Oslo and planned to go to Venhaug for the holidays as was his custom. He had the ticket in his pocket and would leave in the morning. In the middle of the morning he went to the Theater Café; walking through the restaurant he noticed Elias Tolne at a table but hoped he hadn't been recognized. (He wasn't that lucky!) Tolne was one of those vague characters who float about in the periphery of everything that has to do with literature, theater, films, and such, but have no definite connection with any of it. When Tolne spoke of well-known personalities he always used first names—Sigurd, Herman, Arnulf, Helge, Tarjei; or, it was my friend Ragnhild, Ase, Thordis, Agnes; this one had said that, and that one had said so and so, but usually it was Elias Tolne who had said it. If he managed to squeeze in at some table where his "dear friends" were sitting, it became rather embarrassing when they asked what his name might be. When Erling had ordered his lunch, and a drink to while away time until the food was served, he saw Elias Tolne approach his table. Erling was civil at least to the extent of answering questions with a grudging yes or no, and though Tolne wasn't sure of himself he nevertheless pulled up a chair. Erling looked away. Tolne kept talking nervously about his writing. As

far as Erling knew the man might at one time have had a book published
and he could understand the little tragedy with Tolne: he had assumed,
as do so many writers, that a book meant fame. That the author as well
as the book could be forgotten within a few weeks, in spite of fine
reviews, was something Erling too had learned with bitter surprise—like
Elias Tolne. The difference was only that Tolne, like hundreds of
forgotten ones, had been unable to digest the fact that anything could
turn out so directly opposite to his expectations. An author was an
author, wasn't he? He had become what is called a misunderstood
genius, and what really kills such a person is his deep feeling that he is
the victim of some incomprehensible injustice. He cannot see that the
dream was a dream only. Beside this, Elias Tolne displayed only too
clearly the very common "father-relationship" to his publisher—Father
had not made the dream come true, Father hadn't been understanding,
hadn't been good. The publisher can be a much better feather in the hat
than the book when the author is able to say *my publisher.* It is like
honey on the tongue, and if the author has a book thrown back at him he
keeps silent about it and has the same feeling concerning it, as if he had
been caught exhibiting himself, or stealing a lamp shade. Actually
nothing has happened, there is no law that says publishers are always
right; nevertheless violence has been committed against the beautiful
picture of the author and *my publisher,* those two who ought to be seen
dining together at a corner window, exchanging great and wise words
with meaningful countenances. No one any longer had faith in Elias
Tolne, and he had taken on the bragging obsequiousness of the failure
who can no longer conceal from himself that everyone is avoiding
him—because no one enjoys inhaling the stale smoke of defeat and the
crushed one's insidious envy. One ought to forgive, overlook, it sounds
convincing, it is right; but right also it is that one gets completely fagged
listening to the failure's complaints and would rather be some other
place.

Elias Tolne was talking about himself, about all the injustice; he spoke
as the fallen one often does from his fringe position—banalities one
couldn't answer without feeling silly: Have you seen Sigurd recently? Is
it true about Arthur? The other day I ran into Fostervoll. (Well! one
with a last name!) I hear Johan is writing a new play.

Erling looked up and said, "I live in the country—to tell you the truth,
I don't know any of those people. Well, of course I know Fostervoll."

Tolne scowled at Erling: "You mean to say you don't know Johan
Borgen?" he said.

"Well, yes, I do know Borgen."

"Have you seen him lately?"

What was there in one's personality that prevented one from saying: Please, why don't you disappear! I want to be left in peace, you silly ass!

Elias Tolne returned to his own writing. It hadn't dawned on the radio people that he made his living writing; couldn't someone give them a hint?

Erling drew back.

Tolne continued: Some writers simply were excluded from the radio; the Authors' League ought to take it up; demand a certain, just allotment among writers when it came to reading and such. And again he jabbered on about personal persecution.

The food arrived. "Get me a glass of beer," said Tolne to the waiter.

"Well, it isn't quite convenient," Erling finally managed to say. "I'm waiting for somebody."

The waiter disappeared. Erling was boning his fish and noticed with irritation that his hand trembled. He avoided looking at Tolne.

"Whom are you waiting for?"

Erling did not answer.

After a while: "May I treat you to a schnapps with your codfish?"

"No, thank you."

"Have you become a teetotaler?"

The bald insinuation made Erling boil. This type of wit was Tolne's specialty; the intention was to make Erling smile and say something. But he refused to comment on his present alcoholic habits. There was a long silence. At last Tolne said, "The other fellows just asked me to find out something from you."

He named them; they would spend Christmas in a cottage at Rauland and had laid in quantities of liquor. "Are you joining us?"

"I'm busy."

"Busy with what?"

Erling stared at Tolne and stopped eating for a moment. Why get angry? There was nothing strange or unusual in the situation; when he hadn't at once taken the bull by the horns and told the man to leave, it had to go this way. He thought over what had been said; just small talk, except he hadn't been able to stop it in time.

Elias Tolne was wondering what the change in attitude might mean and chose the explanation that suited him best—that Erling was thawing out a little. "Where are you going?" he asked.

Erling replied calmly: "To a few friends near Kongsberg."

The sneer came at once. Tolne leaned forward over the table; he seemed to slobber as he said to his dear friend Erling: "Ah—you're going to Venhaug?"

Tolne did not realize he had been permitted an experiment and that the victim was pleased with the result. Erling only looked at him and did not move a muscle. Tolne's eyes started to flutter about, he must have said something that was a mistake, perhaps it wasn't the thing to do to talk about women with Erling? But then his courage returned: "Why don't you call long-distance and tell them you can't come!"

Erling stared at him still for a moment before he resumed eating. He felt the impotent hatred that radiated from Tolne—how stupid it would be to snub somebody who would spread it everywhere. Erling shook his head slowly, giving up without knowing it himself. When he finally had got rid of the man he called the waiter and ordered two schnapps, while Tolne still could hear him. There was a jerk in Tolne's neck muscles.

A sneer had something special about it. Most people lived to regret they had sneered. Not so many years ago they had sneered because he had a child with a street-walker. That time too they soon wished they hadn't sneered. They didn't say so; they said it was fine of him to take care of his daughter and place her at Venhaug. A handsome admission, but with flaws—even while they had sneered he had taken care of his daughter the best he could, that was why they had sneered. Furthermore, they had sneered because he had given the daughter his name, she was known as Julie Vik. Now that too was a feat. As a general rule, it was utterly amazing how it reflected credit on everything one did if, gradually, enough people came to remark over their beers: "I saw Erling yesterday, by the way. A hell of a fine fellow!"

Julie's mother was called Margrete, a street-girl who happened to land as helper in a farm home. There she met Erling, who had rented a cottage in the neighborhood. Julie had never lived with her mother but had been kept for pay in various homes. Erling had managed to find a new home for her several times when he suspected she was unhappy. One day, in December 1948, Felicia had unexpectedly met him and Julie when they were out walking; he was saying good-by to her before leaving for the Canary Islands. Felicia had not known about Julie. It turned out to be an afternoon with much suspense in the air; Felicia was quick to put together and figure out many things she would rather have left untouched: Julie was about thirteen and a half years old, and when Felicia heard this she asked immediately about her birthday. Julie mentioned it automatically, in a toneless voice, the way she spoke in those days, and Felicia looked abstractedly at Erling, while she figured out he had fathered Julie at exactly the same time he had turned his back on *her,* as completely as if she never had existed. He could read the deduction in her look, and she knew he noticed it, but it was never mentioned. The following day she took Julie with her to Venhaug and there she had stayed. The strangely empty and joyless side of Julie had long ago disappeared. In much she had become a copy of her admired friend Felicia, but had been strong enough to maintain her own personality, which broke through now that she was approaching her twenty-third year. Yet, always a shadow over all, the shadow over Julie—

One might have predicted she would be the problem child at Venhaug. There were so many things one might have predicted.

Felicia was heaping coals of fire upon his head, as if this were her favorite sport.

• *Aunt Gustava*

Just before reaching Venhaug he asked Kristiansen to take the side road to Aunt Gustava. The old woman was sitting in her kitchen sorting berries. She could not entirely hide her pleasure at seeing Erling. Her legs were poorly now at ninety but she must get down to the cellar for some hard cider.

Aunt Gustava was, as far as people knew, nobody's aunt. For many years she had helped with the baking on the farms at time of festivities or other events, but most of her time she had spent at Venhaug where, before Felicia's time, she had run things better than anyone else; but she had been cautiously kept at a distance, for Aunt Gustava had a tendency to tyrannize. She came from a cotter's place on one of the neighbor farms and had lost her parents at eighteen—so long ago that youths of today weren't sure there had been such a time. Shortly after being left alone she met a man who took over the place as well as herself, but there had been a long engagement which Aunt Gustava often recalled with caustic remarks. She might also relate how the marriage had turned out. Perhaps he might have become a good man, she would say, guardedly. Aunt Gustava was never enthusiastic and perhaps she didn't remember her husband too well. We had been married about half a year when it happened, she would say (and everyone knew what was coming now). It was raining, she observed. That kind of persistent rain early in

November. He went to the forest at dawn and was carried home at dusk. He had found a spruce which the storm had felled during the night. The roots rose up like a wall of earth and stones that had peeled off the mountainside, and anyone should have realized it would fly back when the tree was cut off. But Per hadn't used good sense that day. If indeed he ever had any, Aunt Gustava would add, as if talking about a stranger who was only to be judged from one single action. Perhaps he didn't have much in his head, how do I know? They found him a great distance away—in the top of a pine! He must have had a real jolt to sail through the air like that; and of course he was dead, but then, he had the disgusting habit of boozing a little in rainy weather. Imagine, he stood on the root end of the tree trunk while he sawed it, he must have been off his rocker that day, decided Aunt Gustava. To fly through the air like a bird! A note of humiliation was apparent in her voice. When she reached this point in the story of her marriage, the listeners might look away abstractedly. Aunt Gustava would mumble something about a big head and small sense, and then it would come: Wasn't there someone called the Flying Dutchman?

Aunt Gustava had experienced another great disgrace. Her son was born after she had been a widow for a few months. On some birthday or other of mine, she would add (with remarkably great disgust in her tone of voice). In that way we had the same birthday. The boy went to the States and for five or six years he would ever so often send me a few dollars in a letter. No one knew what I could do with them, but the storekeeper wanted them, and I'm sure he cheated me. He always wrote he was doing well. Then he stopped writing. Not a sign of life from him after 1916. Aunt Gustava was annoyed with him; that he might be dead never entered her head; she suspected he might have done some stupid thing like his father. Anyway, they were a little off on that side of the family; perhaps he had gone to dig for gold. But in forty years he might have had some minutes left over to write to his old mother. People thought that Per—he was named after his father—should be about seventy-two by now, but Aunt Gustava thought of him as a youngster.

The farmer had taken back the fields but he let the widow live on in the cottage, which had a small garden. There she had lived these many years with her potted plants and her caustic outlook—which apparently lengthens life—and kept an eye on what was happening around her.

Some ten years ago the old farmer had died, at an age that staggered even Aunt Gustava, and this had given her something more to talk about besides the flying husband and the son who didn't write letters. The seventy-year-old son-in-law who had taken over the farm wanted her out of the cottage. This had annoyed her—and Felicia had once said it even scared her. To Erling and others she only seemed angry about it; Aunt Gustava did not wish for any changes in her world. She most emphatically pointed out that she was too old for that. If anyone investigated further it might become apparent that she never had paid any rent, but then why should she? She was born in the house, almost a hundred years ago, and the old farmer had never thought of anything so stupid as to ask for rent. It must be something they had thought up down in Kongsberg.

Erling always enjoyed a visit with Aunt Gustava and often spoke about her to his friends. But he could never quite figure her out; if you asked her if she was satisfied with life she would look suspicious, surmising some trap. Why shouldn't she be satisfied? In a moment she might get back to Per and his flying-stunt, and the boy who didn't write, but outside of this, life was as it ought to be, thought Aunt Gustava.

"She is a lovely parasite," was the way Felicia expressed it. "A parasite with style. She doesn't aim high, but she insists on getting what she wants."

Erling did not quite agree with this; it wasn't entirely correct, he thought. Aunt Gustava had an unusually hard life behind her. She loved flowers, and children loved her. She was helpful. She never carried gossip. On the other hand, she was reserved and sceptical, and had an almost ridiculous interpretation of those two happenings in her life which had stuck in her mind. He himself liked the old lady immensely. So did Felicia, Julie, and all the others at Venhaug. But it was like hitting one's head against a wall, as it were. There was no crack and no door in that wall. She was tart as vinegar, but pleasant to visit with. She was full of cavil, she was tyrannical, and amazingly free of snobbery. Erling had more and more come to the conclusion that Aunt Gustava was a cool number who gave humanity hell, but once long ago had realized that as long as she herself wanted to have an enjoyable life, others too might. Consequently, she was a representative of one of the most ethically enduring philosophies—built on egotism as conceived in the mediocre but practical mind of a farm woman to whom two and two still make four. And Aunt Gustava and children? Was it perhaps so, that children—always unsentimental if no one has ruined them—just liked a woman they realized was indulgent and kind because this was easiest? One who viewed them with such indifference that they realized it was all the same to her if they cleaned out the plum jam or fell down from the roof and broke their necks? Much of what Erling had seen in different homes made him suspect that it wasn't always love that created a sense of security in children, rather a combination of solid nerves and lack of useless interest in the brats' doings. And some people had been born with this.

Aunt Gustava had always been ample in size and after the war she had grown immensely rotund. Comparing her with a hippopotamus might be as exaggerated as to say you have been hit by an atom bomb if you should happen to win two-hundred-fifty kroner in the lottery. Yet, Aunt Gustava did remind one of a hippopotamus, and Erling avoided contemplating her weight. He had seen her for the first time in the autumn of 'forty-five when she already had grown out of all proportion, and thus he imagined her also when she spoke of her youth.

She came panting with the cider jug and poured him a full beer glass. Herself she supplied with bread and cheese from the table drawer which she had pulled out until it rested against her massive paunch. Outside stood the taxi and ticked away, but she was always above such matters. "Now you must tell me everything," she said, and pushed almost a whole slice of bread into her mouth. Out of one drawer and into another, thought Erling, and sipped the cider before he emptied the glass. "You always have such good cider," he said.

"Empty the jug!" admonished Aunt Gustava, while pushing the rest of the bread slice down her throat and arming herself with a knife for another slice from the loaf. "What have you been doing lately—fooling around with girls, you old buck?"

Erling said he had been busy with his writing.

"Writing again?" said Aunt Gustava disdainfully, and pushed in some more bread. "Don't understand people who never do anything. But then, you live a great deal at Venhaug."

Erling laughed heartily. Aunt Gustava chewed and looked at him fiercely: "What in hell are you laughing at?"

It really wasn't anything to laugh at; most writers in Norway might well need a fattening-up time at Venhaug; but that was the way it always was, he thought, suddenly serious. Few or none would have found their way to Venhaug, until they already had security and a home of their own.

"Is it true that you are the son of a village tailor?"

This came almost as if she had read his thoughts; he answered quickly, "Why do you ask?"

"Well, at least that is a sensible occupation—I wish my husband had taken up sewing."

Erling emptied his glass again and rose, he was longing to get to

Venhaug; otherwise he might have listened again to the tale of the man in the treetop.

"By the way, how did they get him down?" he asked.

Aunt Gustava's thoughts were already so deep in the story that she understood at once: "That I have never told because it was revolting," she said, throwing her head back and filling her gaping mouth with a handful of bread crumbs and cheese scraps. "They pulled him down from the pine-top with a logging-hook."

We end up in different ways, thought Erling, as he hurried out through the pouring rain to the taxi. Some are choked to death in a pig-snare, others are pulled down from a treetop with a logging-hook.

• *"Who told thee that thou wast naked?"*

Erling stayed in his usual room at Old Venhaug, which stood unoccupied now. He picked up a newspaper but was unable to concentrate and gave up. On his bedside table a tallow candle spluttered. The rain beat against the windows and splashed on the window sills. A nearby brook had turned into a thundering waterfall. Erling sucked in the living sounds. It was a little after twelve. Someone was entering the house, climbing the stairway; he recognized the sound of the quick steps, the swishing raincoat. A light knock on the door and Felicia stepped in. The water ran in streams from the coat and the sou'wester; her rubber boots glittered. She doffed the wet garments and spread the raincoat over a chair like a tent. She only smiled at him, without saying a word, while she quickly undressed. Her body was brown like a Maori's, and the color seemed even warmer in the fluttering half-light. Her hair spread like a white bird over her head and when the faint light struck her eyes there were sudden gleams. When she placed her cool body next to his he felt for a few seconds a prayer within him, that it might remain exactly like this for long, but even before his wish was conscious they had been swept down the rapids.

Erling spent himself before Felicia and he watched her transformation—her calm and happy face with half-open mouth and blissful smile which with a few spasms was suddenly turned into a Medusa-like fury, a contorted face as in labor pain. Nerves and muscles around the beautiful eyes became lax, giving her the ugly cross-eyed look of a changeling. Suddenly Erling was thrown aside, as when a cross-wave hits a boat. Groaning she fumbled after him and one of her hands managed to get hold of his hair. He was afraid he might break her fingers—they were frozen as in a cramp—but he loosened her grip so as not to have his hair pulled out by the roots. By now he was sufficiently outside to appreciate the more comic aspect of what was happening and he wondered if perhaps at last he could see a sensible reason why people in the old days wore nightcaps. Standing beside the bed he watched her rave on to an end, and he recalled that the winged horse of poetry was the offspring of the sea-god Poseidon and Medusa.

Felicia came to, in a contorted position, looked at him in irritation, and said angrily, "What are you laughing at, you clown?"

She lay down, her head on his shoulder, and listened to the rain, she too. He caressed her body and murmured, "Can you imagine anything more—anything more cozy than a pouring rain in a dark August night?"

"Two people all alone at Old Venhaug," she said, "what could be more blissful. During nights like this I always think of the wild animals and all the little birds; I can so well see the woodcock, and the grouse, sitting on their roosting-branches so close to the trunk; they sit bird-warm and sleep while the wind roars and the rain pours down, and the tree rocks them to sleep, along with other birds in other trees, while a loose roof-tile rattles at Old Venhaug, and I must tell Jan tomorrow morning, for he is very particular about the roof-tiles, you know—'Mend in time,' he says—anyway I'm crazy about you because you haven't been here for so long, and thank you for not showing up drunk—"

"You rave like the night itself, Felicia. Your speech is like unto the wild stream of a spring brook, and nothing is like your sweet brew—"

"Stop it! We are in August. You can compose poetry after work-hours, as your brother so rightly remarked. I woke up early this morning, before daylight, and thought of you. I could think of nothing else but you, and couldn't sleep. It was the same the whole morning, up till noon, I was thinking—today Erling must come; and when the telephone rang I jumped past Julie and grabbed it myself—it couldn't be anyone but you, and it was. 'How silly can one get!' Julie said."

"Meaning me?"

"No! She meant me. 'Have you had a letter?' she said, 'or how do you know Erling is coming?' I was thinking of you the whole morning the day you arrived from Las Palmas, and when I was at your house—all the time I was thinking of all sorts of things about you; and I'm with you just as clearly when you cheat on me, then too I wake up in the night and feel murderous, but this time I knew you were longing for me—men are such beasts!"

This unexpected ending relieved him from having to answer; he would have felt silly in saying he had been thinking similar things about her, and equally strong. He would rather tell her this some other time. If he told her now it would be like listening to someone tell you how sick he has been, and then interrupting to say you have been even sicker.

"Men might be beasts," he said. "Nevertheless, you tramped through pouring rain to get into bed with one here at Old Venhaug."

"Wasn't that why you came to see us?"

"I came for everything Venhaug stands for," he said, seriously. He leaned over and stroked her along her back, for this simple operation was the nicest thing she could think of when she was relaxed as now. After a while she turned over on her back and he continued to massage her. She lay with her eyes closed, as if sleeping, and breathed evenly. Then she grew restless, put one of her arms around his neck and pulled him down on her. Well, this *was* better, he thought; that relaxing business inclined one to piety.

She rose, went over to the chair where his clothes lay, and felt in his pockets for cigarettes. His eyes followed her soft movements; it stirred him more than the first time he had seen her naked (suddenly he remembered Gulnare). Then the roles had been the opposite—he had been married, she had been only seventeen. Now she was forty, but never had he felt her younger, happier, more smiling. There she stood, as slender as the seventeen-year-old, her white halo disheveled, lighting first a cigarette for him, then one for herself—for a fleeting second, in the light from the match, he caught the glitter in her eyes. The avenging angel, the enemy of enemies, he saw just then. Only four days had elapsed that time, after her younger brother's death, before she had taken revenge on the informer.

How distant, so long ago and unreal . . . .

• *The society girl and the tailor's son*

Erling leaned on his elbow and watched Felicia standing there smoking, a far-away look in her eyes. "I was thinking of the war," he said. "It's almost like telling lies when we talk of it now. As if recalling a dream and trying to pretend it was real. Take Jan, for example, trying to tell us about that mission of his. It sounds today as if it had emanated from a distorted mind. At times I have actually wondered if anything of all that really happened. Incidentally, not long ago I dreamed that I was dreaming and woke up and realized that all this business with atomic weapons was something I had made up while asleep. What a relief that no bombs had ever fallen over Hiroshima and Nagasaki, and no more worries about the little boys the Rosenbergs left behind."

Felicia inhaled deeply; she said in a husky voice, thick smoke rising slowly from her mouth, "It's good you woke up to remember them."

"Don't stand there so far away," said Erling.

"I only wanted to cool off a little, Erling dearest."

He started; she had never called him that before.

"Something happened Friday night," he said, "something that made me come here just now, and not in three weeks for example. Come here, Felicia."

She crushed the cigarette against the hearth and crept down beside him. He put his arm around her shoulder and said, "I had a caller Friday evening. Torvald Ørje—you remember, the little Goebbels at Os?"

"Why would one of the unhanged like him call on *you?*"

She lay quite still and did not interrupt him while he told her the story. He concluded: "I became terribly upset. Something happened to me; I felt ashamed that he had dared to come, standing there contaminating my house. Yes, above all I felt terribly insulted, but there was so much that was unclear also. There stood this repulsive person, a murderer of the stupidest kind, and yet I was reminded of the thing we have so often talked about—our share in the blame. These people were the product of Norwegian surroundings, children of Norwegian parents, Norwegians like you and me. We have created them ourselves. Rehabilitation for the traitors? Nonsense! Never for their base actions which cannot ever be forgiven. But we should recognize that we also are not entirely blameless because of the existence of so many of that kind in our country. Why did they fall into the obvious trap? Quisling, as you know, wasn't insane, but he was nuts, he had a screw loose somewhere. How had it ever been possible for him, with his background, to have been placed in a Norwegian cabinet? Neither the Germans nor the Norwegian Nazis had placed him there. And this Torvald Ørje with his dog-head—a worthy representative of thousands of these lost souls—coming to me, trying to bargain with me and pay me with my own belongings! For a few hours after I had thrown him out, there seemed to me no solid ground in *anything*. I didn't even want to stay at home; and then I called you. Strangely enough, Felicia, I tried to find comfort in our meeting that time when I returned from the Canary Islands—no, not in that way, there would be nothing strange in seeking comfort in that memory—but it was strange that you should be here and know about it, and relive the same thing in your mind. I suddenly saw your face shining above and beyond all melancholy I felt this morning. I came here to get help, and I have already found it. I intend to stay only a few days, but I told the lawyer I would be here, and to send my stolen belongings here. Did you know—those pictures hung in Ellen's and my home. You are not involved with them in the same way as I, and you may keep them, sell them, or give them away. Torvald Ørje at any rate must not have them."

Felicia was kissing him and said nothing for a long time. When at last she spoke he wasn't surprised, perhaps rather a little disappointed, at the conclusion she had reached: "What you say about his having contaminated your house brings up the idea I have toyed with so often—you should come and live here. Not that I feel he has dirtied your house, no more anyway than if someone else had broken in and messed it up—that seems to be a special joy of burglars. I can't agree with your notion about that, but it struck me again that here stands Old Venhaug empty, which makes a house deteriorate. Ordinary tenants I don't want. Think it over, Erling. Move in with us. You can't buy the house—Jan would never let it go; it's his childhood home; the family has lived here for untold generations, and besides it's located in the center of his beloved farm lands. Jan is a sort of farm-estate snob, God bless him. But you can take over Old Venhaug, as if it were your own, and you can keep your house in Lier—in that case you would have a retreat if it didn't work out here; a place to run to when you tire of me, and get hold of someone else, which I couldn't stand here at Old Venhaug. And then there is Julie—"

"You shouldn't have taken this opportunity to bring it up again, Felicia. We have threshed it out so many times that neither one of us can have anything new to add. I'll always leave here with a bad conscience, and each time you imagine I'm up to something worse than before. There are many things I won't repeat now, but if I moved in here I'm afraid something might come between you and me. And between Jan and me. Between Venhaug and me. I have for long been accustomed to being alone when I work. You are jealous of my aloneness, Felicia, and nothing good will come from it if you rob me of it."

"Yes, we have talked a lot about it," replied Felicia, "but actually we've never come to the bottom of it. The only valid argument you use against living at Venhaug might be my interference with your work. But I don't believe this either. I'm sure it could be arranged so you could work as well as you do now. I think the whole reason is quite simple: for long periods of your life you have had miserable living quarters, perhaps even none; when you were young you were forced to live with people you despised; this led to a desperate wish to live alone with no one around; there mustn't be the slightest hint of interference. It has come to a point where you see ghosts at high noon if you can't be entirely alone in the house. You are so afraid one might come and disturb you that you bite in advance. Don't be angry with me now, but this is the tailor's son from Rjukan that shines through—and deep inside, you are more afraid of interference from me than from anyone else, because I'm the society girl, the kind who least of all must have anything to say. I think you should throw overboard those last remnants of the plebeian. I doubt if you can do it completely, and in a way I don't want you any different from what you are. All of us love you. You haven't a soul in the world who is closer to you. Nor will you ever have. When we suggest you move in with us and live here at Old Venhaug, I'm sure you can have it exactly as you wish. Your freedom will never be curtailed because we live on the place."

He did not reply. He kept caressing her, while he thought: The net gets stronger and the mesh smaller. One day I won't be able to move a hand.

Stroking her forehead, he said: "Perhaps another ten years, surely not more. Then I'm old. You are twenty years younger. You don't look ahead far enough, Felicia."

"Much further than you think! Where else could you live as an old man?"

She pressed herself close to him: "I love you as you are. You might try to love me a little, the *me* that I am, without all your reservations. No one chooses his place of birth. You have a burning needle somewhere in your body—but now I think it is time you let the tailor's boy give up the ghost."

Erling withdrew a little. "Don't you think we are talking about exceedingly unimportant matters? I have adjusted myself to the fact that things went as they did in Sweden. That's the important thing as far as I'm concerned—I've adjusted myself. I was trying to get you away from Steingrim, and felt I might succeed if I got you into bed. I was wrong. You fell for Jan and married him. I was at your wedding. Perhaps you remember that I didn't touch a drink that day, only raised the many glasses to my lips. I was on guard against myself, although I wasn't really afraid anything would happen just there—at the triangle-wedding. However, never has there been a more ill-natured guest at a wedding feast. I kept watching you—and reciting Welhaven to myself—his *Asgardsreie*. I think it was well I wasn't drinking, reciting that poem; it might have lighted a fire in a drunken brain. I could have made quite a show of myself. And—as in the poem—been pulled by the hair up through the chimney and vanished, all the women surrounding the

bloody groom. I was wondering if you were all sane; there were only two
sober men and one woman when the party broke up—you and Jan and I.
Then you had a child with him. I've always suspected you didn't want
one with me because—"

"Because?"

"Because I was sick. Because you thought I was crazy. Because you
were wrong in analyzing a neurosis that might mean a little of anything,
and you took it to mean insanity. But things were also so mixed up that
you took me back because I *was* sick. You rejected me and accepted me
for the same reason—but it was Jan you married."

"Must we dig up all that again? That about sickness you haven't held
against me before. I wasn't wrong, but you weren't crazier than hundreds
of other Norwegians in Sweden at that time. It wasn't your sickness that
decided me. It was simply that Steingrim and I had agreed to live
together. I was tired, and confused also. All that killing along the border,
investigations and searches everywhere; I needed a place to bathe, to
sleep—and *I had given you up many years before.* Your sickness might
have been added to all the rest, but it was never the deciding factor."

She started to sob. "With Jan I could get peace. He wasn't demanding
every moment, the way most men are. What you have just said is so
unworthy of you. I and that little French girl (what became of her, by
the way?) were the only ones to look after you and keep you from going
under with sickness and drinking—and you mustn't think it was easy.
But I would never have married you, even if Jan hadn't come along.
Never, never. Because you are an unlucky bird with women. It is simple
enough to figure out why: first you were scared to death of women for
many years; then they just fell for you for many years. Either situation
was equally bad. And I was involved in both situations. When you took
me as a young girl and I fell madly in love with you, then you were only
a Martin Leire—"

"Felicia!"

"Then you were only a Martin Leire! And when my turn came again,
in Sweden, during a different period, then you only wanted me as a
trophy. You were sick, that is true, but there was enough of the devil in
you that you wanted to take a short cut instead of getting well. You
yourself refused any serious attempt to get well. You wanted Felicia
Ormsund, so people could say: 'He still has got it, has Erling Vik—there
he is with Felicia Ormsund.' But *that* was out of the question. She didn't
want you as long as you—in one guise or another—acted like the son of
the tailor. She wanted a healthy and grown Erling who no longer took all
the hopeless short cuts. And yet—she didn't wish to become dependent

on *that* Erling either. For this I must tell you—I knew what I had done for you once before: when I was very young I gave you courage to meet women; that time when you were exactly twice as old as I—you were thirty-four. I was very young and full of expectation. You crushed everything in me after I had helped you. You went to other women with what you had become through me. *He?*—anybody would have thought had they heard it—should *he* be afraid of women? Yes, you were, and you left, and misused the chance you had been given, you misused it like an ape. Then all those years went by and we met again in Sweden, and in your sickness and blindness you wanted to misuse me once more. But it didn't work out, Erling. You say you adjust yourself to circumstances as they are and that is all. Well, I've done the same, but to me it isn't all. I have been able to forgive because I could see the background and because I was in love with you. But if you are honest with yourself you must realize you have never forgiven me for what I did in pure self-defense. Perhaps it *was* you I wanted. I won't argue about that any longer. Anyway, you have a daughter at Venhaug, and she is crazy about you. It's only reasonable that you also live here."

Erling decided not to speak, but it was difficult. A long pause followed. They studied each other's faces. She stroked him gently over the cheek: "Erling," she said, in a voice half-choked with pain, "do you know, in high school I was called Felicia the Chaste? And I wanted to live up to the name they teased me with. I didn't want to be like the others. One day I said angrily to another girl, I didn't intend to imitate anyone except myself. She spread it about and they all laughed at me, but I did mean it even though I had expressed it poorly. It wasn't any purity or virginal ideal I had in mind; I was—and I am not afraid to say it—*I was proud*. No stain on Felicia Ormsund! And by the time I met you I had gained my end—I was the queen in that damned hen-house, and the girls knew I could have had any boy I'd liked. Now you know it, you silly Erling, who came like a bull in a china shop and took the maidenhead from the society girl, and then forgot her for years. I could never rid myself of you. There is something wrong with you, Erling, something completely out of line. All the women you have known you have made unhappy. But that was not your object—you didn't have anything in mind at all; I don't even think you ever realized that it was the stupid revenge of an upstart. But you became my great love. Whether near or far away—you were always there. Actually you haven't made *all* women you met unhappy, for the exception lies here beside you. Yes, you were always there. It burned my soul when you cheated me. For a long time I thought I had become another person, but it was only that I was growing up and didn't know what it was all about. For this I must tell you, Erling, I am the only woman you have met who is strong-willed. I remember the day I cut out Cecilie Skog—I must have since I am the one lying here. I was and remain Proud Felicia, and your evil spirit couldn't break me. For there is an evil spirit possessing you, the *Werewolf* you have talked so much about. The Werewolf is after your soul—I have felt it for years. You didn't *make* your victims unhappy, but they *became* unhappy. I also see it this way—one day a pyromaniac got into your forest, and you discovered him too late. I'll show you sometime the thirty acres of our forest that was burned down in June. Somewhere within you there grows such a forest. I became aware of it in time, and took care. Other women got lost in your burned forest, where no birds were singing and no heart beating. There lay only the decayed corpse of a lame and smoke-blackened tailor. Erling, I have the most intense desire to take care of you. I have always had it, and you know your society girl is kind. Mayn't I give you Old Venhaug and look after you? You can always take off and stay away as long as you wish and carry on somewhere else. I know so well what you think, in part at least—*what will people say*—which always lies there and smoulders within you. But that I understand better than you, and you needn't pretend it is me you want to shield. People in a place like this imagine many things which they don't really believe. It would never dawn on them—as is written—that anyone could sin with a glad heart and smiling lips. They know our way of life is different from theirs, and if they see anything they can't draw logical conclusions from by their own rules, then it just doesn't exist. I knew what I was doing when I hugged you so wildly in the yard when you arrived and Jan was watching—I wanted to give a demonstration of sisterly love."

"It would be different if I lived here?"

"Better, yes. No one would think anything any more, even if some had tried before. They don't think one can change the laws of nature, and what they possibly think seems to them so unnatural that—"

"You talk like a child."

"Don't speak condescendingly about children—and if it's Jan you are thinking of you know how he is; if people only are peaceful, his forgiveness knows no limits. 'Let's be decent,' he says, and you know as well as I, Erling, how much there is behind his simple words. The art of living he knows better than either one of us."

Erling said, with a forced smile, "Yes, I remember the report he delivered to the gang when he had dutifully liquidated Jan Husted, according to his own thorough and philosophical turn of mind."

Felicia snuggled up against him: "Since you mention it I'll tell you how he happened to be chosen: Jan himself asked me to suggest him. He knew I was going to volunteer, and he didn't think that would look good. Now I know why he had figured out that it would be best both for him and for me if he once took a chance instead of letting me go a second time: he already had his eyes on me and hoped he could catch me for his wife."

Erling lay silent a moment, then he climbed out of bed and fetched a bottle of wine. "The glasses might not look crystal clear," he said, "but I did rinse them."

"You should let me take care of those things."

"There you go again. I would never have any peace here."

She dug her nails into his thighs until he yelled. When he had filled the glasses he sat down on the edge of the bed, but discovered to his annoyance that she suddenly had fallen asleep. This was one of her peculiarities. He sat down in the easy chair and kept drinking wine until he fell asleep where he sat. A pale dawn was breaking as he awakened. Again the rain was splashing. He jumped up and said, "Get up, Felicia! It's almost daylight!"

At once she was wide awake, and he wished he could fall asleep and wake up like that. She made a few grimaces, trying to make him smile; he would have liked to give her a good spanking. "Well," she said, "there isn't much fun having a man who looks like one on his way to the gallows when one wants him!" She recited:

> Ride, ride to church,
> Decked in gold and silk,
> Gold and silk and a cape so blue,
> And a little horse for the rider too,
> In summer, in summer,
> To church!

He sat on the edge of the bed and watched her pull on a pair of panties so thin he could have rolled them up and pushed them down into his vest pocket; then, in spite of his sleepiness, he must tell her the most pornographic story he had ever read. Everything was relative, depending on age and circumstances. He had been about twelve or thirteen when he had read something in the local paper about beards. It had caught his interest, for all the men in the neighborhood had long beards, and he was hoping that boys might grow voluminous beards the day they returned from church after confirmation. He wasn't sure how this would take place, and he suspected some boys might keep it back if they didn't want it right away; he wasn't going to do that.

What he had read was a news item from the great world. A number of prominent ladies had been interviewed concerning their opinions about beards. One was an actress and to Erling's consternation she insisted that she preferred clean-shaven men. What was the use in growing up then? Yet, this great actress had not been fanatical on the subject; she agreed a man might wear a small mustache, if it were well perfumed. "All women know why," she had said, with an infatuating, mischievous smile.

He had guessed the meaning of mustache, but not what all women knew, and his pondering upon this had given him voluptuous moments when alone. Since then he hadn't bothered with pornography, he said; it always had to do with garments half on and half off. Nowadays nudity was called pornography. It seemed no one liked it that hints and shady allusions had disappeared; everyone needed them.

It disturbed Erling that it was full daylight, even though not clear; it was raining heavily again. But at last he listened to her departing steps down the stairway, so sure and definite, the swishing of her raincoat. Through the window he watched her cross the yard between the tall white birches, saw her climb the broad steps at New Venhaug, enter the open veranda with its rain-reflecting slate floor, open the front door. He went to bed and pulled the down comforter over him, entirely weightless, it seemed. He lay for a while and recalled the many nights here with Felicia, over a dozen or so years, even before New Venhaug had been built. He succumbed to sleep, and dreamt that he was walking from Old to New Venhaug with her youngest daughter by the hand. They walked the same way as Felicia had done a few moments ago, and it was raining like then. Jan was standing on the glittering veranda slates and smiled at them, and behind him at a window he saw Felicia's face. Her eyes were burning. He became frightened; Jan took the child by the hand and remained standing where he was, but Erling disintegrated, evaporated as it were. He woke up groaning, with a feeling of complete impotence and imminent tragedy. Not to live, not to die, only to be blotted out as from a blackboard. And now he remembered how Felicia had stopped a moment at the door before leaving: "Erling, you have convinced me that you must live at Venhaug," she had said.

In the open door she had stopped again, turned half around toward him, chuckled to herself, showing her broad teeth: "Of course you must live here! Why should you men have the prerogative of seeing the Werewolf?"

And this became yet another dream, more portentous than the first one, though he suppressed it quickly as soon as he became fully awake, and dared not recall it until later in the day.

• Felicia with the birds

Felicia looked up from a bowl of black currant berries and said, "Jan dear—I've asked Erling to come and live at Old Venhaug."

The children were playing outside while the rain let up for a spell; a whole swarm had gathered from neighboring farms. Intermittently they would rush by the windows like a flock of frightened sheep, their shoes clattering on the flagstones, yelling at the top of their voices. How are they able to, thought Erling, and looked at Felicia. What was she up to now?

Julie brushed a few berry-stalks from her slim fingers as she looked from Felicia to Erling and then to Jan, who sat lost in the Sunday morning radio concert. Jan came to slowly, as if arriving from some other place. He walked over to a window and looked out toward Old Venhaug. If he had heard what Felicia said he might already have forgotten it—one couldn't be sure. Now he was looking at something outside, they could see from the motions of his head he was trying to get a better view. "Well," he said, with a last look at the interesting happenings outdoors, "if Erling wants to, all right. It stands there anyway—why not? Or perhaps—why? It wasn't Erling who suggested it."

He looked thoughtfully straight ahead. "There is one drawback. If Erling should move here and didn't feel at home—? Then it would have been an unsuccessful experiment for him."

Jan left the rest hanging in the air, for anyone who wished to complete the thought, and started walking across the floor.

Felicia picked up another cluster of berries and Julie did the same. No one spoke. Jan was as far away as before. Children shouted in the yard. Erling did not wish to move to Venhaug. That is, naturally he might hanker to—at least sporadically—but that seemed to belong to another dimension. He ought not to. So it was. It would be wrong to say that Jan might adjust himself to anything; in his case it wasn't a question of adjusting himself, rather an almost total neutrality. The problem was with Erling himself. He wanted long days and nights alone—and he was not sure Felicia would accept his aloneness. She said he would never be disturbed, but this he didn't believe, and he would only be sitting waiting for her interruptions. He must *know* that no one was coming.

He wanted to put a bottle on the table when it suited him (even as an occasional guest he must more or less hide his supply at Old Venhaug). Felicia had the same attitude toward liquor as most educated people insist they have, which in reality means no attitude at all; she thought he should drink like "other people," meaning herself. Like all "decent people" she didn't realize what she was doing when she put a bottle on the table and then removed it. *Anyone who doesn't know the God of Alcohol is bound to behave stupidly with bottles.* Another thing—he wanted to eat only when hungry and not when others said it was time for eating. The few times he had lived what is called a regular life he had all day long felt himself so stuffed and nauseated that his brain worked slower and slower, like a clock running down audibly. Felicia would never cease popping food into him. If he failed to show up some day she would feel forced to look in—he might be sick. Well, even if he were dead, what could she do about it? Within a week she would suggest an extension telephone to Old Venhaug.

Felicia knew what he was like. Take care of him, she had said. Men must be taken care of, and they *liked* it, otherwise they would have no joy from their escapades, those silly fools. Be taken care of. One might get wet feet. Once he had taken a Norwegian lady about in London; sitting on top of an omnibus, during the rush hour, she had remarked, thoughtfully, "How difficult it would be to keep an eye on one's husband here!"

"You are an ungrateful character," said Felicia, inspecting her fingers, sticky with currants. "I offer you a house with eight rooms, big kitchen, lots of closet space and everything, and furniture too, you can have a comfortable bed, and a nice view of New Venhaug. And you start to sulk. Can't you understand I've tried for years to give you something? Now we have moved out of Old Venhaug and there it is!"

"You have forgotten to offer it without strings, Felicia."

This was only gently malicious in intent, but nevertheless her suggestion did have the drawback that he never could invite a guest, without bringing him over to the manor, eating with them there, sharing every acquaintance with them, which would force him to leave home more often than before. There was no use mentioning it. He could never lead a private life at Venhaug. There Felicia and Julie sat with their ideas. He knew Julie agreed with Felicia. She always did. He had once called her down because she took sides automatically.

Nothing was said for a long time. Felicia was thinking about a visit to her greenhouse a few days ago; she had gone in, locked the door and walked over to the opposite end and peeked out through the ventilator. It was sufficiently open for her to see through four of the horizontal slats, giving her a view of the path that led to the clump of silver-tipped spruce where quantities of old junk had been piled up to be out of sight.

Felicia's greenhouse ran from north to south. The double glass roof slanted from the high east wall steeply to the low west wall. In the east wall a wide, yard-high window had been built of the same construction as the roof; the lower edge of the window was about six feet above ground. The house had a high ceiling because Felicia had insisted on this; she wanted birds in there also. And the one who pays the piper can have what he wants. The panes in the steep roof were of greenish glass, and double so one couldn't see through them even when the lights were on. In summer all windows were given a coat of whitewash to temper the sun's rays. Inside there was a path down the center between the two cement slabs that ran the length of the house. The heating plant was just inside the door, on the north end, opposite the main building some two hundred paces away.

Felicia had begun to dream of a greenhouse when she was fourteen or fifteen. In their garden at Slemdal they had an aloe that was too large to bring inside in winter; then it was moved to a gardener's greenhouse. One day her father had asked her to look in at the gardener's on her way home from school and arrange to have the aloe moved back for the summer. She encountered a boy in the garden who pointed to a greenhouse where the owner was busy with something. She had been greatly taken by the artificial summer in there and had made a long visit with the old white-haired man who was pruning plants. There was a beehive in there, and the bees flew about from flower to flower. He told her that these were especially friendly bees, and at first she had thought he was making fun of her, but he went on explaining that there was a great difference in the temperament of the bees from hive to hive. "All come from a single queen," he said, "and if her disposition is unfriendly, then this trait is inherited by all her descendants, but if she is friendly then her children are friendly too. That is my explanation, but animals are like people—you can't be too sure about anything." He walked over to the hive and placed his hand cautiously on the entrance board. Soon the fuzzy little insects were all over his hand, their wings buzzing, but they seemed as contented as pups. When he slowly lifted his hand they flew off and attended to their chores. Felicia asked if they recognized him. He looked at her with his kind, old-man's eyes and said he didn't know; there were so many theories. "Do you know what a theory is?"

Yes, Felicia knew what a theory was.

Well, then, there were many theories. He himself was of the opinion that there were people whom animals liked, be they bees or birds or horses, and other people whom animals did not like. "Look at the little birds there," he said, and nodded to a large cage. "They too like me, but unfortunately they have to be in a cage now, otherwise they would eat the bees." He put his hand into the cage, and the birds fought with each other to perch on it. "You understand, they are at liberty to fly anywhere they want when I move out the bees." Why were the bees there? He explained to her about pollination, and here in the little greenhouse's concentrated sample of nature she understood at once all that had been completely incomprehensible when her teacher had made her poetical allusions. But then, the gardener was telling her facts, calmly and directly, as if speaking to an equal who just didn't know the facts. Felicia felt she was blushing when so much more than the gardener had said dawned on her. She had not been in ignorance as to what took place with people, but it had been a painful knowledge until this very moment when nature in its whole was taken in. She said, eagerly, "The kind bees—they are helping the flowers because they can't themselves?" "Well, one might put it that way," he said, and smiled to himself, "well, yes, that is correct. But some flowers don't need any insects to help them, there the female flowers are fertilized with the aid of the wind which carries the pollen along with it." She asked, "But if it happens to land on another kind of flower?" "Then there is no result, unless they are very closely related," he informed her. "I've heard that tigers and lions might get offspring together, but if someone tries to tell you that this happens when the animals are quite unlike then you must never believe it. Only silly people believe such."

Felicia had been so taken by the old man that for a time she thought of becoming a gardener. At the same time, but without having formulated it in so many words, she had learned what it meant to adjust oneself to life's demands in one's own little circle and be happy there. And he had had this effect on her by his mere being, sitting there on his stool. At last she must leave, she shouldn't stay too long. In the door she turned and said good-by once more. He was still sitting there, looking after her with a sad smile she always would remember. She forced herself to hurry away, for she had wanted to run back and hug him, and one didn't do such things. Many years later she could at will recall the smell of growing earth and feel the moist warmth with the old man looking after his plants among birds and bees. And, strange to say, some ten years after this encounter she had thought of him one evening, as she passed a group of Germans marching across Valkyrie Place, and she had become so terribly depressed that she had to cry because they were allowed here in the old gardener's homeland.

In April 1947, she had got her first pair of finches. It had been quite simple; she had seen them fly in and out through the ceiling shutter. This was propped open with a small stick with a string. She sat down back at the fireplace and pulled the string when both were inside. Then she covered the opening with wire so the shutter could be opened for airing. When the babies were hatched she experimented by removing the wire, and it worked out well; the finches flew out and in and supported their babies themselves. When the fledgelings left the nest she replaced the wire. Now she had seven finches that wintered with her. When new broods were to be fed she removed the wire again. It became her custom, every August, to shut up as many birds as she wanted for the winter. Later some confusion had arisen over the seasons: some started to build nests already at New Year, and she had to supply baby-food during the winter. Others, which she had shut out, returned from abroad and came back to the greenhouse. A few years she had been forced to wire the opening until sufficiently many gave up and built nests in other places outside. Birds were always fluttering about her when she came to the greenhouse and they alighted on her head and shoulders. She had built a bird-bath from an old copper pan and there they splashed about. She withdrew entirely within herself when she watched the bathing birds and had a flock of them on her shoulders and knees.

Tor Anderssen had undoubtedly been spying on her long before she discovered it (when would the others discover it?). He had happened to overhear her when she was telling Julie that she usually spent her time in the greenhouse with her clothes off. It was shortly after Julie had come to Venhaug. Felicia was embarrassed when she realized the gardener must have heard most of what she had said—he was on his knees with his tools in the bushes close by. But it didn't bother her for long; already that same evening she felt quite unconcerned about whether he had heard her or not. But it must have been at that time that she gave him the idea. She could recall his surprised look then, of one who had heard something unbelievable. Probably the thought had not come to him that a woman might be undressed even in the bathroom. The Kinsey reports were the most boring books she had ever read; they gave her the impression of a tedious and pallid foolishness which most people practiced and which she couldn't see the necessity of forbidding or protecting anyone against. If it was like *that* she would refrain voluntarily. But it had made an impression on her that many men were of the opinion that nudity was perverse and actually unimaginable when making love—and made the act difficult if not impossible. They seemed to believe the very thought of it was something the police should handle.

There was hardly any doubt that Tor Anderssen had felt he was dreaming. There, in full daylight, Felicia had said that she often took off her clothes in the greenhouse, and enjoyed walking about naked while she tended her flowers and talked to her birds. Or reclined on a straw mat and read a book. It was a pleasing sensation to be in air potent with growth and warmth, to inhale the smell of earth and plants with finches chirruping around her. She had said that just so did she imagine Paradise, albeit on a larger scale—and by the way, she was curious to know where Paradise was located; according to Holy Writ it was somewhere on earth with guards posted outside. But the guards one might get rid of with modern weapons, at least scare them off. Surely, Paradise must still be where the Bible had said, for its destruction would have been a happening that undoubtedly would have caused enough of a sensation to be known.

Felicia had spoken of Paradise and nudity in such a way that less than ten years later she might have been prosecuted for it. Possibly extenuating circumstances might have been found in the fact that her unsuitable remarks had been educational in intention, even if misguided, and had under no circumstances been intended for publication. She had gone beyond hints when she read one of Erling's poems, a ribald piece he had composed at request for a wedding and for which he had been promised ten kroner. It was called "To Kristine's and Nils's Wedding in Mo in Rana," and the contents, which fitted the occasion like a hand in a glove, might be understood through the lines: "Of future bliss one well may hint, but not be more precise in print." Only one handwritten copy was in existence, beside the one that had been mailed to Mo in Rana. It had come about because someone in Rana had a son called Nils who was about to be married to a girl called Kristine, "and you know, Julie, they wrote your father and put ten kroner in the letter and said they wanted a wedding poem." If his fee was less, he might return the difference in stamps. And Erling had not been able to resist, he had sent the poem, and the ten kroner also, to Mo in Rana.

Felicia had indeed meant to shock Julie a little, certainly not the gardener. It had bothered her that Julie in those days had exceedingly narrow views of almost everything, having been terrorized almost to idiocy. Felicia had drawn a deep sigh the day Julie at last was able to laugh. From then on Felicia shortened the rations of depravity and injected it only in quantities she considered absolutely necessary to bring the cure to a conclusion. It was an unintended side effect that Tor Anderssen had stationed himself at the ventilator.

The greenhouse had become her own world, and she could picture herself in it even after she had grown very old and everything at Venhaug had become different from what it was now. She knew Jan and Erling often thought of death. She herself never did. Old age she might sometimes look forward to with something resembling longing; she had once got it into her head that perhaps one could endure oneself better when advanced in age and wisdom.

She wanted to put her stamp on Venhaug, which she loved. She wanted to remain here after succeeding generations had taken over and she could sit with her birds and look down into the well of memories. She dreamed ahead to a grandson who resembled her and who was master of Venhaug; she dreamed of great-grandchildren who would call her Old Felicia with the Birds. She would sit alone and recall the men she had loved, and she would remember her father, and her brothers who had died so young. She would sit alone among youths in days to come, a remnant of all the past that had become a dream. She would live out each of man's ages in the same way she had lived out the years gone by of her mature age. At Venhaug she would remain. Here she would wish to be remembered as long as Venhaug stood. After that she didn't care. Eventually people at Venhaug would say: That happened in Felicia's time. That took place while Old Felicia with the Birds still sat at Venhaug.

Tor Anderssen had been looking stealthily about him; now at last he dared emerge from the little clump of trees; he approached, staring intently at the ventilator.

Felicia had watched him, smiling. Today you have to find another game, you shaggy wolf, you have to wait until tomorrow, or some day when it suits Felicia.

She did not touch the ventilator, she simply turned her back on it and walked away. She was in no hurry, she wanted him to see her, and let him think what he wanted, for she was leaving.

She banged the door shut behind her, locked it, and walked up toward the manor house.

· The identity

At last Felicia dropped her hands on her lap and looked at Erling. She didn't speak; people one knows well one doesn't recall from especially many situations, rather, one's clear impression is from a few. Erling was aware that Felicia had been sitting silent studying him this Sunday morning. She looked at him only to make sure he was still there, he felt, while she was pondering something she was unable to solve. She drew a deep breath and attacked the currant berries again. Julie was sitting with half-open mouth, breathing evenly and audibly. She never took her eyes from the currants. He looked at her with the eyes of an expert to whom nothing was surprising. He himself would have turned around to look at Julie. There she sat with her secret. And he returned to his own, the sneaking old feeling that he couldn't trust his own identity. For a moment his eyes followed Jan, who walked and walked, slowly but without stopping, as he had done at Old Venhaug also, as he had done during meetings in Oslo while the Germans were in the country, even if he only had a few yards of floor space. He had seen Jan continue his walking-motions when standing, unable to move. Many times he had had the feeling that Jan was walking away from his identity. That he wasn't there at all. Then his lower jaw might hang open a little, exactly as now. Erling discovered that Julie was following Jan's walking feet while she picked up cluster after cluster of currants.

Was Jan on his way to *his* Erlingvik?

I am one who doesn't know who the *he* is that I call *me*. I don't know, and no one ever tells me. In my dreams I am told to go home to Erlingvik —and there is nothing I would like better, although I am frightened when told so. I don't know when I gave a name to the place or the concept and dimensions of Erlingvik; I recall vaguely that I could get to it if it had a name, but even so I didn't find the way home.

"What are you thinking about walking there, Jan?" asked Felicia.

Jan swam unusually fast up to the surface and said, "I have just figured out that it is exactly thirty-nine and a half years since I made a slingshot. It was in the gable room back there at Old Venhaug."

He had been only thirty-nine and a half years away this time. Some other time he had returned from a star.

Erling was afraid of losing his present identity—even if it were a false one—and he remembered that for a while it had actually happened, while he was a refugee in Sweden. Looking back at it now, fourteen, fifteen years later, through reversed binoculars as it were, he felt that it had been rather interesting to lose a borrowed identity. If you lose your false passport you are in a difficult situation. He was on his way to pick up his new ration card at Vasagatan, and kept fingering his passport in his coat pocket until it was soaked with perspiration. He was moving slowly along in the waiting-line, more and more afraid he might shout the truth about his identity. Over an hour he had been standing in line and now there were only a few ahead of him, but he knew what would happen when he reached the window—he would lean forward and shout to the girl sitting there: I am not I!—He had had no choice except to leave the line and walk away, afraid of being apprehended before he could get out of reach. He managed it the following day—he had to have food even if he wasn't he—and then there hadn't been such a long line to give him time to work himself up, and the girl hadn't noticed him, hadn't seen that he wasn't he. He had felt himself to be like a circus artist forced to balance on the brink of calamity, and only his outside shell had walked about in Stockholm. He would never have got along at all if he had not for so many years been thought of as mad in the common everyday sense of the word—that is as one who might rise to the rank of genius when one of the senior geniuses died.

He recalled the dream now, the last one this morning, after which he was almost too frightened to go back to sleep. Indeed, they were two dreams, but he felt the first was only a sort of prelude to prepare him to dream on. A girl was lying on the floor and he had pulled up her skirt; between her legs she had a diminutive head of Molotov, who looked surprised. Erling had become confused, not knowing what to do next. Then the girl hid Molotov behind a hand mirror in which Erling could mirror himself, but the face he saw he did not recognize. The dream that followed had been worse. He had had a visit from the saber-toothed tiger. Someone pushed him through a door into a room where he was to be interrogated. An older man was sitting on a dais behind a pulpit. He looked like Hindenburg. Behind the dais was a dirty plank wall. Only the two of them were in there—the guards had locked the door behind him. He was standing before the judge who raised his heavy head and asked who he was.

"My name is—" but he started to stutter and continued with this until finally he spewed up a name. He spit out the last syllables of it and saw that they were covered with stomach juices and bile and something still worse, and he was afraid to wipe his lips for fear the judge might notice it. Then it was his height, color of hair and eyes, and a few more questions, and he replied as he always had, as could be read in all the passports he had had, but he knew he was lying, nothing had ever been correct. There were more questions, about occupation, parents, background. He replied in detail and truthfully to everything, with increasing fright, and tried to make himself believe he had nothing to hide, but the judge must have known who he was and knew every word he uttered was a lie; it was something he had invented long ago, and might as well not have done so, and he could have shouted out and demanded that the judge tell him who he was, and whose personality he had assumed and which he himself perhaps was now; or perhaps he was dead. He didn't know who he might have been. He guessed at two or three he had known, but didn't feel it could be any one of them, they were themselves and not him. Was he no one at all? The something that stood here and reported that he was, might be only a thin shell around something, a shell that said something that the shell at times had believed, but all was lies, even though he never had intended to lie about it. And there had been something about a mirror also. "Turn around and look at yourself in the mirror," the judge had said, in derision. "Then you'll see how well you fit the description you have given of yourself."

But Erling hadn't dared turn about, because he saw how the judge's heavy face began to change. If he too is someone else, then perhaps he is me, thought Erling, in fear. The judge looked down at the floor—perhaps he wanted to hide his transformation—his eyes grew so big Erling could see them in spite of his head being lowered, eyes which exuded something while they increased in size, and they turned and looked at Erling under the judge's gray hair. The eyes were still expanding and slobbered like the jaws of a beast. Lines and bags were forming in the cheeks, the underjaw fell down, the cheeks protruded. Erling wanted to shout that he would confess who he was, but he was unable to speak. He wanted to turn around and look in the mirror and see who he was before the catastrophe took place. He had not noticed any mirror when he entered, but there must be one there when the judge said so. He wanted to kneel and pray the judge to look in the mirror and tell him who he was, but now he had lost his voice. He gathered all his strength to turn about and look, but as soon as he managed to move ever so little, before he saw the mirror, he heard a sound from the judge's bench. He looked up. The judge had vanished, but from behind the bench the saber-toothed tiger was approaching him, its eyes like burning coals, the tusks growing down from the upper jaw, crooked and a foot long. The floor creaked and groaned under the heavy weight of the beast, but only a low whisper was heard as the soft cat-paws touched the boards. He cried out in terror and woke up. Not even much later, sitting in the taxi on his way back, had he got over his regret at not looking in the mirror to discover the solution of his riddle. The sound of running feet, many voices that were after him before he would be liberated from his dream, white, upstretched arms as from a cellar opening, a hand touching one of his ankles, and someone, far away but clearly and loudly calling: "The salvation is in Erlingvik! Go into yourself!"

• *An approximate nothing*

Erling had started to help Julie and Felicia with the currants, and he said: "You ought to put a bottle of wine on the table."

She stripped the berries from the stalk in her hand and looked at him, only looked; her eyes said nothing. "Why not," she said, finally, and brushed some rubbish from her fingers. She looked at the clock as she rose, and returned with a bottle and four glasses (but Julie didn't want any). She looked again at the clock. "You were correct the first time," he thought, "I know it's early in the day"—and then their eyes met.

Erling was rather irregular in his shaving habits (if Felicia mentioned again that he should move to Venhaug he would remind her that he never shaved during a work-period). More or less jokingly Felicia used to say that she took it as a signal for the evening when he turned up newly shaved (all women know why, the famous actress had said, with a charming, mysterious smile). She had hinted she took it as an exactly opposite signal when he one day had said he wanted something to drink. Another time she had quoted Viktor Rydberg's veiled remark that Bacchus had no children. Erling had wondered what she might offer this time, and he had hoped it would be white wine, or their own hard cider, but it was sherry, and he knew it meant as much as: Have it your way—empty the bottle!

He poured, raised his glass to them, and sipped. Jan also took a drop and walked on with the glass in his hand. Erling drank half of his glass, picked it up again immediately and emptied it.

Felicia picked up a handful of currants and hummed to herself:

> I got myself a hobby-horse,
> His name was Abilgray,
> A straw sheaf was his head,
> His tail was made of hay.

"Drink, Erling!" she said in the same tone of voice, and started another verse.

Jan put down his glass somewhere and each time he passed the place he discovered it, equally surprised. "It's great to have a glass of wine on a Sunday morning," he observed. "It goes with the morning concert."

Gudny and Elisabet appeared like a gust of wind, slammed the door and brought with them a cat and a dog they were jabbering something about; they had stopped a fight, it seemed, and it was hard to understand them when they finally spoke of their errand—to remind Jan he had promised them and their friends a ride in the car. They forgot about both dog and cat, and when the latter tried to hide behind the wood near the hearth but found the place too narrow it attempted to escape through the chimney. Felicia managed to throw out the dog, scolding all the while; and then the cat, which didn't belong at Venhaug, jumped through a windowpane and was gone. It surprised Erling every time he heard the twelve-year-old Gudny imitate Felicia's voice. The two similar voices were now scolding each other. "Stop that circus!" said Jan, annoyed; he had fetched a broom and a dustpan to clean up the shattered glass. "Get out, brats! And keep the animals outside—I'll be with you in a moment." "Such foolishness," he kept muttering to himself when they had run outside, their voices mixing with the others. "Drag in a cat and a dog to tell us they'll fight. I'll fix the window later, Felicia, I think I have the right pane. Such brats—they should have a good spanking!"

Jan's standing expression was that they should have a spanking. This he had from his father, Felicia had said; he didn't spank anyone either but said one ought to; Jan was strong for traditions.

Elisabet had been five months old when Erling had seen her for the first time in 1950. He wasn't sure where to place babies in their first stages; but since they didn't bother him, neither would he bother them. He might sit and watch babies for long intervals, but didn't think much about them; it was like looking at a bird nest, or the nest of field mice, and drinking in the life-warmth through his eyes; but what he actually looked for was that something in babies that made women jabber in chorus and go on like parrots in the jungle. Indeed, a baby was something especial. Someone had to defend a being that couldn't fight for itself. He would do it himself if need be. But it concerned mostly the mother. One must be careful that this valuable belonging of hers came to no harm, for if it did she would be quite wretched and not easy to deal with. And one should consider too that soon that little bundle would be a human being one might have contact with. Better wait and see; there was no contact with a baby. This was a notion only women fell for and they did so loudly enough. An unborn child was dead silent. After it was born it started to cry. Otherwise no perceptible difference. It was lucky a foetus didn't cry, like a chick in an egg. It might not have been so strange if, as a general rule, unborn babies cried when the mother was careless. It was wrong of people to accept everything as obvious; it robbed them of much joy. The moon and its peculiar passage across the heavens would have struck them dumb if it had appeared for the first time the day before yesterday. What made the difference was that it had been there so long; now it was only the moon. What was remarkable about it? Well, there was much quite remarkable about the moon, but never mind since they couldn't see it.

That time, in 1950, Erling had been interested in Gudny, as he had been before he left for the Canary Islands. She was between five and six when he returned, and had the same big, round owl-eyes. Already she had started to imitate the speech of others, but this she had not perfected until she was about nine or ten. Gudny had sometimes made him uncomfortable while she still was only three. Now, at twelve, her owl-eyes could penetrate right through him. When looking up he might meet her eyes, and they continued to search him unabashedly. It was not an unfriendly look, but he had reacted to it more or less the same way since she was quite little. It was as though he possessed a knowledge others didn't have and which she wished to have eventually.

Elisabet was now seven and went to school also. She resembled Jan but had all Felicia's restlessness. A young monkey, as it were, throwing herself from branch to branch while the old ones sat steady, calmly blinking at the sun and peeling their bananas in peace. Big sister Gudny had from birth been a calm child, dignified as a highly placed mandarin, but it was only a bluff. She had got her looks from both parents—and an ability to imitate both them and others that could make one speechless. She need only observe a person for a few minutes to reproduce a picture of the whole personality. Some people refused to say a word when she was present, but then she would take her revenge in a mimicking portrayal with nasty overtones. In school she was feared and even became the teacher's great concern; he had spoken to Jan about her, complaining that he couldn't turn his back on her before the whole class was in hysterical laughter, and however quickly he turned toward her, there Gudny was sitting as serious and innocent as ever. She could without the slightest effort imitate any dialect or tone of voice she chose. The delicate strokes by which she underlined people's little peculiarities were like the sting of a red-hot needle to some. In her way she was a friendly child, and quite obviously in love with her father. She had a certain weakness for Erling, too, but could torture him so with her caricatures that only with great effort could he control his anger. With Felicia she could be completely merciless, but was unhappy if she thought she had hurt anyone.

It is said that a person doesn't know much about his own voice, or has only mistaken notions about it, because the echo in the skull, along with other disturbances, interferes with the function of the hearing organs.

Thus most people are surprised when they hear their own voice recorded. Erling had begun to wonder, however, what were the facts in the
case, when Gudny could speak with any number of voices, thousands
theoretically. The imitating of other voices must cause as great an echo
in her skull as her own voice did.

Gudny had assumed power with this art of hers. If she wanted to get
her way, irritate, or insinuate herself, it was usually enough to answer
others in their own voice. But if this wasn't enough she used a third
person. With Felicia she invariably used Jan's soft, slow dialect. Or she
might call from another room in Erling's hoarse voice: "For God's sake,
Felicia! Give her what she wants so we may have peace!" "You mustn't
do that!" said Felicia, angrily. "That's forgery!" Julie she had taken under
her special protection: "For she is made so that she can't get even," said
Gudny. "That sort of people one mustn't tease."

"Tell me, Gudny," said Erling one time, "are you quite sure it is *your*
voice you are using when you believe it is yours?"

It had been one of those moments when Gudny could become so
strangely soft. She threw her arms around his neck and replied unexpectedly: "How do you think I can stop a thing like that? I would like to
so much."

"You mean you cannot?" he asked, as much surprised that she wanted
to, as that she couldn't.

"No, I cannot stop it, and I think it is silly. I would prefer to be
Gudny only."

Erling hadn't known what to say, but it struck him that Gudny was
not alone in doing something she didn't like, and never stopped doing
just that. It had seemed to him Gudny felt lost when she crept into
someone else's skin. "I would prefer to be Gudny only." Was she too,
afraid of losing her identity? Lose it forever if she didn't take care? Was
what one called personality perhaps not so securely anchored as one was
inclined to believe? It was possible that behind such an opinion hovered
a suspicion that one never had had any identity or personality, that one
lived in an illusion, a swindle. He might feel as if he didn't exist at all,
never had existed except as a bluff for a bluff, a sort of mirror-room of
bluffs that mirrored bluffs and more bluffs, a fateful formation that
functioned somewhere in nothing, zeros following zeros, a nothing that
bred nothing and never ceased to breed nothing, an industrious, laboring, untiring nothing which could lead only to nothing and one day
dissolve into another nothing. A delusion, an unreality held together by
another unreality, something that was life's beginning and its dissolution,
something that had not the ability to die, but could easily disappear, and

people would remark: What became of him? It might seem to them he hadn't been there at all, and those who thought they had known him might, from shame, keep quiet about it, or say: It was just a story I told, and you must have been very gullible not to check in the records whether he actually had been there. Hadn't it always bothered Erling that his base was something that approximated a zero? Hadn't his life been peopled with beings he only had brushed against in the periphery of his Nothing? Didn't names daily pop up which he had heard third- or fourth-hand—a carpenter on Therese Street, or a sailor in Horten, he had only heard the names, but now the names appeared with great agony, and he could think of the unknown persons for days—

• "—or anything that is thy neighbor's"

Felicia and Erling were alone in the room, and he said: "It's a long time since you mentioned anything about that little shortcoming in Julie."

Felicia bit her lower lip thoughtfully and did not reply at once; then she began with an extenuating circumstance: "Fortunately, so far it's only here at home she takes things. I would have been told if it had happened anywhere else."

"Tell me about it—I don't like to ask questions."

"There is a change. That time it started, long ago, it was mostly I who was the victim, although it did happen others also missed things. She acted more like a sleepwalker in the beginning. Now it never happens that anyone but me has things stolen. The fact that nothing is stolen from Julie—if we now should assume that it is *not* she—can have a good reason. It would be almost impossible to steal from her, because of the location of her room, and also because she is so careful with her belongings. I must mention *that* too. But there is no doubt who the thief is."

She stopped a moment.

"I feel, in a way, so uncomfortable about what I say now: my underwear disappears if I don't watch out."

It was apparent she considered this as an indication that the thief was a woman. Erling said nothing, but he thought that this was no indication at all. He realized there was nothing to prevent a female kleptomaniac from appropriating women's clothing under certain circumstances. The disease might be very complicated. Yet, a female thief stealing female garments led one primarily to think of an ordinary thief. Much more often male fetish-worshipers practiced that kind of stealing.

"During the last half year I've lost a number of things of no particular value, except for two rather valuable ones. They were those earrings you brought me from Las Palmas seven years ago, and the pearls Jan gave me on my fortieth birthday. I have not mentioned it to him, but a couple of times since, I should obviously have worn them. He too must understand. No one else has lost anything."

Both were talking in low voices, listening for the faintest sound.

"And it couldn't be anyone else?"

"No. Anyway, it would have been impossible for anyone else to get to the rings and the pearls—except Jan, and that, I believe, would be going a little far. To be quite frank—if I reported it she would be picked up."

"It seems amazing that my daughter should develop such a tendency —here she has for so long found all the love and understanding anyone could hope for."

"Yes, but she didn't find it when she needed it most."

Felicia hesitated a moment, then continued: "I can put it this way— almost a hundred percent of what I lose, Jan has given me; of actual valuables only the earrings came from you. When you say she gets so much love here there shouldn't be any reason for this sickness—mightn't one suspect she continues to steal from a sort of habit? She began stealing love, and the old, senseless technique is carried on. You know better than anyone, Erling, that old habits are difficult to change."

She looked at the bottle and shrugged her shoulders.

"She is using her old technique," said Felicia with a little change in her voice, "because now she is after another love she also doubts she can get: the gifts I have received from Jan ought rightly to have gone to someone else."

"Well, that's one interpretation," admitted Erling, but thought in the same moment of the underwear; perhaps Felicia had thought farther ahead than he at first had suspected.

"I look at it this way, Erling; when it started it was love and understanding in general that she hungered for. Now she doesn't like it that you give me presents, and Jan must under no circumstances do it. And something else: her caresses of Jan are quite innocent—seemingly. But she is almost twenty-three, Erling."

She laughed, and her laughter was honest enough: "I'm not at home in many sciences, but there is one I know: Julie is in love with Jan."

"She knows our situation, Felicia—do you think that might strengthen such an idea in her?"

"I'm sure of it. But only in the dark part of her brain. In her enlightened part she is too wise to draw such a conclusion. Such 'rules of three' are indications of sickness, or in any case too childish for a sensible, grown person like Julie. I know almost all there is to know about Julie awake—and a great deal about Julie dormant. You must realize I am half mother and half sister, she is half sister and half daughter."

"And Jan?"

Felicia smiled: "How does he react? He and Julie are in the same situation—with this unimportant difference that Jan thinks it too silly to steal. 'Forgive me,' he says, 'I believe those were your cigarettes.' "

"Now listen, Felicia, don't try to tell me Jan is in love with Julie."

"Of course he is. Otherwise he would have discovered her proclivity long ago."

"Balderdash!" exclaimed Erling, and when Felicia fell into a paroxysm of laughter, he said angrily, "I think you take the whole thing a little too much as a joke."

"I've never been able to see anything funny in Julie's kleptomania, Erling. The poor girl is under a burden which might lead to the saddest consequences. I do *not* think she knows it. This has been repeated several times and that makes it anything but funny. In one way of course, she knows what she is doing, but she keeps it in a sort of closet without light. I don't know what complicated names there are for such things—I'm only trying to tell you something there is not the slightest doubt about. It is related to somnambulism in some way; come to think of it, she does walk in her sleep at times. But it doesn't check entirely— too much has been taken when she was awake. Remember, she and I are always together, or practically always. No one knows her as I do. She is completely innocent. Once I explained to her the word kleptomania, when she ran across it in a paper—it was shortly after she had come here. 'How stupid,' she said, and read on without further comment. You may be sure my eyes were open."

Erling did not doubt Felicia's eyes had been open. When were they not? She had eyes in the back of her head. But—wasn't Julie equally sharp about her disease, and aware of whom she was up against? Erling smiled in paternal pride at the thought Julie might have fooled Felicia. Felicia's eyes were indeed open. She said, "What are you smiling at?"

"I'm smiling because you apparently think of it as a joke that those two are in love with each other."

"How else could I take it? Would it be becoming to Jan Venhaug's faithless wife to start crying?"

"You haven't exactly cried, but I've certainly been made to suffer when you thought that I had been out with—"

"That's entirely different."

Erling shook his head. Obviously it was something different, since he wasn't married to Felicia and there were some things he need not talk about with her.

"For one thing," she said, "it's entirely different when you chase other women, because Jan likes only a sensible and good girl like Julie. There is no comparison. Secondly, love is so many things. Those two keep flirting in all innocence, yet not so innocent as they themselves believe. What could I do about it? Tell them something they wouldn't enjoy knowing, and thus make myself nasty? In the third place, you have no business dissipating and then coming here with all sorts of tales about being tired and having colds."

She slowed down, and he felt it was high time. He recognized her peculiar smile, indicating deep seriousness: "There are times when a woman is forced to think men are Sunday-school children—I don't mean those little hypocrites one meets everywhere in life, I mean those one reads about in the Sunday-school papers, those amazing ones. You are unable to look into the future, and therefore you are surprised at any happening a woman with an ounce of brains has anticipated all along. Julie came here when she was fifteen, brought up in a children's home and any other place she had happened to land, poor soul. She was on her guard like a homeless, mangy dog—suspicious, difficult, confused, ever ready to lie, ever ready to crouch under the whip. Such was Julie when she came here, but I realized the girl had possibilities, and I went after her with all my might. She turned into a nightmare to me when it dawned on her that I wasn't going to birch her or use vile language. It would have been much easier to keep her down where she was. Well, we got over that stage, but it took three years for her to find herself. And at last we arrived with the Julie who is now twenty-two. It was obvious she would worship Jan, idolize him, adore him. I knew it before the poor child had come to Venhaug. Anything else was absolutely unthinkable. It was also unthinkable that such unabashed devotion would leave the object without response, especially as the girl has plenty of what my grandmother used to call male-appeal, and furthermore was trained by me to make use of her advantage. Unfortunately, I did not forsee that Julie was a kleptomaniac or had any other character defects, as perhaps I should have. As far as I know now it would have been quite out of the ordinary if something like this hadn't developed. It grew from stealing love in general to—a specialized stealing of my husband; perhaps it is a compliment of sorts that she has kept her stealing of love inside Venhaug. I have been defeated in my educational effort and I must take my punishment. As you see, I haven't been able to make it thoroughly clear to Julie that love one cannot obtain through threat, through purchase or theft. It is something one is given on time. It has no price. Today Julie knows this very well, but in some one of her cellar chambers she still harbors a dream-like misconception, a simple, childish impulse. It is my fault she hasn't been able to root out this devil, this stupid imp, and crush it."

Erling kept silent. He felt uncomfortable when Felicia pulled up—by the tail as it were—that part of his past which had to do with Julie. It didn't shine.

"Julie will see the light, if she hasn't already. She can put her best foot forward if it is something she really wants. She wouldn't be your daughter if she could much longer manage an existence as a kleptomaniac nun. One day she will appear in my room and say, 'Felicia, here is silver and much else I've saved to buy Jan—' and then suddenly her mouth will fall open and she'll say, 'What kind of nonsense am I talking, Felicia! I must have been walking in my sleep.' "

• Julie Erlingsdaughter

Julie and Erling went for a walk in the forest, where the first signs of autumn were visible. The paths were moist and the skies gray. They could hear the children calling after them "Julie! Julie!" as they stole away. It was the same story each time she and her father wished to go for a walk alone before he left.

They seldom got into a real talk; Julie stuck to inconsequentials or preferred to say nothing. Yet she was open and sociable. She gave him many spontaneous proofs that she loved him. She might hug him and say: "My Erling! my Erling!" But that was all. She never confided in him. When he was at Venhaug he could always see that it was Felicia and Jan—and the children—who long ago had become her intimates. When she was with any one of them she chattered on and on. He sighed without knowing why; not with regret though. It was well the way it was. He missed something that Julie couldn't or perhaps wouldn't give him—a little intimacy, a little gossip about herself. He had no intimates. Felicia—well, that was something else. They had reached the point where one knows almost everything about the other—except for the locked-up part; and then there was this undercurrent of warfare. They never reached the stage where the one would win over the other. They used up a lot of time figuring out what mental reservation one used in this instance or that, as if they were foreign ministers at Venhaug and Lier respectively. The position of each was weak when it came to diplomatic exchanges for both would begin to laugh if either one threatened reprisals.

With Julie he felt the self-consciousness a parent often has, even when the relationship with a daughter is more normal than it was with him. He had seen little of her as a child and, if he had, he might have ruined her life. At Venhaug his visits were those of an uncle, and she had early been conscious that they didn't concern her primarily. His relationship with Felicia she had discovered at once with all the clarity a suspicious child of dubious background has. At a tender age she had learned that she was an illegitimate child of parents equally dubious. Under the pressure of this, and the hostile moralizing and blasphemous piety of her surroundings, she had soon begun to wonder what it was all about. He himself had had less to say than he liked to admit. There had been something degrading in the fact that he had been unable to arrange for his daughter as he would have wished, even though he used connections in high places as far as he could. When he had refused to return her to the orphanage after she had come to Venhaug, Jan had taken upon himself the controversial aspects of the problem, while Felicia made off with Julie to an "unknown address" from which she terrorized a dozen officials via telephone, foreclosed on a long-time mortgage somewhere, and in similar manner scared another dozen—causing the whole business to die down in some way that Erling had never inquired into. He supposed Jan had been forced to sign certain papers of nonsense which someone quickly had filed for the records. Regardless of how many rules and regulations had to be ignored, the fact remained it was difficult to refuse a home like Venhaug to a child in Julie's situation. All Erling knew of what had taken place was of a negative nature: there had never been talk of adoption. He knew nothing definitely about what Julie herself had felt or thought in all this, but it didn't matter; it was little enough in comparison with the rest of her sad childhood. A few times he had happened to overhear how she and Felicia exchanged ironic jokes about him; they had carried on like a mother and a grown daughter about the family's somewhat comical lord and master. It had given him a feeling of security, although it was not entirely pleasant to realize that Felicia had presented Julie with a rather distorted picture of her father—and that this picture amused Julie.

"I happened to see an envelope in the fireplace addressed to Julie Venhaug," said Erling.

"Yes, I sometimes get letters with that name."

He was waiting. He didn't continue. It was always so. A casual remark never led to a talk, and she herself never started one. It was like inquiring from an official institution; they replied exactly to one's question, if they deigned reply at all; exactly to the ounce, or fraction of an ounce, of one's inquiry. It was a matter of complete indifference to Erling whether or not she was called Venhaug or Vik or whatever name, as long as it wasn't an epithet of derision. He only wanted her to come to life. But she just confirmed what he had said and then kept silent. With some irritation he looked up in the treetops:

"Have you thought of calling yourself Venhaug?"

"No."

"Are you feeble-minded?"

"Why?"

"My dear Julie—say something!"

"What do you want me to say?"

Erling looked at her; he could never get over his surprise that Julie was such an imitation of himself in female form. It was like looking himself in the eyes at twenty. "You are indeed my daughter," he said.

"That's what everyone says."

"Please, Julie, tell me a little about yourself. If we weren't so closely related I'm sure you would enjoy doing it. All people like to talk about themselves. Must I pay court to you to make you talk."

"I have noticed fathers don't pay much court to their daughters. Not at all in fact."

"I hadn't thought of that."

"Well, there you see."

"Perhaps you have something, Julie. Fathers like to be courted by their daughters."

"I have seen quite a little of family life in this neighborhood, Erling, and even if I haven't had a mother to pick on me I know that wives pick on their husbands. They aren't considerate enough, the women contend; their husbands don't court them any longer. And the daughters have to stand by and listen—they who never have been courted by the father."

At least I've got her going, thought Erling. It sounds rather interesting.

"A father speaks from above and down to a daughter, or he scolds her.

It might not mean too much but it makes her feel like a drag. I'll sue for divorce if I ever get a husband whose daughters wouldn't climb in his lap, or if he quit courting any one of us."

"Is it different at Venhaug?"

"Yes, Venhaug is different, the girls flirt with Jan because they know he likes it and is never too busy to flirt with them. I guess it could be called spoiling the brats."

Julie had picked up a twig and was striking at nonexistent mosquitoes. "You want me to talk and talk," she said. "Here you come to visit and talk and talk to Felicia and Jan, and I have to be a good girl and listen. When we go for a walk you order me to talk. You never tell me anything. I would like to tell you a lot of things. Not that I have so much to tell, but once you are gone it strikes me that a man never can be at ease with a woman who is his daughter. It's all very well for the man of the house to be amiable and considerate toward the maid, but the daughters notice the difference. Even if the man doesn't recognize it or doesn't always think of it, the maid is fair game; the daughter isn't. Obviously not the wife either. But if the two of them are only a necessary evil or a yoke around the man's neck, then mother and daughter ought to get together and walk out on him. They couldn't do that in Nora's time, but Nora was a prognosticator whose prophesies have come true; we don't have half as many divorces as we should, though. As yet it is only the daughters who leave home."

"I think you are right in most of what you say, Julie, but that kind of relationship you have dreamt about between father and daughter could never fit in with you and me. It would look silly if a father who earlier has been rather dignified with his daughter suddenly should start to flirt with her at twenty-three. Besides, in our case the circumstances prevent the realization of your ideal."

"I understand, but I was almost grown when I came here, and from the first moment Jan treated me as his own child, and I don't think it'll change."

Erling did not know what to reply. What had been reported apparently depended on the eyes that had seen it.

"Obviously," she said, "you and Felicia made me terribly jealous at one time. I want you to know I got over that long ago."

He might have said that perhaps she ought to have taken Felicia's jealousy into account, but he didn't know what he might ruin by so saying, and anyway he had no desire to say it. "It is so much easier for Jan," he said. "He has no bad conscience on your account."

Julie smiled as she replied, "I've never known your conscience to be particularly bothered, and I'm rather glad for it. When I came here I dragged along a whole wagon-load of bad conscience. If your conscience is black, at least be grateful it sticks like a piece of sturdy tar paper. And as far as Jan is concerned—how can anyone know how easy his conscience is? Or what do you think?"

"I don't always know what I think. But I must tell you, Julie—it isn't what you have said that has made my spirits rise, yet I am very, very glad you said it. Most of all I'm glad we finally got to talk to each other. How about trying to improve, both of us? I have no illusion that you'll tell me only pleasantries. Nor am I accustomed to such. I promise I'll try to change in much, and with good will, not because I'm commanded. You're right in saying I have been rather unapproachable, but I've seen no other way before. You said you had been jealous, but no longer. If all this is true, then you must realize that—shall we call it love?—can be equally great even though different."

"I learnt that long ago. It was only as if I weren't entirely a daughter either."

"As a compensation you got two fathers instead."

He was not mistaken about the deep shadow that passed across her face and he regretted the words he had happened to let slip. For a moment he felt ill at ease. There could be no doubt of what his remark had released: the other woman at Venhaug had taken the two available men, and let Julie have them as fathers, she who hadn't had a mother and only a fraction of a father.

It was impossible to say if Julie had divulged something she herself was conscious of—that she loved Jan—or that it only this moment had dawned on her. She collected herself surprisingly fast and he couldn't notice any change in her. He had wanted something special with her today, he had wanted to lure her into a certain trap—and now she had gone into another. She was walking beside him, again with a touch of impudence, the impudence of a wagtail. Either she had talked herself out of everything, or she had nothing to talk herself out of.

"You must have noticed, Julie, how it interested me—what you said about fathers not flirting with their daughters."

"It interests me too very much. I've observed a great deal here in the neighborhood, also elsewhere. And Felicia hasn't kept me in ignorance, as you know. I have also read some. Perhaps I've got most from Felicia, though, it's difficult to say now after so many years, but never mind where one has gathered what one knows. I know I have read that it is rather common for fathers to fall in love with their daughters, and the mothers with the sons—and find response. This is possible, but I must say it is a love that could have peculiar manifestations."

"Such matters are always difficult to talk about," Julie continued. "People get twisted up in a lot of reservations and forget what they have just said. They start to defend themselves against something no one has intended to accuse them of, because it is so touchy. One must absolutely not believe the father loves the daughter in *that way,* or the daughter the father in *that way,* far from it. It is rather thus-and-so but what this thus-and-so is the person involved doesn't know. And perhaps it's only talk. Either they do fall in love, and then it is thus and not some other thus-and-so. That they draw a limit is obvious, and we don't need all those thus-and-so's to prevent us from believing healthy people have intercourse with little children. I *have* seen fathers who actually flirt with their daughters, and it's rather repulsive, for flirting is flirting whether people are related or not, and it only amuses others who themselves aren't too normal."

Julie thought for a moment and then went on: "We are not talking about abnormality and therefore everything is simple and clear—the family is nature's own school in the art of love. This is natural and reasonable and wholesome and beautiful and has been defiled. You can't doubt that Jan is quite naturally in love with his little girls and they with him. When I get children I intend to love them intensely. No one is going to talk to me about thus-and-so. I know what it means to live in a temperature below zero, day in and day out, the year round, and I am glad I'm aware of it—but that is not the way to learn it. See what happens in families everywhere—natural joy is suppressed, people have been tortured so long with the opinion that love is sin that at last they suspect themselves until they reek from it. Nowadays girls are a little more free, but it is only noticeable because there was no freedom at all before. We are still our fathers' and brothers' slave-women—"

"Our fathers' and brothers' slave-women," Erling repeated. "Perhaps so, but it sounds like a quotation from the Bible of Antichrist."

"I must use the words that fit best, no matter where they come from. Do you want me to make up my own language? When Felicia says such things they don't sound at all out of line, and they aren't. Fathers and brothers are their sisters' guardians. Did you ever see the girls try to run their brothers' affairs! But the boys say—with their big blue eyes—'Of course one must keep an eye on one's sister.' Why? It's only nonsense. 'Can you imagine your sister marrying a Negro?' the men ask. If I had a brother (some say I do have) and he would wish to marry a Negro girl, I can't see it is worse than for her to marry him. It is his own business. I would say: Hope they will be happy! Should I be my brother's keeper? Why in all the world would I want to be? I have no more responsibility for him than he has for me. All this nonsense about looking out for others! Yes, Erling, it could be that the one who has been pinched hardest sees clearest and is wisest."

"Don't bite me! I agree with you, and you know it. I am terribly sorry things had to happen to you once, the way they did, but if I wanted to be a little caustic myself, I might say you escaped from all this that you're getting worked up about."

Julie bit her lips until her mouth was only a line. She stopped walking and asked, "Who was Gulnare?"

"I have never told Felicia anything about Gulnare."

"Sooner or later Felicia finds out everything."

"God only knows why she must unburden herself on you!"

"I ask her myself. I want to find out a little about my father. Who was Gulnare?"

"Gulnare was my great love."

"The real big one?"

"Yes, the real big one."

"How long ago was it?"

"In 1915."

She looked at him, her mouth open: "That's forty years ago!"

"Yes—but this can't be the first time old people tell you time passes. And youth can never understand that a time was before they themselves existed."

"Can one never forget one's great love?"

"No."

"I thought so. And then you became Felicia's great love. Too bad you couldn't have had it together."

"Then you would never have been."

"What of it? I would never have known anything about it. It might've been just as well. Didn't Gulnare want you?"

"Yes. Something ruined it."

"Why did you desert Felicia?"

"Because I wasn't all there. Anything else?"

"Are you happy, Erling?"

He thought a moment. "Well, yes, I am quite happy."

"Is there anyone whom you honestly love?"

"I realize you're giving me a sample of how unpleasant it is to be interrogated. Yes, there are quite a few. It is a disappointment to me that no one believes it."

He took hold of her arm: "Let's walk on."

He thought: Would this girl not know if she were a kleptomaniac? Would she not be absolutely sure of it if she were in love with the father she now has at Venhaug—when she shows such a lively interest in a similar situation? My daughter is too clear in her thinking not to know herself in every detail.

A snake at your bosom, Felicia, but it doesn't bite you. Yet it still might.

"I would like to give you a present, Julie. Is there something you particularly would like to have? Don't hesitate, speak up. Some jewelry, or something—"

It was an experiment, but it fell flat.

"Are you trying to flirt with me?" She smiled. "You have given me so many things; they only accumulate in a drawer."

This turned her thoughts to money and other possessions: "I make my own clothes, from Felicia's discards. In that way I save a lot. Felicia is rather frugal, but she spends a good deal on clothes. Queen Felicia isn't quite as bad as Queen Elizabeth—she might wear a dress more than once, but—"

"I save lots of money that way," she reiterated, "for I think it is stupid to be poor."

"Do you believe poverty is only a matter of stupidity?"

There was a new intonation in his voice.

"To me at least it is. If I have my health I'll never be poor. I realized at once that here I could learn to run a farm, and I have."

"You were a child when you came here, yet you say you realized it at once?"

"I realized at once that it was so when Felicia told me, 'Don't ever be poor, Julie. For the time being you can learn here how to run a farm. There is no respect for the poor,' she said. 'If you learn to do something exceedingly well you'll never be poor, but you must do it better than others.' That's what she said. And it is true. Felicia knows everything, and she is not poor."

"Felicia had money, Julie."

"And knew how to keep it, Erling."

There was a painful silence and he waited to see if Julie would break it. He himself was not known for his ability to save money.

"I'll save money," said Julie. She repeated it, as if aside: "I will save money."

"For something big and unusual?"

"Well, one might say that."

Now she was about to begin again, he thought, and then—*period*.

"Are you angry with me, Erling?"

"Angry? I? I'm only thinking how terribly nice it is when you keep talking. You haven't done so for a long time. Now tell me what you are going to use your capital for."

"I want to have a sum of money. Felicia and Jan know I'm saving ten thousand kroner as a start. I have a long way to go. When I reach that sum Jan will do something with it. Place it, he says."

"Well, I must say! It does seem that the apple falls far from the tree. And when you have those ten thousand they will surely have gilt-edges with Jan's handling of them. And then what?"

"Let them be where they are. And save more money, but also buy whatever I want. I don't intend to spend more than three quarters of what I earn. One quarter must be put aside—at least. I'll follow that program for twenty years, after I have saved the first ten thousand."

"When did Felicia make up that program for you?"

"Not long after I came here."

"You only had pocket money then."

"Felicia said that was money too."

"And you thought it was a good idea?"

"Yes, I started at once. It happened—"

She stopped but resumed presently, "It happened I was crying in bed one evening and Felicia heard it. She came into my room, and it was then she explained all about money and said, 'Then you'll have some money if *you* should get a brat!' "

"And all this you didn't consider anything to talk about?"

"Felicia said it was nothing to repeat, but I rather like to talk about it now. She also told me a great deal about her brothers that evening, and about Jan, and you—and then she tucked me in tightly, and hugged me, and said that all that silly stuff they had fed me in the orphanage about the Lord on High, I should try to forget as soon as I could, for it was only nonsense and make-believe so that the big ones could keep the little ones in line—although it might well be there was a God worthy of following, in which case they must have hidden Him well. That was all, for that time."

Here he had been wondering how he could lead her onto her disease, and now things appeared which did not fit in with the sickness, or with anything. Where were Felicia's eyes? If Julie's kleptomania were to fit in here, then one had to reckon with a somnambulism so great he couldn't believe it. And he couldn't help noticing the pointed connection which the supposed kleptomaniac tendencies and Felicia's pedagogic methods had with *him*. And there he stood, caught in the trap. Was it any wonder that *this* daughter, after the treatment she had been exposed to, should become a kleptomaniac? On the other hand, he could not object to the fact that Felicia had taught Julie a little common sense about money. It was only that everything Felicia undertook, if it had even the remotest connection with *him,* threw a little pepper under his collar. Suspicious as he was—and he thought he had reason to be—he had also been thinking about what she had revealed to him when he had returned from Las Palmas and she was with him at Lier: how she had pretended to herself night after night for years that he would come back to her at Slemdal. It would have been like her to fool him now and then and not show up when they were to meet, but this she had never done. Did she think perhaps she had fooled him enough in marrying another man? It didn't quite check; long ago, in one way or another, she ought to have tried to get even with him—if for no other reason than because she had confessed to him.

Julie started to talk again, in a low voice, choosing her words carefully: "A few years later she said something to me that I will tell you. We were out in the garden picking raspberries. She said she had the day before put me in her will, and if she died I was to get as much as I had saved myself, but only up to a certain sum, which she didn't divulge. If I were married by then I would get nothing, unless I had a pre-marriage agreement about my own money. Since then we have never spoken of money."

"Felicia will never die, Julie."

"I don't think so either."

He had known Julie was in the will but hadn't thought much about it. Felicia, who never would die, was always busy making documents as if she might die tomorrow. To him it seemed another one of her hobbies. The details about the savings and the pre-marriage agreement, she hadn't mentioned to him, nor how much money was involved; and, unlike Felicia, he was not interested in the distant future.

She herself had a pre-marriage agreement. What she had inherited was emotionally tied to her. She alone was to look after her dead brothers' estate. Like everything of that nature it didn't seem well thought out, but there was something nice about it that Erling could appreciate. One often heard of penurious widows but there might be a deep cause beyond the miserliness. In Felicia's case it had been so arranged that her inheritance from her brothers was not to be touched by her; it was set aside for the succeeding generation, and even the thought was foreign to her that it was her rightful estate. What Jan had taken, or been given, for new buildings and farm-machinery was from Felicia's own inheritance, and she held a mortgage on Venhaug for it. Erling could never understand that kind of separate accounting, which he considered superfluous papers, unless divorce was anticipated. He had told her so, but she had replied, wisely, "I might die, and Jan remarry; then all mine goes to the children. With one exception—what goes to your daughter," she had added. "She is in my will, partly because she is your offspring, partly because she is the one she is, but you get nothing and I give nothing to other charitable institutions either. I don't count on dying, but then, people can die any time."

Erling could not recall that he had ever thought of saving money— quite the opposite. A person who had not discovered what he wanted to be when he grew up could hardly plan on saving capital. Erling had given up thinking about what he would be, for probably he would be nothing, but at the age of forty-three he had still been probing what work he should choose in life. Gardening had always stood close to his heart, preferably some specialized branch, like cucumber or tomato growing. For a while he thought of devoting himself to the production of fruit wine; the idea of a small farm with an orchard had appealed to him during the war years. But there were many other possibilities; he might become a teacher in a Folk School—in literature or history. This notion had persisted until 1944. The only thought behind all his speculations was that he must be his own master. Then it dawned on him that he was almost fifty, rather a late age to choose one's career.

In his early days he had always been influenced by the views of his brother Gustav, he who should have been a tribal chief in Africa and a high priest of formalism on the side. Erling's tribal feelings were weak but somewhere in his conscience there was a feeling of guilt for having failed his class and its call to colors. He hadn't entirely allowed himself to be taken in by all the sure and steadfast ones, although he knew they were at least steadfast. Their inane fight for shorter hours and funeral expenses was an expression of life-agony in its most trivial form; there should be walls so one couldn't see too far, and so one need not experience horrible moments like Mr. Babbitt's: "It was coming to him that perhaps all life as he knew it and vigorously practised it was futile; that heaven as portrayed by the Reverend Dr. John Jennison Drew was neither probable nor very interesting; that he hadn't much pleasure out of making money; that it was of doubtful worth to rear children merely that they might rear children who would rear children." As a counter-balance to Mr. Babbitt's insecurity were Mrs. Babbitt's pious words that all misery derived from running after other women instead of carrying one's cross in Christian patience. It was possible to imagine that Gustav and his likes some time, in their poverty and insecurity, had decided to ape the steadfast who appeared so secure, and had adopted a conviction that they adhered to in their work, in politics, in religion. Something hidden deep inside them made them feel increasingly afraid of *smiling* which made them fight for more coercion and more prohibitions, which daily made them more rigid and more immune to all the things that eventually might have brought them peace. They did not completely dupe themselves, but they influenced the new and insecure generations.

Each person is the result of millions of happenings, a few great and noticeable, the rest almost imperceptible, but everyone has been exposed to them as to atomic radiation.

Some might realize what their aims are but for years they must spend their time defending themselves against the radiation and trying to build protection. No one must move outside his own frame. If a young woman, or man, wanted to become a journalist but didn't directly spring from such a background, the blood would rise to the head of all the family: there was no institution that guaranteed to make you a journalist, and the editor of a paper could not promise you anything definite; let's see what you can do, he would say. There is no promise that one eventually would become *wholly competent;* everyone shook his head if one asked when one might expect to become an editor, or if an impartial seniority was practiced. Indeed, Erling himself had made an attempt at journalism, but had soon been forced to give up, or, rather, the editor gave him up. Erling had, in his youthful cynicism, and equally youthful naïveté, tried to find out what was most important in journalism. He had been hearing, among much else, that readers were only interested in calamities on a truly grandiose scale—"No, young man—the public wants real *murders,* and to tell the truth, *we—*" it was the editor speaking—"we should ourselves employ a few murderers, but unfortunately that would backfire when other newspapers discovered it, so we can't do it."

One day Erling had been given an opportunity to try his talent on something that looked like a murder, but soon all the circumstances indicated only a common accident. He was very young, and very serious; he felt he was satisfying the editor as well as the readers when he turned in a double headline, stopped in the last moment by a horrified city editor:

THE MYSTERIOUS CORPSE IN VIKTOR STREET
Hope Is Fading That It Was a Murder

He was fired, with the explanation that he had tried to publicize the internal concerns of the paper.

Julie had led him far away from what he originally had sought. He wondered if he should venture another attempt. To talk of her kleptomania now seemed to him complete nonsense.

"Let me look at you, Julie!"

He took hold of her shoulders and looked her steadily in the eyes. She smiled and blushed a little, and then she lifted her hand and stroked him gently on the cheek. He let go his hold. It was impossible—what Felicia had said about her. Yet, objects disappeared; someone must be taking them.

He stood still and looked down at the ground. He could imagine Julie in a sort of trance, a self-hypnosis—and he thought of *that other* Erling Vik.

"Julie," he said. "Answer me honestly one question. I ask because it is something I have had to fight—" and there was a shade of truth in what he said. "Try to think carefully. Has it ever happened to you that you have felt, in some strange way, that you have just come from some other place? As if you had just awakened from another world and that it is gliding away from you, the way a dream evaporates when you wake up. But I'm not thinking of a dream. Have you ever actually thought that you had just returned—for example to your room—from some place you already have forgotten?"

She thought it over: "You mean as if I had been lost in my own thoughts?"

"No, that's not what I mean."

He could see that Julie was thinking it over seriously. She knit her brow. (For how long had people knit their brows when thinking, or growing angry—and why?) "No," she said at last. "No." She laughed. "I don't flutter away through the air like those ghastly girls in the *Arabian Nights* and disgrace myself with rich merchants and sultans on beds as wide as prairies. If that is what you mean? I'm afraid your daughter is most ordinary."

"From all I have heard about how dreadful youth has become since my time, I don't think you are ordinary at all. If I'm not mistaken, you have not yet had a boy-friend and you'll soon be twenty-three."

"You're wrong. I'm so ordinary I have had one. But then he proposed marriage which would have meant that I must leave Venhaug. I discovered I wasn't that much in love with him. Apparently he wasn't the right one anyway; he got so mad it was unbelievable—'Can you beat that!' he said. 'Someone like *me* offering to marry someone like *you!*'"

Erling winced.

She continued, "I've never heard anything like it. But you must under no circumstances tell Felicia. Even though it's all finished now, she might well get it into her head to finish it once more, and *some* things of mine I like to have to myself. And besides, as long as she doesn't know about it, the boy can see that she doesn't know, and it's good for him to walk about and wait for her to find out."

"Wonderful the way you express it, Julie, but aside from your manner of expression, you do take after your father."

He was watching her. He felt a little annoyed on her behalf and he couldn't keep his thoughts off her unpleasant experience. Better not make too much of it, though; but had that boy perhaps been an unconscious attempt on her part to free herself from someone else? Perhaps she had realized vaguely that if she were ever to marry it must be at Venhaug. He looked at her again. It was impossible to believe she was the scarecrow Felicia once had brought to Venhaug. Felicia knew her business. But who was the kleptomaniac at Venhaug, or, more plainly, the thief? What was it Felicia had said?—it happened at times that she detested Julie. She had said; "All her cringing and fawning, all they had made her become at the orphanage. I've always detested a weakling, I can't be in the same room with one. It makes me sick when people belittle themselves and complain. It is still worse, of course, if they brag and pretend to be important, but that sort of weakness makes it easy to brush them off with good conscience. I don't know why people are the way they are, but I can't bear seeing them as failures. I realize that at times adversities might be so great that there has actually been no chance, but I can't forgive them nevertheless. Of all shortcomings weakness is the most unbearable. I can't look at such degradation. One autumn day I went to the forest to see what Jan was doing; I took the dog along to get his scent. We found him busy marking trees. When we had talked about this and that and nothing, I asked him what system he followed—he seemed to blaze all the trees that looked ready to topple over. 'You're right,' he said, 'I'm going to sell some rubbish-lumber.' I've often since thought of that word—rubbish-lumber. It has popped up like a picture when I've come across miserable creatures—truly, rubbish-lumber, I've felt. I'm annoyed at the weak as soon as I lay eyes on them, they irritate me, bore me. How I could stand *you* that first time in Stockholm is beyond me, it was so horrible, but in some way it was a link in the chain—and how I could endure Julie those first years is still a riddle to me. Who wants to pick up rubbish that has fallen off a cart? I don't believe many care to—unless perhaps it gives them the upper hand; people who have no desire to bully are reluctant to help others. I couldn't stand Julie, the cringing fawner and hypocrite she was. Her next stage was difficult too, a sort of humble dog-devotion because I did not use the whip she was accustomed to. I must tell you about an incident at that time which acted as a sort of stimulus—a lady called me one day from Kongsberg; she was passing through and she wanted so much to know how things were with Julie. She gave her name and I had heard it before—Julie had often told of her as a person she feared more than any others. I felt this was a good opportunity to learn something from the other side, so I gave her plenty of tether and she was willing to play with it. I lured her out on the thinnest ice and there she crashed through. 'That horrible brat!' she said. 'Completely unreliable and she has to be watched every moment, and well, well, Mrs. Venhaug, you must have heard of her *background*?' I let her go on for a while until I got tired and asked in my sweetest voice if it was her usual practice to call foster parents to tell them they had potential criminals in their house, and if she was really so sick with revenge over being repudiated that she had to commit an outrage on a child's reputation? Julie was indeed a remarkably lovely child, I said, and furthermore our conversation had been taped, and God help her if she didn't leave little children in peace! Anyway, after that incident there was no thought of giving up Julie and admitting such a werewolf was right. Jan was the better of us two, his control and compassion were even greater than I had expected. When I look back on it now I have the strongest misgivings that such wrecks can be saved. The hard time I had with Julie shows me that in practice it must be impossible where many children are involved. It is unrealistic to think one can rehabilitate people *en masse*, especially when they have only cold disciplinarians to guide them during their formative years. And now you see Julie as she is today—the boys make eyes at her, she is beautiful and balanced, everybody is fond of her—but one can't get away from the fact that she has turned out to be something between angel and nun, for the time being at least. She looks beyond young men; she is chaste because she is tied to Jan. She steals blindly everything Jan gives me and locks it up in sturdy trunks." Felicia had chuckled: "Well, this must stay in the family. And she has made herself useful; if she ever should leave us I don't know what we would do; I think she must be beginning to suspect it herself. But this other thing—well, one day last winter some of us went to a little lake to do some ice-fishing. I cut a hole with the mattock and when I got through, the pickaxe hit another layer a foot below. That made me think of Julie."

Erling glanced at Julie's calm and thoughtful profile and saw a sort of miracle—a young and strong human being who would never have been except for him. Had Felicia determined Julie was a kleptomaniac and that settled it? A person *could* be a kleptomaniac or a pyromaniac for more reasons than one, but could one make that statement except in the conditional? One person might drop dead after drinking a quart of liquor in half an hour, another might do it in twenty minutes and get extremely drunk, but with no other consequence than a decision to swear off. At Venhaug things did disappear. One of the symptoms of a kleptomaniac fitted Julie. Felicia had not said whether or not she had more to go by than the description of a kleptomaniac. She had insisted that if the police were called in, Julie would be arrested. Yet, it was only the old story that if one started to suspect a thing at a certain time, it stayed as a thorn in one's flesh.

He now asked Julie how she got along with the children.

"Very well. They're very nice, and I learn a lot about the interests of a twelve-year-old."

That remark gave him a jolt ("I myself have never been twelve").

She knew quite well what she had said and realized it had hit deeper than she had intended. She went on, "We are really like sisters. Fortunately it turned out that way after I had got over my worst time here and realized I could stay. I wasn't accustomed to grown people speaking the truth. They probably intended to tell the truth, in the orphanage, but if one statement didn't suit, later they changed it. I don't think they knew any better. It seemed obvious to them that when one thing or another didn't suit them any longer it wasn't worth anything. Just like the Great Powers, you know—they repeal an agreement in one day that was intended to last for fifty years and not be revoked then without five years' notification—isn't that the way they do it?"

"Yes, that's correct."

"They don't do that at Venhaug. I happened to overhear something after I had been here a year probably. It was about my room, that it would be more convenient if I had another one. The second one wasn't quite so nice, but they agreed to arrange it one way or another and then it would be as good. It was Felicia who said, 'We can't talk to Julie about this—she would feel she had to say yes.'"

"And you found some excuse to ask if you could have the one they had been talking about?"

"No. Felicia called and asked me to come and help move some furniture, the things they had just been talking about. She was whistling the whole time, as she always does when in good humor, and I had no reason to say anything. The episode helped me a great deal—I was no longer just another piece of furniture. Felicia told me I could arrange things any way I wanted, as she sometimes does with the other children. I was treated like a daughter in the house, and it isn't empty talk; in fact, it has never been mentioned. They let me discover it for myself. But I do a lot of work, without being asked, and I enjoy it. And I am starting to have my own opinions too; that came when I began to draw a salary. Yes, the girls and I are like sisters. Gudny is my girl-friend of younger years, Felicia the other way; we are like three generations. One day it escaped Gudny she would rather have me for mother than Felicia."

"How did you react?"

"I said it was nice to hear, for it was. Children say so much they forget at once—as long as grownups don't hammer it into them with beating and scolding. And that's what grownups do—tie their children to some mental post. In another family a girl might have been spanked for not preferring her mother. Here I could even tell Felicia about it. She laughed heartily and said, 'Oh, *you!* You really have a way with the kids!' "

Erling told her about one of his problems with the Venhaug children; perhaps she might advise him? When he came he always brought something for Julie and the children. It wasn't necessary that he brought presents to Gudny and Elisabet, but they would notice it if he didn't. And sometimes they asked for them. But they didn't seem to care for his gifts. This hurt him because he was afraid there was something behind it, he didn't know what. And it was getting harder to choose presents, especially since he felt they were not very much interested in gifts from him. "But I am their friend, don't you think? Elisabet sits on my knee and I read the funnies to her. Gudny carries on about anything she wants to know. Children don't act that way if they dislike you. But I can't play with them, that I know. I never have. I never have been able to throw children into the air or swing them around by one leg. I can't enter into their wild games the way Jan does. I am well and strong, but I'll be fifty-nine in March when you are twenty-three. I still swim, but not long distances. I can stand on my hands against a wall, but it makes my eyes go black. I don't like to jump up and down. I can get in a passable kick on a soccerball if it's lying still and nobody is trying to take it away from me. A soccer player consoles me by saying this is not a sign of weakness but more like a miracle."

"I say with Felicia—one needn't feel sorry for you. You have it as you want it. I've never heard of anyone as free as you are. You can be glad you are not a sportsman, and all children know there are some grownups who don't play. There might be something to what you say about presents, but nothing to make you unhappy. The children get regularly all they need. This is good, very good one might say, but it robs them of the joy in getting presents that poorer children have. It is your own joy at receiving a present that you recall—"

She thought for a moment before she added "—and perhaps mine."

"But there is something else you should realize, Erling. You have been coming here off and on since 1945. That meant both children lost you time and time again when they were little. Suddenly Erling wasn't there. You failed them again and again. If they are a little reserved about your gifts it does not mean they reject them, for they have forgotten the reason for their reservation. When they were quite little they saw in it an attempt by you to buy absolution for your sins: you paid because you had been bad and deserted them, and though this was good it would have been better if you hadn't sinned."

"Are you starting in now, too, Julie? Tell Felicia I'd like to see her hanged!"

"Alongside the watchmaker with the cork leg?"

"Don't tell me Felicia has been telling you indecent stories about your father?"

"I don't know about that—she says you told that story to three hundred people, while she was waiting for you and you never turned up. I have great sympathy for poor Olga as well—the one you wanted to boil in the iron wash tub."

"I was only fourteen or fifteen—"

"Yes, you were rather precocious."

He let it pass and said he had had a letter from her mother.

"I don't want to meet her," said Julie, shortly.

"You have never been even a little curious?"

"No. All she wants is to come here. I've had letters from her too. She mustn't come here. I don't like her letters. How long since you saw her last?"

"Many years. She has fallen quite low—been in jail many times. Terribly mixed-up. Lives in a thick fog of liquor. What did you write her?"

"I didn't write at all. What could I say? What could I reply to a person who threatens to tell Jan Venhaug about my father unless she gets money? The only thing I ever had to do with my mother—I wrote her a wretched letter from the last orphanage, and she never answered me."

"You never told me that."

"I couldn't. By the way, who would have told her that I'm adopted and will inherit a million?"

"Certainly not I."

"It was the envelope of her letter you saw in the fireplace. You mustn't hear from her often if you didn't recognize her handwriting. She also wrote that now she hears the blood calling."

"How does that sound?"

"Horrible. She wants to come here and put matters right as soon as I send her money for the ticket. It wears her down that her daughter is without a mother's watchful eye in all the world's sinfulness. On the other hand she might consider a monthly allowance. The whole thing was very vague, extremely vague."

"Burn her letters before you read them, Julie. You can feel safe as far as she is concerned. She would never make it even to Kongsberg—never. If you did send her the money for a ticket she would drink it up. She'll never in this life get anywhere outside Oslo, unless she has to be sent there. Possibly she might manage the trip itself, but she doesn't have enough strength or ambition to get out. She is gone, except for a few spasms."

"Don't let's talk about it any more, Erling. I've never seen her. She didn't answer my wretched letter. I have never had a mother and am too old for one now. I don't care for any people except you here at Venhaug."

(*You here at Venhaug. Don't care for people except you here at Venhaug. I am one of "you here at Venhaug." Thank you, Julie. Felicia must be entirely mistaken.*)

He asked, suddenly, "Would you take it hard if I died?"

"I have thought of it. It will be difficult when you die. Why won't you live here at Venhaug?"

"Like other decent people, you mean?"

"Please, Erling—why don't you move here? I do think you're silly at times—you get that big house and we could look after you a little."

"Take care of the dying one?"

"Nonsense, Erling, you know well you'll live to be a hundred. Jan often says, 'Erling—he'll live to a hundred!' All of us want you to come here—the children, the dog, everyone. We have always felt that way."

"I can promise you I won't live to be a hundred. And when it comes to the question of my moving here for good, I think my own opinion ought to be taken into consideration a little bit. You are the motherly kind, afraid my feet may get wet. Felicia would be after me—it's exactly the same thing. You're putting me in a bad humor, Julie, and I suspect you are out on Felicia's errand, even though it may be your idea too."

"You shouldn't say Felicia would be after you and cause trouble. She loves you. And if one should look into which one of you has caused the other the most trouble—"

"Listen, Julie! I've got along surprisingly well for many years, even before either one of you was born, but you women always feel a man must get along in the way you consider best for him, for only that can be the best way. If I should move in here I would one day leave in terrible anger, and then you know I would never come back. You know Felicia has some magnificent thoughts in her head. One of them is to increase my burden of gratitude until I'm squeezed flat. But I can't be squeezed flat, I'll burst."

"You're the most suspicious person I'll ever meet."

"That's a pretty strong statement. You can't predict whom you'll meet, it might be something worse than your father. I—"

He stopped suddenly as he noticed a magpie fluttering a little ahead of them on the narrow forest road. He had a newborn interest in magpies, and said, "God knows what gets into a magpie to make it steal silver."

"It has never taken any silver in all its life."

"How do you know that?"

"How do *you* know it has?"

Erling felt uncomfortable. Had he come near the mark?

"I don't know anything about that particular magpie," he said. "Excuse me if I hurt the feelings of that magpie—I thought it was a well-known fact that magpies stole things that glittered, silver spoons and such."

"Hasn't it occurred to you how strange it is that they should steal silver spoons? Who would throw silver spoons where the magpies could get to them? Do you think you could fish for a magpie?"

"Fish for a magpie? I don't think I understand—"

"Yes, fish for one with a silver hook; it glitters also and should attract them."

"Well, yes, but—"

"Have *you* ever seen a magpie stealing anything glittering?"

"No, but—"

"You and your 'yes, but' and 'no, but.' It must be something you have read," she decided. "Magpies don't steal inedible objects, I have tried them myself, with all the different silver spoons we have, well polished too, but not a single one has been interested in a spoon. Try it yourself. Put a spoon and a herring side by side and see which one the magpie picks up. Well, you needn't try. It is lies and nonsense all of it. When people have got an idea in their heads they can't get rid of it. One must investigate things oneself."

Like a thorn in the flesh, he thought.

Julie added, hurt, "Magpies don't steal silver any more than I do. I have tried with bracelets and beads, too. They don't want them. I've put out a great number of polished objects where the magpies gather and they leave them alone. It's only fairy tales. Some thieving devil must have invented it. I like magpies, they are nice birds, and they don't steal. Nor have I ever met anyone who has seen them do it. Never. Some people brag they have seen all sorts of things, and say they have seen this or that many times, but always *too* many times. They only tell stories. People who lie always have to exaggerate. No one at Venhaug has seen them do it."

At Venhaug no one has seen it, thought Erling, and said, "You become almost fanatical in behalf of the magpies."

"The whole story might well have started because when a magpie flies it looks like a couple of silver spoons fluttering."

"Well, well—this sounds like a poem."

He wondered if her surprisingly energetic defense of the magpies was a denial of something quite different. She had not divulged herself but something struck him: Why had she not touched the subject of stolen objects at Venhaug? *She must surely know.* Yet never a word. She knew exactly what there was in the house. Why didn't she say something? Was she protecting someone? Was she playing her role superbly, yet not daring to ask about missing objects? When she knew things disappeared and no one ever mentioned it to her—no, no one could deny that she knew she was suspected. But why then this heated defense of the magpies?

He said, as if into the air, "I guess you're right. But think how much they have been blamed for, the magpies."

"They have never been blamed for anything," was the astonishing reply.

"Listen to me, Julie—"

"You better listen to *me*, Papa dear. You have never seen a magpie steal anything, nor has anyone else. Therefore no one believes it when they hear such stories. Do you think a thief would get far by saying it was the magpies? No, Erling. He would have to try that somewhere else than at Venhaug. Nor would you believe it. You must realize it is only nonsense."

Felicia had never during the years been able to show proof of her suspicion. I am a poor detective, he thought. I'm too involved. A policeman on this case would not have had a daughter nor intimate friends to blunt his judgments. He would have listened to all Felicia's arguments and then said, That might be, Mrs. Venhaug, but how do you draw the conclusion that it is Miss Vik? And the scales would fall from Felicia's eyes, and she would in horror discover that the police report would state that she had nothing to offer except that said young lady had been in an orphanage.

Would Erling himself blindly have agreed that the thief was his daughter—if she hadn't been in an orphanage?

· 1942

Erling had never forgotten Felicia Ormsund. She had been in his thoughts many times during the eight years that had passed, and he had often wondered what had become of her. In Stockholm, when he espied her at the little refugee restaurant, he felt paralyzed. This was for several reasons. He was miserable because of his broken marriage, he had been drinking more than ever for a whole year, he was sick, he avoided people, he was in a sort of male menopause. He both felt and was considered hopeless.

First of all he must find out if she was married. He asked guardedly from a Norwegian sitting at the next table: "That girl back there, at the pillar, I seem to recall her—what is her name?"

"Felicia Ormsund."

"Yes, of course, but that was her maiden name. Hasn't she been married?"

"Not that I know of, but then she's only twenty-five or twenty-six. There's been no lack of suitors, though."

Erling looked down. She seemed almost as young as in 1934, during their intermezzo. She could still have been taken for a teen-ager, except for the eyes and her experienced bearing.

He realized she had recognized him at once and that her eyes returned to him again and again. How fortunate he hadn't been caught unawares. People walked about from table to table and talked to each other, and through the corner of his eye he saw that she sat alone at times. But he couldn't make up his mind if he should go up to her. Many persons in here knew both of them, and he had no idea how she might receive him. The way he had treated her at seventeen was hardly to his honor, even though there were excuses enough—if Cecilie could be considered as an acceptable excuse to Felicia.

And then there was his fear of everything—of *everything*, which again rose within him violently, and he looked in various directions for an escape before he would have to greet her.

She rose, approached his table, and stopped short in front of him. He looked up absent-mindedly and played slowly at being surprised: "Well! if it isn't—"

She was looking down on him and said, "How are you?"

Her look was searching, observant. She must have heard all sorts of gossip about me, he thought, fury rising, while he was torn by a mixture of shame, misfortune, childish pride, and explosive anger.

"Don't look as if you intend to swallow me," she said amiably. "May I sit down a moment?"

"Of course!" He became eager and courteous. "Sit down, my dear Miss Ormsund! How are you? When did you come across—Felicia?"

He felt he shouldn't have been so formal—as one refugee to another. He became gloomy and on his guard. He saw that she was not so pale as at first: so she *had* felt nervous!

That gave him courage again, and he began to talk rapidly, the words stumbling over each other. He saw her lean back in her chair, saw her astonished gaze—

He suddenly stopped talking and his hands searched about for nothing.

Felicia had slowly risen to her feet. In his abnormal fear and suspicion he could read the thoughts of others better than a normal person—and he could hear Felicia's thoughts, as she stood half-turned away to leave but with her eyes still on his: He is not drunk. He is sick, he is very sick.

He dared not raise his face as she left but his eyes followed her quick footsteps. Passing by her table she picked up her handbag and left the café. He sat petrified and dared not move. Self-pity overtook him: Isn't there one single soul who can help me? Why doesn't anyone care for me?

It was then that his brilliant idea had come to him: He would in secrecy go to some place where no one knew him and have his face lifted. Hadn't he from day to day observed how his features more and more resembled congealed lava? *There* was the solution! Become young again!

· *1934*

It was a day between winter and spring in 1934 that a fluid group of people had gathered in the Theater Café in Oslo, people coming and going. Felicia arrived in company with a lady who knew one of the men of the group. Chairs were being moved wherever needed. Some of the crowd were having dinner in the midst of the confusion; others only drank. Erling had been responsible for the get-together that day. It had become the sort of affair where everyone borrowed money from everyone else, or went scouring for booty around the café and came back with ten crowns maybe, or maybe empty-handed. The young Felicia, no longer in her schoolgirl dress, had changed places a few times and was now pressed into the leather seat close to Erling. It was eight o'clock, he had been there since eleven in the morning, and now he wanted to get some air and motion, go to some other place. It was then he started to snare Felicia, and in a few moments they were in the cool, fresh air on the sidewalk. His head started to clear, he hadn't really been drunk. He suggested they go to Blom's, but she said no, it would be much better to take a long walk; a long walk was the last thing he wanted.

As ill luck would have it Felicia was alone at home for a few days. That was why she had been able to stay so late in the restaurant for the first time in her life. It turned out they went for a walk to Majorstuen and then took the tram to her home in Slemdal. He took a taxi back to the city between four and five in the morning, and had made arrangements to meet her again in the evening. He had not intended to break that engagement, but during all the excitement he had forgotten that he was to give a lecture that evening. When he called her over the telephone there was no answer, otherwise he had intended to ask her to come along. But he could have left a message at the café where they were supposed to meet, and this he had not done. He slept a few hours, went out on some errands between twelve and one, folded up in a friend's apartment around five, with promise to be called at seven-thirty. At eight-thirty he stood behind the speaker's lectern as per agreement, shaved, showered, and sober. Those were the days of youth and strength.

The experience with Felicia Ormsund had been only a passing one, but could have developed into more. To her it remained a fact that a man had had her and then broken his engagement to meet her again. Today he knew exactly how she had taken this and how humiliating it had been to her. His only defense might be that he never had tried to defend himself; but even this explanation evaporated when he realized he hadn't dared to.

In those days he occasionally let himself be persuaded to give a lecture, in spite of knowing that it was always a fiasco. So it turned out this time also, but in a way unlike others. Later, his lecture had been talked about a great deal, and of the three hundred-odd listeners only one had not been furious, had indeed been uproariously entertained and had gained a great deal from it, among other things a divorce. None of this had touched him very deeply. He took few things very seriously during those years—but it had hit him rather hard many years later when Felicia one night at Venhaug had told him she had known all the details from the very first. The story pursued him even to her. She used a strange image in relating it to him: During those days I felt like a beautiful new summer dress someone had dirtied and torn to shreds.

The lecture he was to give dealt with sex. It was at the time when Marxism and psychoanalysis carried on their *crimen bestialitatis* together, the result being an unholy and repulsive mixture somewhat similar to what the Folk Schools daubed together of Christianity and Nationalism—something like deposing the Virgin Mary for Satan's grandmother. Oil and water are each in themselves excellent, but if mixed there is one great problem—how to separate them again.

It must be made clear in this lecture that actually he wasn't too sure of his position in the sexual field. He also knew from attending similar lectures on sexual problems that the listeners' faces were not burning with expectation; it seemed speakers explained again theories long ago accepted, as so often happens. The listeners would be experienced people, hoping to receive absolution for something they had experienced long before the man on the podium had come to instruct them. Erling quoted to himself the words of Stig Sjödin: "What if all the lecterns could arise and defend themselves!"

The Question and Answer column in the Journal of Sexual Advice was in those days on an entirely different level; it was carrying on welfare work in a sexual slum—here was a salvation army of young doctors fired with honest indignation concerning existing conditions.

The opposition to all this was an undeniable argument that always was effective. It was that people had managed to reproduce themselves since the morning of time—then why suddenly all this education? Such platitudes had a certain force, but they failed to take into account that part of the educational activity was directed toward stopping senseless reproduction, and the rest was aimed at circumstances very far removed from the ones people had lived under since the morning of time.

Now, so long afterwards, Erling, sitting at home in Lier, read of new theories concerning the length of time Man has lived on earth; it was considered now to be much longer than assumed earlier. But time does not exist, he thought; it is something we have invented in our cobwebby thoughts, a sort of help-notion like many others which wither away facing the incomprehensible fact that another summer has passed never to return. Anyway, during the so-called time that had passed or evaporated since people first appeared on earth (one could be sure it was *long* ago) they had indeed managed to reproduce without the aid of books, and would undoubtedly manage in the future also, and it was obvious and it cried to high heaven, that they were beginning too late to regulate their own destinies.

That time when he was to deliver this lecture—it seemed to him now it must have been in the morning of time—all this had not quite crystallized out of his established ideas. He had promised to give this lecture that was to become such an extra burden to Felicia. He had thrown himself into the subject and written twenty pages which would sink into literature's dead sea once he had flung them to a gathering that had said they needed instruction, in spite of the fact that this was pure nonsense. It was a boring lecture; he yawned while he wrote it. The title he remembered only vaguely, something about sexual excesses, a subject people usually didn't yawn over. He recalled he wrote something about using reason, a surprising but rather unconscious self-knowledge for him in those days. It contained all the foreign words he had managed to lay hands on, which so often create the warm masonic-language of the initiated, while the simple masses gape. His effort would bring in one hundred and fifty kroner, not to mention the honor which had been especially emphasized in the invitation; he, in return, dishonored the audience.

He was received with the usual display of compliments and given a seat while the chairman stepped onto the podium and introduced him as a prominent person. The audience applauded dutifully as he rose and strode to the lectern. That trip was fateful. It was only a few paces long but while covering them he was struck by something about sexual excesses: in a flash he happened to see them from an entirely different point of view—namely that they did not exist at all.

It was an inspiration, a revelation. Ever since he was half-grown he had listened to a lot of talk about sexual excesses and had added what he could, as if he were one of the initiated. But what actually were sexual excesses? He had never in his life encountered such a phenomenon. He couldn't honestly say that he had participated in anything that could be called sexual excess, never. It was only something he had jabbered along about, written about, and now he was to speak on the subject.

He had encountered sex, and profited by it, but sexual excess? One can have one thing or another to excess, thought Erling; liquor for example could land you in jail with no memory of how you got there. It could be called excessive to be drunk, dead drunk, or hopelessly drunk.

But a sexual experience was sating and sobering, and no one wished it to excess, even if able.

However, this was a belated discovery since he was already standing on the podium. Instead of this lecture on sexual excesses, which was to be one in a series of many, he now remembered enjoyable experiences which could under no circumstances be called sexual excesses—memories of a fragrant wheat field and a fragrant Helene, and other places and other girls whose names were not Helene—in rented rooms, behind locked doors, and wherever it had happened to take place over the years. Only one among them had been a virgin, he thought distractedly, and she had been the last. He had also had experiences that were utterly painful, but these were excesses to a much lower degree, if one now could speak of degrees when they weren't excesses at all. For example Olga, who had disappeared into a built-in iron wash tub, while watchmaker Hermansen with the funny cork leg had silently hanged himself on an iron hook outside the door. Erling became confused at the recollection of Olga who had yelled so terribly, and he began to finger his nose, as he did when alone and thinking deeply about something. He discovered what he was doing when the finger already was on its way and he scratched his head instead. They couldn't possibly think that the experience with Helene could be called an excess? And again his thoughts circled: When one had experienced the pleasure, there was no need for excess, one had no desire so soon again. It was not an act one could overdo and then store for some other time when needed.

He felt like yelling out at the top of his voice.

Of course he had never practiced excess; he had only stood up, brushed off his clothes with his hands, or lain down to sleep, depending on time, place, and other circumstances, as well as the nature of the surroundings.

One should learn how it feels to get up on a podium and only then discover that one has twenty pages of miserable nonsense to read about the pope's nonexistent whiskers—to realize that such a lecture can never be delivered, though it might be forced out by torture. It could not be delivered to an audience of presumably sensible beings. He began to perspire.

It was bad enough the way things were, but then a new misfortune hit him in the head. In his increasing confusion (he stood quite still staring at his hands) he recalled his idea of introducing a new lecture-form. It must have been because the situation was so hopeless; here something new was needed. He managed to mix this problem with the impossibility of sexual excesses, a tremendous concoction which in one well-aimed blow struck out the Folk School's National Christianity (or was it the opposite perhaps). He turned the pages of his script and coughed, to create some sound at least. Then it was silent again, until the audience in their turn began to cough. Erling said nothing.

On the right down in the hall sat a woman in her early thirties. While Erling was contemplating how to renew the lecture-form and why anyone would have wanted him to talk about sexual excesses when they didn't exist, his male eye, in spite of his confusion, told him that she apparently had come unescorted. He wet his lips in deep thought and kept his silence. On the first bench sat a number of ladies and gentlemen of formidable appearance. In a general way he recognized them; they were ogres of discussion societies. They considered themselves authorities on any subject, and Erling knew that when he had finished each one in turn would rise and pick him to pieces. They never doubted their ability to crush any speaker. Their remarks were long and well thought out. He had once made the remarkable discovery that not one of them owned a bean.

He looked again at the young woman, and then he heard someone say quite loud: *One can never be sure.*

It was he himself who had said it and he quickly closed his mouth which he had left open. It had caused a mild disturbance in the audience—every speaker's fear; he had awakened them but in a way that would have been better undone. Now started a curious play; he looked severely at the people in the hall and they became silent. He looked down and a whisper began. He looked at them again, and it became silent. He never learned how long he might have kept this up, because with one jerk—and he didn't know how long a time had passed—he started the lecture. He began in confusion that no one was aware of, in a bubbling revenge for his *faux pas*. And he started with the story about Olga and the hanged watchmaker:

"I would like to tell you how my fourth love affair ended. She was fifteen, her name was Olga, we were about the same age. Olga was kitchen maid in a hotel in my home town, and the daughter of a man who was sent to prison because he had stolen a barrel of coal oil. The judge had said he could not give him a suspended sentence in view of the barrel's value, but I have not looked into the cost of coal oil in 1913, as I have never been interested in figures. Olga was round and plump and I felt she had exciting thoughts about me. Perhaps she did; what she thought of me later I would rather not go into. Because what happened was quite unexpected for her, and I wouldn't be surprised if she later became a nun. That sort of sex might give anyone a severe psychological trauma."

He could see on the faces in the audience that they took this to be an introductory story, an example that would be dealt with more definitely later.

"The hotel basement had concrete passages, exactly wide enough for one to feel the walls on either side with the finger tips if one walked with arms outstretched. From these passages doors led to food cellars and various supply rooms. The doors had enormous padlocks, all except one which led to the laundry room where I had seen the girls in steaming air busy with the wash. Unfortunately this room was at the very end of the building and there was no light in the passages. It was like walking through catacombs. My gift of persuasion was not particularly developed in those days, but nevertheless I had managed to make Olga see things my way, and one evening we stole through the passages of this hotel to the laundry room. This we should never have done."

Erling made a pause for effect, and he could hear the proverbial pin drop to the floor. He continued:

"In this laundry room was a built-in wash tub, and this was involved in my plans. There had been no fire under the tub that day, and I might as well tell you at once that it was empty. I struck a match and noticed that the big wooden lid was in place, but this lid had an unfortunate protruding handle also of wood. And the handle would become a hindrance, so I turned the lid upside down. This I should not have done either. Indeed, I ought not to have done anything; I should have been sitting home with my parents working a crossword puzzle. This would have been best for all concerned.

"I managed to get Olga onto the inverted lid—not an easy task—and climbed up after her. In my favor it should be said that I was terribly nervous, although I had not the slightest premonition of what actually was to take place. The lid was not built to resist great pressure from the underside, and I had turned it over. With both of us on top, it caved in and Olga disappeared among splinters and nails into the bottom of the tub, while I remained lying across the tub, for my position was such that I could not fold together and follow her to the bottom.

"With this happening both Olga and I momentarily lost our senses.

"The fact was that she had become wedged in the bottom, and she started to howl in the most heart-rending manner. I was sure it echoed throughout the whole hotel. I quickly climbed down and thought to escape. I didn't do so at once, though. I still had enough sense to realize it would be best to get Olga away also. She might bear witness against me. While she kept yelling loudly and wildly in her—shall we say—sex-fear, I struck another match. I beheld a horrible sight: only her round face, pressed between her feet and her fingers, stuck up from the tub. I was unable to do anything, and, scared to death, I felt for the door. Then I started to run in the dark, feeling my way with my outstretched arms. Olga's cries pursued me through the passages, the echoes increased them until it sounded like pigs being slaughtered. I could also hear the commotion upstairs in the hotel, and then I ran into someone. I jumped back and hit at my antagonist for I had no time to lose. My fist hit something but I felt it could not be a human being. I struck a match for the third time and discovered it was watchmaker Hermansen hanging by a cord. That made me lose whatever sense I still might have left. The watchmaker was dancing around on his right leg which barely reached the floor. This was his cork leg. The left one didn't quite reach down to the floor, it dangled inside an empty crate he must have kicked over. Unconsciously I yelled out and threw myself down on my hands and knees to get past him, his feet dangling against my back. But something in the cork leg caught in my jacket, and in my confusion I thought the watchmaker had got me by the collar. I rolled over, yelling to high heaven, while Olga was yelling at the top of her lungs in the laundry room. I caught hold of the leg that had become entangled in my clothing and pulled and tore, and if he wasn't dead before I must surely have finished him off. At last I got free, crawled some distance on all fours, and escaped, while Olga's groans faded behind me.

"I joined the group in front of the hotel where wild rumors were circulating: the watchmaker Hermansen had pushed the girl down the wash tub to boil her, but had been overcome with remorse and had hanged himself. They never obtained any explanation from Olga—she steadfastly maintained she hadn't been there at all. Such a position was rather untenable, but she didn't give in."

Erling did not stop after telling the ending of his fourth love; he went right on explaining the impossibility of sexual excesses, because they were contrary to biological and other familiar natural obstacles. And, furthermore, the lecture-form was inexcusably antiquated as a means of information. Of all this there had been nothing in the advertisements of the lecture, nothing in Erling's script, nothing in the program, nothing anywhere. He spoke fluently, without stumbling a single time, talked for more than an hour, and finished his performance with a most courteous bow.

During this whole peculiar performance he had been apprehensive. Undoubtedly, in some way or other he had been successful even though he wasn't sure how or why. The learned members of the "Ogre Discussion Society" did not applaud. He looked down on them for the first time since he had begun and realized he had insulted them. They wanted to see him hanged beside the watchmaker. There they had been sitting at the Theater Café and other places where they gathered, preparing themselves for the lecture, reading all there was to read about complexes, and had been ready to jump on him. Then this lecturer Erling Vik talked outside the announced subject—about new lecture-forms, about the childishness of believing sexual excesses were possible. "Has anyone in the audience ever heard of such?" he had pleaded. "I would like to be given a description of sexual excess. I cannot imagine what it could be."

He had shaken their world by questioning the value of lectures in general; the very existence of these members was based on lectures. He had brushed off sexual excesses, removed the crutch from under their lovely, problem-filled existence. What would they have to live for if no problems existed?

The chairman rose to thank Erling, as is customary. He looked angry, almost blue in the face; he was a student of criminal law.

Erling was sitting at home recalling the story once more. In trying to remember the confused situation one might forget the most important angle at first, perhaps overlook something of the most essential. Thus it was that sometimes a witness changed his testimony. But if every nuance was to be included in remembering a happening then it must be thought through many times. Each might seem like a new version, but actually it was only different layers of the same story, or the same story seen from different angles. It would only cause great confusion to attempt at one time to include all that had taken place.

When he had stood on the podium and communicated so painfully with himself without saying a word, finally bursting out that one could never be sure, he had actually come to the conclusion that, in spite of his own protests, he must follow the script. Otherwise he might as well jump down from the podium and escape. For this other thought—about the new lecture-form and the impossibility of sexual excesses—he hadn't thought through nearly as well as was necessary, and one can't use inspiration the moment inspiration comes over one; only prophets speaking in tongues could do that. Then his eyes had again come to the lady on the third bench to the right.

He recognized her type, although there are many variants. Not so few women are treated badly by fate in early youth—at home, in school, everywhere—until they approach thirty or so, when they take revenge.

Among other things they have suffered from being ugly, or seeming stupid because their looks did not conform to conventional ideas of beauty, or because they did not care to participate in idle talk. They had turned inward, with a thought-world unlike the others—or plainly, they *had* a thought-world. This put them apart. Young as they were they might envy the others their easy manners, their ability to talk without having anything to say, their ability to make friends and intimates, while they were sitting alone. Many of that type begin to grow when the others begin to go to seed. The girl who gets along easily is without weapons when the first blooming is over, and one day she looks about in consternation: Well, I used to be so popular—why no more? She looks at her husband and doesn't find him exciting any longer, and he obviously doesn't think she is, and now there is no excitement in anything, and the dishes are waiting, and one returns yawning from the movie. Then they discover that the ugly duckling of yesteryear is sailing forth, a swan now, her turn now. She who has had everything easy suddenly feels cheated, but never discovers what has happened—namely that she never was exposed to the hard pressure which forces one to build up a reserve. Now when the glitter of youth is fading she discovers she has neither exterior nor interior. And there the swan sails forth; now she is popular, think the hens, and one hen cackles to another, "But she never looked like anything!" And then the hens hear that among other things she is so witty that she makes the men laugh, but all they can do is to read advertisements about ointments against underarm perspiration, and if they buy a jar perhaps it has no effect.

Erling knew that the lady sitting in the audience to the right was a swan who had been an ugly duckling, and he also realized that his behavior was becoming too noticeable, for he had eyes for no one except her—and it was she who that evening revised the lecture-form. She was of strong build and had an abundance of dark fluffy hair. Her forehead was broad, which perhaps made it look too low, her brows thick and dark, the eyes ice-blue. Her nose had a twist upwards. She looked steadily at Erling with something resembling a smile, a provocative smile one might call it. And then something astonishing happened; it was as if his soul left his body and disappeared into her eyes—and this soul of his had eyes of its own, noticed in passing the hollows of her cheeks, so much resembling the cheeks of sculptured high-caste young Egyptians, and his soul looked at her high cheekbones before it disappeared inside her head, but what it did there he did not know; he had to stand and wait for the return of his soul. Was it then so strange that he couldn't get a word across his lips? Now her mouth opened imperceptibly and out flew the homing soul and returned to him. It seemed his soul had been out on an expedition of discovery, but it kept to itself what it had seen. But also, like a carrier-pigeon, it had brought her thoughts to him: "God only knows what that man is up to?" It was then his words had escaped him, clear and loud: *One can never be sure.*

(Felicia! She had received a detailed report the following day, she who had been sitting alone in a café, waiting. There had been no end to the scandal, and it was to grow worse before he got his full deserts.)

A shadow of surprise passed over her face, but then she suddenly opened her mouth and laughed soundlessly. Her teeth fascinated him, they were strong and broad; he thought in passing, they could easily bite off a thumb. With a definite gesture he pushed the script to the very right-hand corner of the reading-desk, took a step backwards and sounded off about Olga, the built-in iron wash tub, and watchmaker Hermansen. But first he had said: "I will now prove the impossibility of sexual excess."

The effect would have been the same had he fired a gun. Something seemed to flutter through the hall while three hundred necks straightened up and bent backwards as if sitting on the same spinal column (he wished he had had an ax but now it was already too late). From then on he only looked at his new friend, not a single time did his eyes meet anything except her face, neck, and shoulders.

For a moment he had a feeling of being dropped from the moon and having to find his way in these new surroundings. He was only vaguely aware of what happened in the hall, his eyes did not leave her, it was to her he talked, no one could be mistaken about this, and many necks were stretched. His look was directly at her for over an hour. After the startling beginning his voice became calm. He wondered whether he should commune with her informally or formally; perhaps better be indefinite. One could never be sure.

This was his revision of the lecture-form. It made it more intimate, but as it turned out no one else liked it. It was an unsuccessful revision.

Not a single time did he lose the thread; he could hear his own voice, firm and clear. The lady of his heart did not move head nor finger, not a facial muscle, and as the lecture progressed and he managed to escape alive from the catacombs—where Olga still yelled in the tub and the watchmaker ghost-like lunged with his cork leg—he could see how she collected herself, mobilizing her will, to clear the situation. Later he could see how her face began to radiate pleasure—to heck with the other three hundred, her eyes sparkled towards him. (Half a year later it seemed incomprehensible to him that the two of them could ever have gone their own ways.) He felt overwhelmingly as never before that one could be inspired by another, and he saw she knew what he felt. A few times it seemed the words he was using had been transmitted to him from her. When his voice fell, or he hesitated for a second, he saw her grow nervous, and she sent him desperate messages without moving a muscle: You must carry through this nutty idea without making a fiasco of it! Because it would be mine too! You must find words for all the things that never have entered your head before!

That evening hardly anyone in the audience could have believed that he and Cecilie never had seen each other before, that he had never intended to divulge how the tailor's son had gained his introduction to sex—which had left its mark on the whole life of the speaker, had indeed encompassed horror that could be expressed only jokingly. He had ironically mentioned a trauma; through this he had intended to make fun of the ridiculous tone of the pretentious debates, but did anyone of the three hundred actually know what a trauma was? Had they realized what was the result of the agony when Olga had disappeared into the wash tub and that dastardly watchmaker had hanged himself outside— just in the moment one was to experience the miraculous? Had they themselves gained their erotic introduction by having been grabbed in the neck by the hook of a dead man's cork leg? Each time he reached a point in his explanation of the impossibility of sexual excess he could hear, now that the audience had grown warm but no less astonished, how the laughter rose from a rustle to a storm, forcing him to wait, almost annoyed, before he could make himself heard again. The professional debaters on the first bench shrugged their shoulders, as they learned to do in their club. Deep within him he felt afraid of losing the thread of his dissertation, since there was no hope of returning to the script. But the thread held. He decapitated Casanova. He made mincemeat of this one and that. Without hesitation he dishonored Sigmund Freud about whom at that time he had rather vague notions, he disemboweled St. Augustine, made a lightning-visit to Sodom, but consistently he ended his sentences with potent oratorical questions: "Tell me, do you know"—turned to Cecilie—"how one goes about practicing sexual excesses? We are *unable* to. It is only all those jealous preachers imagining things about us. It has been said that the Roman Empire was destroyed through sexual excesses, but that idea, I'm sure, must have been invented in an overheated monastery."

The chairman shook hands with him when he finished, for one must stick to etiquette. He said it had been an unusual evening, but he regretted that the lecture on the program had—

He became angry at being interrupted by the audience, for they had to express themselves somehow because the advertised lecture had not been given, so he announced that there would be a fifteen-minute recess before the discussion period. He tried to tell Erling about coffee, or beer, being served, but the lady had risen from her bench and Erling walked towards her. She said, "I feel the three hundred pairs of eyes like the pins in the Spanish Virgin." Erling said, "Let's go this way."

They went into a side room where there were only a few people who stood chatting and who stopped short to look at them. "This way to the Cloak Room," he said, and found a door that led to the street. He motioned to a taxi and said to the driver: "Just drive on! We'll give you the address in a moment." Someone came running after them, and Erling urged the driver, "Get going! Hurry!"

The taxi started with a jerk—he felt for Cecilie's hand and asked, "Where do you live?"

She didn't reply but leaned forward and gave the address to the driver.

He knew now that a certain riddle probably would follow him to the grave, but it didn't matter since the riddle was wholly his own and could not interest anyone else: How had it been that during that time he had done his best writing? A few times, he recalled, he had concentrated on something for longer periods, once three months, another time for half a year. But though his memory was dim, the result of this particular time was available for anyone to read, and how time and health had allowed him to consume such quantities of liquor as he had done and how he had time for all the nonsense and scandals—this he couldn't grasp, especially as he had never worked with liquor in his system. Indeed, he had tried a few times but when he saw the result the following morning, it was so frightful that his fear of anyone seeing what he had written while drunk pursued him even in his drunkenness. Liquor led to a vulgarization of thought and word that aroused the deepest shame in him. But these confrontations with the products of his own liquor-brain had never contributed to temperance in him. However, they quickly taught him to stay away from writing when drinking.

This did not lessen the riddle; he had been drunk practically every day for ten years. The only explanation must be that he had worked intensely after having slept off one drunkenness before beginning on the next, but he couldn't remember. When he once asked advice from a doctor, a good friend of his, he had been told: "You have never been an alcoholic—you're a drunkard!" This raised an echo in him and he knew the truth was never far away when something raised an echo. It was about the same with him as it was with the maid Elvira whom Felicia often referred to: the only thing needed to keep her sober was for the cupboard to be empty and the bar far away.

· The one who wants everything he sees

Felicia was lying in bed, her hands behind her head, thinking about this: When Erling gave that lecture on sexual excesses and a kitchen maid from Rjukan, two of my girl-friends were in the audience. Meanwhile, I was sitting with a glass of soda-water, being insulted by the personnel in a cheap restaurant, and I walked crying the whole way back to Slemdal. I dared not take the chance of letting anyone see my face, not even a taxi driver. Of course, I thought also I was pregnant. I, Chaste Felicia, had not painlessly got over having lost my maidenhead; it still hurt when I walked. My own little girls won't have a similar experience, nor even Erling's own daughter, that much sex education I got at least. My two girl-friends kept talking a lot of nonsense I didn't understand. But they had been greatly entertained, not realizing how much scandal it caused, that lecture. They knew nothing about my experience with Erling, and I don't think anyone except the two of us knows about it to this day. Well, Jan knows there was something. Steingrim knew also. Only that it was something. In those days I was afraid he might expose me, but I don't believe he would have. Then it struck me Erling couldn't talk about it because he must have forgotten all about it—that was a week later and then I closed up like a clam. It was a misfortune that had struck the brat called Chaste Felicia, a truly great misfortune, and worst of all, perhaps, that he had forgotten everything.

I was terribly afraid I might meet him and perhaps see a grin of derision, or hear him say something degrading; he was said to specialize in that kind of treatment. I can still vividly recall my fear in those days, yet it is more than twenty-three years ago. I was hopelessly in love with a man I should have despised, detested, forgotten. I don't set any store by good advice about divorce and God knows what when a woman is stuck with a hopeless man. Or vice versa. I would rather see all the busybody advice-peddlers hanged. They come running in droves too when there is a doomed man to be helped to his death. The only ones who can really give advice are those who have lived through the thing themselves and know what they are talking about.

I got it into my head that I had not come up to expectation, stupid, ignorant girl that I was. Stupid and green he must have decided I was.—Enough of her! Next, please! "She was useless," it said in Hans Christian Andersen about a drunken washerwoman, and I could hear Erling say, "She is useless." It was a humiliation that smarted and smarted: I was useless to the one I loved, so being useless I wanted to die. When we kissed good-by we agreed to meet; I was so happy I almost fainted. Then he called a taxi, walked out, and forgot the whole thing.

I was right. Anyway, that was just about the way it had been. I felt misused, beaten, degraded, unable to mobilize any pride. I could have cried my heart out, year after year until the war came. Then I banished him, because "something is bigger than you and you must fight for it." But he was only banished to a dark closet; I couldn't banish him farther. And then one day at a meeting everything was turned upside down when Erling's name was mentioned. Some caustic remark escaped me. The room was very small, I sat in a corner pressed against Steingrim. A few flinched but pretended not to have heard, went on to something else. But Steingrim pulled out a little black notebook, wrote something on a leaf, and let me read it: "Do you know that E is Brekke's golden boy, that it was he who liquidated Hartvig Lien?" I sat with my mouth open, staring at the page, which Steingrim took from me and pushed resolutely into my open mouth, saying, "Some people eat the prescription when they can't get the medicine. Swallow it now!" And I chewed on the dry paper, it stuck in my throat, I could taste it for at least an hour before I got some water to wash it down. Our group had nothing to do with Brekke, and ought not to know anything, except for information that might be useful to us, and what Steingrim had done was wrong—but from that evening I felt more of an equal with Erling. It was quite complicated; I became his equal because of something *he* had done. Suddenly I was no longer the little girl he had laughed at. That gave me courage to walk up to him in Stockholm, but also the courage to move in with Steingrim the same day. From being an equal I rose far above a sick man that day in Stockholm, but fortunately I soon was on equal ground with him again—he saw to that. But it was too late. And then, that depressing Stockholm crushed what could have been between Steingrim and me. Since then Erling and I have played on a sort of seesaw, and neither one of us knows why.

I remember how I used to walk about Oslo to catch a glimpse of him—and was scared to death I might. I saw him many times quite closely, usually with that dark, distant look of his, but also a few times when he was pure sunshine. My heart hammered each time I saw someone in the distance I thought might be he. I didn't give up until, after many complicated difficulties, I had learned the name of the woman; she was married to an engineer named Skog and her name was Cecilie. I didn't mind her being called Skog, but Cecilie! I felt as if I had imitated her name: Cecilie, Felicia. The two *i*'s in the names, the same number of syllables, accent on the same syllable. I felt small and mistreated that people might think I had tried to imitate her and that someone might recognize it.

I had never tried to imitate anything in anyone, I had not chosen my name myself, and no one could talk about something they didn't know. I dwell on this little incident because I happened to remember my thoughts about it when I looked into poor Erling's sick eyes that time we met for the first time in Stockholm.

Cecilie Skog became my feared prototype, she who had removed me as if brushing off some fluff from her sleeve. I couldn't imagine measuring up to her. Now I know well that my obsession about having imitated her name came to me because I methodically tried to be a younger Cecilie Skog. Even later, when I heard of the drama that had taken place, when Engineer Skog had tried to throw her out of their fifth-story window and only by a hair's breath escaped being flung out himself—even then I dreamed that it was I. Perhaps not so strange, for I know there were other girls who identified themselves with her, even though they had never known the apple, shall we say, of the quarrel. We were so occupied with the doings of these amazing people in their amazing world that we envied them and never saw their actions as scandals. It was a wonderful play among the gods, and it was long before we were to understand that these stories represented the dubious sort of romanticism seen by a person who doesn't realize the actors are all plastered.

There was another story Erling was mixed up in which the police, thank God, never managed to solve. There were four of them, four men with a girl who sold beer in her apartment after closing hours. All went well for a while. Then they realized she overcharged them for the beer. So they rolled the girl up in a carpet and tied her with a curtain string and left her in a corner. Arriving on the street they espied a parked motorcycle. They carried this to the girl's room a flight up, and Erling had related what a job it had been; they managed to get it into her apartment, where they removed both wheels, tied the cycle to the stove, started the motor, and ran away. Everyone in the whole apartment house woke up, people gathered in the street, broke into the apartment, and found the girl standing in a corner rolled up in a carpet and the motor making an infernal racket at the stove, the floor littered with empty beer bottles. When one knows what real drunkenness is like, no stories are worth listening to. But we girls, living in our world of fantasy, identified ourselves with the girl in the carpet. When I myself did so it was with somewhat different feelings, since I was both the girl in the corner and the motorcycle at the stove.

I learned when it was over between Erling and Cecilie Skog, but for me there was never any hope. I learned much that time. First of all I learned to tell whether a man was going through a stage when any attempt to tie him would be futile. I observed that precisely when all attempts are senseless, then women want to be the saving angels. They get nothing but shame in return. Anything else is nursery tales. When a man is in such an orbit nothing can knock him out of it, not even force, for he starts whirling again the moment the ties are loosened. With Erling something remarkable has happened much later: he is the only one I know of who was weaned forcibly without knowing it was done with force, and when you don't know you can't fight back. He never stopped drinking, but without knowing why he suddenly stopped being a drunkard. Before the cure he was generally drunk, after it generally sober. This happened after I had met him in Sweden.

At home they never learned what had happened to me, but on my eighteenth birthday my father said that I suddenly was grown. One might well call it so, if the feeling of having failed to measure up, and all other feelings of shame, mean that one is grown. I read books on sex education; I did so with a good schoolgirl's studious thoroughness and discovered that I had failed on all points, and been both active and passive at the wrong time. This was not encouraging. O Lord! A few years later it dawned on me that one who actually had been natural and honest as I had been with Erling, must never afterwards look into the records of double bookkeeping. For it is my candid opinion that many healthy young people grow up warped because they take the medicine intended only for the sick. It was part and parcel of those strange days that I wasn't satisfied to discover that the man had rejected me, and from this brutal fact fought through my pain. All search for explanations is futile because half or more of the answer can be sought in the man who has disappeared. It is not printed on the lower half of page 63 of some book, why he, instead of keeping his appointment, started to go with Cecilie Skog.

The strangest of all was that I seldom, perhaps never, gave a thought to his wife Ellen and the children. Strange? It is always so; his wife is accepted, not his mistresses. Men are equally confused; they accept their mistresses' husbands, no one else. Erling broke down when Ellen—she had never been faithful as it is called—made a clean break and married someone else. "The one who wants everything he sees, must often cry when others smile."

• The underground demon

After Erling left Venhaug it would be about two weeks before Felicia again turned her greenhouse into a stage for something more than her daily chores. Her desire to face the beast would come over her early in the day, and before leaving for the greenhouse she would have been burning with restlessness for many hours. Only during the first few minutes would she make the feeblest attempt to resist, then she gave it full sway and let it rage at will. She did not notice that Julie was particularly observant of her those mornings when no news of a visit from Lier was forthcoming.

When it came on her strongly, Felicia simply followed her impulse to have another "private séance" in her greenhouse; in dark joy she delayed it as long as possible. There was only one aspect of this thing that worried her: it very seldom happened that she waited in vain for the underground demon, but when this did happen she grew so depressed and icily miserable that the others noticed there was something wrong with her. She herself felt it was contrary to her nature that she should react this way; she dared not look herself in the mirror, felt like a haunted, disgraced sister of Cain. It was worse because she could not accept her reaction, couldn't stand feeling inferior, it mustn't be acknowledged that it was shame she felt. She would escape from it, never participate any more, but after a few moments she was unable to get any farther than to abuse Tor Anderssen to the best of her ability and enjoy her knowledge that he too suffered; when he failed he would have to pay dearly.

There had been a wave-like rhythm over the years, not unlike a marriage that after many tribulations finds its form. Her werewolf might for long periods be almost discarded, as a woman in a depression can grow tired of her husband and view him with the same disinterest as others. Then it would come on again, she would stumble and go under, as if bathing in an open sea and unexpectedly being washed over by the breakers. If he was with her then, peeking through the ventilator, all was well; if he didn't happen to be in the vicinity to grab his chance, she felt as if she were again going through those heart-tearing weeks at Slemdal when she had realized she would not see Erling Vik again. Her thoughts were smothered like a tree under the burden of snow, her head swam. Then one time she was possessed of an idea. She went to Oslo where she first sought a gynecologist and then a psychiatrist. Could she have reached the menopause? Neither one of them thought so. They consulted and said definitely no. She told the psychiatrist about certain fantasies that pained her, holding nothing back. He did not think this was particularly disturbing, which pleased her very much; but when he suggested she take up some work as a counterbalance, she became disturbed again. "I work sixteen hours a day," she said, "and I need six hours sleep." That she was married to an estate-farmer he hadn't somehow connected with work. Now he laughed good-naturedly and apologized: "Well, anyway you're healthy in body and soul, and your fantasies are rather moderate. If you became apprehensive it was just because you are so terribly healthy."

She returned home. Whether it had anything to do with the doctors or not she felt completely indifferent to Tor Anderssen and all that. One month later, however, she was in the midst of it again. And it was rather amusing when she didn't—when she didn't fail in her lust to lure the moth to the light. Surely he would come when he had the chance? After all, he had other things to attend to, just as she did.

It had been rather calm for a time now. We've got past the honeymoon, she taunted herself. But she was excitedly happy when she went to meet him, and it ran its course as all the successful times had and the way she now thought it would always continue. She had perfected some practical details that would make the disappointments more rare (besides they were no longer quite so horrible when they did occur). The greenhouse had many lights to stimulate the growth in there, but now she also placed a lamp and a reading table in front of the heating plant. She was careful to turn it off when she left, but as soon as she entered she turned it on. Tor Anderssen soon noticed this and followed the signal. She invented some other signs as well, and consequently she could have him waiting at the ventilator whenever she wanted him. Thank God she wasn't too often in that humor, and really, it didn't interest her whether he peeked or not.

Felicia was standing at the ventilator, waiting expectantly. Now it began, as she had so often seen. There was a slight motion among the silver-tipped spruce, a few branches were cautiously pushed aside, she saw his eyes, staring at the ventilator. His mustache hung down over a twig. He straightened up and looked about, slowly like an animal on the scent, then stood still for a long time. Both the animal and the hunter know that a motion is more visible on a landscape than an object. For a few minutes the man stood immobile, then he turned his head imperceptibly, looked at the ventilator. He was pale. He was always pale when he stood there. She read in his eyes the same fear she had often read there: Is anyone watching me through the ventilator? Now he looked at the greenhouse corner and took the path which in the shortest time would hide him again. She studied the lean, greedy apparition as long as he was within her vision, then she ran soundlessly along the walk between the flower boxes. The birds fluttered about her. She picked up the watering can with the thin spout which could so exactly direct a stream of water between leaves and flowers without hitting them, and watered the roots of each plant. She stopped in front of the heating plant and lit a cigarette. She knew she was attractive in her tight yellow sweater and the full plaid skirt that made one think of a dancer. She blew a few smoke rings against the ceiling before she laid down the cigarette and loosened her belt. When she stood with the skirt in her hands and folded it neatly over the back of the chair, she lived in the dream that never could become a reality, the one Erling once had taken from her. It wouldn't have mattered that he took it from her if he only had been faithful to her, if he only had kept his appointment and become her lover. Chaste Felicia had nourished what she called the dream of her wedding night—that silly girl-dream she sometimes laughed at when it came to a grown woman and gave her no peace. It must be the right man, she thought, the absolutely right one, the one she had never made a clear picture of in her daydreams. Then came the night when they were alone. She called it the wedding night, and well it might be, anyway the night when they met to make love for the first time. He was in bed waiting for her. She sat on the edge of the bed, undressing slowly, not a little afraid, until he pulled her down beside him and spread the blanket over them with his other hand. Farther she never could go, because she didn't quite know how it would continue—and what had happened that evening with Erling was not conducive to a prolongation of her dream. She didn't get a clear picture, it was rather fuzzy, and the bliss in the dream had not been realized. No reasoning had helped her later and she knew no dream could be a fulfilment. She knew that every anticipation is a mistake—but often provides more than anticipated if one is lucky. She knew one couldn't plan another person's behavior in advance and figure out so and so must happen. This was unrealistic; unexpected details would intervene which no one could have anticipated. Such was life. It was so obvious, so clear, so incontestable, so well expressed in the old anecdote about the deaf man whittling an ax handle. The replies this simple man gave were in response to questions asked him by wanderers along the road, but since he could not hear the questions he replied to questions he himself would have put, had he been passing by. But the questioner was always someone else, not at all interested in the ax handle. Felicia needed no one to tell her her dream had been an ax handle, and so she had shed many tears over this fallacy. She would have liked to die with her dream. She had been cheated of understanding and attention when she had made the great surrender to a man. For he had flung her down on the bed, pulled off her clothes with too experienced hands, and taken her like a wolf-man, she hardly had known what had happened. Afterwards, however, he had been considerate and she regretted nothing; she had even regained enough courage to ask him to stay a little longer when he said he must leave; and he had stayed a while and they had talked and been cozy, even though she was rather torn and frightened. They had parted at the foot of the steps, she was crazy from happiness, cried and laughed and couldn't let go her hold of him. When she went upstairs she had looked at herself in the mirror—she was white like chalk, her hair hung like a drunkard's.

Perhaps she would never again have thought of her dream if he had come as he had promised. Probably she would have laughed at it: That was how I used to dream until I met Erling Vik! But he never came back. I must have been a sentimental fool, she thought as she pulled her short, transparent underskirt over her head. What a bandit he was!

Nothing had helped since, nothing could replace what she had lost, no one could help her turn history back twenty-three years, let her be seventeen once more and meet Erling Vik better prepared. Meet steel with steel when a rather intoxicated Erling nonchalantly tried a sort of rape—and kindly explain to him that such behavior did not suit her.

Felicia was all the time fully conscious of the demon's eyes on her. It is like a movie, with a wedding as the happy ending, she thought. It isn't decent to play it to the end. The peeker is a decent person too; he doesn't spin out the film all the way into the bed, either. His love is chopped off on the edge of the bed. He goes courageously forth to his wedding night fifty, a hundred, many hundred times, but there it ends. It might happen he is satisfied with one peek-bride, like my wolf there at the ventilator. I offer him a sort of ventilator-relationship. It is a kind of marriage, and I've seen worse. He stands out there and sees me prepare myself for our wedding number fifty-three, or is it thirty-nine. Even in our marriage it sometimes happens that the wife is difficult. Or that the husband has gone out for a beer. This kind of marriage between a peeker and an exhibitionist is no more remarkable than conventional ones. The wife must not know that the husband peeks, for that would not be chaste of her, and the husband must not know that she is undressing before him for her own pleasure, for that would be less chaste. You men are such silly apes; even if you stood with your head in a sewer you would babble about woman's chastity.

That business of undressing, or dressing, she thought, too often degenerates into something unattractive, either because one is alone or else because one gets careless when with a too well-known bedfellow. To undress in front of a peeker is like a lesson in a charm school. She wondered if Tor Anderssen suspected that she knew he was there. She didn't think so, and it didn't matter as long as he never could be sure. Men tried not to believe that women were up to tricks. They invented stories to the contrary, but that was something else. They *wanted* to believe that only they were interested in shady things, because the woman must be pure. Under no circumstances would they give up this sick notion of theirs, and if something occurred to make them disbelieve it—well, that only happened once, and the culprit should be punished, preferably beheaded. They had made nakedness a sin to enjoy, eye-lust at ventilators and keyholes, but what sort of sin and lust would it turn into if the woman inside knew, and perhaps sneered? Such they would have no part in. To a born thief there was no excitement or value in receiving a gift. The woman must definitely be peeked at without her knowledge, otherwise she wasn't chaste.

Felicia had known many men, but she was aware of no woman of her age who had had so few. She had learnt that surprisingly many attempts at rape were actually expressions of morality. It was assumed that the woman enjoyed it, but her honor must be kept intact, and this was accomplished by hitting her in the head with a hammer or whatever was at hand. One man had once tried to tie her down on the sofa they were sitting on—he had a cord with a loop ready. She had neutralized him immediately because she thought he intended to strangle her. She became quite speechless only when he said, "Silly—I wanted to make sure you were not to blame!" Men spared no pains in defending woman's chastity, not even when they took it. She had actually been asked if she would like a strap around her wrists so as to feel helpless. Felicia was forced to wonder how often rape was an act of morality. With a crushed skull no one could sin. Artificial insemination was the latest attack on the sixth commandment, and it must have been a blow to the medical chastity-preachers when a British court called it whoring.

Felicia was naked. She pushed her feet into her shoes and started to water her flowers while the birds fluttered about her. She chatted with the finches while her thoughts were with the man chained to the ventilator. In a moment like this he shared her greenhouse world. She had entered the mountain of the underground demon. This might be any man with an inclination for peeping, and when he was the demon himself she could not resist him.

When she returned from a journey where she had met Erling she did not for some time hear the call of her demon, not even at Venhaug if Erling had been there recently. Erling was the antidote; she didn't know why, but she wanted him to stay at Venhaug.

Felicia pretended to talk to her birds but the words were ironically directed to Tor Anderssen who stood outside, swallowing her with his eyes. "Our marriage is a complete harmony because you're so stupid. And because neither one of us peeks anywhere else. We're faithful, you and I; we can't get a divorce and marry other peeping partners. If we don't have each other any longer we must live peeking-chaste to the end of our days. That would be something for Erling to write a tragic poem about.

"I might have myself analyzed. For Tor Anderssen's sake of course. If he didn't like peeking so well."

She thought she knew the peeker Tor Anderssen thoroughly; he had never had a woman although he was almost fifty. If it had at some time been in his thoughts it wasn't any longer. What he saw in the greenhouse must persuade him that no woman was obtainable for him. A woman was an illusion. However much alive this illusion was before him he would never be able to think it was real. He was a man of the type who constantly must have proof that women exist also without clothes, yet each time he went away equally dubious. Each time he stole away from the greenhouse he must be seized with the same sober feeling one has in the street after leaving a movie: outside it wasn't exciting at all, and inside it hadn't been true. Indeed, it was more convincing in the movie than it was in the greenhouse; in the film no rich, elegant lady walked about in the nude, three or four yards away from him, birds on her hands, flowers in her hair. It didn't even touch his consciousness that others might have seen Felicia like that also. It was a secret—amazing, terrible, besides not being true. Each time he was equally overwhelmed at seeing the unbelievable once again. He had nothing to compare it with except a ragged old magazine with blurred pictures of naked girls who weren't entirely naked at that. And that was only on paper.

What took place in the greenhouse made him dizzy. He had dreamt all a man can dream, and that isn't little, not even for a stupid, unimaginative man, but it only further persuaded him that the miracle in the greenhouse was unreal. It was the princess on the glass mountain he saw—even though he hadn't earlier imagined she was naked—and he dared not appear as the knight. He would never be seized with such daring. His consciousness was filled with vapors—were women really created like that? (He must peek once more.) People had children, one couldn't get away from that fact. It was recorded that he himself had been born. In his cottage he sat down and looked at his parents' pictures which hung on the wall above some pussy willows he had picked for Easter. He didn't think they looked like that, either one of them. He tried to visualize his mother in the greenhouse—if she had still been alive—but it was impossible. She would never have looked like that. The explanation must be that there were many kinds of people. His thoughts roamed helplessly to Zulus and Chinese. It must require special gifts to be intimate with another kind of person; perhaps kings or presidents might have a lady like this one. Perhaps if he hit her on the head, or made her drink some potion—but he couldn't think what sort; all he had was spraying fluids for the garden—something to make himself invisible, and her unconscious. He had studied closely how one would go about undressing her. He found a piece of paper and drew the contours of a woman's body. (Felicia was sure of this.) Then he dressed the body from the inside out and indicated with arrows garments, buttons, and other details, as if he were going to the saddle-maker in Kongsberg to order a new harness. Now he could follow the description if there was any trouble putting on such funny things. It mightn't be a bad idea to get hold of a few of those garments. For training. Then he would have to go farther away than Kongsberg; he was known there, and he didn't want to make himself ridiculous. Perhaps he could steal some garments. But he had only stolen during the war when it was allowed. It hadn't been so bad in those days.

To walk about in the greenhouse and securely enjoy the other one's fear—a fear not unlike the troll-king's who dared the sun and the daylight and church bells and left his mountain hall to see a woman, who used him for what he considered a great sin against her; how many times had she dragged him here, he without a will of his own. She was inclined to forget that she also acted with no will of her own; the difference was only that she was secure.

In all kinds of weather he had stolen along this same path. The year round one could see how well used it was from the spruce grove to the greenhouse gable. In winter the snow was tramped down and Tor Anderssen had long ago given up hiding his tracks. He must live in permanent fear of someone noticing them and thinking: Who walks here every day on what errand? Jan, for example, who never missed a sign of animal or human being, even of Tor Anderssen himself, wouldn't he ponder why a well-trodden path led to no reasonable goal? He would immediately investigate, not suspiciously, only curiously; he would discover at once that it led from the gardener's cottage to the ventilator, and he would check if one could see into the greenhouse, into Felicia's holy of holies. She would discover an annoyed pull at the corner of his mouth; he would immediately figure out the best way to correct this business. The ventilator would stay where it was, but the capable Jan would in fifteen minutes have invented some means of closing the view from the outside. He would say nothing to the gardener, perhaps not think much about the incident. But what would Tor Anderssen do? Move away without any noise?

Only children at play would come back there. No one when snow covered the ground. But there was a pile of junk in the clump of spruce. One day Jan would need a piece of metal or something from the discarded machinery, that was all it was good for. Or perhaps he would hit on the idea of selling the junk, to get rid of it. Tor Anderssen could be in no doubt that something of the sort would happen one day and he might be caught in the act. Felicia, secure and unsuspicious, would be inside among her birds and her flowers; no shadow would fall on Caesar's wife, and the troll-king would be unable to get to his mountain again. No one would ever know how she had lured him and sent out her silent calls.

And perhaps it would be well if someone came and tore asunder this bond, and if she too were stopped by a closed ventilator.

· *The Steingrim circle*

One time a few years earlier Steingrim Hagen had stayed at Lier with Erling for a couple of days, which they had spent mostly in talking and drinking. There were not many Erling dared bring home; some were rather inclined to stay on, and ignored a gentle hint to get going. Others were too eager to return. Norwegian lack of formality had many advantages, but it could also become a plague: a man could not feel secure in his own home. When a person one knew relatively well stood at the door it could be rather embarrassing; one couldn't deny one was at home, nor say one was busy and that it was inconvenient; the caller might feel hurt, and in any case, work would be disrupted whether one asked him in or endured the nervous upset that would be the result of a refusal. Possibly intentionally such callers didn't telephone before coming, and he felt embarrassed for them and had to pretend he didn't see through the deception. Moreover, telephoning wasn't so good either; one had to return to work after having said *no,* and this *no* kept ringing in the head as a refrain against work which on the contrary needed positivism and *yes* in every fiber. Artists might be considered enviable, being masters of their own lives, but they in turn might envy some others. Businessmen and industrialists could throw a silly, unintentionally insulting letter into the wastebasket and go on to the next thing, and practically all their undertakings are definite problems which demand exact solutions. Anyone disturbing an artist actually steals the yeast from his bread, making it go flat and hard as a piece of wood if he attempts any further work that day. First he must use important time to wash off the interruption and the peace-disturber. Artists should meet even their friends on neutral soil—in a café, with cheese and wine under their sensitive noses. Interruption is an accident, like breaking a finger, because an artist, or a scientist, cannot shuffle his interest from one subject to another easily. Many others have the same problem but they can succumb to office work or simple drudgery. It is the strength and the *fiber* of the ability to concentrate which is the deciding factor in a person's fate.

Erling had once lived with his family outside Oslo. Behind the house was an overgrown garden. It was his refuge when he wished to think through something, but he soon found it was a lost paradise. Among the neighbors were a few who also worked at home as their own masters, but unfortunately they belonged in what has been nicknamed the practical life. They would come into the garden and say: I noticed you weren't working and thought I would talk for a moment.

They were innocent, they were honest, Erling liked them. They realized it might be real work to write—but now he had a hoe in his hand. They hadn't learnt one could write with a hoe in one's hand, or a spade, or while lying on one's back staring at the clouds. How to explain to them that it was just now one was writing? He realized why artists must be considered selfish and odd. It was always the same: he stood there fumbling with the hoe as if he had some unfamiliar object in his hands, became embarrassed, lame, worn out. A freshly flaming fire was extinguished beyond hope: visions and logic, inspiration itself, all the material that in the evening would have taken shape on sheet after sheet—sheets that one after another would slide across the table, flutter to the floor with soft, nightly sounds, while the hours passed without being measured by the clock.

"I realize you must rest your brain occasionally," the fine neighbor might say.

Rest the brain? That was what they understood; they thought the brain could be given a rest. They should only know how it felt to have a brain. They should only experience the fear that the brain one day might decide to take a rest.

Fortunately there were a few who could not disturb each other, because they belonged together in the same way as changes in the weather belong to nature. No one of the Steingrim circle could disturb or arrive inconveniently. They comprised one of those human circles which surely no one has tried to analyze, or perhaps they haven't been discovered by the sociologists; anyway they did not fit any definition familiar to Erling. Such circles have nothing to do with acquaintances or groups of friends, much less the family circle, and absolutely nothing with organization. They were formed and existed for a few years (during the war) and gradually they became a sort of constellation, and by then the ring had become so strongly forged that any attempt by an outsider to gain admittance would in advance have met the same fate as an attempt to disorganize Orion's Ring. Perhaps the absolute strength of such a circle lay in the fact that its members were individualists. They created wholeness and unity even when they formed the group; it arose without intention, without planning for use or usefulness, like the Belt of Orion or the Pleiades. No meetings were called, they were not a club, not a society, no one could be voted in or out, no dark secrets existed, no skeletons in the closet, and no guests were brought along, for transportation to the Pleiades is rather difficult.

A stir in a few human minds, the nucleus of the circle-to-be, attracted over a long period of time the very few that could belong, men or women, sex did not seem to be the determining factor. There were seldom more than half a dozen in the group. Erling had noticed that such a group seemed to have difficulty of survival if one member died, but sometimes it happened. The Steingrim circle survived. But no new member could be admitted—one could never get in if one hadn't grown in during the maturing years long ago. If a member died, the circle would only survive if the member had been such that he survived as a living memory.

When during the war we needed help or advice in our underground activities against the Germans, did we go to our friends and acquaintances? Well, perhaps we might have considered asking them, but did we actually ask them? Yes, if it so happened that any one of them was a member of what I call the Steingrim circle. In time of stress such members were seen in their true light. And where are the Steingrim circles today? Dormant perhaps, some members distracted by family or business involvements, but the circle is not dead. It comes to life when a demagogue exceeds the line. Such rulers are hardly aware of these groups; they are of the opinion they only have to fight established groups, which demagogues of all times have been confident of obliterating. But in these cells the dormant yeast of all layers of society lurks constantly and is ready to rise when the mighty ones become too arrogant. Then the head of state delivers a statement to the effect that he does not appreciate the *method* of the *irresponsible*.

Irresponsible one might ignore, it is the demagogue's way of saying he is the ruler. The *method* of turning to the people in a democratic way, instead of writing a petition which would land in his waste-paper basket, this is a most uncalled-for notion of his subjects.

And who are the irresponsible, or the irresponsible elements, when the chief speaks from on high? They are the minority among his own voters, who pondered their responsibility even when electing *him*. And he didn't like it. He suspects that they elected among many evils what seemed to them the least evil. And he absent-mindedly sketches a coffin for democracy while he reads.

Of necessity all such groups, or Steingrim circles, have something in common, but this is seldom apparent to the outsider; indeed, the very existence is often not known. The members of the circle need not even consider themselves a circle, and when they do the individual might wonder what holds them together. They can't give any clear explanation of its origin, or when it actually began. Thus the amazement when it strikes, and with strength no one had suspected.

• Until we meet at Erlingvik

When Steingrim left after his visit with Erling he borrowed a handbag full of books he wanted to read, political literature and travel books. Half a year later he packed all the books into the bag again and made it ready to be sent back, or perhaps he had intended to bring it with him on his next visit. Anyway, this was one trifle unaccomplished when he no longer wished to live. One of Steingrim's relatives forwarded the bag to Erling and it stood unopened for more than a year. One evening at the end of August, after he had returned from Venhaug, Erling decided to open it.

While putting the books back in their places on the shelves he opened one because it had no title on the cover. It turned out to be a sort of account book which Steingrim had used for a diary. The cool, guarded script was Steingrim's and he had written his name in the upper right-hand corner of the first page, which otherwise was empty, except for the date: September 9, 1945. The book was dated until June of 1956.

He walked over to his writing desk, lit a cigarette, and looked for a long time at the book. Here, then, was all that was left of Steingrim Hagen. How or why the book had happened to be included in the bag, no one would ever know, and perhaps it had been a mistake. Or perhaps Steingrim had put it in with the intention of going to Lier.

The thought never occurred to Erling that he should give it up. On the contrary, perhaps Steingrim had meant for him to have the book and purposely placed it in the bag. Methodical Steingrim had tidied up thoroughly before he took the pills; he had emptied the desk drawers, burnt the contents, put his books neatly in order, and had mailed a letter to the police after the mailbox had been emptied for the last time (it was a Saturday evening, the letter would not be delivered until Monday, he did not wish to shock his maid when she came to clean on Tuesday). With such prudence Erling believed he could not have overlooked the diary. Besides the three lines to the police he had written on a sheet of paper "Keys to the Apartment," which were placed on his desk. These were the only written instructions he left behind, nothing else at all, either written or oral, nothing. He died as he had lived, undramatic and a little disgruntled. The landlord would want the keys—well he could have them. No need to frighten the maid, and was there anything else he had forgotten? He might have felt in his pockets to be sure he had matches. But concerning the catastrophe he was about to perpetrate, no further telltale marks, even though Steingrin Hagen must have pondered it as deeply as a human being can. When a person left this earth he might as well say the opposite, that the earth went under for him; Steingrim had envisioned this and made it happen.

There were less conscientious suicides than Steingrim Hagen. One of that type might one day explode a hydrogen bomb over London in order to feel, for a fraction of a second, the consolation of fellowship in disaster.

"I must not read the diary this evening, or during the night," Erling said to himself. "I'll look through it tomorrow morning—a sober morning with my fried eggs and coffee."

He stood staring at the book; it had life in it as it were, it seemed to breathe calmly and evenly. He shook his head slowly as he did when something engrossed him deeply. Will I find the key to Steingrim here? the Steingrim no one knew? He recalled what Felicia had said: "Actually I didn't know him, although we had lived as man and wife in a small apartment for almost a year. There was one facet of his nature he never expressed. If I woke up during the night and watched him sleeping at my side I realized I knew no more about that man than I had known the first time I met him in Oslo. And he would sleep like a dead person—his face was closed like a wall even more so when he slept; he was on his guard even then."

Erling recognized the picture, but he had seen that face in a different light also. To Erling it had not always been a wall without cracks, but he wouldn't hurt Felicia by saying so. Yes, Steingrim's face had been like a wall, but there was something Felicia had not seen and so much the worse for her—she would have been richer in a great memory. He had a feeling that with Steingrim she had experienced only defeats, she had never won over him, never had he let her through the wall, she who could raze all walls or walk right through them. Nothing could have brought her greater happiness than if she could have been the one to blow the trumpet at the walls of Jericho. She had not discovered that in one's relation with Steingrim, neither assaults nor the sound of trumpets had any effect; he only pushed forward his reserves to the wall. It was not in her nature to sneak into a Jericho by stealth. Yes, Erling knew— Steingrim had grown colder and colder until he seemed frozen to the bottom. Then he had left Felicia.

Erling had twice seen Steingrim smile, and he was inclined to believe he alone had seen this. Obviously Steingrim had learnt to display a grin, like a vacuum-cleaner salesman. He was sufficiently intelligent that he might also have learned to stand on his hands, and that time when he acquired his sales-grin (probably before a mirror) he must also have learned how to wiggle his ears. But no one would have thought of saying he had seen a smile on his face. Erling had seen him smile and he would never forget it. He had never imagined one could see such a smile on the face of a grown person. It was the smile a mother first of all sees in the face of her month-old baby, a light breaking through from unconsciousness, indicating that finally and indubitably a human being has been born! Erling had expected Steingrim to start out of the chair—the child's first attempt to jump down from its mother's knee, a sort of excursion into space, the tiny hands closed and waving. But Steingrim had remained sitting calmly in his chair looking at Erling until the inner light was turned down and extinguished. The second time he had seen Steingrim smile had been a day in July, 1945, when they were sitting in a ditch somewhere along the road at Asker, their borrowed bicycles beside them, sharing a bottle of whisky. Steingrim had obtained it from an American officer he had snared and flattered for over an hour. Neither Erling nor Steingrim was particularly interested in cycling but they had

got it into their heads to see a Norwegian summer from bicycles with no
Germans about any more. They stayed longer than they had intended
there in the ditch for when they were ready to leave it appeared that
their bicycles were quite drunk.

This recollection gave Erling an idea. He picked up a screwdriver
with a bent point, walked over to the corner, and stooped down; he stuck
the screwdriver into a hole and opened his secret cupboard. Whenever
he did so he thought of Felicia. She had been very clever in discovering
it that time. And *she* kept after him about settling down at Venhaug!
Next time she broached the subject he would remind her of a certain
snooping. He closed the safe and returned to the table with a bottle of
whisky. He thought a moment—straight? or with coffee? He went to the
kitchen and turned on burner number three and put on water. He never
drank whisky with soda or some other mix, and since he didn't like it he
could not understand that others did. Whisky with good coffee—everyone
must know this was best! When Felicia came into his room at Old
Venhaug and there was a bottle on the table she didn't say anything, but
her look told him enough. I would have liked to see her face when she
broke into my wine-cellar, he thought. She must have gone to a lot of
trouble and she was sure to know that I would see she had been there.
Well, let him know, she must have said. When nothing is stolen he must
know it's me. Then the tears had come to her eyes, and in a fit of anger
she would have given the wall a kick.

The wine-god had no children. Carefully interpreted and partly
rewritten from the language in use when everything had to have a name
other than the real one, this line must have meant that neither Bacchus
nor anyone else in the Dionysian company was much of a lover—but
then, tomorrow was also a day, and not all days were dedicated to the
wine-god or to whisky. Except for a few times in his early youth of
blessed memory, when he did not yet know that one could not mix work
and drink, he had unsuccessfully tried it. Liquor was a cuckoo-fledgling
that pushed everything else out of the nest. Now that he was near sixty
it was a false notion in Felicia to put all the blame on the wine-god. He
would make a nice drawing and hang it on the wall with the sentence: *I
am not forty years old.* More honestly not even Viktor Rydberg himself
could have expressed it.

It was eight in the morning when he awakened in his easy chair (it is
almost like a bed, he comforted himself). His eyes fell on a bottle on the
table, surrounded by rings from the glass and the coffee cup. About an
inch of whisky was left in the bottom. Cigarette stubs and ashes were
scattered all over. He had on only the right shoe, the other one was lost.

A glass plate was tramped to pieces on the floor in a mess of tomatoes and mayonnaise. Good to be at home, in one's own chair, one's own house. He pulled off his clothes, went out to the currant bushes and poured water over himself. The lost shoe hit him in the head; it had been in the bottom of the bucket. He dried himself, put on pyjamas, and went to bed. Peace and rest flowed out to the extremities of his body, the tension in all his nerves eased, and he could feel Felicia's friendly hands as he went to sleep. He awakened a few hours later, at peace with the world, cleaned up the room, and drank some coffee. At first he tasted it suspiciously, even though he had brewed it himself.

Erling started to leaf through the diary. He soon discovered it was a potpourri of the most widely separated subjects, from political observations to purely private matters, besides addresses, telephone numbers, quotations, references to newspapers, books, and magazines. It even included a few halting attempts at poetry, of little credit to the author; this he must have realized, for below one of he poems Erling read: It is remarkable that some can write verses which don't make people laugh when they want them to cry.

Steingrim in his poetry-attempt had apparently only wanted to try how it felt in his hand and his head when writing something that didn't require a full line; he had found no reason to continue such waste. Perhaps he had also given up because he appreciated good poetry. Quite apart from Steingrim's lines and some rather curious attempts by others, Erling had never understood why people without the talent spent their time making verses; he found it inconceivable they might have any joy in doing it.

Erling came across his own name and read: "November 17, 1947. Yesterday Erling and I met at somebody's out in Asker. Late at night we walked out on the balcony for some air. It blew hard and was dark. We stood against the wall and did not feel the wind, only heard it roar about us, like on the leeside aboard ship. We had been drinking, and perhaps it was the nasty weather, like in a detective story. Anyway, I asked Erling what he finally did with the one he had liquidated before he came to Sweden, and who never was found. Erling cowered over his cigarette and match; I thought it was stupid to try to light a cigarette in such weather, and I think he did it to gain time and not have to answer me roughly. I would never have asked if I hadn't had too much to drink— and my asking it in that place, where I had to roar above the wind and a lot of people inside who might hear. It was stupid. Then I grew mad at him when I saw his face in the light of the match before it blew out—he is forty-eight, he ought to act his age. He straightened up, his cigarette aglow; it annoyed me that he had been able to light it. I asked again, I was irritated because he didn't seem to want to reply and perhaps because I had asked in the first place.

"He leaned toward me and said between gusts of wind: 'He is in a place no one knows but me; it's called Erlingvik and no one will ever find him.'

"I was drunk-mad at him by then but said nothing more. When I woke up here at home this afternoon I remembered what he had said and felt it was uncanny. It had made me think of the entrance-road to my home, which was lined with tall trees.

"Perhaps Erling only meant to say 'Shut up!' which he had every right to say, but the answer was strange, the whole thing was strange. It was very strange that I was standing there feeling he was talking about the entrance-road at my home where I never dared walk, always had to run; a place that has some meaning and which one is afraid of; something that has become a terrible part of oneself. Well, both of us were drunk."

There was nothing more about the incident. Erling could not recall the conversation on the balcony during the meeting at Asker but it must have taken place. He himself must have used the word *Erlingvik*.

It reminded me of the entrance-road to my home—

One morning long ago, many years before the war, he and Steingrim had been sitting talking, he couldn't now remember about what. They had got onto happenings of childhood that had left unusually deep impressions. Someone had written an article about modern authors exaggerating the importance of childhood impressions and enlarging them beyond actual facts, and that this probably was due to the influence of "that doctor in Vienna whose race-need for originality at any price had not hesitated at the absurd." (We have got no further today, thought Erling—now, in 1957, all that is written in America or the Soviet Union one need not consider seriously: it is ridiculed in one half of the world or the other.) Erling had ignored the reference to the Jew Freud; even before his time literature had been filled with child-descriptions which indicated that in childhood, obviously, character and viewpoints were formed. It was only a few hundred years later, during Freud's systematical investigations, that one realized what an insult it had been. People who claimed that "the grown person's grave conflicts obviously are of greater importance than a few scattered impressions of childhood," had suppressed everything, then, except some "scattered impressions"—there must be oceans they did not wish to remember; besides, they were talking pure nonsense when they refused to understand that the same experience is not of the same importance to the strong as it is to the weak person. There was the old story of the cure for the blacksmith that killed the tailor. Erling remembered a pair of high leather boots someone had given him as a child; they had not kept the water out so his father had had them repaired—which, he emphasized, cost plenty. After the repair they were too tight, but Erling had not wished to mention it lest he hurt his father. Then the old man had discovered it anyway and was unhappy because Erling had suffered from wearing too tight shoes. When the father reacted this way it made Erling even more unhappy, for his father must have suffered when he no longer remarked about all the money he had spent for repairs. This experience was still with Erling: a feeling of shame at having made his father, he thought, throw away money for repairs, and the sorrow over the crushed dream of fine boots. Of course it was true, as the psychologists maintained in different words, that if an unhappy experience was pushed into the corner and left there it did not evaporate because it was kept in the corner; on the contrary, it grew the whole time with its owner and retained the same relationship to him. But—a deep memory of sorrow did the same thing. The sorrow also kept its proportion. Besides other unhappy memories, death had struck close to him when he was twenty-one. He had been quite beside himself with grief but long ago it had turned into something that almost didn't seem to have happened, while the memory of a younger brother who died when Erling himself was a child, remained as a tragedy, albeit eased and distant; but obviously he carried it with him and was as conscious of it as he was of the tattoos he had awakened with one morning in Cartagena some forty years ago.

Steingrim had been listening, his eyes now alive but his face otherwise as closed and vacant as ever. Now he spoke up: "I have a memory I never can get rid of. I never talk about it. There is always something that prevents me from doing so. Perhaps it is too sensitive a memory. It has to do with a tree-shaded road at home."

With this Steingrim shut his mouth and said nothing more. Erling knew it would have been futile to ask Steingrim further when he assumed that attitude, but in this case there was nothing to ask; Erling had many times heard the story of the "avenue of trees" and what had happened there—when Steingrim had been drinking so heavily that he couldn't remember the following day what he had said. Now he only remarked, "You specialize in awakening curiosity, and then, unlike others, you shut up like a clam."

The last time Steingrim had told the story had been at Lier about a year and a half ago. Erling had not been able to say that he had heard the story before; indeed, Steingrim seldom repeated himself, and there was always a certain caution between them, perhaps a fear of crushing something. The only time they had approached anything resembling a misunderstanding must have been the incident at Asker, which Erling had just read about—and he couldn't even remember it, had never known about it until today.

Steingrim's story always varied a little, but not sufficiently to indicate he contradicted himself; new details might be added, old ones forgotten. That he spoke the truth no one could doubt, though perhaps not a plumb-line truth, rather an intensive fantasy-creation of childhood which covered all he had experienced in life and which had become a reality in a higher sense.

As was his habit, Erling had written it down.

"Steingrim's avenue of trees. A road with old linden trees on either side led from the main highway up to the farm. Between the trees on either side ran a hedge of hawthorn. Father had kept the hedges down, never allowing them to reach higher than a man's height, perhaps he wanted to be able to see over them. Over the years the hedges had grown to be about a yard thick and were cut square on top. I imagined them as two narrow roads I might walk on. The thorns were as big as darning needles, points about an ich long. I can see those hedges before me as if I were looking at them this minute, even though they were cut down soon after my parents discovered what I feared there. I really don't know if this was the reason for cutting them down. We burned them in the biggest Midsummer-fire we had ever had. A man came and dug up the roots, many wagon-loads of them, he wanted to plant a hedge at his house, and so it didn't cost Father anything to get rid of them. No one else in our neighborhood had hawthorn hedges.

"In early summer when it was still twilight all night the hedges swarmed with moths. I believe this was mostly in humid weather; at dusk you could see a cloud rise over the hedges and across the road, visible a great distance; then there was a nice, pungent odor from the hawthorn; I remember I had a notion I could eat that smell and satisfy my hunger. Father said those insects were a terrible pest but I thought they were beautiful. They laid their eggs in the bushes and the larvae were held together in some gossamer that ruined the hedge. I don't think I have ever seen anything more beautiful than those yellow moths hovering around the hawthorn during warm, moist summer evenings, but I always feel a little peculiar in talking about it—although it seems quite natural when others do. Write poems about it, for example, or just describe it.

"Our road was about a hundred paces long and rather wide. It was a wonderful feeling to walk along it from early spring until fall; always something was happening in the hedges, especially when the moths were there, but also a great many songbirds built their nests there, and I was aware of the family life among them. They became quite accustomed to me every summer. I have never been much for animals the way many people are but they soon discovered I wasn't unfriendly. I liked for them to think I wouldn't hurt them. In winter the road was depressing; the hedges looked bare and dead, there was slush in the ruts, horse-droppings and other dirt, until the snow covered it. One winter there was so much snow that the hedges disappeared entirely and only the tops of the linden trees waved above the drifts as I watched from the window.

"I have figured out it must have been shortly after I became eight years old that I stopped following the road and instead ran across the fields. Quite near the house on the right-hand side it seemed a man would push through the hedge and try to grab me. This only happened when I was on my way home. He was a big fat man and I never really saw his face, but one time I had seen his eyes and didn't want that experience again. His eyes were outside the face and after me. When I entered the road at the bottom of the hill he would crane his neck out of the hedge and look for me. I never knew how he managed with all those thorns. I didn't think anyone else had seen him; it's difficult to say why I thought so; perhaps they weren't meant to see him. I didn't think of him as a ghost. Actually, I don't know what I took him to be. I never saw him in any other place. It was only late in the day he was there, about dusk, or a little before. I didn't know if he was there at night, for then I never went there, but I was afraid he might break into our house. Even now I have an eery feeling when I remember how afraid of the dark I was at that time. Now I'm not. I presume I used up my whole supply of darkness-fear when I was eight.

"But then I would start to run across the fields when I was on my way home to avoid him. It wasn't easy to run through a rutabaga-field, or when the rye stood tall. Soon my parents discovered what I was up to and scolded me, but they couldn't make me walk the road when the man was there, soon not at any time. Mother saw how disturbed I was and kept talking, just talking to me, and finally I told Mother because she kept insisting. They tried to talk sense to me now that it finally was out, but I refused ever to walk on that road; I took another road that led to the opposite side of the house. I never saw the man there but I was as frightened as ever. You should have seen him when I ran across the field before anyone knew about him but me! He poked his head out of the hedge, even over it, he must have been standing right in the road! The day after I had confided in my mother, Father took me by the hand and walked with me to the place where I had seen him. I explained to my father how he had looked across the very top of the hedge to espy me. I remember how I held on to Father's fingers while we stood there. My father looked about in the hedge but didn't say much; in fact, I don't remember he said anything. But he looked very seriously at me. My father was a serious person."

A big fat man in a thick hawthorn hedge, thought Erling, who wanted to grab Steingrim when he was eight years old. One who poked his head across the hedge and looked for him when he ran over the field. Good Lord, haven't we all experienced the same sort of thing, but perhaps not just like Steingrim. Someone appearing through a wall, leaving no hole behind him, to grab you too. Or one evening on the forest path you turned quickly about and something got away, but not fully.

What was it Steingrim had written in the diary?—"I thought it was something eery he had said. It made me think of the road up to my childhood home." If we are to meet, Steingrim, you and I, let's swim side by side into the bay at Erlingvik. Don't ever let's meet on Steingrim's road.

• *Nature distributes her bounty unequally*

Erling read from the diary:

"From the very first day in Sweden a dark instinct directed me to everything that further contributed to my depression. It did not matter what I undertook. If I sat at home, alone, I was torn by thoughts that made me even more depressed. If I went out I met people who told me the worst things they could think of. If I picked up a book, preferably very old, which I felt might be peaceful and neutral, the dark instinct still directed my hand. One day I came across an old newspaper in the library, it was from 1858, and in it was an article by Viktor Rydberg about the Norwegians—he was on a journey in Norway:

" 'Nature distributes her abundance unequally: tactfulness and delicacy are not characteristics of all nations, and openness is hardly attractive when it displays coarseness and a desire to exalt one's own deficiencies through emphasizing the shortcomings of others.'

"He writes futher: 'The Swede has a right to be proud of his nationality: he belongs to a people who, though few in numbers, nevertheless has carved its name on history's most beautiful pages.

Among the races of the globe he is the chief representative of the Scandinavians, and their bastion in case of danger.'

"And a third quotation: 'First of all we would have expected the Norwegians, who ever since the days of Gange-Rolf have been devoid of history and are destined in the future to share good and evil with us and who never can expect any historical significance except through us—we would have expected that the Norwegians above all others would be interested in their brother-lands's past and would be pleased with the honor of being a common nation with Sweden. In this we are greatly disappointed.'

"The quotations practically follow each other, in the above order. A comparison between the first and the two last is disgusting when the words come from an otherwise prominent person like Viktor Rydberg. Even a well-developed brain works with a rusty nail in some corners when it is operating on a nationalistic level. His disappointment that the Norwegians have lacked the delicacy to sun themselves in the deeds of others, seems real. His ability to judge both his own situation and that of others seems to sway in the direction of power. The German surprise at our failure to appreciate their occupation of our country was highly evident, particularly in the beginning. Once I saw a Dutch-Indonesian conversation-dictionary which contained only words for abuse, accusations of theft and similar doings. Until recently Danish children could read in their schoolbooks that Iceland was a vassal country of theirs. Protests were in vain: national humiliation was considered an honor.

"I could not help making comparisons while in Sweden. My conclusions indicated the Norwegians can be happy with their fate. A quirk of history gave us a free farmer-class, however many the attempts at suppression, and in spite of some dark blots on our freedom. Another of history's gifts: the Norwegians have no other people on whom they could practice their desire for power—perhaps this above all made the Norwegians individuals. They never suffered the moral degradation of collective bragging. A nation's freedom can never become absolute, neither externally nor internally, but it can approach perfection if it is not its brother's guardian.

"Not that the Norwegians were to appreciate their inner resources to any great extent; they perpetuated a four hundred-year night when apparently nothing happened, because there were no kings to write about. But in due time the Norwegians will assimilate their misfortune at not having had a history that ran its course like all others.

"We have never had an eternally smarting wound, like the Swedes with their Charles XII, a misfortune that must be glorified with all the resources of that nation.

"Norway must learn to accept her history, not bury it, not falsify it, not lie herself away from it; rather, with self-restraint look back and unearth all her supposed defeats and analyze them once more.

"Vidkun Quisling was a sick and distorted picture of all sick Norwegian inferiority-feeling, with a bodyguard that worshiped Hardrader —dead a thousand years—changelings begotten through Norwegian envy of all nations that had been or were under the whip. Quisling was the exponent of the inverted dream of being in chains like everybody else. For what was his dream but the dream of a slave to be rewarded with praise from the big ones; a fervent desire to step up before the great Mogul, in gold-plated helmet and shining armor, and swear him fealty with a thundering voice in the Old-Norwegian tongue. In secret a pleader for defeat, in the open a calf with his tail straight in the air running into the burning barn. Always the same thing: humanity's blindness considering defeat a gift and a faith-testing; the acceptances of defeat in individuals are like important junctions where we stop and choose the road. Defeat must be brought into daylight, not dug down, for it is through defeats that one becomes a man. The one who never understands his defeats remains a buffoon; he carries nothing into the future, he is like a woman of the sort who believes she can live on her sex into old age and doesn't realize her bitter mistake until she notices the sneers that follow her in the street."

· Et tu, friend Steingrim

Erling caught sight of his own name and read:
"It turned out all right, even though it was wrong of Eyvind Brekke to choose Erling as a messenger. That time, in early 1941, Erling was on the way to becoming an alcoholic, and several times he seemed to be on the verge of delirium tremens. Besides, one could say he suffered seizures in trying to tear himself away from Ellen; he both wanted to, and not. They were like a pair of Siamese twins, torn by a mutual and unquenchable hatred, yet unable to find anyone to swing the axe. When they were separated from each other in Sweden both of them submerged in a pool of blood, partly their own, partly their antagonist's. These were the sorts of things that occupied us in Stockholm; when I got to London I discovered on the first day that they busied themselves with similar matters there. Erling told me he had planned three books about the same

people; the first volume how things worked out for them the first dozen years after the war, the second about Norwegians in Stockholm, the third about love, politics, and liquor in Oslo up to the day when the Germans came and usurped at least the politics and the liquor. I told Erling I did not intend to read those books, if they were ever written, for no writer could do it without putting his own light under the bushel, and this is not done among authors. If one put twelve writers to work on the same subject in order to obtain a full picture, and each one wrote his work alone, they would only agree on two points, namely that twelve foreign cities would all be called Stockholm, and that each one of the writers would have personally and singlehandedly won the war.

"Well, I told Eyvind Brekke he had made the wrong choice and it would turn out badly. A person who was an artist in so high a degree, and in so high a degree had an artist's temperament, was always in the midst of a private war, and furthermore Erling hated the Germans more than anyone else I had met; such a person would have been the last one I would have suggested for this mission. 'The man is my friend,' I said, 'but that doesn't matter; I know you cannot trust an alcoholic, and Erling Vik is one *now*. One can't say if he can ever get over it.'

"Eyvind Brekke said he had never seen Erling drunk, something that didn't surprise me, knowing that Brekke went to bed at nine sharp every evening.

" 'It doesn't matter when I go to bed,' replied Brekke, 'for an alcoholic is never sober at six either.'

"I reminded Eyvind Brekke that Erling Vik had a wife. She must be noticed, that was her vice. Anything she heard would be carried further, 'in confidence.'

" 'True enough,' said Brekke, 'but Erling knows that better than either one of us.'

"I mentioned again Erling's hatred of the Germans, which was well known long before Hitler came to power. 'Hitler *will* come to power,' he had said, 'otherwise the Germans are no longer Germans.'

"Brekke said Erling of today was no worse a Fritz-eater than thousands of others. 'But I can see your point,' he said. 'It's not in our favor that one of our group is known to hate the Germans. However, exceptions can be useful too; I have need of someone with a hatred that is old and tested and genuine.'

"I tried to bring up Ellen again, and said I wouldn't have taken the chance.

"What Brekke now said made me give in, but I was not convinced: 'You must realize, Hagen, I've taken all these matters into consideration.

If Erling Vik divulged anything to his wife, it would indeed be a serious matter. People of her kind are worse than a dozen informers; they do not intend harm, it's only they never shut up, and this must be taken into account. People of her sort—and this holds true of men also—are the most dangerous ones, until the mate discovers we are at war. Erling knows this. He tells her nothing. Obviously he is going to put her on the wrong track, and so it is in our favor that she is the one she is. She can actually be useful, she too, just in that way. The informers are Norwegians every one of them. Not a single one who knows Erling will suspect him as long as his wife has nothing to spread about.'

"Eyvind Brekke was right; Erling never revealed himself. Ellen never got wind of anything, not in Sweden either. When I came across the border shortly after him, I hoped he would tell me something of his experiences; he never did. In August, 1945, I told him I had known right along. Then we divulged to each other many circumstances not known to both of us. An immense amount is still in the dark, but it's of little importance now. Indeed, this was true already in '45. Erling did not report an attempt on his life in 1941 when the man later was brought to justice, a bastard called Torvald Ørje who specialized in reporting people he himself wanted out of the way or wanted to see in Grini. This man is free now, like most of his ilk.

"I should have been proven right about Erling, and I feel in some way I am. It was abnormal that he didn't leak information. He had never in his life kept anything to himself. Yet, had I told Eyvind Brekke this, he would have replied: 'This time he will.'

"And Erling who never had kept silent before, did so this time. Brekke told me after the war that Erling actually didn't know too much, but he had many addresses, more than seventy. Most of the names Erling must have forgotten but some it could have been possible to get out of him. Perhaps he kept silent because one lone address didn't sound very exciting. Eyvind Brekke had expressed it in his own way, in a message he managed to smuggle out of Grini; he felt that he himself was doomed, and in any case they had crippled him for life. Yet he had time to think of others. His message went through the city like a joke: 'Send Erling Vik to Sweden at once! Assuredly he knows nothing, but God knows what he might say!'

"It would have had dire consequences if they had managed to get out of him the nothing he knew. Many lives would have been lost, Brekke said.

"Erling had of course known a great deal, and picked up more later. But he was and remained leak-proof. He found himself sitting beside two of the 'names' once in Stockholm, but he didn't let on, and they didn't say anything; it wasn't only our side that sent messages across the border.

"Later, I found it comical that Erling was used as money-courier, he with his eternal shortage of money. That was the poorest war-joke I heard.

"Now everything is so changed. Both he and I have become different since then. Many of my arguments against him have fallen by the wayside. Only one is left, and I never used it against him, for Brekke would hardly have understood it. One must never divulge absolute secrets to a writer; it would be unjust to him. His function is to solve secrets, this is his endowment and it can never be otherwise. He must divulge the secrets in words, as the painter does in color. The writer is a catalyzer, if indeed he is anything. He is no priest who must keep silent concerning what he hears in the confessional. It is easy enough to say he must keep to himself what might hurt others, but his nature is to divulge. Nature always breaks through education. Assuredly it is not the common truth he would divulge, the one they look for in court cases, but nevertheless pieces of the original and ordinary truth-clump might be exposed. What he absorbs with any one of his senses is in his case added to his experience, as it is with other people who *can* absorb experience, but in the writer's case it also goes into a sort of crucible where it mixes with anything related to it. One day it is worked through and comes to use, and by then he is unable to say where he absorbed it, and what is a personal experience and what isn't. If one confides something to a writer and demands he put it aside in some storeroom to lie there unused and sterile, then one likens him to the man in the Bible parable who buried his talent. One will realize one has asked the impossible.

" 'Sometimes I use a model,' Erling told me once, 'but it isn't good to say so. People in general make no discrimination between model and portrait. I would indeed feel unhappy in practicing portrait-making, which is impossible anyway. Attempts I've seen are terribly stupid; the events might be all right but do not fit the canvas. The picture becomes false. I must tell you something peculiar, Steingrim: those who are afraid of being depicted are not even usable as models. All sterile, useless stuff. And this is true in the same degree with people who want to be written about. Both categories are like the queues of stupid girls who plague film stars. Furthermore: a person who believes he has been used for a portrait is a simpleton; he has never been intended as, cannot even be used as, a type. On the other hand, one actually used as a model might shake his head and say: Well, perhaps some resemblance, but it isn't me. This I will admit, though: I might in the midst of something let my tongue slip and produce a piece of undigested, vulgar truth.'

"It is that piece of 'undigested, vulgar truth' that so easily escapes the writer, and remains hanging in the air, meaningless. I would like to know how often Erling has let his tongue slip purposely. He himself says never.

"The writer must open himself and display everything. Compare as his opposite an official, who resembles his own secret file and is proud of his mask (which makes an impression on people not worthy of being impressed), a face like a locked file, the type which often grows old early, poisoned by the junk he can't bear to part with, even during vacation.

"Now I've almost proved myself wrong, but the writer does want to expose, it is his nature, he easily says things even when he doesn't mean to. He is not the right man to carry secrets when the country is at war. I believe Eyvind Brekke felt that just in this case he could trust Erling for a special reason: Erling must have had a special motive, probably a strong even though somewhat tarnished motive, to keep silent. *He has not committed violence against his nature.* There was something behind it."

Erling pushed the diary from him, leaned back in his chair and looked out through the window. He recalled his conversation with Eyvind Brekke. Yes, Steingrim, you were sharp; there *was* an ignoble side-motive in my patriotism.

Brekke had been sitting oppostite him across the narrow table, watching Erling. He had said: "No, Vik, it is impossible."

And then, immediately after, coldly, perhaps with a mite of compassion in his eye, "Not with the wife you have."

Erling had looked back without flinching: "I had thought something like that. But if I now say that this very thing is something *she* has driven me to? Finally to be able once again to do something she knows nothing about, can't spread around and embroider, nothing she can use to make herself important."

Brekke threw him a glance. Then he started to sweep up some bread crumbs with his right hand, gathered them into his left, and then threw them on the table again: "I don't know if I like that motivation, but I believe it might hold."

Erling had thought for a moment that Brekke still was hesitant, but that was only because some people walked close by them. "Keep the address and the time in your head," he said. "Never write down anything unless you absolutely have to—"

• Martin Leire

"May 19, 1952. I saw Martin Leire for the last time in November, 1943," Steingrim had written. "It was on Kungsgatan, fog and rain, one of those hopeless late-autumn days in a Scandinavian city when everything seems to conspire to rob one of happiness. It was between five and six, the shop-window glitter reflected on the wet street, the lights cut into the fog like a sickness.

"As I passed the entrance of a hotel, a taxi eased to a stop; its door opened and Martin's death-pale face appeared. In his company was a very young girl, as pale as he, and both quite drunk, their eyes glassy, their mouths half open. He recognized me in spite of his deep drunkenness and seemed embarrassed at the meeting. The girl too climbed out of the taxi and swayed on the sidewalk. A rather indifferent pickup with a face that must have looked stupid even under more favorable circumstances. With great difficulty Martin managed to pay the driver and turned to me, his legs wobbly, his matted hair falling down under the hat which was on backwards. He was fighting his inebriation and mumbled something about having arrived that day and would leave from Bromma in the evening. That could only mean he was headed for London. He had stayed in Skåne for some time but had never written, not even now when he would move on. It had annoyed me a bit even though we had seen little of each other for a long time. After some scandal in Malmö he had gone underground, and it surprised me they wanted him in London. On the other hand, he had had good connections, at least before the scandal; these people ought to have helped him, if for no other reason than to get him out of the way for their own comfort. Or, he might have received his orders, to be deported, as we called it. I knew of several such cases. It was one expediency to keep Swedish authorities from interfering.

"Our meeting was infinitely painful. His feeling of shame broke through his half-conscious face, his unsteady legs, his futile attempts at a few casual words to an old friend, his apologies, explanations—nothing could hide his intoxicated condition. He stared helplessly at me, at the girl, at the doorman. I said something inconsequential and hurried on. At Stureplan rain began to fall in earnest, and I went in and sat down at Sturehof. It turned out to be the worst evening I ever spent during my Stockholm period. My old friend, the inclement weather, bad news from all quarters—all together hit me on a day when I was already down and more lonely than usual. Toward midnight when I had returned to the closet where I lived, I broke down and cried. The following day I went to Sturehof again, for my breakfast. They had a large variety of newspapers there, and I intended to read for an hour to gain my equilibrium after such a depressing night. And then the headlines cried out to me that a plane had crashed. The time, the place, and the fact that no names were mentioned told me that Martin was gone. I called several places before I got hold of someone who knew me and was willing to talk; Martin had been on the plane, he had been killed.

"Nothing from all my war years has stayed with me in so gray and hopeless a light as those happenings. The deciding factor is always how deeply one is personally involved in a happening. I was already through with Martin Leire, in the sense that I would never have looked him up again; in another sense I know I will never be through with him. I got to know him in my loneliness when we both were young. I was drawn to him again and again, but loneliness alone is no good foundation for friendship. He killed something of the best within me, or at least was to blame for its non-development. *Blame* and *blame*—it was I who constantly sought out *him*, this big, strong, shallow person with whom I had nothing in common, no, not with that Martin Leire and his vulgar talk. So bitter can it be to be alone that I time and again returned from visits with my best friend, feeling like vomiting. He was from the first to the last day a stranger to me. It was I who was his audience when he came dragging home with each new and charming seventeen-year-old girl— even when he was over forty—and whispered to me aside God knows how many times, that he would never sink as deep as Erling Vik, myself, and some others, who were satisfied with old women of twenty-five or over.

"The young girls still liked him, even with his thinning hair and vapid eyes.

"I wrote I was through with him and would never have looked him up again, had he lived, and I believe it is the truth, for when I was with him after the Germans had come he bored me to tears. Yet, one never knows. I have long ago confessed to myself it was a relief to know he was thoroughly dead, but it bothers me in some way that he took the plane quite drunk, after his last drunken bed-play with his last and equally drunk seventeen-year-old. It all seems, even to me who always consider cause and effect, almost *too* horribly pat.

"While I was sitting at Sturehof, looking at newspapers I couldn't read, Birgit Orrestad and her little daughter came in to eat. The girl's name was Adda. Birgit had obtained a job at the legation and was well liked there. She was seldom seen out, she was a conscientious mother and didn't care for liquor like the rest of us. There were some of that kind. They created a certain notice by leading a quiet, sober life. I have observed that moderation in all types of enjoyment, *without* an urge to convert others, is quite common in women of a definitely warm and charming nature. They are moderate on all fronts of life. They can listen and talk little. They accept the foulest story without a blink but would never repeat it. They take little interest in morals but act as if they had some. If they finally have an adventure you can be sure they go through the doors soundlessly. One confesses one's sins to them and they don't use their knowledge. They themselves never confess.

"Birgit Orrestad and her daughter we used to call 'Birgit and Adda the Etruscans.' Who had given them that name I never learned, but it suited them remarkably well. Birgit had the same long, curious neck as a deer when it lifts its head and spies about, but she also resembled the sea serpent one sees on old prints, raising its head above the surface, taking in the situation. She had also a touch of women-figures one sees on sarcophagi-lids at Palmyra. Yet mostly a young giraffe. Birgit was of a very fair complexion, she never used powder or lipstick and she dressed rather indifferently. Her eyes were almond-shaped and contemplative. She reminded one of a boy. She seldom said anything without being asked, and one could never be sure of a reply. Everybody was a little uncertain about her. Was she beautiful? Yes, she was. She must have been about thirty. No one knew who was the father of her daughter. A few had asked, but she had only looked pondering at the questioner and said nothing. One woman had taken the chance when alone with the girl and asked her, 'What is your father's name?' and the girl had looked seriously at her and said, 'He has changed his name.' The woman was forced to smile, a little embarrassed at the child's guarded look, the exact miniature of the mother. Indeed, she was so much a copy of her mother that the possibilities of a virginal birth might be considered; the same jerky motion of her head on the long neck, like a camera being focused. People became somewhat confused sitting at the same table with mother and daughter. The Etruscan Birgit seldom talked to anyone except her precocious daughter, the Etruscan Adda. Their eyes *stayed open*. Is it possible that I have never seen either one of them blink? One nearly always thought of some animal when looking at Birgit Orrestad, the Etruscan. A young mare. A dragonfly glittering in the sun.

"It was good to encounter the two; it was some time after I had left Felicia, who could be so trying in her eternal attempts to help.

"Someone had it from Oslo that Birgit had not been married. The name of Adda's father as I said had never been mentioned. It shouldn't have been too difficult to find out but no one had bothered, it seemed.

"I went out and bought something for Adda and sat down with them for a couple of hours. The vapors in my head had eased a little when I went home and started to read. I liked Birgit and would have shacked up with her, but I guess that's not for me any more. It gets so complicated. Those things called passion, sexual excitement and the like are foreign to me. I am like St. Paul. But I perform what is expected from me; it is as exciting as holding hands. I can do it as often as they want and I never tell them it bores me. Yes, it is difficult. I prefer female company to male, and I almost wish it weren't so. For I have some kind of shortcoming that causes me to be mistaken about women catastrophically."

Catastrophically? thought Erling. That was a strong word for Steingrim to use.

The sun was streaming down on the table where Erling was sitting with the diary. A reflection glittered in the glass of whisky he had poured himself, against his custom so early in the day—perhaps an antidote for the many gray days in Stockholm so long ago.

So that was how Martin Leire had seemed in the eyes of his friend, he who never had mentioned him after the war. Not a single word. It made Erling reflect that Steingrim never had used a belittling word about a woman, not even about Viktoria to whom he still was married then, while she told every new acquaintance how terribly Steingrim had degraded her by talking about her behind her back. This he had never done. He had mentioned her only seldom, and only in passing, neither kindly nor unkindly.

He recalled how she had tried to get him, Erling, involved in a slander-campaign she had just started against Steingrim, based as usual on her statement that he had ruined her reputation. Erling's stony silence had at last stopped her and she had not come to him again. But it did not deter her to find that none of Steingrim's friends were willing to listen to her. It was a sort of mania with her, and she attached herself to the most unsavory characters to orate about Steingrim's shortcomings. She understood—as far as she was able to understand anything—that she had been accepted as Steingrim's wife but did not understand she must be decent if she still wanted them as friends. From pure habit she continued her persecution of Steingrim among other people who only were familiar with the name Steingrim Hagen and perhaps felt honored that his wife was willing to air the family closets with them. Erling had heard more than one report of how she carried on, unable to stop once she got started, until the listeners were struck dumb with such nervous chatter, not particularly interested in her but undoubtedly curious about what went on in Steingrim's bed. This they were informed about—while Viktoria talked and talked, until the silence of the listeners grew too intense for her to endure; when she would leave, ashamed and revengeful, perhaps feeling that it might be rather herself than Steingrim she had thrown to the dogs.

The silence Steingrim had let fall over Martin Leire must be rooted in a shame he felt both for himself and for his friend. This seemed apparent from what Erling just had read. Similarly perhaps Steingrim's silence about women had the same cause. "For I have some kind of shortcoming that causes me to be mistaken about women catastrophically."

How strange to persecute a man precisely for something he never has done! The usual procedure is to find a feather, which is turned into a hen. But here wasn't the smallest piece of down. There could be no explanation except that Viktoria had inverted the situation: she could not endure the silence about herself, since Steingrim refused to talk about her day and night, and thus her slander was also an expression of a dream-fulfillment. Unless in her unholy simplicity she was unable to individualize and had never seen her husband other than as one among many, a faceless fool; and took it for granted that he went out of his way to blacken her name.

However, she was dangerous in her way. She represented "the revolt of stupidity," and Erling had never underestimated her evil nature. When Steingrim committed suicide and causes were investigated, Erling had not been the only one to remember Viktoria.

Now he was recalling the time before the war, his acquaintance with Martin and Steingrim, the latter becoming his friend after the war. Both were dead now, neither one reaching forty-five. So many had died, remarkably many when he actually figured their number, while he himself still enjoyed life on earth, had his health, and was what is called, with all its modifications, happy. That he wouldn't wish to change places with any one of the dead was understandable, neither would he wish to change with any one of the living. Of course, his life had turned autumnal in a way, many yellow leaves had fallen, but the sun could still dance, and his lack of youth was a matter of computation rather than something he felt overwhelmed by.

• Viktoria Hagen

On April 9, 1946, Steingrim had written: "I had had many jolts before we were married but it seemed I didn't really wake up to all the dirt until we were legally joined. After the so-called honeymoon we had dinner one evening with cabinet minister Nerbø and his wife. I had become quite interested in a conversation with Nerbø and a few others; we had talked about South American politics. This was quite logical since one of the men had just come back from Peru. Returning home my wife and I didn't speak much; as far as I remember I didn't open my mouth.

"I had observed that a man's criterion as to whether a relationship would last depended on his ability to overlook his sweetheart's first stupidity. Perhaps the opposite is true also. If one is really in love one can easily overlook a *faux pas,* however great. If one is not, well, then one is through with her the first time she acts silly. This, Viktoria must have done before, undoubtedly, but in everyday life I am not observant of foolishness. This evening I was. Toward the end of the dinner I got into a bad humor because I noticed Viktoria's uneasiness and annoyance; her mouth is so repulsive when she is annoyed. She had acted in a peculiar way the whole evening and before we left she was almost disgusting.

"When we got home I picked up the evening papers. Then I poured a glass of cognac and left the bottle standing on the table; I was in the usual gray mood after a dinner; I had in mind a couple of glasses and then to bed.

"Viktoria was standing at the fireplace and had lit a cigarette. 'If that is supposed to be a cabinet minister's home it isn't what I would call exactly elegant!' she blurted out.

"I looked at her over the paper. I had long been aware that in one point I must be patient with her as long as we were married (at that time I didn't think exactly of 'as long as we were married'). It wasn't only her paucity of words; the few she had she could use in a most disturbing manner. As for example now, when she said the hosts' home wasn't exactly elegant. It was not impossible that she meant they lived like Spartans or something of that sort. But by starting with 'if that's supposed to be a cabinet minister's home' she indicated to me that this time, fortunately, she had managed to express what she meant. She had expected elegance from a minister, whatever she meant by elegance (I visualized the worst). Twelve rooms, each one an antique shop, or even worse. Without realizing it she had been a guest in a home.

" 'And me going there in this dress,' she said and threw her cigarette into the fireplace (which I was not allowed to do). 'I might as well have worn something casual.'

"We had been eight at dinner, all in evening clothes, although the men had worn only tuxedos. That must be it, then: there hadn't been a hundred guests, silver service and crystal glasses and God knows what else Viktoria might have read and imagined constituted a luxury home. How will this work out? I thought to myself. She is furious. Doesn't she realize she might have to revise her preconceived ideas; if this does not strike home with her when she comes eye to eye with reality, then there is no hope. I can't begin with her education from the very beginning, and especially not when I realize she is common, a hussy with nothing in her head except cheap movies she has seen.

"I felt, however, I should explain to her that we had been in a home with atmosphere, a place where people felt comfortable.

"Somewhat embarrassed I looked at my paper again; I couldn't make myself say it. If she didn't feel it herself, well, then she didn't. I thought I could in that very moment hear Astrid Nerbø say to her husband: 'Tell me, Johannes, *what* is it Steingrim has married?'

"Well, I might have brought a girl who had just left her maid's job to marry me. It wasn't *that*. Astrid Nerbø herself had worked in an office, lived in a rented room where she cooked her food, and had invited both Johannes and me to have tea with her in the old days. Viktoria had a much *finer* background than Astrid, if one now must talk about such stupid nonsense. Viktoria was a snob of the worst kind, and suddenly I cowered in fear at the thought of what I had got into; Viktoria was furious because she would be unable the following day to tell her girl-friends about Minister Nerbø's elegant dinner party—but *she would do it anyway!* She would furnish Astrid and Johannes Nerbø with an elegant home. There would be no shortage of embroidered linen, silver and crystal pieces, and orchids, and God knows what dishes she would ruin our stomachs with. I suddenly wondered if her name actually was Viktoria, if she hadn't originally carried a simple, pious name, like Britt, or Anna. No, then she would have had to falsify her papers; and our marriage wouldn't be legal either. Oh Lord, how my imagination played with that thought for a moment! Innocently to have lived in sin, and then be able to pack and walk off, in the name of law and morality.

"It must have been a pure accident, her name. She was proud of the name Viktoria. It means victory, she would say, probably to show she knew at least one foreign word.

"That day we had been married for three weeks. I rose from my chair with the tense self-control that can lead to broken windows. I cursed myself, I had to get out of the house, get some air, move about. I looked at the clock. It wasn't yet eleven. Cabinet ministers have early habits. I mumbled something and remembered I had been drinking: I can't kill her while drunk, I must wait till tomorrow.

"Viktoria sneered: 'A minister ought at least to think of his prestige!'

"I noticed her surprised look when I grabbed my coat and hat, still on a chair, and disappeared through the door. It took four months before I moved away from her.

"The following day I was sitting alone at home, working on an article. I felt indisposed and weary and thought nothing was worth the effort. I know everyone feels that way at times, that it is caused from fatigue, or poor digestion. I have not seldom felt that way. I am not what one might call a witty man. Probably I am considered boring, and I can't protest. I kept doodling, and it started to resemble Viktoria's face, I thought. I took a new sheet and tried to draw a picture of her. I'm a poor draftsman and had never before tried my hand at portraits. The result frightened me, I don't know why. Ridiculously enough, I told myself it resembled Viktoria more than she herself did. I suppose I felt I had caught something I knew existed behind the slippery surface. According to common judgment she is better-looking than Felicia, but actually the opposite is true. And then I started to write. I used my finest handwriting, automatically it seemed. I felt my face assume a sneer. Not that I could see my own sneer, but I thought it must resemble the delusion-of-grandeur grin one sees in portraits of old men who have suffered a stroke—the eyes focusing on the nose, one corner of the mouth pulled up, one down, an expression of utter disgust at other people's stupidity. It was about Viktoria I wrote under the picture, and went on for several pages. It was nothing I could have written normally; I felt possessed, not by one but by a whole swarm of evil spirits that hissed and whispered in my ears, they were inside me too, I inhaled them through nose and mouth. Now I would like to have a look at the result. I used a few sheets of paper that just happened to be lying on my desk; I remember the experience as something intimate and yet alien. When I stopped writing I felt better, purged, eased. I drank a little cognac, for liquor carries me on in the same mood I am in. If I'm depressed I become more so if drinking, if happy I get happier. Then I heard her come in. I quickly folded the sheets and pushed them into a book that was next to me.

"This I shouldn't have done; there are always books lying around me and they need not have any connection with my work at hand. Apart from the face I had drawn there was no need of hiding my work. She was never in the least interested in what I was doing; she only asked how much it would bring me, and if it was something I was unable to place she would sulk and say I was no businessman. At first she tried to make me believe she was interested; my mail was searched, and if she was in the house I couldn't send a letter without her having read it. She was suspicious. But she never dreamt of reading any of my boring articles. Politics to her meant stern faces and stuffed shirts, and for once she wasn't far from the truth. 'Why don't you write like others,' she said one day, 'something funny!' I never dared look at her when she made such statements; I felt embarrassed to think others might hear her—which indeed they did.

"I thought I would find what I had written and burn it at first opportunity, but when she was out I couldn't think of the book I had put the sheets in. There was hardly any danger of her opening any of my books—she only used them to stand on when she put up curtains—but it might have been in a novel or a cookbook. I couldn't for the life of me recall what book it had been. I searched for those papers for weeks but I never found them. Every time something was wrong I thought she must have found them."

Erling rose and walked about in the house for a while. He speculated on what Steingrim might have written about his wife—with the illustration—and what he might have looked like as a paralytic—Steingrim with his locked and sensible face, Steingrim who left this world silent and closed as he had lived.

Gifted men, it seemed, often had the most disappointing experiences with women, before they discovered quality. They were looking for women above the average, but encountered in youth so much nonsense-talk that they easily might become afraid of women. One is inclined to generalization, and a young man meeting a hare-brained thing a few times might get the notion all women are chicken-brained. His upbringing has already sown suspicion that she is a lower being, on a level with stimulants one can buy from the druggist with a prescription, or perhaps directly from the liquor store. So it follows as an unworthy reaction that a man ties himself up with a chicken-brain for good; he has reached that stage by believing one must have a woman to sleep with at night, which might be true to a degree, but only to a degree. And then it is written by that light-extinguisher in Christianity, the one who came in through the back door after Jesus' death, yet managed to become one of the apostles, that it is better to marry than to burn. Marriage as a one-man whorehouse.

The trouble with gifted men might originally have been that they were afraid gifted women would be too difficult. Thus, fearing difficulties, they create for themselves a stinking hell, and if the woman still isn't sufficiently inferior, they tyrannize her until she breaks or leaves— sometimes through a window.

Erling stood looking at the wilderness garden he had behind the house. This lush, planless growth was a rest to the eye. Autumn was approaching. Jan is right, he thought. One must not swear at weather or wind or seasons but rather enjoy them. It was only a bad habit, according to Jan; one could get over it in a week, as he had done. All weathers were good, and if you didn't accept them you ruined your disposition.

Jan defended all weathers. "It blows wonderfully today!" he would exclaim, when all the apples dropped to the ground. "What a nice rain we're having!" "You should have seen it when the snow broke through the old barnhouse roof!" he would say, almost appreciatively. "The spring flood carried away the road behind the servants' quarters—it was a most dramatic sight!" "We had an exceptionally nice thunderstorm last night!" He almost purred when he had to get out and shovel snow.

Erling turned about and looked at his bookcases. He was still a little groggy from last night's lonely feast, and the hang-over must be checked. His eyes fell on a book that had been returned after Steingrim's death.

And it would never have entered his head, except for his hang-over, but now he walked across the floor, took down the book from its shelf and let the leaves play against his thumb. There was nothing between them. He emptied another glass but the thought would not leave him: what Steingrim had written might just as well be in any of the books he had borrowed. Erling pulled out all the books again and laid them in a pile. A few minutes later he had the sheets in his hand.

The face at the top of the first sheet was definitely not a good drawing, but anyone familiar with the artist and the model was unable to take his eyes away from it. It was a narrow, nasty face, quite unlike Viktoria's, yet one of those strange creations which a great artist can effectuate with his insinuating lines. It was amazingly like Viktoria; it was a picture of her warped and evil soul. Sharp eyes one couldn't get away from, a venomous face. Erling could not look at it while reading; he folded the sheet to escape the sight of it.

When he was through reading he put the sheets down and shook his head slowly several times. He must reject the thought that Steingrim had written this nonsense while drunk. His handwriting was the usual one, perhaps with a few minor deviations, but neat and cold as ever. Steingrim would undoubtedly have blushed had he found his work and read it. Erling inspected it once more. It was and remained drunken nonsense, yet written by a sober person. It was something a drunkard might orate about, thinking he was funny. Or cuttingly sarcastic. Four parentheses with ha! ha! without the text being particularly ha! ha! Some speculation about selling Viktoria at a slave market. Later, to a day-laborer who might beat her for money so that the viewers could hear how loud she was able to yell (ha! ha!). A few disconnected sentences about a new dress (ha! ha!).

Erling felt depressed; he rose and walked about in the room. Had Steingrim had an attack of insanity before he took his life, and had he realized it?

Suddenly Erling understood how it was; when Steingrim was tired but wanted to finish some work, he would take an amphetamine tablet. This pathological manifestation tallied exactly with an overdose of amphetamine. The same was true of the impression Steingrim later had retained of his work as being remarkable. Viktoria would have recognized nothing except her name. She had actually said once, it would be exciting to be sold at a slave market. Vera Arndt had spoken up and asked what made her so sure she would be sold?

Erling cut out the drawing and threw the rest in the fireplace. Then he sat down and studied the inhuman face Steingrim had created in his hatred; she who had become Steingrim's fate, she who finally found lovers when Steingrim had left her, but never friends. She picked up common, curious men who thought she must be something remarkable to have been married to Steingrim Hagen, but they soon were disappointed.

Steingrim had left her before the Germans came to Norway. "There goes the one who was married to Steingrim Hagen," people would say. They knew very well she was not divorced but it was easier to think of the marriage as being dissolved. She was one of those not unusual cases of a woman acquiring an incontestable though unclear position, through no qualification of her own, after she is put in the limelight by a Steingrim Hagen. And she had not delayed in following him to Sweden when she learned he was there. "It's terribly dangerous for me to remain, I who am married to Steingrim Hagen."

She said the same thing unabashed to the official who interrogated her at Kjesäter where the Norwegian authorities sorted the refugees. Steingrim's lawyer kept pointing out to her for years the immorality of hanging on to a man who couldn't endure the sight of her.

"A man can't just walk off like that," replied Viktoria.

Erling poured himself another glass to regulate his hang-over, and wondered where he might have put the letter he received long ago from Viktoria. She had sent it in 1946 (to his great annoyance), years after Steingrim had left her, and after a five-year world-upheaval. As a rule he did not save such letters, but this he had kept because it came from Steingrim's legal half. At last he found it. Well, it was eleven years old now, written nine long years after her conjugal life with Steingrim had come to an end. He scanned the pages, he had not the strength to read all of it.

"Why must I feel ashamed and uncomfortable?" Viktoria had written. "You always make me feel ashamed, but I have nothing to be ashamed of. I can do everything better than others. I do my duty and I am always well dressed. I don't owe anybody anything. So why do people look at me so funny as soon as I open my mouth? Birgit won't answer me. That witch Felicia begins to tremble at the corner of her mouth. Steingrim hates me, but a man can't just leave the way he did. He said I was a pervert, but I had read in books one could do that. It said also men had need of it. And no one can take my husband away from me. There is only one thing he can do if he is decent—he must come back to me at once. I need some money. I do earn some myself but when he has to pay to live somewhere else he might as well live with me. And I don't like him to pay money to others. They say he wouldn't have to pay if he sued but when he doesn't, well. Perhaps he doesn't want a divorce. It would be so ugly here if I didn't have all his fine books; why couldn't he sit here and read them since he is my husband? I don't know what people will think; I walk up and greet them in all friendliness and they just turn around. I act as one should act but they are all against me. I understand why the girls hate me, because I'm the most beautiful among them. All their men-friends have said so themselves. Yet they turn up their noses. And look at yourself—you ran away from Ellen once. You had to come back to her when she insisted. When you parted it was Ellen who left you. I would be willing to give up Steingrim if I could find someone else. But he mustn't say I am a discarded wife. I don't like that. Mother says that was the worst thing that happened to her and she feels like I do. The girls don't need to turn up their noses; I have had every one of their men, so they have nothing to brag about. I know something about every one of them. That Øystein Myhre who looks at me as if he were sitting on a cloud, he isn't so much of a man as people think. He drank himself out of the whole business, and in the morning he was gone without a word, and I can understand he feels it was rather embarrassing, but I have heard such things happen to men, so he needn't run away every time he sees me; I could comfort him by saying I know how it is. Nor is it true I had anything to do with *Nasjonal Samling,* but there were decent people among them too, and I could agree to All-Help before Self-Help, and so could anyone, but it was wrong to have that Quisling as their leader. Yesterday I met Jasper Arndt, and then I must say the cup ran over, but it doesn't matter what he said, and Vera needn't imagine her husband spends his evenings at meetings, some of us know better—"

Erling put down the letter and pondered the phenomenon Viktoria.

It was a burden he carried with him, an unquenchable interest in the nature of stupidity, its rhinoceros strength because the stupid cannot be stopped through shame, nor feel sorry when others feel ashamed for them. They have brains of twine and hearts of rubber, they can walk on water because they don't know any better, and they have skins as tough as hide and souls where plague rats nest.

· *Delirium*

Erling had again been to Venhaug and Felicia drove him to Kongsberg. She followed him inside to the ticket window and stood beside him when he bought a ticket to Lier. She watched the train until it was out of sight. Should she call up Lier tonight? No, that she couldn't. She had no acceptable excuse. Nor could she ask Julie to call. Erling would take it the same way regardless of who called from Venhaug. He might just say: I don't appreciate control-calls. If he was there. But he hardly would be. If he wasn't there she could do nothing. If he was there his voice would turn ice-cold and it might be a month or two before he showed up again. It was bad enough that she had followed him to the ticket window, indeed stupid; she had seen he had not the slightest doubt why, and of course he had bought a ticket to Lier.

Why had it hit him so unexpectedly? As a rule she could feel it in the air for two or three days in advance, and it had happened she had managed to avert it. When it came to full explosion she could only let him go. There were some things she didn't wish to have take place at Venhaug, and suddenly he would have disappeared anyway.

Early in the morning he had come over to New Venhaug; he had walked about restlessly, looking at the clock. Jan came in, threw a glance at Erling and walked out to Felicia in the kitchen. "Where is Julie?" he asked. "I think in her room," she said, and didn't look up. "Well, I suppose so," said Jan. He stood for a few minutes with his hands in his pockets, looking out in the yard.

Then he cleared his throat: "I noticed it as soon as I came in the door. You'll take care—"

"Of course," she said, without turning about.

At Drammen Erling did not change to the local but remained in his seat and bought a ticket to Oslo. A few weeks passed before he returned to Lier. Then he dragged himself heavily up the slope to his house. He was tired, cold, his feet hurt. His bag was heavy. He felt chilled and wondered dully why, since there was still a little summer in the air. He lit a fire, hurriedly as best he could, his joints stiff and aching.

He stood close to the fire to warm up a little while the water was coming to a boil on the stove. He felt like a ghost. In the mirror his face looked lined and gray. It had been bad, this time, and he was apprehensive of the demons he would meet. It was a good thing he was home.

It didn't feel like a sickness. He was empty. His teeth were of iron, his stomach a gravel pit. He supposed he should eat but the thought of food nauseated him. He wanted coffee but knew it would taste terrible. Sleep, sleep! Slowly he shuffled over to the bed, picked up a couple of blankets and hung them before the fire. He walked with infinite slowness to the corner and performed his trick with the secret cupboard. He took out a bottle of whisky and sat down at the fire. A warning voice almost shrieked inside him that he should turn off the stove and not wait for the water to boil.

He switched it off, returned to the fireplace, and sat down at the low table. He slumped down, feeling like death. The tall glass he emptied gave him an attack of heartburn and he shuffled over to the cabinet for a pill. It eased the burning immediately and he poured another glass. Like the first it lay in the stomach and had no effect. The whole time his nerves were tense at impending calamity. He knew he was on the brink of a delirium attack but felt gratified to think he would escape a cerebral hemorrhage. Walk the tightrope through the dark with the balance pole. Balance himself past the demon. Wasn't something moving back there in the corner near his cupboard, his secret liquor cabinet? Or inside the cabinet? He stared that way and stiffened: there stood a footstool. He had never seen it before. Was it there when he picked up the bottle? But he didn't have any such stool; a most ordinary stool at that.

Perspiration started to break out; then it struck him it must have been Felicia who had driven up and brought him the stool. How silly! He didn't need it. He felt a stab inside his head. He was walking slowly along a street and knew he must not make any sudden motions or turn his head. Only walk slowly and look down. Something rose up before him and remained hanging in the air at the same distance as he walked along; it reminded him of an old-fashioned barometer with clear black lines marking the degrees up to one hundred. The heaviness in his body was difficult to describe; he seemed to be filled right out to his skin with something heavy that had been poured into him and had congealed. It didn't hurt though, nor was the weight particularly uncomfortable. On the contrary, it gave him a feeling of showing off, not unlike carrying a log on one's shoulder, impressing people with one's ability to balance it. The barometer hung before him. The red indicator rose slowly toward one hundred. Only a few degrees were left. He watched it carefully. It stopped one millimeter below a hundred, and he read in black letters on a level with the top degree: *Delirium Tremens.* He was not afraid. Still—better walk slower.

The indicator trembled a little at the top. Quo vadis? he whispered for he dared not ask in Norwegian. No doubt about it; the indicator was sinking, only infinitesimally, but it was moving toward ninety-nine. His heart started to think by itself and whispered to him that his burden was too heavy. His head was heavy, too, but it balanced proudly. It bragged a little to itself: A good iron head! He moved cautiously over to a shop window so people might think he was interested in sanitary goods, like shiny pipes, cranes, a green bathtub, and four white toilets trademarked Niagara. But all the time he watched the barometer. He wasn't afraid for a moment, only interested, and it felt good to be interested in something. Good to have something happen again that could so thoroughly engross him. Wonder what a barometer of such strictly personal use, and a yard tall, might be called? Wasn't it called the alcohol-meter? Now it showed a fraction below ninety-nine.

He walked slowly to the next window, which displayed a wonderful collection of leather straps, riding quirts, handmade shoes. The alcohol-meter stood immobile in the air above an instrument of leather with a pair of round glass openings. It might be a pair of spectacles for an immense animal, a buffalo for example. The indicator reached exactly ninety-seven now. It was sinking, but very slowly. The next window offered spades, hayforks, a garden hose with sprayer, and other tools for people who poked about with flowers and vegetables. He noticed a pair of hedge-clippers with red-lead handles. The indicator hardly reached ninety-four. It struck him it must reach zero, or one, to show a person's decent condition. He walked on, crossed the street cautiously, and came to a cellar door with a sign *Wines;* he opened it and managed to get inside but yelled and screamed—he didn't want to see what he saw. He backed off and landed in something like clay that his feet got stuck in. It was better there but he was cold. There were several newspapers about and he read: The World Council of Churches has asked Billy Graham to come to Geneva in the middle of July to supply the chiefs of state of the Great Powers with a spiritual basis. Billy Graham has declared he is willing to accept the task.

He hung on to the chair, he must sleep, sleep; he poured himself another glass but his mouth hung open while he drank. It was cognac. He had thought—

It was a cognac bottle that stood on the table, and he felt relieved, for then it meant only that he was drunk; the liquor had worked after all. It was what is called an atypical drunk when bottles changed with contents and all. Pathological intoxication. Excessive liquor consumption. And what might Gustav call it? Elephantiasis, probably. Cholera.

He shook the bottle to see if it would vanish. It didn't. It was cognac. An unusual brand. He had never seen that label before. Probably some prussic acid had been mixed in, Felicia must have managed that, better call Venhaug and tell them all was progressing according to the program so she could stop worrying. It was nice of her to worry about him and think of him. Julie was the same way—

It was difficult to manage but he called Venhaug. Some talk about Jan having bought a motorcycle. He was sitting in the same place, drinking; he realized he hadn't called, after all. It jingled and then came Felicia's voice, it could be so deep, as it was now when she was serious: Are you at home, Erling?

At the same moment something grabbed at him. He turned violently and saw a gray shadow disappear into the floor. He started to shake.

He looked suspiciously around and replied: Well, as long as you ask. I believe I'm here in the house. Can't you find something for me, Felicia. I started the fire, it was so cold.

He thought a moment and added to the air: and so strange.

A bald dwarf with long tusks and narrow face was sitting back there on the stool. He looked at Erling and said with a sneer: Peder P. Helldale was born at Søndre Land October 30, 1769, and lived only a few minutes because the midwife had drunk a bottle of strong plum-liquor. The mother was a poor widow. Erling moved his lips but couldn't get anything across. The dwarf looked about the room and at the ceiling with an all-knowing grin: Olle Grøtterud from Rjukan, on March 27, 1931, jumped out of a window from the jail in Hønefoss and smashed himself flat. A post mortem indicated he must have fainted before he reached the pavement.

Erling realized it was Snorre* sitting there, wishing to tell him Norway's history. Cold sweat ran down his face and smelled obnoxious. Snorre went on without moving, only his lips moved a little around the long teeth that resembled knives and forks: You have prophesied in your brother's name. You are changelings, you two, but don't worry, Gustav doesn't want to change back.

Erling let out a howl and the little man wasn't there.

It's he who keeps poking in the cupboard, thought Erling.

He twisted an old newspaper and dried his face without realizing what a devilish appearance the printing ink gave him (it was something a demon had thought up to make him kneel in horror before the mirror half an hour later; Felicia had given him that mirror, but she only wished him evil). He sobered up a little. There was no stool in the corner. He looked at the crumpled paper. In a column that was still legible he read about Billy Graham word for word. It was the liquor-god who wasn't very smart today—all he could scare him with was happenings in the news.

The door opened—*the wrong way!* He cried out. It was the portal of hell when it opened the wrong way! The portal of hell was in his house in Lier.

A hell of a discovery, he thought suddenly, and looked about wide-eyed—but then there was something behind him. He yelled again, he wanted to get away, but couldn't get anywhere for there wasn't any anywhere. The door blew open the right way and in came six pallbearers with a coffin. They put something slippery and cold and living under his head and he yelled, but it was only placed there so he could watch the pallbearers and see what they were up to. They sat down at the table and ate the food they had brought with them. Each in turn drank from the bottle. One started to howl like a dog and a piece of bread dropped from his mouth, there was something about that bread—

All six assumed stiff iron-faces and whistled like dreary civil defense sirens. Someone had poisoned them and it was their death-song they were howling, they knew it by heart. They did not free Erling before they died, all six crawled on hands and knees out through the door and left the coffin behind. The piece of bread that had dropped from the mouth of the first howler started to move. It reached the edge of the table

---

* Snorri Sturluson, Icelandic historian and poet (1178–1241).

and fell to the floor and turned into something gray that dragged itself toward the coffin.

Erling was sitting in his chair. A fear so tremendous it would be impossible to endure seized something inside his head. How much was real of what took place? Would things always be mixed up from now on? Would he never be able to tell which of the happenings actually took place? The piece of bread emerged back there where the dwarf had been sitting; a bit of clammy, dirty, nasty bread, actually evil, disgusting bread, it dragged itself painfully back to the old chest which hadn't been there before, flattened out and squeezed under it, and became an eye that stared at him from under the chest. When he had a moment of reality—or what he desperately hoped was reality—and waited shakingly for new horrors, he could not control his inclination to investigate phenomena, and he thought: this is being registered while it takes place, exactly like dreams. How could consciousness take part in such, if it didn't also stop it? No, here was one observer who had nothing to say, one consciousness unable to rise to its own plane and call out: Get thee hence, Satan! Tears streamed down his cheeks, as something yellow, fluttering rose from the floor—is there no one to help me, I can't stand any more—

But in his lucid moments, which came like patches of blue in a stormy sky, he cursed and gritted his teeth like an epileptic. He didn't ask for any help, come what may; he would not give up, he would die if he gave up—and he started to yell again.

I have never in my life been afraid of anything, he thought, and pushed the matted hair back from his clammy forehead—with one exception: an insane person. Someone I knew to be crazy tried to get inside once, banged at the door and looked at me right through the wood, a man of flesh and blood I knew, a man with an honest name and a place to live in. Never have I been so terribly afraid as then. I am afraid of crazy people, not any others, not of anything else.

His thoughts went the compass round for comfort, for something to squelch the fear that might come, fear that his brain would rush off by itself, like a car on slippery ice. For a moment he tried to cling to the memory of a night's adventure in Stockholm with young Vera Poulsen, whose name now was Vera Arndt—forbidden territory—and he found a pleasant memory that brought rest. It had been early in spring, probably in the middle of April; at dusk he had sat down on the shore of Glommen, not far from Arnes. The evening was mild and light, a pungent fragrance rising from the earth. He ate from his lunch basket and drank warm coffee from the thermos. It tasted a little of metal. He took a drink afterwards and surrendered himself to the beautiful evening—

But the earth opened her mouth, he fell through and was in a land with a burning sun. Now I'm dying, he thought. But it was only something that had burst in his head and he had fainted, or perhaps gone to sleep. I'm dreaming, he whispered, you can't fool me, I'm getting well again, I'm lying here dreaming. He could have cried from gratitude when it felt as if the hunted brain might come to rest again. With great presence of mind he ordered his troops and hoped they wouldn't notice his being a little abnormal. The men couldn't find the rope to tie the girls' hands behind their backs in order to drive them to the slave market. He only had one long rope and that was too good to cut up. One must keep expenses down. The last shipment had been poor, pure swindle, and one must report it. Insulting to send such well-shaped samples to an experienced merchant like him who must realize at once that everything important was missing: there was no fizz to any of these lifeless girls, either front or back. Well, take this rope anyway, he said angrily, and tie them up in one bunch all together.

He hit them with the whip when they complained and then they stopped, even though the rope couldn't have hurt less because he whipped them.

At the market place he scratched his head. He was a clever man. Put all six of them on the block, he said, then they might impress through their numbers. Well, not so bad, if you were nearsighted. Has anyone seen stupider heads? Turn your backs, all of you! he yelled out.

He examined one of them a little closer once more. It might be sufficient to examine one carrot of six, all alike. What's your name? She giggled and said her name was Viktoria.

As if that would be of any help, he grunted. Turn around!

She had a sort of beauty, like the others. A synthetic sort. Perfect in appearance, but without gunpowder. He shook his head and cracked his whip irritably while he took inventory: breasts and hips right, shoulders good, back satisfactory, behind fine. Worth looking at from all angles, all equally boring. Arms and legs cheap, glossy standard type. Face tries to look attractive, framed with blond, common hair, ordinarily put up. The stupid asses even thought it would be enough to have a hairdresser fix them. Well, he thought absent-mindedly (he had just sold a few suckling-pigs), one needn't offer them for breeding purposes, but skinny as they were and raised for a different purpose they wouldn't bring in much if sold by weight either. And the high taxes and one thing and another.

He sat down on an empty box and eyed the collection disapprovingly. If he could only sell them the way they stood, with their backs to the customer. But buyers always wanted to turn things and find faults. There wasn't a thing they refrained from putting their noses into, and in his line there would be no object in hanging up a sign: Merchandise Must Not Be Touched.

He concentrated again on the carrot farthest to the right, the one who bore the artistic name Viktoria. Viktoria, indeed! *Sieg heil!* Her name could be changed, of course—no, no use, they always took such curious names, they had so little liberty, and too little sense to use it. He recalled with annoyance how in his younger days he had been cheated by an old merchant who had said that in the dark all cats were gray. He had quickly been cured of that delusion.

Aside from some inconsequential minor differences all six were exactly alike, a source of pride to girls of that sort. He could confine his melancholy appraisal to Viktoria. Well, the sack might be good enough, but nothing in it, he couldn't get away from that. No cat in there. Someone ought to invent something to give a spoiled product that little spark, the life, the aura. Silly—he sat here growing lyrical as the Koran from pure shame. That one there had looked at him as she had seen the others do. It was a disgusting sight. He didn't understand these modern times. with mass production among the girls, this destructive rationalization. It was different when he was young. Now they could obtain all sorts of spare parts for Adam's rib, but lacking the paradisiacal fragrance of manifold delicious fruit. Girls without topsails (in his youth he had been a great seafarer) and no evening wind in the shifts.

People came and looked at the prices of his merchandise; they had no faults to find, but once they had stated this they walked off. Later in the day Erling climbed up on the block with the girls and removed from their backs the price tags they had hanging in a string around the waist. Anyway, he must try something else, people would climb up on the block and lift the tags to see if they were hiding birthmarks. He cut the price in two and put up a sign: Close-Out Sale. Then he sat down on the box again and drank a mouthful of beer. Still business was slow, and the price was slashed further, for he couldn't keep those girls to feed, nor could he starve them, that made them look so sulky, and he couldn't whip them to make them look happy. Fortunately, at last he got rid of five of them to some underpaid office-workers, and Viktoria stood alone. She shivered and had goose pimples from inferiority feelings, when the sun set. The other merchants were taking down their tents and people were returning home to beat up their wives, but look! there comes finally

Steingrim Hagen walking across the square. And he bought Viktoria at bottom price and got the rope in the bargain. He thought she might get the idea of running away.

Erling had raised his hand to stroke his long beard, but it wasn't there—look! the damper stood ajar, a fumbling hand emerged with long emaciated fingers. It felt about for something along the fireplace wall, next to the damper, but couldn't find it and withdrew. Nebuchadnezzar was on the 'phone. A Spaniard came in and stooped over a stone on the floor to sharpen his knife, while staring at Erling. He had Felicia's eyes when she rose and soundlessly approached him in her low-heeled shoes. Erling started to yell again. A naked foot protruded slowly from under the blankets on the bed; he wanted to hide behind the blankets hanging before the fire, but he was unable to move, could only yell and howl—

He wept helplessly as he saw Steingrim climb in through a window at New Venhaug, he himself standing impotently in the yard. Steingrim had a knife between his teeth—but Felicia only laughed inside. Now he noticed it was whisky standing on the table and he wondered dejectedly if he could manage to get into bed before anything more happened. He took the bottle with him, reached the bed, and took off like a rider in the night for three long, bloodcurdling days.

• No regrets

Pale and hollow-eyed Erling picked up the telephone and called his friend Øystein Myhre. "How are the finances, Øystein?"

"What's the matter, Erling?"

"Can you let me have a couple of hundred?"

"What is it? I can hear something is wrong."

"Nothing much."

Øystein sighed. "Well, well—I saw you in town a few times."

"I've had an attack."

"How long?"

"What day is it today, Øystein?"

Øystein whistled and said, "You're at home then? It's Thursday."

"I can't leave the house, Øystein. Can you manage to send me the money?"

After a short pause Øystein replied, "No, Erling, I don't want to send the money with someone else. I have the car today and I'll come up to Lier myself. O.K.?"

"That suits me very well—only, it doesn't look too good here. Things are broken and—"

"Who has been with you?"

"I think I've been alone."

"Will you promise to stay put 'til I come—in a couple of hours?"

"It is entirely out of the question for me to go anywhere. I must owe whoever brought me home, if I didn't pay for the taxi in advance. It stinks of liquor—the bottles I didn't empty I must have crushed with a hammer. Could you bring me a little red wine?"

"I will."

"You know—for tapering off."

"I understand. Go to bed until I get there."

• Into Felicia's world

Julie Vik, or Julie Venhaug as people in the neighborhood mostly called her, kept a great deal to herself, but she did not feel lonely. During the first years she had slavishly imitated Felicia, but how much had stayed with her of her older friend's point of view was of course impossible to tell. One could not get away from the fact that she had accepted most of Felicia's opinions as her own, but assuredly it would be a mistake for her to think that she knew everything that concerned Felicia Venhaug.

Felicia was in the habit of thinking aloud, and too clearly. When alone with Julie she always did so, and this might lead Julie to believe nothing was hidden; it seemed to the younger woman Felicia held back nothing.

What Julie heard she absorbed like a fairy tale, almost her own. Her father was dissected and described—a rare experience for daughters, who generally hear such only from a mother intent on blackening a hated mate. Here it was done in a way that made the daughter like her father so much better because of his faults. She never doubted that Felicia was deeply in love with Erling, but it was difficult for her to accept a relationship so contrary to established rules for love and marriage. She hoped one day to be married herself and could not reconcile herself to a marriage such as Felicia's.

It was a fairy tale she heard. She learned subconsciously how an oral tradition is created and almost word for word is handed down to a later generation. Felicia was not averse to repetition and thus Julie heard the same happening many times, and incidents also were repeated in other connections.

She still felt dazzled with the world she had been permitted to look into, as unlike the one she had known as a city in flames is unlike a burning rubbish-heap. It made her proud and inspired self-confidence—but since she was a wise girl it also evoked her critical appraisal—that this woman, so far removed from anything she had been able to imagine in her confused surroundings, could confide in her because she was fond of her and in love with her father. She could never rid herself of the hope that Felicia would turn out to be her mother, and that that other horrible mother was someone who had been paid to assume the shame because Felicia had only been seventeen or eighteen and had such a severe father. It was through Felicia's eyes she saw the world, and with a much calmer temperament. In her looks she was strikingly like her father and resembled him also in other ways. But in the important traits of her character it didn't seem as though she would ever take after him. At least Felicia didn't think so.

Julie might sit with her work and repeat to herself all Felicia had told her, in the same way as teen-agers have their favorite poet; or she might feel that she herself was a part of it and had experienced all:

"Mother died the day before I was ten, and after that it was always as if I had become a mother to Harald and Bjørn. It bothered me to hear it for I had always dreamed of being a boy. I would have preferred to be one of my brothers but I could never decide if it should be Harald or Bjørn. Harald was almost exactly two years younger than I, but Bjørn was only one year younger than his brother. Sometimes I felt it would be silly to be Bjørn for then I would be one year younger than Harald, but then again it might be nice to be his little sister. At other times I thought it would be nice to be Harald and act the good big brother to Bjørn. In that way my love went in waves, and I couldn't rid myself of my daydreams until I met Erling. From then on it was only something half-forgotten about an old love.

"Harald and Bjørn became fast friends when seventeen or eighteen or thereabouts. Of course they had always been friends, but before that time they would get into the worst fights with each other. As young men they always stuck together, and when they first dated they found girls who were close friends, and paired off in greatest harmony. That foursome used to spend many evenings in our home. I remember how it annoyed me that I was treated as some sort of an aunt; a girl turns older than her years when she has young brothers; she should have a big brother to make her feel young. Perhaps girls subconsciously fall in love with their fathers to gain something called eternal youth; it's said to be quite natural, and that explanation might be as good as others that have been invented. Obviously it was quite ridiculous that I became jealous of those two girls. They didn't take anything from me and they were not the worst the boys could have found.

"There was no doubt but that Father wanted them as daughters-in-law and this added to my discomfort. Yet, I realized all was as it ought to be. They were daughters of people he knew, well-to-do like himself. The father of one was a doctor, the other belonged to that mysterious profession called businessman. But after one year the whole thing came to an end in a dramatic mess, and each one of the four soon found consolation with someone else. Father said nothing, he seldom said anything, but it was easy to see that he felt a little uncomfortable with two new girls flirting in the house. People said he had aged when Mother died but I have no memory of that. To me he was always the same, to the very day he died, late in the fall of 1940. He was a little stooped and had a face like a friendly wolf. As far back as I can remember I had loved him terribly and unhappily. I felt so sorry for him I would sit and cry by myself when I thought of him. I couldn't imagine my father ever had been happy. And it does sound a little strange that he started to age when only about thirty-four, but many people have told me so. According to my information, that is when a man should be in his prime; he has his desire and his humanity well balanced, and he has passed the age which Kinsey records as most ruttish, yet has a mature heart. But things are always out of line when a person isn't viewed as a whole. To me a man halfway between thirty and the dangerous forties is always in full bloom. Then he has the world by the tail as never before and never again, however much he may think he can improve with the aid of position, money, influence, and power. It is a dangerous age for him if he is weak in the head: his horoscope has been drawn, all experienced people can see what he is good for—or not. Women ponder him from a wider angle than before, as male, as an ornament in society, as a triumph over other women, as a prospect for the future. If he misjudges what is happening to him and forgets that this age is a period of trial, then he is in for a rough punishment. I think a thunderbolt killed Martin Leire when he had wasted his gifts. It may be unjust but it's tempting to look at it that way.

"After all these years, Father and Mother would by now only be sixty-four and sixty-three years old. The last picture I have of Mother was taken in 1926, the year before she died, and there she looks a woman much younger than I am today, a woman who never was anything but young. My wish that I could have known her grows stronger every year. I read once that even parallel lines must meet somewhere in infinite space.

She stayed in people's thoughts and they talked about her, and eventually they talked to me, and her stature grew. Her pictures show a superior woman with great kindness—my eyes fill with tears each time I look at them, these feeble reminders of something that is so close to me night and day. She is not dead. It is incomprehensible that I don't remember her in any other way, don't retain the slightest memory of ever having seen her. And I was ten when she passed on.

"On the contrary I have a clear memory of Father, who was robbed of his courage to live when he lost her. He never said so in so many words, or perhaps he felt there was nothing to say. Nor was he a great talker. There was a mixture of melancholy and banter in his brown eyes, and occasionally but very rarely he expressed himself with dry humor, especially if he felt someone exaggerated. He was moderate in everything. Only once did I hear him repeat what might be called a joke, and that was on his deathbed when he knew the end was near. He desired to speak with his lawyer, who came at once in his car, so fast I realized he must have run away from whatever he was busy with. Then Father fought a desperate battle with fever and unclear thoughts; there was something he hadn't brought up to date in his will—it was a last and desperate effort for his three children, but he made no provisions that interfered with our freedom of action. When all was over Father adjusted himself for the last time in his bed and said to the lawyer: 'Now Lie, I expect you to plead for me when you follow.'

"I am sure Henrik Lie will do so, but he is still with us. I was told how devoted I had been to Mother and how they were apprehensive about me when I was told she was dead, and that makes it even more difficult to understand how she completely vanished from me within a year. I can feel her presence and something tries to come to life when I look at her pictures—then I sense the shadow of a great sorrow, not mine, another sorrow than my own. She comes so close she completely envelops me, and I might be seized with a terrible fear that she no longer is, that I can't recall her face, never remember her voice that was said to be so beautiful. In the pictures I can see her clear, big eyes and what might be called a sensuous mouth. She looks at me as if she wished simultaneously to reproach me and forgive me for having forgotten her. She was only thirty-three when she died; Father lived to be forty-seven. Mother died of pneumonia, which in those days still was quite dangerous, Father from some sickness in the blood which they hoped to cure to the last, but he suddenly grew very feeble and died in a couple of weeks. I had expected it, after the Germans came. He didn't have much resistance. I think hopelessness got him that day in April; he felt he didn't care any longer after that. He would stand stooped at the window and look at the German soldiers marching by. Then he would shake his head slowly as old people might do at a grave where a young person is being buried who had to leave first.

"When I was fourteen, Father considered getting married again, but no one mentioned it and for a long time there was nothing exactly to indicate it. But a woman of fourteen feels such things in the air. One evening Father brought the lady home. Harald and Bjørn greeted her courteously and withdrew to their wild-west stories; I noticed them throwing glances at her on the sly. I was supposed to act sociable, and I felt at an immense disadvantage. I would never be able to compete with this strong, beautiful woman. I was shaken as one might be after a bad accident, and fought my strong impulse to rush up and throw my arms around her neck and cry, but also to shout and to hurl things at her, a cup or a pot or anything. Point for point the same thing was repeated three years later when Cecilie Skog took Erling from me.

"I'll never forget Harald's crushed look when Father introduced her as Mrs. Haraldstad. Mrs. Sissel Haraldstad.

"I knew in that moment as sure as the sun shines, I would forever remember Mrs. Haraldstad's face, even if I never saw her again, but *not my dead mother's face.*

"*That* would forever be denied me, but I would remember the face of Sissel Haraldstad.

"And so it has remained. Two women have cut me out, Sissel Haraldstad and Cecilie Skog and to this day I am afraid of them; I shudder when I happen to recall them. They appear in my sleep and laugh at me.

"Many times the eyes of this lady happened to fall on us, the two silent boys and myself. One single time when she looked at me I realized she said a great many things to me with those eyes. Today I know it was mostly of me she was thinking—that she with her experience could read me like an open book and that her eyes said: Why not do it, Felicia? I cannot push myself onto *you* in your father's house.

"Father walked with her to the station, telling us he would come right back. This he did, too, but not until they had had time to talk it over. Only a few minutes after they left, Harald and Bjørn went to their rooms without saying anything. They never mentioned the evening later, and I believe I knew them well enough to say they didn't say anything to each other either.

"I pretended I was reading the newspaper when Father returned. He walked about the room aimlessly for a few moments, then he pulled out his keys and opened the liquor cabinet. 'I'll take a crutch,' he said. It was something he did seldom. Father was very moderate, like Jan. 'You want to get me a glass and the soda, Felicia?' he asked so kindly my eyes filled with tears. I realized I had cut out the stranger-woman.

"He mixed a grog and I noticed it was dark brown; its usual color was light brown and sparkling, and I wondered why the difference. He replaced the bottle and locked the cabinet, because our maid—she was nearly sixty and we had inherited her from an old widow who had died—could not control herself when the cabinet was left unlocked. When she first came to us, shortly after Mother's death, she would sometimes get drunk. Then she acted like an old gypsy reviving her stormy, youthful days. Otherwise she was quiet and capable. Father took it mildly the first time, not quite so mildly the second, and the following day he pointed out to her that his particular brand of cognac was rather expensive. He always attacked a problem sideways like a crab. Elvira broke down and asked permission to sit down, and during tears and sobs she admitted she could not leave it alone: 'But it isn't as bad with me as you think, Mr. Ormsund. It's only that I need the crutch of the cabinet being locked,' she sobbed.

"She was right, and from that day a drink in our house was always a crutch. But Elvira must often have tried the cabinet door, for twice she found it unlocked, and then the mess started all over again. Elvira danced for us and announced jubilantly that it was Mr. Ormsund's own fault. She was overjoyed because now she need feel no shame the following day. I always think of Elvira when Erling drinks more than is good for him, but he doesn't get happy like Elvira.

"Father sipped his dark grog and said nothing until the glass was nearly empty. Then he raised it with the last few drops, and I could see from his moist eyes it had taken effect: 'Skol, my Felicia!' he said and smiled. 'We'll always manage, we four.'

"I cried almost the whole night through, and afterwards I felt like a criminal. In a way I still do, but time lightens the imprint of one's own evil deeds also. Now that I am the same age as Father was then I realize more clearly than ever how older people might wither under the tyranny of children and youths. Has she thought of me and perhaps hated me? Does she hate the one she stepped aside for, but who never herself showed any such consideration? Does she know of me today, does she sit at a window when I am in Oslo and follow me with her eyes? Does she muse, there goes Felicia Ormsund Venhaug who was so mean she begrudged her father being a man—and how hasn't the covetous Felicia grabbed for herself?

"There is so much I have learned since I grew up, about Father and Mother. I've been obliged to think how very much Jan's and my marriage is a repetition of theirs. All of us children took after Mother we were told.

"Not that Father and Jan are alike. They are as unlike as two men of the same race could be, and Father would turn in his grave if he knew I had married a man who spoke a dialect. Yet he was broadminded and perhaps he would have been pleased to learn it was too late to throw me out.

"One wintry night I returned from Old Venhaug, the snow crunching underfoot; earlier there had been a new moon, it had set now, but it was half-light with snow and stars. I felt warm and joyous in the crisp air, and when I reached the cozy sitting room at New Venhaug I had no desire to go to bed although it was after two in the morning. I found some cigarettes and a glass of wine and sat down in front of the fire; I happened to sit facing the two large pictures of my brothers. First my thoughts lingered for some time on my arrival at Venhaug—November 3, 1945. I recalled Jan's expectant and perhaps a little nervous smile as he stood there waiting for me to say something—would I maybe not find it good enough? Now it is almost impossible for me to recall how I felt, standing there with our sleeping child in my arms, looking about the sitting room of Old Venhaug. But I had a feeling that many generations of dead ancestors were accepting me; I had a feeling of security and assurances with all these faces of the ancient family watching me, having gathered for just this purpose. 'You smile so nicely, Felicia—can't you put the brat down some place?' said Jan. That was the welcome that scamp of a father gave his first-born, and then she was laid in an old love-seat, and I was laid on an ancient sofa that never had been constructed for so reasonable a use; it was so comical and so beautiful that it has been worth remembering, even though we never tried to do it on that sofa again. It's the only time I've heard Jan swear. He doesn't usually swear and carry on like Erling, nor is it in his nature to use the bawdiest words in the language in the heat of passion. I must say Erling's erotic lyrics are not intended for children's books.

"I sipped my wine and looked from one of my brothers to the other where they hung and watched me from their portraits. Harald had picked up the nickname The Pious One, and as Bjørn was interested in metalwork he was called The Blacksmith. Harald had really chosen his own because I used that name for him; I don't think he was particularly pious but he wanted to specialize in religious history. 'I have for sons a religious historian and a blacksmith,' my father used to say with his tired smile, but I don't think this implied any disappointment that neither of his sons was to carry on his work. He would never have dreamed that I might do so, and the subject was not even broached; I was afraid I might see first his surprise and then his forgiving smile. I knew only too well I was just a daughter in the house—I studied, yes, but only as a pretense; I would one day marry someone, or become plain Aunt Felicia. He was that way in his thinking, and it was quite out of the question to oppose him—even when he had said nothing."

It was obvious this was something that had bothered Felicia.

"While I sat there looking at the portraits and sipping my wine a strange feeling took hold of me that Erling and Jan were standing behind my chair and also looking at the portraits. I didn't turn though, because I knew so well they weren't there.

"It struck me that I had never known any men who were younger than myself except Harald and Bjørn. Yes, it struck me, yet it was something I had always felt and known. I had never felt younger than my father, nor younger than the teachers in school or the older pupils. I knew people my own age, like Erling and Jan, but no younger acquaintances or friends.

"But didn't I, now? Didn't I have my own children, as well as Erling's young daughter? No, a calm voice replied within me, you know no younger persons except those two dead ones. All others are your contemporaries.

"Isn't there then anyone who is *older* than myself? No, I couldn't think of a single person older than myself either.

"I felt this so strongly and as something I had always known that I must try to analyze my fantasies a little closer. It was a sort of exciting search for something inside my head—a search for the key to my own life.

"I heard a floor board creak in the upstairs hall and then someone coming down the steps. It must be Gudny who wanted a bite to eat; it wasn't unusual for her to come down to the larder at night. But it was Jan, in his slippers and pyjamas, his hair ruffled.

" 'I was awake and felt you were sitting here,' he said, and pushed his fingers through his hair. He saw me look at the portraits and asked, 'Am I disturbing you?'

"I fetched some wine for him because he sleeps so well on a glass of wine; I had to tell him about my strange sensation concerning Erling and himself while sitting there looking at the pictures. He took a sip of wine and said, 'I had thought something of the sort.'

"I dared not look at him. I didn't know what he had thought, or what he was thinking now, but something was implied in those words. I knew also I had had the same experience with him many times before—not concerning the same thing as now, whatever it might be—but this: that Jan knew more about myself than I did. Strange though, it had never made me feel uncomfortable with him; on the contrary, it had inspired in me a feeling of security, of being at home with Jan. He has also been aware of things I thought were my deep secrets, and it sounds paradoxical but it has made me cry in joy. With Erling I have never encountered anything similar. When Erling thinks he has discovered something— mostly wrong—then he becomes insistent and annoying like a policeman who must force a confession from somebody. More than once I have wished to tell him to mind his own business. Leave me alone, I've thought—have *you* any right to plague me?

"Once there was something I wanted to say to Jan and I found him alone in the barn, grinding turnips for the cows, sweating and turning the crank; some of the help were sick with influenza. He wore dirty overalls and a handkerchief on his head with a knot in each corner.

"He sat down on a box and looked at me. He brushed away some dirt from his face and said quietly, 'Better not tell me, Felicia.'

"I can't imagine that he knew what I had in mind. He couldn't have known. Then I talked of other matters I hadn't intended to take up with him, and we walked over and looked at a calf that had been born during the night—I had been up to see about it myself. It was dry now and perky even though it didn't as yet quite know how to use four legs. We talked some more and he gave me a hug before I left, and it turned out that his judgment had been right: I shouldn't have told him. What surprises me is not so much that he is that way, rather that I, so self-willed, find myself liking it. I have seldom felt so happy as once when he and I went bathing in a pool at Lagen and he carried me like a child to the edge. It was so wonderful that only for a moment could I get up any anger when he unexpectedly threw me into the water which was very cold.

"I was staring into the embers of the fireplace and did not wish to ask. By and by I will understand what he means, I thought, I nearly always do. Yet, I was so anxious to ask the question that I brought up something quite different: 'What made you think I was sitting here?'

"He had kicked off his slippers and was studying his toes. He has quite ordinary toes.

" 'You might at times say a *little* more than you do, Jan.'

" 'Yes, but—but these matters are only inconsequentials,' he said in surprise. 'I couldn't sleep. Then I went into your room since I couldn't sleep alone, and then—well, you weren't there. I went back to bed, and then I heard you here, and so I came down here. Have I left out any of the details, Felicia?'

" 'Don't make me start crying, you devil!'

"He rose and shuffled out of the room. I heard a vague jingle and he came back with a whisky-grog. It was dark brown. So unlike him. Absent-mindedly he drank from the glass a few times, without saying anything, but I could see the liquor had affected him—he is not accustomed to drinking. He leaned his head back and poured down the last of the drink—and started laughing at me. He plain and simple laughed at me. Then he said in his most ordinary voice: 'Now stop your vigil below those pictures for tonight, Felicia. It's almost half-past three and I see you're getting cold.'

"I followed him up the stairs like an ashamed schoolgirl, and I have never more closely relived my experience of twenty-three years ago with Erling, that evening when he and I walked up a staircase.

"It is the only time Jan has ever frightened me; he took me like a soldier in a sacked town who rushes in with his weapons, stomping through the house in his creaking boots until he finds the girl in the last room."

• Japanese water color

In the evening Erling retired to Old Venhaug early. A little later Felicia yawned and put away her sewing. She was tired, and said she was going to bed. Soon one could hear the faint sound of water running into her tub. Jan went upstairs and to bed in his own room; he usually took his bath when his work was finished.

Felicia emerged naked from the bathroom and tripped on tiptoe along the broad hall to her own room. Quickly she fluttered her nightdress over her head and crept contentedly into bed but felt a little annoyed as she dozed off because she was letting sleep displace such a feeling of well-being. She started at once to dream she was walking through a summer spruce-wood where it smelled of pitch and the sun warmed her skin. She stretched backward a little as she walked, thrusting out her breasts and gaining an even balance. How lovely to be only twenty and walk about naked in Japan. All the Japanese were at work, poor devils; on such a beautiful day they ought to have been with her in the forest, enjoying themselves. Something tickled her left hand; she stopped and noticed a blister was forming, and then the skin parted pleasantly and a brown-fried fish poked its head out. She took it by the gills and pulled it out, it felt so remarkably pleasant, but she couldn't think what to do with a fried trout in the middle of the morning. Dubiously she put it down in the green grass and continued as before. The forest opened up and in the distance to the right lay Fujiyama with its sharp yet soft lines. The sky had turned bluer and seemed higher now that Jan had managed to make the Russians and the Americans agree to raise it. It had also been such a beautiful day when the telephone rang and God asked if he might speak to Jan for a moment.

The crater of the volcano was tilted so she could see into the oval opening and the light pillar of smoke that rose. People were known to have climbed the sides of Fujiyama, but no one had continued to climb up the smoke pillar and sit on it. Except possibly Jan. She laughed until she shook. To see him, shy as he was, sitting on top of the smoke pillar over Fujiyama in his new fine suit and with a hat on his head.

She felt ashamed and blushed a little at having laughed at Jan in Japan—and at the foot of a holy mountain at that. Always one did the wrong thing. She walked down to a tempting brook and lay down in the lovely grass at the edge, first on her back, then on her stomach, then on her back again. One must make sure one tanned evenly, she thought, and was reminded of the brown-fried trout. A moose bull came down from Fujiyama. He stood across from her on the other shore, watched her before he lowered his head to drink the clear water. Then he raised his head again. From his lips water dripped down into the streaming brook. Felicia thought it was strange she wasn't afraid of such a big moose bull, standing there only a few yards from her, and she having no clothes on, and then she blushed. It must be unfeminine not to be afraid. She tried to but didn't succeed. The bull winked at her with one eye. The old sinner's flirting—for he must be an old sinner—was so ridiculous she could laugh herself to death, she kicked up her heels and laughed at the dear old gardener who had told her so many new and interesting stories she couldn't go to sleep that night but only think about how kind he was and that she must become a gardener. Here he stood and touched her so pleasantly, and it was indeed pleasant, then, to be fourteen. All the birds fluttered up from her body and played in the air. She felt the wind from their wings on her breasts and the air glittered with hummingbirds, but she must have been naughty, she had laughed at Jan in Japan. The moose bull made a flying jump across the brook and she tried to yell but it only turned into muffled lowing and she awakened. A surprise dawned on her: of course she had yelled, but it had been a false alarm, plain cheating: she had almost burst from joy when the bull started to jump, and then, unfortunately, she had been awakened by her own hypocritical cry.

She turned on the light and sat up in bed. Her conscience bothered her that she could lie alone and enjoy herself so much. She had been aware of Jan being shy when she said good night to him. And she hadn't taken the hint because she was tired. Shy Jan—after fifteen years! *Tired* and *tired*—she had had strength enough to go to a movie in Japan, in a way, and alone, and had imagined she was twenty.

Felicia rose and rinsed her mouth before she stole out through the hall and to Jan. He was in bed reading a book which he let drop when he saw her. She noticed how he squinted a little, a reaction she recognized so well in him when he was pleased.

She put away his book and wormed herself into bed: "Do you know, Jan, I can still blush. I have blushed twice tonight. Could you imagine that?"

"No."

"And then I've been to Japan and laughed at a moose who came down from Fujiyama and thought he was something. He winked with his right eye and so I didn't notice the other one. He reminded me of someone and then I realized it was the old gardener at Slemdal, the one with the birds—"

She stopped suddenly.

"There is another gardener who is more real," said Jan presently.

Felicia stiffened. But she must say something, find something to say, anything, otherwise he would wonder—if he didn't already know—

In her agitation she dared not speak.

Jan must not have noticed anything for he said calmly, "I get a little angry when he looks at you that way. I almost feel an urge to ask him to control himself. I have seen him stare at you like a beast in heat."

She exhaled cautiously.

"I think he is a really disgusting character," said Jan, "and no one knows what goes on inside him. But if something ever gets into his wooden head it stays there. He was a tool during the war . . . . There is something about him I don't like. When he came here in 1945, then things were different—but . . . . Well, I don't think I would have let him come a month later. And the contract he got then was too advantageous to him—it doesn't make much difference to us by now, but there it is."

Felicia coughed a little to try her voice. "What is it mainly you have against him?"

"I don't know what to say. He does what he is supposed to do. Always has. You know I approve of people I don't have to keep telling what I expect. I'm sick of people who can't perform according to agreement but have to be constantly reminded. You remember that dairy worker we had."

Yes, Felicia remembered him. It's hard on the nerves to repeat each morning what must be done during the day. One morning when the hungry livestock made such a noise it sounded as if the barn were on fire, Jan had told him to leave on the instant. Enough was enough. Furiously he had paid his full wages, feeling this was the simplest and cheapest way.

"I've never had to tell Tor Anderssen a single thing," he said. "But I wish he weren't there."

Jan put his hands behind his head and looked at the ceiling: "Sometimes there are things one knows but can't do anything about. I would like to get rid of Tor Anderssen. He has never had a woman and he exudes rape. He is puritanism's farthest outpost."

Jan started, and listened. "What was that?" asked Felicia, and listened, too. "I thought—"

Jan slid out of bed and walked soundlessly toward the door. She saw his firm body from behind and thought how strong he was, a man of iron. He opened the door, looked down the hall, and listened. Then he ran with spring-like steps to the staircase and down.

He returned but stood a moment, naked, in the open door and looked once more down the hall. "Hm," he said, "I could have sworn—"

He closed the door and came back to bed. "It must be that the house is so new—it still keeps laboring, still talking to itself."

She could see he wasn't convinced, but at last he seemed to forget. She lay close to him and noticed how he slid into rest. Jan worked hard from the moment he arose in the morning until he went to bed. He liked hard work. And because of this he could hardly keep awake once in bed. He had been reading when she came in; he must have been expecting her, then. She smiled as she watched him go to sleep. When she was with him she never left until he was asleep. She never tired of seeing him go to sleep. She could not tell why every time it was equally nice and peaceful to see Jan sink into sleep. Anyway, it was among the most wonderful things she knew.

It might happen that he came in to her, but only very seldom, almost never. He had been looking for her the other evening. It had been many months since the time before. Always I must—

She ceased her caresses, waited a moment, and pulled herself silently from the bed, walked out into the hall and closed the door behind her. Inside the door of her own room she stood for a moment and looked at each individual object before she closed the door behind her. Once more she inspected her belongings on the bedside table, before she opened cabinets and drawers. She remained staring down into one drawer. She knew where her things were and noticed at once what was missing. She locked the door and went to bed.

While she made herself comfortable in bed, Jan quickly passed her door, hugging the wall in order to avoid creaking floor boards. He used the same technique as when he approached animals at play—to get where he wanted while the one not supposed to hear drowned out other sounds. He walked down the steps, listened again at the bottom one. Without striking a light he crossed the room and felt if the veranda door was locked. It was, the key on the inside. Then he felt window after window in the whole house, and at last the kitchen door. All were closed and locked from inside. Once before this evening he had made the same inspection, with the same result. He stood silently in the darkness and pondered. Long ago a problem had arisen which appeared insoluble. Had Felicia also thought of it, but kept silent about it? *How* was it possible there was a thief in the house and for many years now they had been unable to catch him in the act, or even discover who he was? In a way Felicia could be forgiven, for she had suspected Julie and her mind stopped *there*. Jan was inclined to agree with Felicia, but he wanted to know, not only think he knew.

Jan was unsentimental; he told himself there were only two at Venhaug it could not be, namely himself and Erling. Rarely, very rarely, did more than two weeks pass without something disappearing. Even though Erling was quite clever he could not sit at Blom's in Oslo or at home in Lier and steal from them at Venhaug. And it could not be any one of the servants for they did not stay at Venhaug at night. If it had been any one among them, he or she would long ago have been caught in one of Jan's many traps. There remained only four—Julie, Felicia, and the two little girls. To Jan it seemed equally bad whichever one was the culprit. Felicia? Jan was not blind to Felicia's diversity. If she experienced any of the black-outs she suspected in Julie (Jan felt sure Felicia never would do it with a clear head) then she would have a motive strong enough to blame Julie.

• Vigdis

Jan was twenty when he fell in love with Vigdis Lauge, who was of the same age as he and the daughter of a shopkeeper in Kongsberg. They met one evening when there was a dance in the barn at one of Venhaug's neighbors. She was living for the summer with her parents and two of their younger children at an abandoned cotter's place belonging to that farm. Guest-Haug it was called and had, according to tradition, once belonged to Venhaug.

Already during the first dance Vigdis complained because she could not anticipate any real summer vacation when she must look after her brother and sister constantly. The parents spent a great deal of time in Kongsberg taking care of the shop; then she had to work for three. Jan sympathized with her courteously, but after five minutes' acquaintance he noticed her turn sulky when he made the mistake of asking her if it could be such heavy work to look after a sister of seventeen and a brother of fifteen. Couldn't they more or less take care of themselves? He soon discovered that there was some truth in her summer being ruined and what part the children played in this: she was ruining her disposition by picking on them and trying to make them wait on her. Moreover, when her harassed mother wasn't there to wait on her she might have to lift her hand herself. Vigdis destroyed everything around her and terrorized everyone. The younger children were in revolt and paid back in the same coin; they took care of themselves. She could do the same or shut up. The power she once had had slipped through her fingers, and this she could never forgive. Two years later Jan realized he ought to have fallen for the younger sister, but by then he had turned philosophical and it was Vigdis he remembered. It had turned out as it often does with the first hot love: he never forgot her completely. She remained a long-ago picture of youth and light summer nights that clung to some deep corner of his heart. It was a severe blow to him when the affair broke up, but he couldn't forever sit and mope over it—and he began to run after other girls as a sort of distraction. Besides it is embarrassing for anyone to be so terribly unhappy.

In the beginning it had been with him as with most young men in that situation—there were no visible faults; later one might discover some unfortunate trait, later still, many more; and then the whole thing bursts, and it appears she had nothing but shortcomings. After not seeing her for a long time, and meanwhile discovering there are other girls in the world, the whole episode settles, and she becomes a woman one used to know once. Four or five years later Vigdis was living in Kongsberg, married to a railroad man, and Jan had heard she was happy—or could have been. The fly in the ointment was that she would remind her husband time and again that she could have been mistress at Venhaug had she been so inclined.

Jan wasn't so sure of this; her disdain of farmers had been obvious. They had no shops, it might be far to a movie. Fortunately it had been dark when she suggested that perhaps some time in the future they might dispose of Venhaug. Jan still shook his head at the memory. Only after stupid Vigdis discovered it would not have been a social disgrace had she married the heir to Venhaug did she boast she could have had him. By now he realized that had she happened to come to Venhaug she would forever have held the disgrace over him. Once when he and Felicia were waiting for the bus he had espied her ogling Felicia (stupidity never stays young! it had struck him). It was a stare filled with gaping hatred. He quickly looked in another direction, reflecting that he had always escaped the worst disasters. He felt her thoughts like an announcement on the bus's timetable—if they could be called thoughts: this Felicia Ormsund who had become a farm-wife in spite of her good looks and elegance, how stupid of her with a big house in Oslo and money, plenty of money people said, enough money without that big house, such a shame, the way she carried on and put on airs out here, when she could have gone to the theater whenever she wished and could have married anyone she had wanted, and then to marry a farmer, so far out in the country, far away even from Kongsberg, and far too young for Jan Venhaug, though really she wasn't so young, at that.

Felicia had been interested in some children playing about them, and now she said, "Silly how some women never learn the simple trick of staring at people without staring at them. Did you notice that fat woman over there on the corner? One would think the most common wench would learn how to act in youth—and she must be at least fifty-five."

"She'll be forty-six in a few months," said Jan.

"Well, I suppose you know everyone here."

In the midst of his annoyance at the staring Jan still recognized his old gratitude to Vigdis. Not that she in the least deserved such a feeling. She had quite involuntarily and unawares changed his life twenty-five years ago. Poor creature, there she stood and felt herself cheated, cheated the way stupid people feel cheated when things take a turn not to their liking, whether it is a matter of importance to them or not, and whoever is to be blamed. Jan was infinitely far from feeling any triumph—not only that he had escaped a woman who could let her body go to ruin thus; a man like Jan felt gratitude toward a woman who in her simplicity had taught him something, gratitude that she, with her little mind, had belittled his love and kept him on this silly and repulsive plane until he realized it and escaped. When all turned out for the best Jan Venhaug felt neither triumph nor grudge.

Felicia had heard of Vigdis but did not know who had been staring at her. It amused Jan that Felicia once had so looked down on Vigdis that she now didn't recognize her. It had been on the train. Felicia had returned from the ladies' room and sat down beside him with her book. Then Vigdis happened by, sulky and red in the face. Jan and she had never recognized each other with a greeting over the many years. "Did you notice that character?" asked Felicia. "I almost felt she would pursue me to the toilet. It was Mrs. Venhaug this, and Mrs. Venhaug that, but I didn't have time for her. 'How lovely it would be to see Venhaug again!' she blew after me as I slammed the door in her face."

In his mind he could see Vigdis at Felicia's Venhaug and he managed to change his laugh into a yawn. The always curious Felicia had not even cared enough to ask what sort of character it was who had wanted to be invited to Venhaug. He held her hand and she squeezed it while she read on in the book. What had she taken Vigdis to be, if indeed she had taken her for anything? It was then he understood better than ever one of Erling's reactions to Felicia. Erling had thoroughly experienced being looked down on by what he considered to be society girls, even back in Skien and in Rjukan. It must have been worst in his sensitive years, when he was about thirteen and the family moved to Rjukan. His father had imagined it was some sort of gold-rush camp there in the year 1912. The Vik caravan had arrived and evoked laughter and derision which Erling never had got over—it had been bad enough before they moved there. His limping, bald father with his wild beard, his deaf mother with her crooked neck, and his mother's father who lived with them and who had no hands; and that immense flock of brats—"pale as corpses to show the dirt the better," Erling had expressed it in his dunkenness, telling about the migration from Skien to the dangerous and foreign Rjukan where for the first time he had seen an established upper class.

Undoubtedly Erling had said more than he had intended that time— and more than he could remember the following day. Jan had met people who knew the family, even if not present at the arrival in Rjukan. They had been most deeply impressed with that hairy, dirty parody of a human being without hands, holding the liquor bottle with the stumps of arms when he quenched his thirst. The peculiarities of the family were soon on everybody's tongue. Vik the Tailor used an amazing book-language, interspersed with many home-made words. People would bring him garments to patch; and when they emerged from the little cubby-hole where he sat looking so important they would spread his political observations about. Some of his statements still survived in Rjukan.

When Jan had met Vigdis he wasn't blindly in love at first, and according to his reckoning it wasn't quite proper for a girl to be so easily had after only a few hours acquaintance.

But then, he had actually been aggressive. It was only the following morning this dawned on him, as he lazed in bed—because it was Sunday he might have said, but knew better. He used to rise at the same time every day and had done so all his life. When little, unlike other children, he felt no desire to sleep longer because of something mysterious called Sunday, and when he grew older and understood what a Sunday was, he had already his own animals to look after—the play had become reality. Each morning he would tend to the animals before he had breakfast. Yet he knew that nothing would happen if he stayed in bed and took it easy. His father would automatically tend them if Jan didn't show up; or any one of the hired help who had been trained by the early-rising father and son. There was no danger that any beast need wait beyond the expected time.

Jan had a feeling of overwhelming well-being, a sating of all senses, completely rested after only three hours' sleep. He pushed his elbows into the mattress, closed his fists, stretched himself, and yawned loudly. His blood worked and sang, and never before had he been so conscious of his own body as this morning, every bone and fiber in it. He put his hands under his hips, lifted his lower body until the toes pointed at the ceiling, he enjoyed looking at his well-shaped feet, legs and thighs with taut muscles. He parted his legs until they formed a large V through which he looked out the window at the swaying birch tops. Here I lie and watch the birches between my legs on the morning of July 2, 1931. I feel I could go out and push the barn off its foundation. He started swaying the outstretched legs in rhythm with a song he suddenly remembered—but he didn't sing too loud, one mustn't make a fool of oneself:

> My lass and I go dancing
> Out in the fields in spring.
> My cap I raise to her

And we join arms and swing.
My song is for my lass alone
In the summer evening clear.
Sing falleri, sing fallera!
Come, rest with me, my dear.

When Jan during the past years looked at Julie, his thoughts had sometimes gone to that young and long-ago Vigdis. God help me, he would think, if that creature should suspect my thoughts ever came near her!

He knew Vigdis believed so, but believing is one thing and knowing is another. Jan had learned that a woman once worshiped had difficulty realizing she might not still be. In really serious cases she creates dream-like myths that the man lives in greatest misery with the wife he has, and this can become a fixation that leads her to the most ridiculous speculations if she isn't too happy with her own lot. If Vigdis knew he was thinking of those old days, she would never understand that although she was involved it had nothing to do with her; it was something that remained built-in as in a niche, a remembrance with a name, as certain poisons might accumulate in a skeleton unable to escape from the body. Now all was distant and diffused but it might awaken a dream-like desire to repeat that pattern, make a secret arch over the past years, over Vigdis of today—that horrible scarecrow!—back to the Vigdis of 1934.

He remembered best his aching jealousy, but not as something bad. He must suppress feelings of today to recall how painful it had been. Now all had changed into something peaceful, sun-sated and summer-like, reminding one of a Midsummer bonfire in a distant, hazy night. That far-away Vigdis had not even been left her own face, nor could he have recalled it with assurance of correctness. She had now assumed Julie's features. This she actually didn't deserve.

There remained with Jan a sort of shame-feeling about that love story. People might wonder how this one or that one could have fallen for such a one, but they refrain from mentioning what they themselves have fallen for.

Jan had told Erling about most of the story. It wasn't exactly like him but he wanted to put it in words for once. Nor had Erling referred to it again. How love also could be degradation and shame! It could be all sorts of things.

He had told Erling unemotionally and monotonously. How much in love he had been. Helpless, eager, completely in the hands of a girl who had lowered herself to a peasant boy. Jan was not one to enjoy cheap triumphs, but he had wondered what went on in Vigdis' rumpled head when he returned from Sweden with Felicia. And Vigdis had, even before the war, changed her mind about farm-boys: one could stay away from the barns and all it meant and Jan had bought a car. He could recall her words of twenty-three years ago: At least you might discard your dialect-talk when my girl-friends are around.

"Were you rough in your talk in those days?" Erling asked, suspiciously.

"Rough? I talked my inherited tongue, that's all!"

"Well."

Erling did not look up when Jan said she had misgivings about *marrying below her class* but fancied that Venhaug could be sold. Those words made Erling prick up his ears: Had *she* really meant anything serious to Jan?

"Excuse me," he said, "but what was her father, then? Postmaster General or something?"

"He had a grocery store, you know, one of those little stores in Kongsberg. They had one girl to help them behind the counter."

"Did they have money?"

"Money? You mean a fortune? They had nothing."

"And she said *marry below her class,* or is that an expression you've invented?"

"It is word for word what she said."

Jan told about his consuming jealousy, nights without sleep, derision and broken promises. "Why don't you give her a good beating, that must be what she wants," one of his friends had said. Jan had looked down, unable to reply.

Erling asked outright, "Were you afraid of not getting anyone else if you gave her up?"

Jan laughed gloomily. "Far from it. I've never been afraid of girls the way some are, the way you have told me. I could've had my pick, they all knew I was the heir of Venhaug. If it had been a question of just any girl. But Vigdis was good-looking. Of course some others were too. That her face was completely empty I couldn't see. Or maybe, I don't know. It was that other business, you know—I burned for her. Like a lit Christmas tree. If she only hadn't talked so—so unkemptly, if that's the word. And not been so vulgar-genteel. I have some appreciation for form and language, wherever I got it from, more than you have. Well, as to form—she was worse than Viktoria. When one falls in love not everything fits right with body and soul. Body, yes, but the soul of Vigdis was worthless."

"In other words, it was all strictly animal?"

"Strictly animal. You hit it right, and there is something wrong when a woman is useful only for mounting. But the Vigdis affair makes one wonder. For although that was all, and although each time I got up I wondered what in the world I was doing there—"

Jan pondered. "Well, in spite of it being so, a dream remained from it. Of course erotically colored, but a dream nevertheless. Where had it come from? A dream one might have about somebody one has been deeply in love with and who had been given both body and soul. When it was all over I couldn't get away from the fact that all that business about the erotic—even apart from the soul—yet had something in it, all by itself—the stuff old Pontoppidan writes about. I can imagine that the sexual part amounts to sixty or seventy percent of the value, as a matter of fact. But the other thirty percent should also be there. Otherwise a person's thinking apparatus must be very low. Even if only five percent is left for the soul, it's got to be a mighty big five percent.

"By and by the shame and the embarrassment took over. One can not forever go about and blush for shame over the one one loves. I broke abruptly, almost the way one decapitates someone. This didn't suit her. I realized it should have been she who did it, if it must be done, but I couldn't wait for that. Although she has made a few attempts we have never spoken to each other since. She sent a close friend of hers to see me, one of her kind. I looked at her but didn't reply with a single syllable. She wrote. I managed to burn the letter unopened. She telephoned. I put down the receiver. Every minute of the day I was near giving in. It was pure hell. A hell of jealousy. As hot as the real one. Until I saw it through. I've told you before I dared see it through. So however I turn it I am under some sort of obligation to her and I enjoy my ungratefulness."

Jan was silent a moment. Then he laughed: "She never managed to grow up anyway, she had nothing to grow with, she only grew older. Someone must have told her she had been silly not to get her talons into Venhaug. I dare say many people have enjoyed telling her so. I know of at least one case where she became furious at someone because this person had failed to tell her earlier that a farm might be something after all. It's incredible—well, I mean I have been incredible, to her. She was after me every way she could think of, and I heard a story of how unhappy I was supposed to be, and that I had misunderstood—

"Well, that's how stupid and disgusting it was from the beginning to the end, in every way. But the jealousy finally burnt itself out. When one has held the devil by the throat and looked him in the eyes, well—"

• The dove hunt

It was a morning in the middle of October and the day promised to be raw, possibly rainy. Erling came into the kitchen, gloomy and morning-sulky. He screwed up his eyes against the bright illumination and wondered what need there was for so many lights being turned on. It was only half past five, he had stumbled across the yard in darkness and sworn because no one had thought of turning on the outside lights. Did they take him for a cat? Erling was not in the habit of showing himself to anyone when just out of bed. He couldn't stand people then, least of all himself. Jan, the gardener, and some youths had already assembled in the kitchen, all disgustingly awake and talkative. Well, the gardener kept his mouth shut, his jaws worked like a feed-cutter, he ground bread with his head, a most repulsive sight; why didn't he turn his head since he couldn't eat decently? Erling pulled up a kitchen chair and stared in annoyance at the bench where Jan sat and poured a cup of coffee for him. He drank the coffee and waited apprehensively for someone to speak to him, but apparently they had been warned and talked as if he weren't there. He slowly overcame his first morning-orneriness while he drank the coffee. It could have been both stronger and warmer. No one except himself could brew coffee nowadays. He espied the milk pitcher, poured the large earthen stein full, and raised it to his lips with hands still trembling with anger. He ignored Jan's faint smile to the others as long as he was left in peace. He emptied the coffee cup and looked around sullenly for the pot. Where in hell had those idiots put it? He wouldn't ask for the coffee pot but picked up a slice of sausage and pushed it into his mouth. His heart began to calm down. He chewed, raised his eyelids, and looked around murderously for the pot. It stood at his elbow. And when he finally got his bearings he discovered a large plate of fried, steaming eggs. With the fork he shoveled a couple over onto his plate, tore them to pieces, and ate them. Still another degree calmer he refilled the coffee cup and emptied it with a few swallows. He poured himself some more coffee and at last felt peace rise in him slowly, not unlike the feeling of some warming matter spreading to all his organs and turning him into the everyday man Erling Vik. Rain started to stream down against the window beside him; it too was friendly and calming. His breathing became deep and even; he felt it no longer as some sort of nuisance in the upper part of his body, rather as a sensuous suction down to his legs, to his fingers, from the stomach. He reconquered his body as he had been forced to do every morning since childhood, forced to do as far back as he could remember. Only as a grown man had he realized that many others had a similar problem, and that he and his like were a flock punished with moral-preachings because of an inborn peculiarity, a peculiarity they themselves suffered from as if it were the mange or a clubfoot. Before he realized this fact he had struck out in fury at any living or dead object that crossed his path. It had helped him greatly when he realized that this morning surliness of his was a sound, natural reaction to the demand of starting all over again, and that it was the early birds who were crazy enough to greet a new day with welcome:

> The blessed day which we now see
> In goodness dawn to us,
> It shines from Heaven more and more
> With comfort and joy for all.
> So do we know, we children of light
> That night has passed away!

Did you ever hear the like! Thus they chirruped, those morning birds. Nothing in the world could make a sane person more furious than someone barging in bellowing: "Get up, Hans! Get up, little Hans! The lark is already singing!"

Or get up and beat the drum.

He remained sitting yet a few minutes, staring into his coffee cup, before he started to poke about in his pockets for tobacco, his head still bent down. Only when the cigarette hung from the corner of his mouth did he rise like the others and pick up his outdoor clothing that he had dropped in the corner. His leather jacket increased his feeling of calm and warmth. Now let them beat drums to their heart's content, although he rather wished they wouldn't. He pushed the cartridges into proper pockets where they wouldn't get wet, and added a word to the conversation now and then as the men checked their guns. Jan was very cautious and wanted others to be careful. Never aim a gun at anybody, whether it is loaded or not. This was his morning-song—to people who had been big-game hunters before he was born. Today they would shoot doves. Five youths were in the kitchen, in great anticipation of the hunt, although not one of them would ever dream of eating a forest dove. Eight men to hunt doves, ready before dawn. Felicia was responsible for this. People of mature age like himself should go on a dove hunt a few hours before dusk. There was more atmosphere to it then, and one could get closer to the birds as dusk fell, and especially as they were feeding just before roosting. But perhaps doves were like certain people, more alive in the morning. With that statement Felicia had interrupted: if several people hunted together, the morning was the right time. It would grow lighter so one could see better and better; just the opposite was true in the evening, and that was when people shot each other. Even though no one had paid much attention to her opinions about anything concerning hunting Felicia had with more persistence than ever driven through her thoughts. Well, had they gone last evening at least it wouldn't have been raining.

All this Erling was commenting on cheerfully as they were getting ready, stomping about in rubber boots, feeling pockets to make sure of matches, pipe, tobacco, cursing the rain—well, perhaps once out in it . . . This gave Jan an opportunity to say one shouldn't curse any weather one could be out in; Jan was always chivalrous to the weather. He had the same attitude toward the different times of day, and now that Erling had his circulation going, Jan defended even the morning hour. Erling agreed that the morning hour could be very pleasant, provided one hadn't been in bed during the night. They got into that especially pleasant mood that blossoms among a group of rested men who—sated and satisfied, pipe in mouth, gun on arm—are out on the same errand which has nothing to do with girls. In their hearts each one was equally embarrassed that this great gathering concerned only a few doves. It should at least have concerned the siege of some neighbor farm.

Everything people undertake, even the smallest thing, has a background of causes that date back to time immemorial; but to be precise, the latest and most apparent causes for the dove hunt at Venhaug in October, 1957, must be traced to the outbreak of war in April, 1940, and the death of King Haakon seventeen years later.

Jan Venhaug, a graduate in animal husbandry, before the war had made journeys to foreign countries. There he had revised his ideas about food. This could be a long chapter, but let's stick to the doves. He had reached no farther than Copenhagen before he found dove on the menu. He was to have the same experience in many other places before he discovered that Norway was the only country in Europe where the delicious dove was in the same class with the magpie and the buzzard when it came to game food. He obtained the recipe for the first dove he ever tasted: "For 6 people take 3 doves; pluck and draw. Save brains and giblets. Place in each dove 8–10 seeds from fresh grapes; salt birds, wrap in bacon, and brown on spit. Use first very strong heat, and as they begin to brown, spray gently with good cognac. When birds are attractively brown, lower the heat, or finish in oven 20 minutes. Baste generously with game bouillon. Meat should be left pale red. Toast six slices of bread. Take brains and giblets, mix with cognac, boil a few moments, crush in a mortar, strain. Season with salt and pepper and set aside. Put the toasted bread on a plate and spread with the sauce. Split the doves, put one half on each piece of toast and serve."

With the arrival of snow the doves disappeared from the Venhaug forest, and in spring they nested early. One brood after another was hatched until August, but beginning in the middle of that month one could pick off a few any time for dinner. Jan started to study the habits of the doves; and as a consequence he planted a few peas in some openings in the forest. He also strewed some peas above ground so the doves always found something to eat. Since then he had shot forest doves every year, except during the occupation years; but this was the first time he had gone hunting in such a large company. Jan had always preferred to hunt alone. Because then no one counted his misses, he would say, but the fact was that hunting to him had always been more of a meditation and friendship with the forest than an actual hunt. He liked to roam about and pretend he had an errand.

The morning he heard over the radio that the king was dead, his thoughts, like those of many others, went back to the spring of 1940; if there were any dormant ideas about Norway as a republic they must have died out in those days. He himself had always been a republican but failed to see why the king's title must be changed to president. This was actually all the republicans were fighting about, those few that survived after 1905; now it was no more than a matter of semantics. He realized that the disadvantages inherent in birth-succession were generously compensated by the absence of eternal fights to determine which demagogue was the greatest scoundrel in the race for the top position; in fact, since 1905 the republicans have had only two candidates of importance—Michelsen and Nansen. And he refused to speculate on the rush for patronage that would have ensued. The only changes he considered reasonable were, first, freedom of religion for the head of the country (that old restriction about his being a Lutheran would hardly increase his piety). Secondly, females must have the right to inherit the office. Thirdly, the human right to a marriage of his own choice must be restored to the king; anyway, he must not necessarily marry a foreigner. But on the last point Jan had begun to have his doubts. If they only refrained from spreading far and wide that it was a love-marriage one could believe it might be.

In any case, it was the war years Jan remembered at the time of the

king's death. Concerning the national mourning that had been proclaimed he shared the sadness one feels when an old gentleman goes to
rest, the man who first said no to the Germans, and later to Norwegians
who thought they were unable to stand on their own feet.

Jan had been sitting in the kitchen when Felicia and the children
came down; he had been up early and had chanced to hear a bulletin at
half-past six. He told them what had happened, and the children were a
little confused as to how to take it that the king was dead. He helped
them by telling them a prominent man had passed on, a very tired and
very old man had gone to his rest, and there was no reason for sorrow;
except sorrow at death in general, not for the one now taken away.

To say this last to children was justified, he thought, because to them
death was something so distant their thoughts were unable to grasp it.
But was it right and true to say we had reason to feel sorrow at death, at
our own death? He had been looking out through the window, across the
wide yard toward Old Venhaug, with its tall, autumn-yellow birches, and
he had shaken his head slowly. It might sound flippant to say one would
not wish to miss one's death since it was so ordained one couldn't escape
it either. But he had long known he would not wish to miss what was the
most incomprehensible to the individual. He did not wish to be without
the knowledge that one day he would indeed die. Not doze off into
something called eternal sleep, not depart to return at the blasts of
trumpets and other noise. He wanted to *experience* his irrevocable
passing, never to awaken again, never be conscious, see or hear any more,
never himself be heard or seen, never. He could not understand that
anyone would wish to miss this definite, total, final drama. That was one
reason he and Erling had become so close: they two were ready to meet
the final drama. Oh Lord, people run to their churches and rage over
their feeble faith or worry about it, because they do not wish to admit
what their own knowledge tells them, or have insufficient strength to see
it as a knowledge good to possess, a knowledge the foremost minds have
fought to convey. (Jesus died on the cross that you might understand
it—he thought he might put an end to that trouble-maker from Sinai.) A
knowledge of the total drama that makes one a human being while one
exists. This doesn't happen until one has seen in a vision the handwriting on the wall. Then there is no longer a Jan Venhaug, and never
will he know if he has been, and that's good.

Julie had also come down. They were sitting talking inconsequentials
until Julie said, "Please, Jan, why don't you for once think out aloud?"

He looked at her with a smile and from her to the others: "I was
thinking something rather ordinary and decent; it came to me when I

listened to the radio. It is still somewhat vague but I'll be glad to tell you: how would it be to invite a few of those we knew so well during the war. Invite them to gather now that the king is dead. Now that in a way something has had a period put to it. If we can say nowadays that anything ends, *period*."

He thought of adding, "Anything except ourselves." But he did not say it.

The children and Julie started to talk about it back and forth. Jan listened absent-mindedly. Compared to the two children Julie was grown-up in a double sense. Twenty-two and hard hit by the war in the early years. To the two others the war was only an empty lesson at school. So shortsighted we are. Why didn't we insist in 1945 on a special school-book beginning with a general review of the then just finished war, continuing with a description of the occupied countries (as well as a description of a people without a country), and then a description of Norway under the iron heel? Now it will never be done. We have committed ourselves to large and small lies to our children—in school. How about telling the story of one of our military chiefs, of German origin, a general who might now have been sitting in the Oslo Palace as Norway's executioner if the fortunes of war had not turned in 1942. Now it will never be told in school. It is remarkable the use we make of schools and schoolbooks. In one of them I read that after the war a Norwegian became the most important man in the world. Trygve Lie—a little Puck travelling by express from country to country.

We live in our own time and with its current banalities, he thought further, but also in a future and a past dimension. Thought spans milleniums back and forth—and comes to rest for a short second on a stupid opinion concerning the world's greatest man. We live in a strange age when people at last have managed to rob words of any meaning. Everything means anything and nothing. The result is that what a person says becomes completely meaningless. An article of today assumes the meaning intended by the paper that prints it, and if the editor should change his opinion, it would never be noticed. Perhaps the editor no longer need go to the office, perhaps he has been honorably pensioned off already. In Sweden, two of the country's leading papers changed sides, and they lost fourteen readers—fifty percent more than anticipated.

Felicia was hesitant about accepting Jan's idea; it wasn't the bother of preparing for the party she feared, even though she took this into account. Her first reaction was simply: Jan is and remains the most innocent person I know. Whom and how many of those people could we invite *together*? We live far away from most of them. A list of names passed through her head, and suddenly she showed her teeth in a smile Jan seldom saw. She enjoyed for a moment the memory of the fight, but her face darkened again when she recalled her brothers, Steingrim, and the other dead ones; she recalled secret as well as open discords which had arisen as a result of the war. How could such a party be arranged to give it any kind of meaning? One couldn't at any rate invite people who long ago had become one's enemies. Nor a great many who perhaps had been important in the final outcome but whom they hardly knew any more. Neither Jan, Erling, the gardener Anderssen, nor she herself had been central figures, far from it; they had hovered somewhere out in the periphery, perhaps as satellites around satellites, but who cared about that now.

Some of the first on the list were gone as if they never had existed. A few were chronic alcoholics at such a stage one could not expect another sensible word from them as long as they lived; they would sit and drink and entertain each other with drunkards' bedtime stories, and would return uninvited once they had been permitted to come to Venhaug. The living must retain the right to wash their hands of the dying. Am I getting old? she wondered, remembering first one, then another—no! I don't want those sots at Venhaug.

Nor some others she could think of—good people all right, but a little out of place *here*, the kind of patriots who might say anything, stunted in their growth, as it were, thinking they knew Jan, which they didn't; and she didn't wish to see Jan take off across the room after any one of them, his neck bent like a young bull ready for a fight. She had seen this happen before. Jan was quick in his movements if anyone insulted her; he never learned to differentiate between women who could defend themselves and those who couldn't. There were people who never looked behind the placid Jan, they knew nothing of how thin was the shell of the farmer who guarded his inheritance. Those two or three she now had in mind were a little stupid, they had seen how far he could go when it concerned the defense of a greater inheritance, but never would they realize there was more than the kind, accommodating Jan. It was the same sort of people who learned to their chagrin that they didn't know Erling Vik. People in this country think they know and can judge a man because he happens to turn over a table at Blom's, and they never change their opinions however often they burn their fingers on their mistakes. They think they *know* the man when they see him out in a car with someone other than his wife. They only see the waste-products of a person. It would take a sledge hammer to make them change their opinions once formed.

It didn't take long for these thoughts to sift through Felicia's head. She said, "You know without my saying how many apprehensions I have, and you must have your own. Of course I would like to, but—"

"There are many buts," said Jan, "and we must think it over thoroughly to avoid unpleasantness. You know we have often thought of something like it, but a gathering in a restaurant becomes just another meeting, with stiff speeches and a lot of trivial talk."

"We could wait and decide when Erling comes," interrupted Julie. "He wrote me we could expect him any day now. There are so many he doesn't want to meet."

Felicia was trying to gain time. She wasn't very keen on having guests, but she would make the effort if Jan insisted. She felt he would soon change his mind. The group from those days was scattered. There would be the problems of children, new wives, and new husbands. The war had been a regular divorce-mill. Then there would be the previous wives and the previous husbands. She thought further, and as a result was completely exhausted. Except for one permanent bachelor, and Erling who hadn't remarried, and of course the dead ones, everyone had discarded wife or husband (one had shot his wife and was now in prison). Her first conclusion was that they must invite married people without their current spouses and together with previous wives or husbands. That could certainly turn into a gay circus. She felt relieved; Jan would jump back as if something had stung him.

She looked at the many names she had written down. There was the bachelor Øystein Myhre. She had nothing against inviting a bachelor. Why had Øystein never married? Good-looking, masculine, gifted, not without money, good position. Girls still made eyes at him.

With somewhat less interest she studied the list of women. There was Birgit Orrestad, who had a daughter although not married. At least she hadn't been last summer when Felicia had lunch with her in Oslo. They might invite Birgit and Øystein. And perhaps Birgit's daughter, who must be grown by now.

Felicia hesitated again; Birgit was still attractive; well, one might say very attractive even. And her daughter resembled her greatly, at least at that time in Stockholm. Her name was Adda.

It was Erling Felicia had in mind. She didn't hesitate to envision the consequences. She would like to invite Øystein Myhre; it was not quite so exciting to have Birgit Orrestad. Well, perhaps. Øystein and Birgit, then. But if Birgit brought her daughter, Erling would have someone to ogle anyway.

I'll suggest it, she decided. I'll mention it. That the others are only a crazy notion Jan will realize as soon as I remind him how terribly mixed-up they are. So much wasted trouble. So stupid they've been. And all those children spread all over.

A recollection struck her; in one case the children had first gone with the father. He remarried but divorced wife number two also, or perhaps she was number three. In any case, the children remained with their stepmother who wouldn't give them up, and legally they were hers as much as her husband's. She was eligible for an invitation, but she had nothing to do with the whole thing—indeed, Felicia had no idea who she was. There she sat, with someone else's children, and wanted it that way. So complicated had situations become for everybody, more or less. But me they'll criticize, she thought annoyed. Fools that they are in their own mess. And some of them—who still will criticize me—will talk about what luck people with money have, able to do anything they want. They dare not, and will not, admit that I have managed with less money than it has cost them. Then they would be forced to see the truth of their own actions. They must invent some special explanation when others seem wiser than they themselves. Those who have money! they cry out when messed up in financial misery which they could have avoided. If one only had money! But even without money they could now have been without debts, if they only had managed their lives without running in and out of marriages and accumulating more and more obligations which shouldn't have been theirs. They borrow from banks to pay off present wives and buy new ones, not to mention sending their children into a maelstrom of trouble. What do they mean when they say I can manage my situation because I have money, when I never have used my money to create anything similar to their debacles and their expensive bank ns? it is I who have managed things as if I were poor and had to watch every penny, while they carry on as if they were majority shareholders in Morgan's Bank, or kept a printing press under the bed and made their own money.

A few days before the Etruscans and Øystein Myhre were expected, the idea of a dove dinner had come up. And now the men set out westward from the farm, up an almost unclimbable hillside. Jan was ahead, Erling made up the rear. As soon as they were drenched the rain stopped. They hiked about an hour before Jan called them together and indicated where each one should take up his post. Below them they could distinguish an irregular opening in the thin spruce forest, perhaps a few hundred paces long and maybe half as wide. It was not yet light, and each one was sent to take cover under indicated bushes round the opening. Farthest away lay the little pea-patch where Jan would take his post. They were given strict orders not to shoot until Jan had fired the first shot; all must crawl on hands and knees to their posts and remain rigid behind their various bushes. All firing must be done against the sky only.

Tor Anderssen and Erling, being the oldest ones, chose nearby bushes. The younger men spread out; they were unable to take this hunt very seriously. "If you see a fox let it run!" was Jan's last admonition.

Erling sat down, leaning on his elbow, and felt the moisture through his clothing. The morning was quite still now. Night-frost and wind had not yet stripped the leaves from aspen and birch scattered here and there against the dark spruce. He heard a sleepy crow far in the distance and cautiously lighted a cigarette. Not a sound from the other seven, and he wasn't quite sure of their positions. The feeling of total solitude in an autumn-still forest put him in a pleasant doze, from which he was awakened in about ten minutes by the whir of the first dove. It came down over the middle of the opening and looked guardedly about. It seemed hesitant, braked with its tail ready to take off again, but then alighted near the withered, rain-beaten peas. Erling's heart beat faster and he knew the others had the same reaction, with the exception of that wooden-head Tor Anderssen; but they would soon relax. One more came down; it repeated the maneuver of the first one. Then three more followed in quick succession. A few minutes elapsed, and still more fluttered down. He wasn't quite sure how many had arrived but he guessed about thirty, when one of them suddenly lifted. Others followed, and the tension was insupportable until Jan finally fired. Erling and the other men fired simultaneously, and the shots echoed through the forest until they died down like distant thunder in summer. Erling had managed four shots and was sure the last one at least had missed. It was difficult to decide who had shot the doves they collected, but of course there was much argument. Tor Anderssen did not enter the conversation. The only conclusion they agreed upon was that Jan had downed two with his first shot; fifteen were gathered up in all. The youths had never participated in this kind of hunting before and wanted to nail down the one who had scared the first dove. But Jan knew his birds: there was always one or another stupid bird that got it into his head to start too early, he said; it was rather annoying, but there was nothing more to be done before evening. He suggested a few other places they might try, but then they must be very cautious, for even though far away the shooting might have warned the doves there.

Farther on in the forest they sat down on a wet, roughhewn log, all in a row, while Jan poured some cognac into a tumbler. They talked forest and hunting while the tumbler passed from hand to hand back and forth along the spruce log. Erling, as usual, felt a little on the outside, not quite belonging in this company; Jan and the youths were of the same sort. It was master and servants unlike anything he had experienced. Nothing condescending, nothing fawning, and a communion in matters intimate to them all; he was ashamed that it bothered him a little to drink from the same tumbler as they.

"Now the drinking is over," said Jan. "It doesn't help one's aim." He handed the bottle to Erling and added: "You take charge of the feed-bag."

The boys broke into laughter, surprised and relieved when all the gossip about Erling and the bottle was turned into an ordinary joke. Even the following day they were still cracking jokes about Erling and the feed-bag, which he himself happened to overhear: "Handed him the bottle and told him to take charge of the feed-bag," he heard through a wall. But Erling also realized that the released laughter did not quench the curiosity in their eyes, the curiosity he had always seen when at Venhaug, and which did not have to do with bottles.

He felt uncomfortable lest Jan had had something else in mind when he used the expression—far-fetched perhaps, so far-fetched that Jan himself hadn't seen it. Let the lecherous billy-goat look after the feed-bag—no, it was too much like speaking of rope in a hanged man's house.

• Bacchus had no children

Late Saturday night Erling had managed to find his way to Old Venhaug, but as he sat down on the edge of his bed to undress he felt very drowsy. He abandoned himself to the imperishable delusion that he might, just for the time being, remove his jacket, loosen his tie, kick off his shoes, and doze for a few minutes until he gained sufficient strength to undress properly. He went to sleep immediately.

If matters had taken their usual course he would have awakened when someone brought him his coffee in the morning, to keep him out of the kitchen. But in an hour or two he woke up hearing somebody crying.

He was unable to clarify what this might mean. It took some time before he realized he was at Old Venhaug and not in his own house or somewhere else. One time in Sweden he had awakened on a sunny day, alone in an elegant, unfamiliar house. Unable to figure out where he was, he was struck with a brilliant idea: he would open the front door and read the name plate. Then the door blew shut and locked behind him. Now he knew where he was, but he was there dressed in only a short undershirt, and he would rather have been inside and not knowing.

"Why does she cry?" he wondered confusedly. "What is there to cry about here?"

He felt for matches and after much trouble he managed to light a candle. A surge of relief swept over him at the sight of the familiar room, for he hadn't been quite sure. Who was it, crying there on the other side of the wall?

A light dawned in the thick darkness of his head: doves, dove hunting—

Now the picture unfolded quickly; it was Saturday night, there had been guests. He searched every corner of his brain for a scandal but couldn't remember one. Who was making that noise in there? No one was supposed to occupy this house except him. Another memory surfaced: someone was to stay over at Old Venhaug—at the same moment something most unusual occurred to him: the whole evening Felicia had urged him to drink—oh that bitch!

He was in that dizzy borderland between being drunk and having a hang-over, a condition you experience only when awakened just after having slept off the top of the drunkenness. Everything in the room turned upside down as if razed by a hurricane. Someone has filled the room with water that I can see through. Water of room temperature. This suddenly seemed to him so funny that he burst out laughing, but fear cut him short, for he realized he wasn't laughing at all, only seized with spasms in his face muscles. Now he must play the detective. Who was crying in there? He tried to get up but fell on the floor. On hands and knees he crawled toward the door, but it was not easy to keep his balance on all-fours either. It was a top-heavy arrangement.

He turned over on his back to gain strength. At least he had managed to stop the wailing in there. With the aid of his magic radiation. "Keep on being silent!" he shouted in triumph.

He heard someone move about and then the door opened. There stood Øystein Myhre in his shirt sleeves. "Well, why are you on the floor?" he asked. "And what in hell do you mean waking the whole county!"

"County-shmounty," said Erling, irritated. "Who are you beating up in there? Come here and I'll push your face in."

Øystein remained standing in the door and did not reply.

"I didn't mean to insult you," said Erling. "Take it easy a minute while I think things over."

He fought to clear his head.

"Listen, Øystein—take the towel and soak it in water and let me hold it over my head."

Øystein did as directed. After a moment Erling lifted the towel from his eyes and said, "Don't help me, you fool! Then my exercise won't work."

"I have no intention of helping you!"

"Why are you so sulky?" asked Erling. He made an attempt to turn over on his stomach. "Let's see now—"

He managed to get up on his knees and elbows. "It'll be too high if you fall again," said Øystein, who felt he was sobering up just watching Erling.

But Erling did manage to get up. "The trick is to evaluate the situation," he said, didactically. "When I left the bed I didn't evaluate my situation. Now I do. Whom did you choke to death? Get me a glass of water! I can't walk that far. I have been drunk."

"*Have been*," mocked Øystein, and handed him the water.

Erling drank, trembling. He walked over and put the glass down on the bedside table. "There you see!" he said, and Øystein discovered that Erling was indeed looking awake.

"Good! Now go to bed, Erling!"

"No—I must find out—I must get to the bottom of this, so I can sleep. Who was it you were beating up?"

Someone suddenly laughed, and a smile fluttered over Øystein's face. "No, my friend, I wasn't beating anybody. I was proposing."

"Proposing? At your age? Has anyone proposed to anyone since 1912? Ah, I see—it's Saturday, it was a Saturday proposal. But why did she yell? How do you go about proposing? That's something I would like to know."

He thought a moment, then he said, "Felicia has made me drunk. Has she made you drunk too?"

Øystein said calmly, "I noticed Felicia was urging you on."

Erling raised his hand, as if lecturing, "She has done so because she has filled Old Venhaug with loose women. She stands discovered."

There came laughter from the hall.

"What's that?" asked Erling, shuffling toward the door. "Have you proposed to a whole flock? First they bawl and then they laugh—"

"Better go to bed," admonished Øystein.

"Never!" shouted Erling. "Have you got a drink in there? Now that you have ruined the night for me anyway with your beastly behavior—"

A woman appeared in the door. She was difficult to recognize in the pale, fluttering light, but soon Erling saw that she was the older one of the Etruscans: "Is she the one you proposed to and beat up?"

"Why not ask him in for a drink, Øystein—please, let's!"

"Dry me off first," said Erling. "He poured the night pot over me."

She took a sheet from the bed and dried him off.

Then they walked into the next room. Erling sat down on one chair and Øystein on another. The two men talked for a while before Erling discovered there were two women sitting on the bed instead of one. Mother and daughter. Erling frowned and asked, "Have you proposed to one and beaten the other?"

Øystein handed him a glass. "I have good grounds for not proposing to my own daughter," he said.

Erling took a gulp of cognac and coughed; he didn't quite follow. "Which one of them is your daughter?—Ah!" he exclaimed. "Now I get it! It was you who changed your name!"

"You're drunk—I've always been Myhre."

Erling sat looking at the three of them and slowly his brain began to grasp some of the story. He emptied the glass, for he was afraid of dropping it; then he inspected them minutely once more. "Well, well," he said, "so that's the way it is."

Then he added, quite sensibly, "What a waste on Felicia's part to get me drunk!"

His eyes were rather dim but he noticed the two women were smiling. Neither one of them had ever smiled in Sweden. He opened his mouth, but shut it immediately. "Øystein," he said a little later, "either I'm more drunk now or I'm beginning to understand something. Or I understand something because I'm getting drunker. Give me another drink, I want to raise a toast to you three, and then you must see that I get to bed and don't fall on the floor. Any floor, anywhere. Skol! What a pity one can't cry when drunk, for then people'll think it's from drunkenness."

He didn't remember a word of it the following day.

• A man without a philosophy of life

Sunday afternoon Erling said, "Early this morning I got a little extra sleep, as the ladies present recommended me to do, because Erling from Rjukan was sticking out here and there under the disguise. When I woke up I took a walk with Julie and Adda. We spoke earnestly about life, which they assumed I must know all about. I recommended they read the history of the Roman Empire, Josephus, Snorri Sturluson, the

Old Testament, Fröding, Shakespeare, and *The Good Soldier Schweik*. They didn't think much of that. They wanted to hear what I thought of life. They wanted my life philosophy, God bless them. I have none. Except that one bends to the conditions of life because one must, and that sounds very simple. Concerning a philosophy of life I have this in common with most people, namely that—at least to themselves—they acknowledge they have none. Contrary to those others, I'm not embarrassed to admit this fact. Once a man or woman has matriculated it would be considered a degradation were it discovered either lacked a life philosophy. But, no matter.

"Many are of the opinion that a life philosophy is something necessary to a respectable individual. They believe others have one and try to make out they themselves are furnished with this spiritual help. Not long ago, in the dining car on the train from Drammen to Kongsberg, someone asked what my life philosophy was, in the midst of pork and beans. With a life philosophy they must have something vague in mind, a sort of belief in some system which they could use as a sort of guide-line, or perhaps a starting point.

"A person with a life philosophy accepts or rejects what he sees in order to create or hold on to a definite plan. For this he is rewarded with words of praise and honor—upright, straightforward, incorruptible—words that sound rather silly when used about others, who are supposed to be dishonest, disjointed, and together or individually downright crooked.

"People with a life philosophy are apt to look down on others who also have one, because they cannot accomplish the impossible: to have an identical one.

"Generally speaking, it would take about a dozen years for one person to define his own philosophy; from there on he might begin to define a few million different views of others.

"It is common to all life philosophies that they make the possessor the epicenter, with his friends being mere adjuncts, and that without this epicenter all philosophies would be crazy, and craziest of all those that pride themselves on being positive. We do not know sufficiently all the elements in any one life philosophy, we do not know what new elements might arise to tumble the whole, and we know nothing about what old elements we must wash off one day. Life doesn't care a hoot what philosophy one uses for it, nor has the Sphinx changed one iota because some slaves lost a few of their lice in his hair.

"Less imposing, but more honest, it would be to say: 'I act as far as I can according to certain simple experiences and inner directives which I hope and believe are right.' Life philosophies have an odor of bad conscience in bad disguise.

"With this I have made myself unacceptable in all life-philosophy company, which undoubtedly I was before and which pleases me. Let me add only one more thing that would make me, if possible, still more unacceptable in that company: people with a life philosophy are so boring I can't endure them. This is something all know but keep quiet about. Who knows, perhaps life's meaning is that we should be bored and sad, but I will have no part of it. Life philosophies resemble most of all frozen flowers on a grave. Religious, ethical, political—all kinds of life philosophies stink up our atmosphere from childhood on. We are not supposed to enter life, and be of it; we are taken by the ear and lead outside, there to shiver and freeze, with no other occupation than to peek through a keyhole at some nonsense placed there for us to look at.

"Like most others I have been partly forced and have partly chosen to assume a rather definite position in regard to life phenomena as they appear within and outside myself—a life attitude, a course of conduct—and I wish I could persuade some of the doubters that this is good enough. Even if they should discover that the term life philosophy in itself is ridiculous as a life confirmation, and its consequent life denial, it might help them to breathe a little easier. If one wants to dress up, one need not necessarily put on a lead hat. All of us are forced to live as opportunists, and our so-called life philosophies are only breastworks for weaklings. They can peek over those breastworks and assume a threatening attitude or throw rotten eggs if their group is large enough. This is called the fight against all evil of our time, fearlessly and openly. God and everyone—not least the former—are well aware that even in the most bigoted family—and perhaps first and foremost there because its members are more interested in being *considered* morally upright than actually *being* such—the thought turns to a doctor or a quack if an unmarried daughter gets pregnant, and they will seek out the doctor or the quack regardless of their life philosophy, which still remains applicable to others. For their own case is special, something they hadn't taken into account when they took on their life philosophy. Individuals have built life philosophies on the theories of evolution, which must imply a knowledge as to where they lead; but even if one knew this one must build on what people are today, not what they have been, or might become. An evolutionary life philosophy, then, can absolutely not be defended, and the same is true of religion, which also, incidentally, no one ever tries to follow. But every great vision, whether evolutionary or religious, can of course be registered as valuable, if only esthetically.

Perhaps we might say that a life philosophy is a guide-line, tied to hypothetical phenomena outside ourselves, and always an unverifiable construction, or a synthesis of many or all unverifiable constructions.

"We hear enough about life philosophies that are supposed to be common for whole nations, but if we investigate them closer we discover this is not true. The Nazis adhered to a doctrine called obedience to the Fuhrer, but outside of this they could think and believe whatever they chose, indeed, did so. Under the Nazis, freedom of religion was absolute, with the one restriction that all must acknowledge the authority of the state, a condition existing also in the Roman Empire. There have never been so many life philosophies as under Hitler."

Erling discovered with surprise that a full glass of red wine stood beside him; he emptied it and continued: "My attitude to life, and especially the human existence, is regulated by the fact that here we are, and here we must make out as best we can. The surest way to gain permission to live the way we wish, is to grant others the same right—and to remember it well when we use this right. This demands uninterrupted inner guard, because it is difficult for us to let others live the way they want. We have a dark urge to force others to accept *our* views, *our* desires, *our* experiences—as I mentioned earlier, undoubtedly because we (and not a bad idea at that) are not too sure of ourselves. We must keep this guard constantly alert within us: Why do I object when he or she does this or that? Does it actually concern me? Does it hurt me? We must always force ourselves back to this one thing: Everything is permitted so long as it doesn't interfere with others. I have, without success, tried to live up to such an ideal, but ideals too must be unattainable, or one might come to rest when the demands have been met. When well-meaning people have tried to create new moral laws to replace the religious ones, they have done so because Christianity's demands could not be met. The line of thought is on a low plane. I try to let others live as they wish, undisturbed by me, and do not forget that this requires great practice and uninterrupted effort as long as one lives. Let *this* then be my life philosophy, since I am not allowed to appear without a label."

• It happened in history's depth

"But I have a sort of world-picture. This too is called a life philosophy, as is almost anything between serious men. Women are less inclined to be solemn about everything. My world-picture can be likened to a small nebula, and what you see is an unverifiable something. And therefore I wish to say that when I use absolute expressions in the following, like *know* and *believe*, then I do so only for brevity's sake and it is not important to me to make others believe. I am trying to find my own way, not to make converts. If I should ever have any disciples they would have a tough time.

"What I know is that something incomprehensible took place far back in the depth of history, but that its date might after all be determined. Not in terms of days and years, like the battle of Poltava, or the discovery of America; for example, imagine the twenty-third of February the year two million four hundred thousand three hundred and ninety B.C. Have you considered how our time reckoning floats on the surface, and how impossible it is to get it, or any other reckoning now in use, accepted internationally? Here at last is a task for what we in our wish-dreams have named the United Nations. We can never obtain a time-reckoning which includes the unfathomable eons that have passed, but at least we can obtain one that has meaning to all; one that isn't tied to national or religious happenings that mark our lack of the conception that time existed before ours. We might count back ten thousand years and call that point Zero.

"Somewhere back in the midst of time, and beyond our ability of comprehension, something happened which unfortunately never can be used as a basis for our time-reckoning. What was it? Perhaps that 'man' became human and spread over the globe from his original home. Perhaps that he arrived from another planet, with which he lost contact; which happened, indeed, quite suddenly. Perhaps it could be established in time, but only through a different conception of time—the way people used to say God in the *beginning* created heaven and earth, before anything else existed. I have pondered much over what it was that happened to human beings, what struck them—surely an impulse to do something else, an impulse that started them to move with ever increasing speed toward a final goal, now not far away, and that final goal is Ragnarok. And sometime again, long after this new Ragnarok, everything will begin from the beginning anew.

"What happened that first time was unbelievable, and since then only once has the unbelievable struck all of humanity at one time: the *universal* and paralyzing fear of the world's destruction, and a growing belief, approaching knowledge, that Ragnarok is close at hand. Because now people have lost control of their destiny. In many instances, and under the most varying forms, they have relinquished their will and right to act in unison. They have lost their courage, but kept their aggressiveness, and put the blame on others, on those across the ocean, who are to be blamed for everything, and may Heaven consume them with fire! Or else they say: We are helpless, we have no voice in these matters.

"We have both sold ourselves and wedded ourselves to destruction—in order that we may, during the short moment allowed us, have a piece of bread while being brainwashed in front of the hypnotic television. No one has ever predicted the truth of what will happen when war breaks out, least of all the military experts. Only one fact holds true today, and that is that no great power wants war within its own borders. If I were asked 'Is there no hope for Europe?' I would still reply 'yes.' The race between the two great powers might have another goal than the one we are told. The goal might be simply that neither one of them wishes to be the weaker the day they have to meet and divide the earth between them.

"But I fear something else, I fear Europe will become the firebreak, I fear that in places where no bombs have fallen the birds may drop dead and children sink down on the roads, while the great silence spreads and our soldiers lie dead around their atom-artillery, no longer with eyes to see it all, see that our world for a moment is still there as before, but without bird-song, and without verdure in the fields, and with no one to plague his neighbor who isn't there either. It won't even leave a smell, for bacteria too will be exterminated. It will be the myth of the tower of Babel returning again. We must die, just when we aimed to be like God and travel into space. And now we arrive at what could be called my third, or fourth, life philosophy: there is much to indicate all this has happened before, and I can imagine people again, perhaps a hundred thousand years from now, spreading out over the globe from a place they later will call their original home, spreading out over the earth from one place where life has survived, and God knows what myths they will drag along with them. Could they be very different from the ones we now have—Cain and Abel, Sodom and Gomorrha, fire from heaven, a phosphorous hell with Satan, a dream of peace in Abraham's bosom, Nirvana, murderous war-gods, portents in sun and moon, wars and stories of wars, castration, the holy phallic worship, the eating of the sacrificial ram, bloody sacrifices to a creator by his own descendants, the world's destruction, doomsday, son-sacrifice, fear and salvation—from whence do we have all memories and myths of such craziness, if all such craziness hadn't once taken place? What we call predictions and prophesying—are they not all remembrances?

"And some time, far in the future, people will arrive at their great well-being again, with television sets, good times with anxiety, and the hope like today's that people will be slaughtered only in other places than their own, in another Hungary, another Korea, another Algeria, another Indo-China—and that the righteous will be set against the unrighteous whom they know possibly less about than about themselves, and finally a new Billy Graham and his decisive battle with the last sensible human beings at Armageddon.

"Once, in the depths of time, people left nature. For a long time they went on walking alongside nature like a scared phalanx, but the phalanx grew more and more threatening as the years grew into hundreds of thousands. People continuously made more daring attacks upon nature until its position weakened, and by that time only a few thousand years remained before the next doomsday when nature would take back all hers.

"Someone has said nature was unable to invent the wheel; it was something Man made outside of nature. One forgets the solar system which is the wheel and the wheels.

"Even the survivors of a coming Ragnarok will preserve the memory of the wheel. They will begin with the sign of the sun, as people have done so many times before, long, long ago. And they will continue with wheels as in the past, with wheel-filled clocks on the walls, with wagons and bicycles, and again they will, in the sign of the wheel, evolve to destroy the wheel. Our right time-reckoning should be one from suicide to suicide."

• Romantic meeting

Øystein Myhre poured some red wine into his glass, pushed back his chair a little, and let his eyes glide over the company. His unusually active look tarried a few seconds on each in turn. His abundant black hair had grayed, but with a rebellious gray that didn't remind one of age, and all knew Øystein's love for ladies; when he was around, other men kept an eye on their women.

"When Felicia called to invite me here, I found it rather difficult to arrange on so short notice; had I known, however, what contact was to be resumed, I would not have asked to think it over: she did not tell me over the telephone that Birgit and her daughter were expected."

He raised his glass to Felicia, who sat with her mouth open, expectantly; she smelled sensation about to break. Now Øystein turned to

Erling. His eyes, always big and bright, were no less so from the drinks he had had or from his high good humor. Øystein Myhre was known to be intoxicated by nature, he needn't drink but he liked to. He had some difficulty now in getting started, he smiled at the Etruscans, perhaps he was thinking of something else, but after a few fumbling sentences he began: "Erling, you spoke of repetition in all matters. I have recently been to Sweden; in Stockholm I stayed at a little hotel where I also spent a night during the war, and as it happened I occupied the same room. Yes, Erling, this is meant to be a short comment on your theory of repetition. Let's forget that you didn't necessarily mean repetition within the frame of a human life. I was awakened by the telephone in that room one morning in 1942. It was very early, considering the day before had been my birthday. I turned over a lamp and some books on the table before I found the receiver. The operator announced a call from Oslo. Remember, this was 1942, October 13, early in the morning. I would not have been more surprised had I been told there was a call from Tokyo for me, it seemed then just as distant. For a Norwegian refugee to receive a call from Oslo was in itself unthinkable. I tried to wake up, and sober up, while thinking back and forth. It was obvious the Germans kept track of which Norwegians had fled to Sweden, and my being in Stockholm was undoubtedly on record. I waited, and could hear hellos from different points along the line, repeated interruptions. The conversation must be listened to in more than one place, and then it dawned on me what a hell I would have at the legation when they found out Oslo had called me. I started to perspire. Keep in mind: it had been a violent birthday, and the call was from Oslo, in 1942. I was not an important refugee, not one of those who singlehanded had saved Norway at one time or another, I had stayed as long as I could and issued false passports. Yet, I realized I was involved in a conspiracy and that the spying against the refugees must be so effective that they already knew in Oslo that I hadn't slept in my own bed, but in a hotel, because I had been too drunk to take the tramcar to Nockeby.

"After some more trouble on the line, a Norwegian voice suddenly came through: 'Is that you, Øystein?'

"Yes, it was I. Then came a long string of words that had me completely confused. 'Are you listening?' this person kept repeating, and I replied 'Yes!' It was the only word I could get in for a long while.

"It was something about fish—yes, *fish*, but I could not comprehend what it meant—all I could think of was a red herring.

" 'What do you think of that?' he finished his long harangue.

" 'Well,' I said, 'except for trout and perch—but who is this speaking?'

"I could hear a gasp, and then he asked, disconcerted: 'Why do you talk Norwegian?'

" 'Why shouldn't I speak Norwegian? I might say that was the reason I came here—so I could use my own language.'

" 'Isn't it you, Øystein?' he yelled, and then he added a surname beginning with Y, which wasn't mine. 'No,' I said, 'my name is Øystein Myhre, and thank you for all the information!'

"I could hear a muffled 'Hell!' and a click as he put down the receiver.

"I didn't know what sort of information I had received, nor did I ever look into it, but when I met the hotel porter a little later he gave me a wounded look. He had heard from Oslo, too.

"I managed to get out of bed, and emptied the first of three weak beers I had been allowed to bring home with me the night before. Then I shaved with a hang-over's slow motion. Then I drank beer number two, washed up, and put number three to my mouth. Just then there was a knock on the door. I opened, and a lady I knew entered. She greeted me with an explosion of insults because she hadn't been invited to my birthday party. She was—well, let's say, about the same age as the younger one of the Etruscans is today, and she had the power of speech. Her sentences flowed like a fountain until I pushed her down on the bed, and joined her, newly showered and shaved; now she only complained of the beer-smell. She was Swedish. I told her no women had been invited to my party, which I supposed was so though I couldn't recollect clearly.

"Well, that was that. When I recently—fifteen years later—came to the same hotel in Stockholm, I recognized at once the room where I had negotiated about fish that time during the war. You see, the room had some of those peculiarities which arise when the architect has some space left over and doesn't know what to do with it, and consequently leaves it as is. It is the funniest room I've ever seen, for it has no shape. But I tell you this only to explain how I could recognize it so many years later. Pleased in a way to be back, I unpacked, washed up, and went out on the town.

"When I had been in Stockholm a few days I was awakened one morning by the telephone. Here I might point out some minor differences from my earlier visit; now it wouldn't have been strange at all to receive a call from Oslo. On the contrary, I suspected at once that it was from Oslo. Nor was it the day after my birthday, although a few Swedish friends from the war years had partied me until rather late, for no reason in particular. Again I knocked ash trays and papers onto the floor before I got the wrong end of the receiver to my ear and groaned Hello! When I finally could hear the operator she announced Copenhagen. No one there knew I was in Stockholm—never mind why, it simply was impossible. This time there was no need for so many interruptions by listeners being put on the line, and I could clearly hear a man's voice from Copenhagen. This person also spoke with furious speed—he must have been thinking of the high rates. He might have saved himself the trouble, for when he started with the word *fish*, my mind simply didn't comprehend. This Danish caller was a specialist in eel, but even so. I stared angrily into space until I yelled that I wasn't awake—and was it eel he was talking about?

" 'Yes, it is eel—and aren't you Mr. Myhre from Norway?'

"We got into a priceless conversation. Keep in mind my head, and my fish-call from Oslo in the same room some fifteen years earlier; there must be something more wrong with the room than I had suspected. 'Is it eel you say? Please, spell it!'

" 'What do you want me to do?'

" 'Spell it!'

" 'Spell it? You want me to spell eel?'

"How many extra three-minute periods this took I do not know. I was perspiring, but then, it's good to perspire after being drunk. It took a long time before some key words opened my brain; I had actually at one time experimented with an unusually fine eel recipe, and the Dane wanted this recipe.

" 'Of course you can have it!" I yelled, 'but how in the world did you find me?'

" 'I called a number of places in Norway—'

" 'Places in Norway?'

" 'Yes—and finally I reached a farm out in the country—'

" 'You reached a farm out in the country?'

" 'Yes, it was a farm—'

" 'What are you going to do with the recipe?'

" 'I've heard it's very good!'

"I gave him the recipe and wished him luck. Unfortunately I didn't take his name. I would like to meet this food-happy Dane sometime and exchange culinary views with him. I have a feeling he must be a fine person."

"This story about two telephone calls isn't very profound," resumed Øystein, "but as a compensation it is true, with no invention on my part about the repetition of details; moreover, it continued as follows: When I was through talking eel, I opened the first of my three beers and poured it down my throat. Here too there is some difference: the beer had become much better since last time. Otherwise I had a feeling that the ritual would repeat itself. I shaved, drank beer number two, washed up, and sat down on the edge of the bed with bottle number three, waiting in expectation. I stared at the door—not that I heard anything, not a sound. But at last there was a knock on the door.

"I know very well I should now deny the truth and make up some anticlimax, like the maid appearing at the door. Everyone knows that no sensible person talks about having seen the sea monster; that is why its existence never can be proven. But sea monster or no sea monster, it was the same woman as fifteen years earlier. In spite of this fact, the difference was great. She had grown fifteen years older and it wasn't becoming to her. Indeed, it spoiled her looks to a degree fifteen lost summers seldom have spoiled a human being. She had had nothing to carry with her through the fifteen years except her purely physical youth, and as a result she had dropped it somewhere in the gutter, for it requires a *mind* to retain one's youth. I stood in the doorway and recalled a notice I had once seen: Undesirable persons are asked to leave the premises without attracting attention.

"And exactly there, at the door, all similarities came to an end."

Øystein looked down at his hands and continued, without noticeable change of voice, "I proposed to the Etruscan last night."

"Which one of them?" burst out Felicia.

Øystein looked at her: "I only wish to add that the Etruscan is older in years, yet twenty years younger than the woman who appeared at my hotel room door in Stockholm. And my proposing to the older one of the Etruscans—who by the way accepted—might have to do with the fact that I am a law-abiding subject and do not propose to my own daughter. Moreover, I prefer a somewhat better-aged product."

His announcement had very different effects on them. The first reaction came from Erling. He had managed to part some of the cobwebs in his brain, thus opening a window to what had taken place the evening before. He complained loudly, "What a sot I must have been!"

"You behaved oddly, but decorously," said the Etruscan Birgit.

Felicia exploded a second time: "You seemed to have drunk enough to—"

"Yes," replied Erling, and looked the other way, "unfortunately I must have drunk enough to stray—"

Felicia was not one to be stopped; after a quick look at Erling, as if to say, Don't make yourself out worse than you are, she called across the table to Jan: "That's one wedding we must celebrate at Venhaug!"

"Thank you, Felicia," said Øystein, "but we already have decided where to celebrate, and only one guest will be invited."

Felicia went over and whispered something to the Etruscans and together they left the room. Julie sat a moment in indecision, then she rose and followed.

The others remained silent. Jan reached for his glass and emptied it; the others did the same. Then they didn't know what to do, except to fill the glasses once more. With great circumstance Øystein lit a cigarette. "Listen, Erling—my double-story was not meant to end in a proposal-announcement. According to your theory, would you say that my first story had taken place even earlier and, furthermore, that it calls for still another repetition? I do realize your theory concerns history in general, but in that case, to my mind, there must also be a repetition of details. Mustn't the theory hold true in the most unimportant happenings as well as in the great events—this about humanity's repeated creation and eternally repeated destruction? Or, isn't it rather so that in an apocalyptic time, all wish to write apocalypses?"

He made a quick gesture: "No, Erling, one moment never has the same meaning as another has had, and history will never repeat itself, either in moments or eternity. Nothing happens other than—well, than otherwise. No one and nothing will arise again. History never repeats itself and never has. Such a belief is a canvas we hide under from pure fear: nothing must happen except what we can imagine; yet, happenings will take place never imagined. Look first at the old nomads, and from them to the moon satellites. People had accumulated knowledge for a million years, until the results deluged us yesterday—in other words, during the last few centuries. You are oldest among us and have in a way seen all with your own eyes. You can remember a world without automobiles, you have seen the first airplanes, kites of sailcloth and bamboo with a rickety motor. And now you live under a manmade moon and you are strong enough to see many more. And now, for some reason, you want to quit and let our world come to an end. You forget—*always* a new element is added, never before envisioned, an entirely new and unanticipated element that changes the path of history. It has always been so, will always be so, in all fields—technical, psychic, all. It will always so continue. We might just as well espouse an entirely different dream—the opposite dream, the dream of returning to an older system, and put up a wall against evolution, anyway try not to get any farther than we already are. It's only an immature line of thought; we have small examples in the attempts to renew old moral conceptions—with the unavoidable result that new ones take wings. A law must confirm existing order, or create a new order, but the latter can only take place in economic and technical fields. In the field of the soul no new way can be planned through a new law, or by reviving one already dead. What has happened in the human mind cannot be undone. This has been known to all great lawmakers, but of course never to a practicing jurist. Those who try to turn us back to something they consider better still remain submerged to their necks in the old mess. That nothing is new under the sun, is, as I said, only an expression of apprehension. Today we have a new moon under the sun, and more will appear, and I might agree it is a tempting dream that they could have been there before—but it remains a dream."

Erling rose with his glass in his hand. He raised it to Øystein and said, tiredly, "I am a very curious man, as you know. I've never felt I've seen enough. But there might be something to what you say. And I'll tell you one thing: I was sitting in a plane several thousand feet in the air, reading about the new moon. I was overcome with a strange feeling— perhaps now I had actually seen enough. I thought of that first plane of sailcloth and bamboo from my childhood, the first automobiles—imitations from some old manor-vehicles with high wooden wheels, and men in top hats. I recalled people advertising for horses not afraid of automobiles; horses then, that would not bolt across the field and break their necks at the appearance of a gasoline-smelling car. I remember the farmer who called out all his help and admonished them to kneel when the Lord appeared in the heavens. But you have got me sidetracked: I am not anticipating the world's destruction at this moment just because I'm toying with the idea. You needn't answer me, but I have never had much faith in—well, I hardly know how to say it—so I'll say it right out: 'I am dubious about ex-wives and old girl-friends—"

"So am I," said Øystein, "and it isn't the broken pieces she and I have picked up to patch together. There never was anything to break to pieces—matrimonially speaking. We have never worn each other out. We start our honeymoon now. Both of us free, at our age—what do you think of that? Strangely enough, each of us, in our own way, has been waiting for the other. This with Adda—that was a nasty trick I played on her. I'll try to make up for some of it, but that is not the reason we're getting married."

• *Alone*

Erling looked down. *A nasty trick I played on her,* he thought, bitterly. *I'll try to make up for some of it.* And how was it Øystein had continued? *But that's not the reason we're getting married.*

He emptied the glass, walked over to the window and pulled back the curtain. By the light of the lamp over the door he could see Julie and the younger of the Etruscans walking back and forth along the veranda, arms round each other's shoulders.

He went out by another door, crossed the yard diagonally toward Old Venhaug; he wanted to be alone for a while. As he entered the hall he could hear a noise above him. What a hell of a lot of crying there was nowadays; it must be Felicia and the Etruscan Birgit. He stole silently out again, but the thought struck him he would have liked to hear what these two women had to cry over together.

Julie and Adda were still walking on the veranda where the autumnal insects kept swarming around the light, creating fluttering shadows. He walked along the fence so the girls wouldn't see him. It always bothered him to disturb people who might have need of talking about their own problems; it was almost a fear, perhaps some remnant of embarrassment at being the fifth wheel. He felt exposed by the light from the lamp even though he well knew they couldn't see him from where they were. He stopped behind some tall bushes, still in leaf, and watched the two who had just now turned and walked toward him. Were they also crying together?

No, apparently not, and now he wondered why he had thought so. Well, they weren't crying then, but each had much to cry over, perhaps as much or more than Felicia and Birgit who had gone into hiding at Old Venhaug. One could be terribly blind to the most obvious; why hadn't he at once understood why Julie literally rushed after the others? Why hadn't he realized the reason for those two girls walking together? Of these two illegitimate children, Birgit's daughter had been the more fortunate, but who finds comfort in the thought that someone else's fate might have been worse. And his own child had been pushed from one impossible foster-home to another until Felicia rescued her.

Rescued by Felicia. And the Little Etruscan had until now lived in a sort of closed conspiracy with her mother to keep people from feeling sorry for them. It had been a joy when her father materialized yesterday, but it was too late, she was grown, she now took care of herself. Erling had heard she had a boy-friend somewhere. But she had gone through her childhood and early youth without a father, and from the moment she could think her own thoughts she had been made to feel there was something degrading in not having a father.

Those two young girls under the light, they had one thing in common —their forgiveness to a father. Julie had grown up like a tree that has languished in poor soil but is moved to an advantageous spot before it is too late. Even that obligation of gratitude Felicia has burdened me with. She demands a high and peculiar price. I owe her my life, I owe her everything, I owe her for the lives of others whom I deserted. She hasn't spared me anything. Great has been your revenge, Felicia, great when you demanded blood-revenge for your brothers, and equally unmerciful has been your revenge on me. The remarkable fact is that you have lived out the revenge as a natural and organic part of your life. What I understand least is how you find the time. Here you came, a city girl, and assumed the reins of Venhaug. Yet, you have time for anything you get your mind on, and you never seem to tire. I imagine you have added the strength and the will of your young dead brothers to that of your own. Many were those who declared a private war against Hitler, but I know of no one who declared him total war as did you—cold-blooded, consuming, uninterrupted, without letting anything else stand in your way. It has always been dangerous to injure you, for then you grow tall and double your strength. Compared with you most others become remarkably ordinary.

• When you have taken the Devil for partner

The guests were ready to leave. Erling was in his room at Old Venhaug, packing. Felicia came in.

"Erling, I know I should never beg you—but it's inhuman never to break a principle."

He stood waiting, his face expressionless.

Felicia knew she must not touch him now; he turned stiff as a post when she tried to persuade him with caresses.

"We know each other, Erling, and you know yourself."

Her voice broke.

"Don't go to Oslo now, Erling. Stay here a day or two, Erling dear. You know what will happen if you go."

Tears stood in her eyes. Erling looked away; she was not in the habit of using tears as a weapon.

She dared not even look at him, fearful of the least mistake.

"Only a day or two, Erling, then I'll drive you to Lier."

He waited a moment, then picked up his things from the traveling bag and put them in order on the dresser. He said, with his back to her, "All right, Felicia."

• Horns for our adornment

"There is something I've had in mind telling you, Felicia. Something one dares not say. Terrible taboo-words."

"If you're going to use dirty words, you can do it somewhere else."

"I'll say the disagreeable with beautiful words; I hadn't thought of quoting from a pornographic dictionary. Anyway, it's your own fault you can't stand those words which I have no intention of using."

"I realize words in themselves can be good enough, whatever they are, Erling, but due to our particular sufferings some of them are apt to awaken memories of our past. When you use them with me the result is opposite to what is intended—but what have you in mind?"

"It is rather difficult to state, and it won't take much to stop me, so please, don't sidetrack me again."

He thought a moment. "I know very well there should be nothing in the way of my settling down here at Venhaug, because—"

Her slight movement indicated she would listen to every word.

"Let's put it this way—I'm a teller of tales and an illustrator. I get nowhere without pictures and examples. Be patient with me now; I'll get to the point eventually. You said Jan knows more of the art of living than any one of us. I won't discuss this—I don't like competitions. But he knows more about practical philosophy than anyone I've met. He has an unusual ability to look experiences in the eye and build his life upon them. He is one always to gain wisdom from damage done. Concerning one definite and very serious experience, three men gained wisdom from the damage. Few would become much wiser from *that* damage. It was therefore rather remarkable that we should know each other, we three. It was Jan, myself—and Steingrim. The other two were younger than myself, but Jan was first to gain wisdom, then Steingrim, finally I. Perhaps I've never been completely honest with you when you have talked about my living at Venhaug. I've never been afraid of Jan in that connection, though you mustn't draw the conclusion we have discussed it. But we have long ago come to an agreement about something behind the whole matter. About some deviltry we have managed to *kill*. Because of this, he and I have never had any reason to discuss anything in a way to make it appear we discussed you."

Felicia whispered, "I know you never have."

"Because there was nothing to discuss; we have the Werewolf tethered. Steingrim saw it, and felt it, but he never managed to bind it completely, and the Werewolf took him at last. This was the logical consequence when he had seen it and not conquered it. Now I wish to tell you about a man by the name of Kare Svaberg. He had the Werewolf at his side, and ought to have seen it, but did not. Men of that sort go insane. Most people neither see nor hear the Werewolf, but become generally poisoned by it.

"One evening long ago, while still living in Oslo, I was at home, talking with Kare Svaberg. It was after twelve when he left and I decided to walk a bit with him. It was a summer night, peaceful and light. He was telling me what had happened to his wife a few years earlier when she had gone to a psychiatrist for her nerves or something. I don't know if you've noticed how helpless one feels when being told about such for no reason; one just accepts it. The matter doesn't concern oneself, and for all one cares it might be a fabricated story which never has taken place. One's sense of criticism does not come into function for there is nothing to stir it; one doesn't feel involved, one doesn't know the people involved. If some small doubt should arise one suppresses it, because one's interest in the whole is minimal. I had no reason to doubt Svaberg was telling the truth, and I would soon have forgotten the incident except that the psychiatrist mentioned occupied a prominent position. Possibly I did help in the matter, but I've no recollection of so doing.

"Svaberg had tried to bring court action against the psychiatrist but without success. The doctors always stick together, he said. Such incidents could take place free of any possibility of criminal action. I said well and yes, and I remember I wondered that he would tell the story; we weren't exactly intimate. If he couldn't get at the criminal, at least he didn't help his wife by telling the story. Moreover, I had some doubts afterward; Mrs. Svaberg was no young thing, though older women can, of couse, be quite charming. But Mrs. Svaberg wasn't that either. I knew the name of the doctor and what he looked like. To me it was not convincing that he needed to use wolf-tricks to get along with women.

"Later, as my interest in the story grew, I would keep my ears open when the doctor's name was mentioned. It appeared he had always been successful with women; it was his special gift, so to speak. When women looked at him they got that weakening in the loins, you know. It is dangerous when such is documented in a court; what is a definite point in his favor becomes in court suspicious circumstantial evidence. Those who preach morality believe others have nothing to do but rape any woman anywhere, even if she were dying from cholera. Common sense should tell us this is the case only with people sexually confused, which morality preachers usually are.

"I believe a couple of years passed before I saw Svaberg again. There was nothing special about him now either, but this time my suspicions were aroused when he related troubles with some other doctor. He just mentioned it casually and immediately went on to something else, but I had a feeling he was on his guard. Perhaps it's an afterthought of mine but he didn't seem sure of himself. Anyway, our meeting reminded me of Leo Tolstoy's bloodthirsty attack against the medical profession in *The Kreutzer Sonata* and *Anna Karenina,* where he speaks of those vile men who choose their work so that they may see young women naked, and be paid for it. If Tolstoy had not been writing in the heat of sexual excitement something *must* have dawned on him. Our diseases are not in the clothing, not even in the pants, and if the panic-stricken Tolstoy thought anything at all, it must have been that it was better for a woman to die than be healed by a man. As you know, there were no women doctors in those days—this too would have been in opposition to a modesty that must be defended, even to the doors of the mortuary.

"At our second meeting, then, I started to wonder about Svaberg. Going home one winter evening I met a musician I knew. That was about the time when I first met you, Felicia. He came from a concert, in tails under his heavy coat, with a fur collar turned up over his ears. He roared to me to make himself heard, there was a blizzard and the snow filled the streets like smoke. He wanted me to go home with him for a nightcap. I could feel the wind through my clothes as we beat our way forward against the stinging, pelting snow. We swung off to a side street where it didn't blow quite so hard, and passed an entranceway where a man stood crouching. I barely noticed the gaunt face as we struggled by; it seemed unusual to be standing out there but it did not call for a comment. A few minutes later we reached the musician's flat.

"His wife was waiting with sandwiches, and something to drink. Then he said to his wife, 'It's unbelievable, but Svaberg is standing out there in this horrible weather.'

"She nodded without saying anything. 'Svaberg?' I asked. 'The face seemed familiar—was that he standing there? What's the matter with him?'

"Then I was told the whole story. It had gone from bad to worse, but for a long time no one had realized the man must be crazy. He did not disturb anyone and it was difficult to do anything. He lived across the street, not far from the entranceway where he could keep an eye on his flat. When anyone entered the door to his building, he crossed over to the opposite sidewalk and looked up to his own windows. Then he would dash across the street and up the stairs. His wife lived in a veritable hell as he searched through the apartment for her 'lover.' For many years people had assumed she was philandering but felt he could at least keep it to himself. The more sceptical still insisted there was no smoke without a fire, even if Mrs. Svaberg was careful with the fire.

"That time I came to the conclusion," said Erling, "she must once have been unfaithful to him; then in his confused and disturbed condition he had invented the stories about the doctors because he couldn't keep it to himself, but later he cracked. I wasn't sure he had gone completely insane—well, Felicia, you have seen for example *me*.

"Then one day I happened to tell Svaberg's case to a psychiatrist. He said, 'One would think you had read the case history. We have him in our institution.'

" 'What do you call the disease?'

" 'It's related to delirium diseases, in my opinion the result of brain injuries difficult to trace. This special symptom we call jealousy-delirium.'

" 'And the background—faithlessness and all that?'

" 'It's wholly unimportant. She would've had the same hell whether she had cheated him or not. Obviously he would have triumphed had he caught her in the act. Had he done so he would have had no need to invent those doctor-stories. I've met her a few times in connection with the case—she swears no doctor has ever treated her with disrespect; he accuses her of being in collusion with them. He even spread about that some had raped her. Now when she dares to speak, she explains it is all inventions of his mind. Anyway, she is rather sickly and entirely disinterested in men. This had further disturbed him.'

"I asked if it was a usual professional risk for doctors, but this he denied. If anyone showed such tendencies it usually ended up in nothing, or pure comedy. He knew practicing doctors who were not even aware that a risk was involved. Mostly specialists were the targets. Perhaps the words special, specializing, specialist worked suggestively on such men, or perhaps they simply found a wider field by letting the wife try as many as possible when she was referred to a specialist."

"What are you trying to tell me with this story?" asked Felicia. "And what is your own opinion about the Svaberg case?"

"It must remain only what I *believe* concerning this faithlessness that all immediately hook on to. Mrs. Svaberg has never been faithless to her husband, and I believe with the doctor that this has plagued him the most. He has felt painfully hurt that no one has wished to share her with him. He has felt himself insignificant for this reason, but does not suspect it. It has smouldered within him. He was a victim of the Werewolf. You ask what I am driving at, and it is difficult to express. But it'll all appear in due time, little by little. It is much easier to explain to a woman one is in love with—when at last one wants to speak up."

Erling felt he had unintentionally said something which would make her listen more attentively.

"I have no illusions," he resumed, "as so many half-educated people have, that I can master a whole list of sciences. My reading is too sporadic and varied, however great. I lack the important elementary basis. I can hold my own with the psychologists, but not the psychiatrists. But what I believe is that neuroses, psychoses, and what we usually call mental diseases, all are different degrees of brain injuries. The names are sufficient as long as one discounts anything but the degree. If we use the expression mental diseases we can say that only those caused by bodily injury or a definitely established bodily disease, have a chance of healing (let's exclude those born mentally weak). The others are incurable, both the mildest and most severe cases. This is due to the fact that the patients have been exposed to problems against which they tore their minds to pieces, and there is no chance to think it whole again. The damage has been done. They are marked for the rest of their lives, and this no one doubts, not even one who leaves the analyst as cured; what has taken place is not a cure, rather a possibility for a new start with a changed consciousness.

"Whether we like it or not we must return to the old concept—for it was right!—that *a despairing person will think his mind to pieces.* It is not true that insanity is lying in wait when our consciousness is blurred by sorrow, mistakes, mistreatment, degradation—and from thoughts and wishes one was so afraid of seeing in clear daylight that one rather sacrificed one's mind. People have always known one can think one's brain to pieces, and one of the methods used to rule people is to force them to think their brains to pieces. The funny thing, though, is that if the brain has been harmed only mildly, the person might grow above and beyond his original ego, and become dangerous as a rational being. Those damages caused through a person's own thoughts can be divided into three groups. The mildest one, which we can recognize ourselves when regaining balance after the damage, the more difficult one, which we can recognize, as well as its size, with outside aid, and then the extremely difficult cases which must be handled by others, until possibly we get far enough to manage the last part of the road by ourselves, back to light, or definitely alone in darkness.

"There is this fortunate thing about it, that all who grow above and beyond the damage they have suffered, gain more than they lose. The consciousness develops into something greater and higher than before around the injured point. Through a remarkable process the injured place becomes a feeding-center, makes us develop, grow wiser—but we can't call it recuperaton. Thus it is that a new and greater life grows round an old knife-wound.

"One symptom remains constant: the melancholy that thrives and grows through all experience, through every development of consciousness. But until the light burns down in old age, nature has endowed life with brightness only. Anyone with eyes can see this. It is un-nature that creates un-lust. Melancholy is the price we pay for enlightened consciousness, and for what we call recuperation, the symptom of the old inner damage. Therefore it is murderously depressing to see melancholic children. Adversities,· mistakes, sorrows, disappointments, as all know, might be so great that they change the course of life. When they more or less are conquered, then we have become greater human beings—but we have become melancholiacs, under one mask or another, often with a shield of humor, sometimes openly.

"The melancholiac will recall the time he barely escaped bleeding to death, and therefore he easily observes the transitoriness of all things. He is right, is even considered wise, but isn't particularly appreciated. The healthy will always say: 'He is so very right, we must die, we must decay—but why take all this in advance? After all, if there's a question of doing wrong against life, or a godhead, then this wrongdoing must consist of taking life tragically.' Thus the melancholiac is right only superficially. Who knows if everything is transient or illusory? Some melancholiacs, indeed, do not believe so, and have become entangled in contradictions without end. It is possible that the type of melancholiac who considers everything ashes, sawdust, and straw, is not at all the wisest, but rather one who has managed to dupe us with a solemnity and knowledge which concerns only details and commonplace. Isn't the melancholiac one who is tied up with his own obliteration, but only to a degree that he must constantly remind others he won't be alone?

"Felicia, once upon a time you encountered that unlucky bird, Erling from Rjukan, and you came away with a brain injury, on top of whatever injuries you already had. God knows we cannot be grateful to whoever was responsible for our meeting; yet, you lost something, and gained something else and greater, and you did not get stuck in melancholy, you rose and broke a hole in the wall and came out stronger on the other side. I had little honor from *anything* that happened during those years, but you yourself say that without all this you would never have become Felicia.

"You have a remarkable instinct, Felicia. You encountered me that time when I had seen the Werewolf but dared not admit what I had seen. To that extent at least I was still quite normal. I had been as submissive as most. But when we met again in Sweden, the Werewolf was walking life-like at my side, baring its teeth. It was just before I dared see what jealousy is—and became well; since then I have been envious of no one. Jealousy dies in him who has dared look the Werewolf in the eye.

"Jan was much younger, yet he had had the same experience long before me. But first you met Steingrim, he who also had had his fight with the Werewolf and managed to keep it clearly before his eyes. Don't you know why he left you? Because he couldn't bear exposing you to people who were still ruled by that monster—that's to say most human beings, so many one can almost say all. His courage failed him. The fact is he retreated from the solid majority. He did not retreat because of me, that you know. But do you know he shied away because he was ruled by—I'm inclined to say—democracy. He wanted us three to continue to be together. He wanted to be with you and share you with a man who at last also had stuck the knife into the throat of the Werewolf and broken the terror of jealousy. But he retreated to save your name and reputation."

Felicia kissed him and said, "Didn't you think I knew that, Erling? Did we need so many years and so much anxiety to say it?"

He looked away from her. "Yes, we needed so much time. The Werewolf is a terror-god. You can stick a knife in him, you can learn to know him and despise him, but kill him you cannot. He is the world-conqueror.

"And Steingrim was an unusually valiant—and scared—warrior. He saw the sneer among the refugees in Stockholm and elsewhere. He who knew the Werewolf and had conquered him as far as that victory can be won, he was himself married to one of the werewolf-pack. He saw the sneer directed at him from all those who, without exception, also had encounted the Werewolf, but in deadly terror had suppressed the sight. He held you too high to expose you to the slaves of the Werewolf; he was also afraid, and then also there was this with Viktoria. Mostly, he couldn't bear to see the sneer that followed you. Perhaps he didn't realize how tough you were. Then there was that little disappointment—he had thought he could have a woman without complications, a hair-raising thought in Steingrim Hagen's head! Then he left you so no one would sneer when they saw you. He became unwillingly moral, and left for your sake—so that you could marry me only. Your underlying feeling— that you only wanted to be sure of me, rule me, unable to endure someone else taking me, but unable to think of me as a legal husband or father to your children—all this was far outside Steingrim's thoughts, I believe."

"Erling, you know yourself that—"

"Steingrim was terribly innocent and naïvely chivalrous, Felicia. Then came Jan Venhaug, whom you knew—you had even killed people together. You knew that he too was a warrior, but one from the farm lands, one who had conquered the Werewolf, whom I hadn't as yet fully comprehended although he was walking at my side day and night. Of us three men I was the oldest but the last one to gain comprehension. In some respects I believe I had come further than Steingrim, and indeed, he was the one to commit suicide, not I. But I was still squirming in my last jealousy-delirium. Don't cry, Felicia! We were three men whom you understood better with the heart than with the head. You would have liked to have all three of us."

"No, no, Erling," she said quickly. "There you're wrong. Steingrim dropped out. I saw he couldn't cope, so I never made demands on him. And now he is dead long ago. I wanted him and I didn't want him. I could never have endured that he must guard my reputation. There was something lacking in Steingrim. He was afraid. He thought it would be easier with someone stupid. I hope you eventually will explain to me what you are driving at with all this talk about the Werewolf—but something like that had got its teeth in him."

"That is exactly what I'm trying to say. And has Jan never talked to you about women, and encounters with the Werewolf—perhaps in different words?"

"I believe there was something about a girl from Kongsberg. I've never been sufficiently interested in her. Once it escaped him that someone had wanted him to sell Venhaug. By then I knew enough. Was she perhaps a werewolf?"

"Nonsense, Felicia. The Werewolf has been with us since the beginning of time, and has no sex. Something that is and has always been alone, has no parents and no children. It is neither woman nor man, nor anything in between. One cannot attribute sex to either the godly or the satanic; the angels have no one to preen themselves for. No, when Jan discovered that the girl cheated on him with 'civilized' city-men, then he met the Werewolf. He 'discovered something,' he said, but did not call it the Werewolf. Then *he* received his brain injury, and turned from a well-grown but rather ordinary birch into a mighty oak. One must use solid and pastoral parables in speaking of Jan."

"Well!" said Felicia, as if hearing something new. "But what about *your* brain injury?"

"Obviously more than one. Many small ones, as they hit all people. Anyway three or four of the worst. Among all they brought me, large and small, was also the name *Erling from Rjukan,* which you learnt before the war. When I heard it myself for the first time, I had already worn it for long. Strange that it should bother me so in those days—it is in the same class as Harek of Tjøtta, not to mention Erling Skjalgsson from Sole—and to one not familiar with the background there was nothing degrading in it either for me or for the hamlet of Rjukan. I don't know who invented it but he must, in his undeniable nastiness, have had a feeling for the fitting. Now that label is gone, as far as I know—because I accepted it in silence. I am Erling from Rjukan.

"Now it doesn't matter what the brain injuries were. The important thing is what they brought me. The sickness made me tired of elegant mahogany furniture when I could afford it. The sickness in other respects let me grow to recognize the difference between a Cézanne and a picture-postcard. The sickness gave me ability and courage to see through and ridicule the puny snobbery of little Erling from Rjukan. An incurable brain injury has opened my eyes to the good earth and the heavens above it. It forced me to use reserves, it showed me the road away from the kingdom of the dead. The road has been long, yet I would not wish to have missed any part of it, absolutely nothing, not even the bitterest shame. The goal I'll never reach, but this too is good—it gives me a sort of eternal youth to have every day bring a new and dear surprise.

"Look at Svaberg. *They got him.* Not the doctors he has in mind—and who would shudder at the thought of having slept with his wife. Nor she. Not the host of imaginary lovers who fill poor Svaberg's brain. The Werewolf got him. At some point in life, at a point not now discernible, he did *not* take the bull by the horns—"

> I lost my way in beastly forest
> Round about the elves' stones—
> The Giant's daughter lured me,
> I lost my way home.

"He must have been jealous sometime, some flare-up once, and he saw the Werewolf, but dared not look at it. He used a chisel on his mind until he split it in two. What now is whirling about in his brain out at the asylum concerns fellowship, sharing, love. Poor Svaberg's dream of joy and peace, suppressed and turned into a horrible delirium in fear of once more seeing the ray of light he had seen. The Werewolf took him."

• Father and son

On the evening of November 30, Jan was sitting up late going over some bills. Toward midnight he felt thirsty and went down to the kitchen, where he poured himself a glass of fruit juice. He sat down on the kitchen bench and drank in small sips while his eyes wandered over the objects round him. He always enjoyed seeing the kitchen spick-and-span, especially at night when the farm's food-factory was at a standstill, as now. He composed in his mind a chapter-heading in the old-fashioned style: "From the Hearth to the Electric Kitchen." He recalled from childhood all the carrying of water, and the limited hygiene as a consequence. He himself had carried hundreds of gallons of water, under the yoke. The well had dried up every summer, and the distance was great to the river Lagen. Even at other seasons this had happened. So they finally had bought pipes, and a pump that always went on strike. His father had complained about such an arrangement, until he grew tired of complaining, hardly able to hide his malicious joy when there was trouble with the pump: "There you see!" The old man was still caught in the superstition that the labor of water-carrying and wood-burning must remain. He didn't say right out that it was God's intent in His unchangeable wisdom, but it was about what he meant: women and children must work themselves to death. Jan tried to enumerate the many fields where people still adhered to custom, because it was custom, and once and for all accepted; and while he every Christmas Eve read the Gospel as his father and forefathers before him, he wondered why people didn't get rid of their peevish God. Was there in all the earth any people so steeped in the catechism as the Norwegians? As a compensation they had deserted religion's heaven-reaching cathedral and moved down into its sewer. The farmer sat on his tractor but thought with his wooden plow, absorbed long ago; and as long as possible he had let his Rebecca fetch water at the well—until Rebecca finally had made life sufficiently miserable for him.

Jan's revolt against his father apparently had taken place quite painlessly. No one except Jan knew about the furious storm that had raged.
One day in 1937 Jan had placed the farm's records for the last ten years
on his father's desk, gathered together with much effort from slips of
paper, bills, his father's own statements over the years, and much else.
He had pointed out all the shortcomings these records contained, the
decline they indicated; he had hinted cautiously that after another ten
years there might be no Venhaug any more.

The deciding impulse to take up the fight had come to him when his
father had almost accidentally let it be known that he intended to sell
some of the forest land.

The fight had been carried on in deep silence. The father said nothing
for a couple of months, but did not force the forest-sale. He started to age
and avoided looking his son in the eyes during the whole time. Jan by
and by arrived at the point where he didn't know what to do with
himself. The silence lay over the whole farm. Father and son no longer
heard human voices, so to speak.

One Sunday morning in the fall Jan had made ready to hunt grouse.
His father asked if he could come along. Jan squirmed under the almost
frightening question, and at last his eyes met his father's. They were
tired and sad; his father stood there silently and was asking reprieve. Jan
had a wild feeling that some victories were too expensive; he would have
liked to throw his gun on the floor and start crying. Instead, he replied
calmly something about having seen these big birds in such and such a
place lately (he hardly recognized his own voice), and his father replied
eagerly that this was correct. As they left the house both knew that eyes
were watching them from the windows.

They walked a long time through the forest and nothing was said. As
soon as they had left the yard Jan managed to walk behind his father,
and when the first bird took wing he called out, "Your shot, Father! I'm
not in a good position."

Then they sat down, each on his stone, and looked at the grouse. His
father pulled out a hip-flask from his pocket and said, "This calls for a
drink!"

Actually neither one of them cared much for liquor. They drank,
looked some more at the grouse, and sat a long while sizing up each
other. It would have been obvious that his father should have the first
shot, and he had never offered Jan a drink before or brought liquor on a
hunt.

Jan kicked the moss with his boot-heel and did not look up as he said,

"I did write down a few lines, and I know well how it could be taken, but I'll never get rid of Venhaug."

His father coughed and said, "Well, I realize as much. I never thought you would."

Presently he added, "It seems matters do repeat themselves—I didn't put anything in writing to your grandfather, I wasn't inclined that way; it happened in the barn; I yelled out at last: 'To hell with Venhaug!' In the evening he told me matters had gone too far when I could use such talk.'

Now a long silence ensued. The father took up the thread again: "I don't wish to cede with 'reserved rights.' That kills a man—and it was not to the advantage of either the father or the son the last time things were so arranged. That you too must think of when your time comes. You have taken over now, and there is little need of papers. I only ask you to get your electric pump first of all—otherwise I'll wonder why you don't get one. That's all, Jan. That's the way I want it. And now for the first time in months I shall enjoy a drink." He put the flask to his mouth, then handed it to Jan. When both had had their fill, the father said, "Jan, it isn't as bad as you perhaps think, but in one sense much worse than such colts as you can realize. I have saved money while Venhaug stood still. You will have your troubles, but tonight when I put everything on the table—it's silly, Jan, but I'm anxious to turn over everything and issue your legal power."

Jan was glad his father had not at that time brought up marriage and heirs. Nor did he mention it later, not until he lay dying. It must have cost the old man a lot to let the subject rest. At one time his father had almost insisted he get married. He had also hinted at some good "wife-timber," fine women in every respect. That time the storm had passed by. Jan had rather expected his father to get furious at the reply he had ready, but when Jan with irritation pointed out that it was he and not the father who must sleep with the girl, the old man started laughing. Jan wondered how his father would have taken the daughter-in-law he got. Yes, Felicia had money. That would have carried weight with his father. And she knew what she wanted. He would have respected that too. But his father had eyes all around his head, and could hear like a forest beast. Some ghastly noise would have risen heavenward had two such millstones been put to grind together.

• "*I gave her Helled Hagen—*"

Jan walked out on the veranda to check on the weather. Earlier in the evening some more snow had fallen but now the night was still and white, with starlight and a half-moon. He looked for the two new "moons" and the capsule of the first which in turn had become a moon itself, but they were not visible. "And God created the two great lights, the bigger to rule by day and the smaller by night, and then the Russians made two somewhat smaller." Jan would have preferred to let things be as they were and that all new moons should fall down again. They disturbed him.

He filled his lungs with the cold, refreshing air and thought perhaps he was among the last to dare drink in the winter night without fear that it was deadly. It had tasted so wonderful ever since he had had pneumonia a year ago. Double pneumonia. He had been delirious for a whole day. The children had mimicked him months afterward: "Oh, I'm so sick, Felicia, so sick, so sick, Felicia!" She had been sitting at his side the whole time, and she was paler than he when it was over. The penicillin had made Jan weak in his knees so he couldn't walk normally for a while, and he was getting quite fed up with his daughters walking behind him, dragging their feet, they too, complaining: "I'm so sick, Felicia!' But the sickness had given him something the children and the others couldn't share: *they* didn't realize the air could have an aroma like fine wine. The doctor had said it was "only" because he needed oxygen so much. Everything good must be labeled "only." He remembered something a boy in school had said when the teacher had birched him out in the yard: "Every time something is real good you get it in the ass." God only knows what the teacher might have done with the air if Jan had said it tasted good.

The moon shone on a line of dark spots in the snow, they continued between the tall birches and on toward Old Venhaug. They were footsteps, he discovered, more noticeable in the new snow, darker in the moon shadow. He also noticed that they had come across the veranda. The tracks did not return. He pulled back his sleeve and looked at his wrist watch. All was dark at Old Venhaug. His eyes returned to Felicia's tracks:

> I took proud Brunhild from Glassberg
> In full daylight.

I gave her Helled Hagen
For companionship.

Jan walked backward and saw his shadow grow smaller and smaller until he had no shadow at all, standing under the entrance light. He stopped for a moment in the living room, then he crossed over to the bookcase and took down Strindberg's *Black Banners*.

Soon he found the place:

". . . that nasty female tennis game, rather bent on hurting the opponent than, as is the case in the real game, getting in a beautiful ball . . ."

"When, as now is the case, the woman has absolute veto in every disagreement between them, then the man is defenseless, and then the lie rules the world . . ."

". . . no, I've never in our circle seen a married man unfaithful, if not forced by his wife . . ."

"Jealousy is the husband's purification-spring which keeps his thoughts free from being entangled with another man's sexual sphere, through the wife. A man who is not jealous, but accepts, is a sodomite. I know one man who enjoyed his wife's affairs and loved the 'family friends' . . ."

"It is only an invective and as such a lie . . ."

The last quotation he had underlined when, as very young, he had come across *Black Banners*. The book had later been lost, but when Felicia brought Strindberg's works to the house, he had in 1946 reread *Black Banners*. When he came to the sentence he had again underlined it—in a sort of pious tribute to his youth, but it was also something else.

Then, so long ago, he had not paid much attention, perhaps none at all, to the context where the quotation appeared. It had only struck the seventeen-year-old as a profound truth that invectives are lies. The remark was directed against the supposition that a man was a woman-hater when he had been married several times and had children with all the wives. Then it was a *lie* to call him a woman-hater. Jan considered the logic more than dubious, but accepted as earlier that invectives were lies.

He felt the whole thing was rather difficult to argue about. If, in certain circles, no husband could be unfaithful to his wife except on her demand, then that flock of husbands must be of a peculiar brand of morality, all with Lesbian wives. On the other hand, male jealousy was supposed to be an expression of purity and a protest against being driven into another man's sexual sphere—and the man without jealousy was a sodomite—an invective so rough that even at best it didn't cover such men's inclinations.

It was remarkable to see jealousy raised to the utmost virtue, this feeling that always was more or less connected with self-contempt, contained in a feeling of unmitigated shame.

Jan went upstairs and to bed. He lay awake for long, his hands folded under his head, and thought *through* the nature of jealousy once more. Jealousy had once almost killed him and he felt he was familiar with it. It seemed obvious to him that Strindberg on this subject had happened to say something quite opposite to the truth. Jealousy in a sexual meaning might be absent altogether, it could be weak, it could have all degrees up to a cause for murder. In some societies it was unknown. Some people, especially men, affected jealousy because they thought it was the proper behavior. Generally speaking Jan considered it had two causes: fear that the desired one might entirely get out of the picture, and apprehension as to what people might say about the so-called cheated member. The first might be reasonable, but it was after all self-worship and not love. The second was to be the victim of a dubious convention. In both cases jealousy was a cry for force in love, something in itself unreasonable, but accepted in law—which consequently should lead to jealousy also being accepted through law. Yet, on the contrary, certain forms of jealousy were punishable. It was a virtue, or something degrading, depending on from which direction the wind blew. It was precisely as degrading to be jealous, as not to be, and anyone smelling it started at once to figure out new laws instead of abolishing old ones. The same people who derided the jealous one, were ready with a whole arsenal of accusations against the one who was not jealous. But how about themselves? Where was the love, or at least some common sense, in this idiocy of thought and feeling? What caused healthy, normal, grown people— often greatly gifted—always at some stage of their lives to pose the question, to themselves and to others whether it was possible to love *two?* The question obviously was answered the moment it was raised. How was it possible people didn't believe their own experiences?

They dared not. Under persistent and devastating pressure they were made to believe they were perverse when they showed signs of being normal. Others again accused them of being emotionally sick because they feared they themselves might be, when actually deep down they were equally sound. What plagued the calm, considerate Jan the most was the enormous hypocrisy. Those fiery, even hysterical, defenders of the one-man-one-woman idea—those were the ones especially marked as tearing the wildest at their chains, or sinning with their shackles rattling. Those who had discovered the two-and-two combination, and felt happy in it, seldom voiced an opinion about something that was a problem only for those yelling. Where was the key to the peculiar riddle that all must act in the same way, not only in controllable matters, but also behind closed doors, even in their beds? Perhaps it was strangest of all that the very ones who stuck to the holy norm because it suited them, never were attacked by sinners of other hues—nor were these people who liked the official norm very aggressive toward the polygamists. It was only the men with obviously unhappy marriages who insisted on punishment for polygamy. In short, people seemed to become tolerant when they were happy in their own situation. Those who stuck their noses into other people's business had nothing enjoyable to stick them into at home.

• The effective ones

Erling arrived in Oslo about noon on January 3, 1958. It was a Friday. He checked his bag at the station since he had no reservation; he telephoned a few hotels in vain and gave up; he would find some place to spend the night.

While he was having his lunch at the Theater Café, the thought struck him it might not be so easy to find night-quarters after all. The one he had in mind to invite himself to, knew she could not expect anything from him after all the Christmas drinking; but he knew that this would not be too important—it wouldn't be the first time she had received him as a wreck. Suddenly the thought didn't appeal to him. It wasn't one of his devil-may-care days. Sometimes still he was aware of these remnants of old and ingrown vanity and fear, which always made him think of his childhood in Rjukan; he could see himself slinking along, in memory playing his psychopathic role of the village tailor's son. Once a tailor, always a tailor.

He sat with his coffee, and a glass, and kept his eyes open for people appearing round the nearest corner of the irregular-shaped dining room, looking for tables or acquaintances; he was careful to make it look as if he was occupied with his newspaper. There were only a few people in the restaurant now, it was neither the lunch nor the dinner hour. When he noticed faces he recognized without being able to place them he became especially occupied with his paper. Others he knew by name and these were easier to handle; he knew how to defend himself against them. Those faces he couldn't place were much more difficult; one might happen to bite people one had no reason to bite. He pulled out some papers and his pen from his briefcase, to make himself appear very busy, and wrote a few lines to document his activity: "In the Beginning I created heaven and earth, and the earth was empty and darkness was over the depths, and My spirit hovered over the waters. I was careful not to say 'Let there be light!' for then someone might see Me."

He thought of Vera and Jasper; he might stay with them. But one didn't ask for such; one didn't stay with one's friends. Everybody expected, as did he himself, that people should call for a taxi when it grew late. It was humanly right to get rid of one's friends. They mustn't be lying on the sofa in the morning and mumble something about borrowing a razor. He recalled one time when he *didn't* stay over. ("It would be such a compliment if you stayed.") But he knew the hostess was a little peculiar; she was positively brusque as she said, "It's upstairs, the door to the left." He went up, opened the door: in bed was a woman smiling at him. He closed the door, went downstairs, and said there must be some mistake, for Mrs. Jørstad was in bed there. The hostess became confused: "Well, yes—she said—she said that—and so I thought—"

In fury Erling had called for a taxi. For some reason he remembered it had cost twenty-two kroner to the city, even in those old, cheap days.

Such a situation would not arise at Vera and Jasper Arndt's. There you were plainly welcome, could talk about sensible matters and enjoy yourself. He started, and muttered to himself, "Speak of the devil!"

Jasper Arndt was standing at the bar, in overcoat, his hat in hand, looking at Erling. Now Vera joined him. They came to his table, asked if it was convenient, and Jasper carried out the overcoats. Vera sat down on the seat next to Erling. She was blossoming with health and happiness. The cold from outside was still on her cheeks, a wave of fresh air wafted from her as she struggled out of her fur coat. Then she started to examine Erling; she was one of those who worried about his welfare. "Are you taking care of yourself?" she asked. The question touched him, but it had also begun to bother him in recent years. He felt it was posed too often. When he looked at himself in the mirror there were times he realized why. It isn't only that I have passed the meridian, he thought, that must have happened some time ago. People are beginning to be friendly, as with a father, or an uncle they like. The same thing has happened as when I lost my youth and only discovered it a few years later. I must have been wearing the frost of age on my face for a long time now, without knowing it. At least for three or four years. Death is thoughtfully looking up at my house when he passes through Lier.

Jasper Arndt returned and sat down on a chair facing them; he liked to have a whole side of the table to himself. He was of middle height, a heavy, blond muscle-man in whom everything was broad; broad face, forehead broad and low, neck and shoulders like a gorilla. Now he fumbled on the table for an ash tray and menu with his long, powerful arms, while Vera watched him with a beaming and affectionate smile. Their friends had been forced to acknowledge that Vera and Jasper were a happy couple. That is something people don't acknowledge without opposition and protest, and for good reason in most cases. Vera and Jasper, then, were accepted as a happy couple—but with watchful eyes fastened on them from the rat-holes. Under certain circumstances it is supposed to appear more convincing to the dubious if the woman is exceptionally attractive, and the man looks as if he could break a telephone pole with his bare hands; and both are known for obvious amiability as long as no one insults them purposely.

Jasper Arndt was an engineer in some firm which built bridges or something, at home and abroad. Erling's conceptions about such matters were usually vague. Jasper had a good income and some money, a car, a house in Smestad. On that point also Erling's ideas were vague. About money he knew nothing, except that he tried to earn some when the bills began to annoy him, or that a check might come in from something he had written twenty years ago and which had been almost totally for-gotten until somebody wanted to reissue it. In that way he was, so to speak, pensioned off, he who had avoided his pension-rights because of a fear of early death; similarly with life insurance and other arrangements that were advertised along the roadsides, pointing to the cemetery, or so he thought. Strangely enough, he realized others did exactly the opposite from the same fear of death.

Vera and Jasper were thirty-five and had three children, all girls, and all five members of the family were life-insured.

Erling listened and looked from one to the other while they talked and ate. Would he ever understand them and all they stood for—Vera and Jasper whom he knew so well? Would he ever understand their energy, their positiveness which was obviously of the happy kind? Would he ever understand people who as a matter of course rose at seven every morning, even when they had gone to bed at four? He himself under those circumstances, equally as a matter of course, would sleep until twelve. Would he ever understand the *effective human being*? He thought of Felicia, Jan, and many others who were vastly stronger than he, even though, for inscrutable reasons, he was always considered the stronger. They kept their hard workdays, yet managed hard evenings like himself. On the other hand, three days in succession, night and day, like himself, none of these effective individuals could endure, neither in work nor in feast.

He had never envied any one of them. He simply admired them, in secret. How could they radiate such health—like Vera sitting there, who had three children, and took care of her big house without help, partied a great deal, was always in good humor, and had time to chat with friends over the telephone. Always in balance, always ready with sympathetic understanding, never tired—and when in all the world did she have time for all the books that interested her?

And Jasper? One couldn't brush it off by saying he was strong as a dinosaur. Yes, a body was needed, but it was far from a general rule that strong bodies were anchored in will power and were effective. As he looked at Jasper he thought here is a man who doesn't even know what the word health means, and never has approached the edge of his limitations. One was entrusted with, or accepted, a problem, and solved it; Jasper would hardly have more to say on that subject, and he would look uncomprehending if anyone raised the question. Or, might perhaps, even in him, a knot have been formed, difficult to explain, something he hid under the industrialist's accepted mask of matter-of-factness, and which might in time slow down his power of action, even though he continued to look energetic?

The question of how best to manage one's time had been a constant problem to Erling, ever since he started to reason as a grown-up, and the problem still remained with him as a sorrow one couldn't do anything about when approaching sixty. The days had always run away from him, and it was small comfort to him that all his life he had had occasional spurts of febrile activity. What might not have germinated out of the thousands of days he had spent staring at the floor, apathetic, unshaved, listless.

Erling had learned it did not pay to ask such people how they had managed to arrive at their effectiveness. Perhaps it was beyond their comprehension that a person could be otherwise, and anyway, most of them were inclined to talk of "pulling oneself together," or even bare their lack of understanding of human phenomena by talking of something they called laziness, the usual way of expressing the fact that a person is wrongly placed and hates it, something that, at times, attempts had been made to correct, through beating, as if this were conducive to greater appreciation. Ludvig Holberg, who was so effective in spite of his poor health (or perhaps because of it?), must have been asked how he managed; otherwise he would hardly have taken up the question and tried to answer it in one of his essays. The efficient one takes efficiency for granted, the same as an arm, or the nose, and does not unprovoked discuss the subject. Nor did Holberg understand it as a question: he only comments that unessentials ought to be pushed aside, and superfluous letters avoided. After that his reflections trail off into nothing and then shift to a subject that can compel his interest: "You wish to know if the cattle-sickness has hit my farm too. Why should I be saved more than others? My cows have quite died out, but my neighbor's dog on the other hand is still alive and well, although I have cursed him more than once for howling night and day. Well, one has to take things as they come."

Well, then we know that much about the cattle-sickness and the neighbor's dog. Holberg must have been yawning when he tried to answer a stupid question in his fictitious letter. This about pushing aside unessentials was the same answer one received from people who uselessly started to ponder problems they knew nothing about. Pull yourself together! they say to people who wish nothing better. It is said of Henry Ford that it "made him heart-sick" to see anyone sit and do nothing. He would have been healthier if it hadn't interested him, and still healthier if that machine, Henry Ford, had understood what he saw.

Erling had been classified as something called manic-depressive. It was a long time since *he* had attempted to classify anyone, himself included. Life seemed to him for every year more of a riddle, a constantly more anxiety-filled mystery. Would he have come closer to the glowing kernel if he long ago had taken another course? Am I altogether a lost man? Someone had classified a mental disease whose main characteristic was a feeling of the unreality of all things, but wasn't this too easy an explanation? The one filled with fear for the unreality of all things, wasn't he on the contrary approaching the gates of reality? He who lives will see—but no one will live, no one will see. I have seen the first airplane, and satellites, but I have never felt one can approach reality through artificial birds and false moons.

I sit here now and register that I am together with two people; each of us has his own line of thought while we communicate with one another. In everything each motion we make is a mystery—why should I not have a feeling of unreality?

Vera was unfolding a paper she had found on the table. "Well, I declare!" she exclaimed, her mouth full of food. "Now Erling is having delusions of grandeur!" She read aloud, choking with laughter: "In the Beginning I created heaven and earth, and the earth was empty and darkness was over the depths, and My—capital *M*—spirit hovered over the waters. I—capital letter, which it should be anyway—was careful not to say 'Let there be Light!' for then someone might see Me—capital *M*. Is this an introduction to some new book?"

"It *is* a sort of delusion of grandeur," said Erling, as Jasper examined the document to grasp its contents after Vera's confused reading. "First I was reading a newspaper, in order to appear busy. Then I realized that wouldn't be enough, and I started writing. I was tired and irritated and had enough delusion of grandeur to decide who was to sit with me. When you came, the paper became superfluous."

"A farfetched compliment," said Jasper, and emptied a glass of cognac.

Vera looked at her watch: "I must get home to the brats. Where are you staying, Erling?"

"I couldn't get a hotel room, but I'll find something."

Vera looked at Jasper: "Why don't I take the car—then you and Erling can sit a while and take a taxi home, when I've got the children to bed."

"You imply two things," said Jasper. "One, that I've drunk a few glasses and should not drive; two, Erling will stay the night with us."

After Vera had left, Jasper asked if it was true that Erling a few years ago had stepped on a plank that was lying under tension and as a consequence had been thrown some ten yards through the air and had landed on top of a filled garbage-truck. Erling admitted this symbolic incident had occurred. It had been at a building-site he had unsuspectingly entered on an errand of nature, but the next time he would not hesitate to outrage that silly notion, public decency.

Jasper sipped his grog thoughtfully and said, "That sort of thing only happens to you. Is there actually anyone who might *wish* to make fun of himself?"

"There's some truth in that," said Erling. "It's part of my life. As a child I hadn't learnt to allow for it; therefore I always had bad experiences. The surprise, you might say. For many years now I have taken into account the worst that possibly can happen. Or the most ridiculous. Or the idiotically incomprehensible. Have I ever told you about the wash pail that disappeared one time in Stockholm? I had rented a small flat. It was completely empty when I came there for the first time, and rather dusty. I went out to a store and bought a scrubbing brush, a mop, and a pail, since I had nothing better to do. Then I started to wash the floor. When I was about half through I turned around, as I had done several times before, in order to wring out the mop. But the pail had vanished. No one had been in the room except the pail and me. And the brush and the mop of course; they were still there. I looked around. No pail. I looked in the other rooms. Nothing. The front door was locked from the inside—there was only that one entrance door. All windows were closed because it was a cold day, and moreover, it was on the third floor. I looked through every one of the closets and the cupboards. The pail wasn't there and was never found. Finally I suspected myself, that I hadn't bought it. So I went down to the store and asked for a receipt for my purchases. I said I had to have it in order to get my money back, which of course was nonsense, but I was so nervous I felt I had to give some explanation. Yes, he wrote out the receipt for one mop, one brush, and one pail. I went back to the flat. The pail wasn't there, I never saw it again. I was careful not to buy another."

Jasper got his grog into his windpipe which caused some commotion, then he gasped, "I have a few thousand invested in a pail factory—you won't get a job there! Or perhaps—if you could conjure away all the pails we sell, after they are paid for. What a pity you don't remember how you did it!"

"I don't like you to laugh," said Erling. "People laugh because it was only a silly pail. If I exchanged the pail for something of great value—a small child, for example—then you wouldn't sit there and laugh. It's now fifteen years since it happened, and I haven't yet quite got over it. It's stupid of me to stick to the pure truth. If I had said it was a rosary that disappeared, no one would have thought the experience comical, and the story would have been equally true. It must have been a nasty devil that spirited away just a pail, but of course, there was nothing else to take. I don't know if you have read Graham Greene's story about the poor writer who had a three hundred pound pig fall on him when he was taking his morning walk in Naples. It killed him and the pig too. The man's son grew up a scum. People turned in the street and said, 'Did you see him? His father was killed by a pig that fell on him. He was an author. A three hundred pound pig.' Be careful, Jasper: out of consideration for your children you mustn't be killed by a falling pig, it must be at least a meteor, or a satellite, or they won't have a chance. Don't ever mix pigs or pails with a mystery."

There was something Jasper wanted to ask, and Erling was again on guard, but what he said couldn't stir him greatly: "Do you think you know Nina Blaker sufficiently?" asked Jasper, cautiously.

"Nina Blaker? Do I know her *sufficiently*? I should think so, since I have no desire to know her better. Is she spreading tales?"

"Well, she doesn't say anything right out; she implies, and that can be worse."

"You needn't say more. It's obvious what she means, but there never has been anything and never will."

"When both sides make their own statements, people believe what they want to believe—and never the most innocent."

"But they must know they can't hurt me with any kind of stories. I'm immune as a wall, and no one can hurt me. You might suffer through gossip, you might lose your job. That curse you have in common with most; that is why it's so difficult for you to understand that all gossip about my kind has the opposite effect to the one intended. Let it be as stupid, nasty, hateful as you please, it only adds further to the disgustingly 'interesting' picture of the author—a picture that for many years now has been of little interest to the one it now is supposed to hit. One of the women who hates me the most, has for years been my best impresario. It is rather unpleasant to say, but to me it proves mostly her inability to free herself, and some remnant of veneration makes me feel sorry for her. In spite of all, one learns to brutally recognize what is mostly to one's advantage, and all you are afraid of is to my advantage. Observe America, where they seek any kind of publicity, even pay to get it, they beg for it, sell themselves for it—for all this, that has been forced on me. I must have fought for years to defend myself, privately and publicly, before I realized I was only pouring oil on the fire. Now my comfort is that all this stinking smoke will evaporate almost the day I die."

The restaurant had filled with dinner guests. At times Erling would look about in the room but quickly withdraw his eyes. "You must realize I envy you," he said. "But I prefer to call it something else."

Jasper Arndt looked at him in surprise and burst out laughing. "What in hell are you saying? Which of us should envy the other, if there's going to be any envying? What I had in mind was some details of your life that I suspect might hurt others. A few details, nothing more. But if I were to envy anyone it would be you. I could stand on one leg and ramble off a hundred advantages you have over all the rest of us. First, the immense gift you have for staying off the ladder where every climber only tries to push the others down. Do you actually believe in the mask I must assume if I wish to keep my position? Don't you live in a world without competition? Don't you live in a place of your own choice? Couldn't you any day it suited you move to another place that might suit you better? Haven't you attained more than you yourself dreamt? Aren't you completely indifferent as to who is nominated for what by the king? Don't you live in happy ignorance of who is elected or rejected by the voters for city government, and have no need of calculating the consequences? Aren't you conscious of the fact that no one else can take your place, and that you desire no one else's? Can't you afford to let others enjoy all the good life might bring them, because nothing is denied *you?* Aren't you a favorite of the gods to have an occupation that does not force you to stretch the law or, morally speaking anyway, trespass on other people in financial matters? Have you ever been forced to bring a man to bankruptcy and throw him into the street, even though you know he has been pursued with calamities? Are you not a fortunate person not to have to call on your enemies with a friendly face? Or receive them in your own house with a so-called friendly smile, hoping to God they will leave as soon as possible? Can't you decide for yourself with whom you wish to share a drink or conduct business? Isn't your freedom of action limited by no other laws than the ones you would have no interest in breaking? Not even your work forces you to bargain! When in hell have you listened to an alarm clock? No one bawls you out when you go to work, no one cries when you leave. Your most remarkable attainment after the war I won't even mention—but even that you couldn't have managed if our Lord hadn't endowed you with His particular blessing. I will not say anything more, for of course it is myself I talk of when I criticize someone else, and who wants to bare himself more than is necessary—"

A man had come to their table and used this moment to ask Erling, "May I join you?"

"No!" said Erling, and turned to Jasper.

They kept silent a few moments, watching the man's feet, before he withdrew.

"Who was that?" asked Jasper.

"Don't remember. But you said—"

"I said a great deal," interrupted Jasper. "Who, may I ask, can do what you did just now? *I* would have to be drunk to do it. I wouldn't be able to sleep wondering who the man was. I would have been forced to rise, angry as hell, yet with an appearance of utmost friendliness, and say something like 'I'm terribly sorry, but it's so long since—' "

"I'm sorry to disappoint you," said Erling, "but this was a special case. That man couldn't have the slightest doubt he was interrupting a conversation of interest only to us. I reacted quite naturally to a piece of insolence which *I* wouldn't have perpetrated on others."

Jasper sighed. "It doesn't change one iota what I said. I have to endure many inconveniences I wouldn't dream of causing others. The point is, *you know* it doesn't hurt you. You know that man can't get even with you, regardless of who he is or what he might do. Now he is sitting where he was before, and is slandering and blackening you—thinking he can kill a legend."

"One more impresario," said Erling.

Jasper pulled out a large cigar that fitted well in his great stone face. "Were you at Venhaug for Christmas?"

Now it comes, thought Erling. He looked away, as if just catching sight of something, stared steadily in that direction, as he replied, "Well, I spend all the holidays there. In fact, we talked about my taking over an old house they have and moving there for good."

Jasper did not reply, and Erling felt his friend was looking at him askance. When Jasper finally made a move it was to call the waiter for the bill: "It's time to leave," he said.

They were standing in the cold outside, waiting for the taxi they had ordered. The big cigar in Jasper's mouth pointed at the National Theater; the smoke mixed with his breath and turned into mist in the frosty air.

"I would so like to say one thing, Jasper. We are friends and I don't like to ask any favors—but you brought up this about Venhaug."

"I understand," replied Jasper, quickly. "But I had reasons of my own. You must realize it's Vera who is interested. It seems women more than men size up other women and what they stand for; and attempt something that might be called identification. A sort of daydream. And then they apply it to their husbands; they daydream until they are all upset. The mistress of Venhaug has become a fixed idea, I might say, and in this case particularly so, since we know the people involved. I don't know exactly how men look at it. With pigs' eyes, I guess. For women it's as if they heard a strange signal. There is something in that signal which they fear—and long for."

He stopped a moment, staring at the National Theater as he continued, "You must realize, beside you I'm a child when it comes to experience—but I forget it when I talk with you, for then you too become thirty-five. Now I will tell you what you might not know, that we of thirty-five look at you as one of our age, and so do even some in their twenties. This, plain and simple, is your amazing attainment. If anyone has managed anything like it before, I don't know about it. And since you now are almost sixty it means you are dangerous. How do you do it, take on the ages of others? When did it start, Erling? Do you feel anything special when it takes place? Well, I guess not; I don't believe you yourself really recognize this peculiar mechanism—the man of all ages and none. I myself, I am less interested in your talk than in what you *are*. Perhaps I'm begging for advice, of God knows what; advice about something I don't know."

He had neither turned his head, nor removed the cigar from his

mouth. Erling stood there in the severe cold and felt hot and embarrassed.

"I believe that's our taxi now," said Jasper. "I'll remember, I'll never
bring up Venhaug again, but I trust you believe me when I say—perhaps
putting it poorly and not well thought through—I wanted to illuminate
something in myself. You must know that even if I were curious I could
control myself. I wanted information and went about it in about the
same way I would in business. I am happy, it looks as if I were very
happy. But there are so many strange things—"

On their way to the station to pick up Erling's bag, and then to
Smestad, only occasional words were exchanged—about the cold, and
the difficult driving conditions.

• Master-Mason Pedersen's wife

"Tell us something nice about love," pleaded Vera, as she made herself
comfortable in the easy chair before the fire. "But really good, Erling!
Something to make my spine tingle. And something very decent, like
real life."

"Then I want to say a word first," said Jasper. "Something I've
thought about a great deal. As late as today. I wonder if sex isn't the only
thing people think of. Those who say they don't are the ones to worry
most about things erotic. But as I say, don't you think it is the one
subject everybody thinks about the most? For example, when I attend
business meetings, I use my pencil industriously—doodling naked girls,
which I put into my pocket before anyone has time to see my supposedly
important scribbles. Once I drew a girl being birched. We were discussing a new metal alloy, I recall. I have a feeling sex lurks behind every
bush, when it doesn't dance around the bush. Mom, *macht,* meat—isn't
it all the same?"

"It does happen there are times, indeed long periods, when one doesn't
think of anything else," said Erling. "It is much easier for the woman—
she is sex personified. She isn't always aware of this—a tiger doesn't
remind itself every moment it is a tiger. Woman is sex personified, and
man is its errand-boy."

"Stop it!" said Vera. "I would like to hear something about love.
Nothing with juicy, pornographic words which crush the sweet expectations. I appreciate the art of hinting, leaving room enough for my own
imagination. That's best."

"Shall I tell you about Master-Mason Pedersen's wife?"

"It depends on how old you were yourself. I've read too many sweet stories about the six-year-old's ethereal love for Mrs. Pedersen."

"I was nineteen."

"And Mrs. Pedersen?"

"She was thirty-eight."

"Do you still see her?"

Jasper had the habit of getting drinks into his windpipe. It happened this time because he was so quick with figures: "Good Lord, Vera! Mrs. Pedersen must be seventy-eight now!"

"Yes," admitted Erling, and looked into the fire. "She must, because she was thirty-eight in 1918, exactly forty years ago. It was she who taught me the woman is sex in person and the man its errand-boy. Moreover, I consider it in bad taste for Jasper to laugh. In 1930 I tried to find Kamma Pedersen. I tried again shortly before the war. The last time was in January of 1953—that's to say, that time I came as a sort of pilgrim to look at the house where she had lived, but had left before 1930; the last time even the house wasn't there, only a vacant site; it had been torn down for a new one to be built. I lived with Mrs. Pedersen for four months."

"You must be terribly old," said Vera, "when your girl-friend in 1918 was three years older than I am now in 1958. You should be looked after—if I didn't have Jasper and the children—"

"Keep quiet!" said Jasper, sternly. "Erling knows all that."

Erling searched his memory and started several times before he found the right words and began: "It is this way," he said, "I have had many lookout towers in my life. I have a feeling most people are so anxious to forget their old lookouts that they actually do so. I have never forgotten my old towers, and if I must tell about Kamma Pedersen, then I must climb my old lookout in Rjukan. A gentleman never admits he has had other lookouts than his present one, or that he saw anything from them. I am not a gentleman, but instead I can tell you a gentle story from my old tower which still stands in Rjukan. It isn't told from today's tower.

"I shall never forget what once was mine. Not my parents, nor my playmates. None. I have over the years worn a path between my towers, and as long as I live I can never tell anything, important or unimportant, without a walk from tower to tower. Some are ivory towers, some towers of Babylon, some leaning towers, and some insignificant hills on the landscape. In some cases I only poke my head up through a hole in the ground.

"Anyway—I had happened to sign on on a boat and had to leave it in Copenhagen. It was shortly before Christmas, the depression had come on, and boats were laid up, and all those things you can read about in books. There was unemployment because the blessed war had come to an end, I heard a man say in a tramcar. I couldn't find a new job.

"It is remarkable how birds of a feather flock together. As you know, I wanted to write, and within a week I had met up with two boys who also wanted to write. How such a *recognition* is possible I don't know. None of us ever announced our ambition with word or sign. Yet, there must have been something, for one day one of them said to me, 'The funny thing with you is that you look like a poet and happen to be one.'

"We stuck together as boys do in youth. Straightforwardly, and without reservations, we acknowledged each other's undeniable genius and read enthusiastically aloud our 'collected works' in a rented room. We were unfamiliar with criticism and enjoyed blissful moments as we debated and visualized our richly promising future. Incidentally, neither one of the other two reached forty; both died their anonymous deaths, emaciated by talents not great enough to break through, and enough drinking and disappointments to ruin their health. I can well understand parents who get worked up when a son or daughter wants to take up art. For almost one hundred percent of those who do, go to hell; and so parents keep urging the youth to realize that painting and such can be pleasant to fool around with in the evenings. Only vaguely do parents understand what is so terrible, namely that the one who goes in for art places all on one card, and has only one. They see the son or the daughter having chosen a road that only rarely leads to anything but ruin, and they feel the youth should *choose* another road, without understanding that there is no other road and no choice. And so I have only one reply to every youth who asks if I think he ought to continue: 'It is not a question of what anyone thinks; if you actually *can* stop, then you'll only amount to something less than third class, and you must stop immediately. But even if you cannot stop, this is no guarantee of your success.'

"Well, as I said, in Copenhagen I couldn't get a job of the sort people call sensible, and I wanted to stay there as long as possible since it was the first time in my nineteen years I had found friends who at least helped me get over the thought that I was the only crazy one. I met several of that kind, some even crazier than I, and some who played crazier than they were, and that isn't good, for they are never crazy enough. Not a few among the ones of my own age down there did have it in them, as time has shown, but I didn't meet them at that time. All those I knew have gone to hell. Only two or three did I keep track of, indirectly. All died. How many of the others died I don't know, but as far as I knew them they belonged to the group I must call the real ones, judging them from the point of view that not one of them could stop, and consequently I believe all are dead.

"All this led me into a chaotic group of hopeful youths and old characters who prophesied over their beers. It was a sort of floating chaos where one could manage to live enough not to die, at least not until one had spent some ten years, I suppose, in the murky atmosphere. Now I only vaguely remember how I got food; mostly only bread, but I have a recollection of some beer. And some cash, I believe, although of the smallest kind.

"It is one of my peculiarities that I always look about for a place to stay. Some of my friends then, as well as some in later years, have looked askance at this, but I have always wanted a place where I could put my head at night and not feel cold. It wasn't clear to me then that the one who sleeps in the gutter is doomed, but I had noticed that it made one a complainer and pleader, and made life so horribly dull. I didn't like that. Once in that stride it was difficult to get out, and one thing and another. I mentioned these sentiments to someone, who took me to Mrs. Pedersen and introduced me as a live-in prospect. I could sleep in the kitchen, on a mattress Mrs. Pedersen warned me must be rolled up by seven every morning, tied with a string and put in a corner. There I lived three and a half months and paid four kroner a week.

"It was not love at first sight. I never started that kind of business myself. Mrs. Pedersen was so much older and was my landlady, and *she was married*. I had heard about affairs with married women but didn't quite believe they existed. Moreover, I was afraid of Mrs. Pedersen. I had been told she would undoubtedly show me the door if she discovered I was a dubious tenant with no steady work, and I must never tell her I was a Norwegian; I had told her I was from the island of Bornholm. Besides all this I was afraid of all persons older than myself—a gnawing sort of fear I never dared admit even to myself until recent years; I still catch myself feeling adolescent and green when encountering grown people only half as old as myself.

"I would imagine the sexual instinct doesn't change much from one generation to another, and the so-called 'purity' set up as an ideal for youth is a century-old stupidity which has created generations of warped and hate-filled people. Every boy I encountered in youth lived in a fantasy about girls. All of them might have amounted to something if there hadn't been these insane prohibitions against the only thing perhaps that is obvious in life. Of course we all talked dirt about what we couldn't get, but which every nerve in our bodies screamed for.

"Before I arrived in Copenhagen I had grown as warped and crooked as is possible for a human being. I agree, there is too much talk of such matters. And the situation hasn't improved. I deduce this from the very few open, healthy faces I meet on the street. How is it possible that grown men fail to realize they are healthy and normal in their desires, and should not be living in fear of derision, for by so doing they grow more and more strait-laced, load themselves with useless honors, and bury their humanity under a display of maleness they don't believe in.

"The Pedersen couple had no children, and this was good, for the offspring would have had to find its playground in the dark yard-well with its twelve privies, each one shared by several families. From the kitchen window I studied in the evening the life of the rats among garbage cans, dustbins, and privies. The tenement reminded me more of a barracks or a prison than anything else. Each floor had a narrow quadrangle corridor, and from it doors led to seemingly innumerable flats; and the most peculiar people emerged into the pale, ghostly kerosene-lamp-light of the corridors. Each apartment had two rooms and a kitchen. All kitchen doors opened to the corridor, and when the entire tenement was preparing dinner, the smell and the smoke in the corridor was so thick you wouldn't have dared enter it unless you were a smoke-diver. The kerosene lamps burned all day long. Water had been piped into the building, with one faucet for each sink, which also served as urinal, and luckily enough, Master-Mason Pedersen and his wife lived on the fourth floor, so there was light in their kitchen, and they escaped the sewage from others; something they were rightly proud of. For since there was no main sewer pipe the contents from the upper sinks emptied into those below. 'How lucky we don't live on the first floor!' said Søren Pedersen. He had an appreciation for the good things in life, drank a great deal of beer, and loved heavy food. He had friendly pig-eyes, a bushy mustache, reddish above and at the sides but yellowish on the underside.

"Much has been said about the immense ability to adjust, inherent in people and rats. They live in the tropics, in arctic regions, in the sewers under Shanghai. I think one might question this ability as exaggerated. One has forgotten to take into consideration the place of origin of the rats as well as the people. People of the refined type did not endure well the concentration camps, and I wonder how you two would have managed to live at Number 5, S Street, Copenhagen. I also keep in mind the opposite—the many years before I was able to sit in a villa at Smestad and enjoy a grog with calm nerves. We may have the ability to adjust, but, generally speaking, it is not the individual who adjusts himself, rather he hangs on to what he knows, whatever this may be. The right to live in the unchangeable is the right of free people in a free country. This description of Number 5, S Street—what was it actually? Well, it is true enough, yet terribly incorrect. It is Number 5, S Street, described forty years too late. Then I would have spoken of the warm kitchen, the friendly Mr. Pedersen, his wife who soon began to offer me a cup of steaming coffee in the morning. I would have told of the many steps heard in the corridor, would perhaps have mentioned some rough, friendly joke the wives threw at me as I passed the doors. If I had dared expose myself that much I would surely have described my evenings, after all grew silent and I was reading by the light of a candle, or dreamed in the dark about girls and the future. At one period of my life I found myself longing back to Number 5, S Street, and felt life had indeed become worse since leaving there. One who *began* in Number 5, S Street, as a child, and then grew into a better milieu might be inclined to see things in an entirely wrong perspective. True enough, he missed a lot as a child; his development might have been delayed, he might have wasted the years he spent in Number 5, S Street, but he forgets he liked to live there and hated to move away. He liked it there because he didn't know anything better. The privies, the garbage barrels, the rats—it was a world where something happened, and one wasn't lonely. To me Number 5, S Street was a step forward in freedom, and had many other advantages. I had escaped from something worse. And it is from this worse lookout tower I want to and must see Number 5, S Street. *It did not smell there.* Only today do I know it must have done so.

" 'You come up here in daytime and sit in the warmth, if you like,' Kamma Pedersen suggested one day, and I blushed. She had realized I was without work. That evening I came home very late and stole in silently. In the morning, after Søren had left, she set the coffee cup down beside me; then, planting her hands on her ample thighs, she stood looming over me: 'You silly boy,' she said. That afternoon I did come back, took a seat cautiously in the sofa corner with a borrowed book and was given coffee and cake.

"An apprehensive man might tell the story of Joseph and Potiphar's wife. Joseph was a clever operator who knew what virtue was worth at the right moment, and I can appreciate the young Joseph's preferring prison to a fiasco. I wasn't as quick-witted when Søren's wife made her plain-spoken suggestion, nor did I take my failure like a man. Or perhaps precisely like a man? I did make a few attempts to talk myself out of the possible failure. 'I'm so sick,' I said. 'You aren't sick at all! Only a little confused.' Then I adopted a hurt attitude, trying to look even sicker, but you see—well, I was just putty in her hands. Half an hour later she slapped my behind: 'Didn't I tell you! It was only confused you were.'

"I never dared tell of my experiences with Mrs. Pedersen, and for various reasons. It would have been difficult to make out I was a great seducer, even though my propensities for lying about such were well developed. But one couldn't brag much about a woman that old—"

"Old!" exclaimed Vera. "She was only three years older than I!"

"Sssh!" said Jasper.

"It wasn't anything to brag about with a woman that old," continued Erling. "I would have to lie about *that* too if I had told of my experience, and then it might have slipped out she was over twenty-one. Perhaps Søren Pedersen was most in my mind; if the gossip should come back to him, he must, according to the books I had read, kill me. It wasn't in that way I wanted my picture in the paper; I wanted to grow immensely old, quite bald, and have people make pilgrimages to my own villa at Ullern. Why Ullern I don't know, but Ullern I had in mind. I must have heard of some great man living there. And there was so much else; I couldn't give Kamma Pedersen flowers. And when I realized I was in love with her, I felt terribly ashamed; my rebellion against the sixth commandment must have been something wild and devilish. Truth must not enter the history of literature. O Lord, what an idiot I was! Kamma who saved me from so much dirt! And what an ass I must have been, dreaming in my fantasies how much better I was than the formidable Søren Pedersen— not that I looked down on him because I had got together with Kamma, far from it; I never thought along those lines. The crazy part of it was that the ones I wanted to cut out must be dukes or great authors, who would challenge me to duels, while the duchess threw herself over my corpse, or my antagonist's, I never could make up my mind which.

"Fortunately, I calmed down in a few weeks after the revolt Kamma Pedersen had caused in my life. I told you, Jasper, I didn't think you should laugh; I owe few people as much as I owe Kamma. You should have heard how heartily she laughed when I told her a few months later I had found a girl. I don't suppose I ever became entirely well, but had I not met Kamma I am sure I would have developed into an invalid."

• Some are more fortunate

It was Saturday and Erling left early, hoping to get something done that day. He took the underground with Jasper. The packed train filled him with horror as he thought of what he had escaped in his life. He was hanging on to a strap, trying to figure out how many trips back and forth in this herring-barrel it would have taken to make up forty years. By the time they arrived at the National Theater station he was almost pious with gratitude. As they emerged into the open, Jasper said, "I had nothing to eat before I left, and neither did you, I noticed. I'll run up to the office, to make an appearance, and in twenty minutes I'll meet you for a bite to eat. I know where I'll find you now that you are awake."

When Jasper returned, Erling had satisfied his morning-after thirst with a pint of beer and ordered one more. Jasper too thought he would try a beer.

Erling said, "This must make you feel like a real bohemian?"

"I don't think," replied Jasper, "I ever would dare let loose on a weekday during office hours. I mean, sitting here talking away the day over several beers. The mere thought of such an experiment frightens me. Not much, but it makes me feel a little shaky. Well, really not fright, I guess, but the feeling comes over me that nothing so meaningless actually could happen to me. Perhaps the same sort of feeling you might get if the thought should strike you that—that you might kill someone. That you actually could think such a thought. A few years ago I happened to come into Majorstuen between eleven and twelve in the morning, on my way to a meeting. I ran into a business-friend—did you ever hear such a horrible word?—and he was drunk. I don't believe anyone at the meeting noticed the shock I had received; indeed, I'm sure they didn't—you know, because of this affable mask one assumes. But I had shivers as if I were coming down with pneumonia. I could picture myself drunk on a weekday at twelve, stumbling along the street, a policeman looking after me hesitatingly: 'Is he going to make it, or must I bring him in?' And perhaps he would bring me in. Help me into the police car. And I would emerge from the jail some hours later, pale, ruffled, unshaven, clothes wrinkled—yet take the chance and hurry down to the East Station district to find a bar."

"I think you are joking," said Erling.

"I do that *too*," said Jasper, and picked up another sandwich. "I also know what you're thinking now—if not exactly, at least something along this line. You think this reminds you of the interest decent women take in prostitutes—or used to in our grandmothers' time."

"In *your* grandmother's time."

Jasper threw a quick look at Erling. "Well, yes, in *my* grandmother's time. I know they were consumed with interest in the uncaged birds."

"Because they got so little themselves," said Erling, rather brutally. "I really feel sorry for both sexes; each had to be equally frigid. Well, even

if people know little about each other—this much I know, that you live
neither with your grandmother nor with a prostitute."

Jasper stretched his arms into the air, folded his broad hands behind
his head and leaned back. He laughed heartily and showed all his white
teeth. "No," he said, "nothing is wrong with me. Only when I meet you,
perhaps my thoughts stray to closed doors. I know *one* thing for sure: it'll
never go wrong with me—I exclude sickness and death, of course—it'll
never go wrong with me as long as I don't let go my hold on my work.
Therefore I'll never let go."

"But you are frightened when you see someone who has let go?"

"Yes, and then I take a stronger hold. After I had seen that man in
Majorstuen I made more money than ever before."

"Then maybe I can help you to make more money, I too?"

Jasper eyed him a moment, uncomprehending, before he replied,
"Don't tell me *you* ever let go of your hold?"

Now it was Erling's turn to laugh. He pushed back his chair and
signaled with his glass for more beer. "Have you never seen me ruin a
day?"

"No. That's something else. You are as frightened as I am of slipping.
Only, you've drawn the line in a way that has no mathematical meaning.
I'm a mathematician. My line is drawn with knowledge. To tell the
truth, I believe yours is drawn from moral points in your mental
landscape. To me it seems most confusing that it works. I've very little
interest in morality; you fight with it like Jacob with the Lord. But right
behind you now sits an older man I meet at times; I can read in his
closed face a tremendous question mark: 'How come Jasper Arndt is
sitting here with that depraved, amoral Erling Vik?' I, Jasper Arndt, who
yesterday signed a fully legal and advantageous deal you never would
have dreamed of signing. A chess-move so correct and legal and watertight it's almost embarrassing, but with one little beauty-fault which has
nothing to do with legal or accepted business methods. If I hadn't
chosen to haul in that fish, all the experts would have realized within a
few months that I was blind. No one would dream that I should reject
an honest agreement because it had the beauty-fault I mentioned.
Morality never enters in, because an advantageous and legal contract is
in itself a piece of morality, in the same way as a cube undeniably is a
cube. But bear in mind, in the same way as we have something called a
business-friend we also have something called *business-morality*. It is
good enough morality for church and community affairs, at courts of law,
and for the speech at my funeral; but at home, or among friends, or for
all I care, together with Our Lord, one ought to shed it in the vestibule.

Among one's own it is not moral for the clever to fleece the less clever."
For the second time he looked at his watch: "Now I must go."

When Jasper Arndt had said he must go, he went. Erling looked after
the rough, heavy man, with his springy steps, and wondered how much
his skeleton alone might weigh. His shoulders were immense, and the
gorilla-arms swung as balance weights. People turned aside at his approach. He was Israel crossing the Red Sea. Erling recalled what had
happened to Jasper's face when he said he must go: it had hardened and
cleared. Three-quarters of an hour ago it had been Jasper arriving; the
man rising to leave was Managing Director Arndt, of Salvesen Steel
Company.

• The Vik brothers

Erling had managed to obtain a hotel room, and Sunday morning he lay
in bed thinking of his parental home in Rjukan. It was strange how one
could never get away from the place where one had spent one's childhood.

He had never seen his parents' graves since they were open and
waiting. His father had died half a year before his mother. At his
mother's funeral he had noticed some twigs of spruce that had been
placed to one side of the grave-bottom; some wood was visible, and this,
he realized, must have been the corner of his father's coffin, which they
had tried to hide with spruce twigs. The surviving children, with the
families they had formed, stood around the hole with the coffin, while
the minister said some meaningless words. It had been a raw autumn
day, withered leaves had blown into the grave and lay there motionless.
Erling had waited impatiently for the service to come to an end. Gustav,
his oldest brother, cleared his throat and took a step forward. "I wish to
speak a few words on behalf of the survivors," he said, and Erling did not
lift his eyes while Gustav said them. Later it had been hard to decide
who had been worse, the brother or the minister. The brother spoke of
the temperance movement. He also touched on the fact that some of the
dead one's children had managed well for themselves. Since he was the
only one with a steady job, and considered Erling a little off, there could
be no doubt as to who the well-managing survivors were.

When the brother had finished, Erling raised his eyes and looked at
him. This stone-dead man, he thought, is my brother. That awful person
with his temperance movement and his good job. He looked down at the
coffin, looked about in the grave, shook the minister's hand, and looked

at his brother again; and at the relatives who lowered their eyes every time he turned toward them. He knew well enough that he was their only topic of conversation when they met: how horrible he was, how conceited, but it would surely end badly. He hadn't heard them say this in twenty-five years, but—

He was as far beyond their reach as if he had been a tribal chief on Borneo. Now he realized he had done something that in their eyes would cast its shadow far into the future: he had failed to bring his wife along, whom they hadn't seen, and he could hear the hundred interpretations they would give to this during the next twenty years.

He had seen Gustav a few times during the years since their parents had died, and he had remembered to send a greeting when Gustav turned sixty, half a year ago. They had nothing in common, but he knew neither of them realized this, and therefore never could accept it as a reason for not meeting and drinking coffee together. It had never been difficult to keep the distance. Erling only failed to make an appearance, and Gustav, being the older, would not stoop so low as to seek out the younger brother. Open breaks had never taken place. Gustav considered himself worthy of veneration, expressed in coffee-calls on Sundays, the presentation of wives, and such. This both Gustav and his wife had hinted at in a manner they considered diplomatic, but Erling had never taken the hints.

Now he wanted to look up Gustav, whom he hadn't seen for at least four years. He opened the telephone book and found that his brother still lived in the same old tenement-house at Sagene. There he had lived since he was married thirty-six years ago: Vik, Gustav, Labor foreman. Gustav was the boss of a blasting-gang, and this was his pride, but he didn't think it looked well in print. He knew everything about blasting away mountains and handling dynamite. "Never a single accident," he would say, "but then, I'm a teetotaler and have never broken my pledge." He wouldn't look at Erling when he said this. He didn't mean to boast; he only insinuated the reason for the younger brother's many accidents.

Erling was ready to telephone but stopped himself. It would entail a coffee-feast with mountains of repulsive cookies, and neighbors with red faces, present and staring. He would rather take the chance of finding them at home.

He thought of his relatives as he rode in the taxi. There was one question he had heard oftener than he could keep count of: "Why do you bother with your relatives? You seem to be more interested in *them* than they ever have been in you."

Perhaps they were right, but when they imagined his family could be written off mentally, too, with what is called a summary decision, he felt they revealed something about themselves. They knew little or nothing about the tensions that had existed; they must have grown up under circumstances where tensions had been so weak that they themselves, so they thought, not only could have gone their own way, but also could have forgotten their antagonists forever if the relationship became too obnoxious. They knew nothing about ties that only could be broken externally, geographically as it were, but never psychologically. When family feeling has assumed an inner state of war it can never be rooted out. One might put a great ocean between, and thus feel much better, but the ties hold, all the unsettled remains, and will remain as long as a single member survives. In a family riveted together through hate, not even death can break the bonds, hate hovers as a poisonous gas over the graves. People who have never lived with such an incarnate pestilence, do not know the forces rampant, that must be killed and made impotent. They do not realize that these are high voltage power lines, with no one to turn off the juice.

To Erling everything had changed character, yet deepest down all was the same. At different ages the problem assumed different aspects but the same problem-complex appeared on the surface. What had lain uppermost now for many years and therefore seemed always to have been the essential thing was the suffering he had endured at the hands of unreason. Through his whole scared and suppressed adolescence he had been among people who spit on logic, connection, cause and effect, insight. Not that he would have recognized such elegant words for these conceptions, but one needn't know the name of something to love, hate, or miss it. He remembered Gustav's washing himself once in the kitchen, the wash bowl on a stool. When he finished drying himself he had flung the towel through the air, so that it landed in a bowl of milk on the kitchen shelf. His fury over the fact that his mother had placed the milk bowl just there was like an outburst from a lunatic. The family had trembled with fear for several days. His mother had prayed and pleaded and promised to cover the milk bowl next time, but Gustav was not to be pacified.

Is it possible to find a logical line in such actions, something that might offer a sensible explanation? Erling, at least, had not succeeded. It was obvious enough that when Gustav encountered something he didn't like, someone must be blamed, and the guilty one must not be himself, not under any circumstances. Never was he the miscreant; he was defending himself against attacks. The warrior must become a *Wehrmacht*. The pattern was clear enough, and Erling felt poisoned by it. If

Gustav should find a ten kroner bill on the street, and someone else saw it simultaneously, Gustav would have insisted on his rights: he had seen it *first*, and, deeply offended and with the indignation of the righteous against the other finder, he would have appropriated the third man's possession.

His behavior could be described in detail, but who would have understood more because of this? There were any number of worthy men who were clever at gathering material about human behavior, and equally clever in calling it a science; Erling had little respect for behavior-psychologists, people who had taken up collecting behavior-patterns instead of postage stamps.

Elfride opened the door, and she did not recognize Erling since she hadn't expected him. Then her features took on the confusion he knew so well of old. She had industriously supported Gustav in the early days when it was the older brother's task to instruct Erling in life's responsibilities and in the unprofitableness of folly. "Look what happened to your mother's father!" Elfride had one thrown at him. "Good Lord!" replied Erling, "but Grandfather had no hands!" "Neither have you, as far as I can see!" Gustav had come to her aid. "I don't see it matters much whether you have hands or not!"

Yet they had never, not even Erling, said anything that led to an irrevocable break. If one of them realized he had gone too far, he would try to cover up at once. Neither Gustav nor Elfride had hesitated to drive home that "of course you must understand you are free to do as you wish—it is entirely your business that you are stupid." And Erling on his side might ask Elfride if she liked his new tie; she would not refuse an outstretched hand, and after carefully inspecting the new tie, she would say that it could have been much worse.

But all this was in their younger days, before any one of them was more than twenty-five. When Erling began to make a name for himself, it turned into an open hatred on Gustav's side. He was not one of the kind, simple-hearted ones who, without objection, accept something they don't understand. His heart was granite. But there was no doubt that his contempt for Erling was honest. Erling was a good-for-nothing who wouldn't work like decent people; he drank, and did worse, and it would be only right and proper if somebody went and told the newspapers about him. Then Gustav started another tune, and it was impressed on Erling what life was really all about. Elfride had added her bit, and she had no more perception than Gustav; but she never missed an opportunity to get a word in about her brother-in-law, when Gustav was absent. This angered Gustav greatly when he learned of it. Indeed, his relationship with his brother bothered him increasingly with the years, for he could never rid himself of the dream that Erling one day would come to him and confess his pig-headedness. The situation had not changed even now, when both of them were grandfathers—Erling, admittedly, along illegitimate lines, something Gustav secretly considered a mitigating fact, confirming all his worst expectations—and there was no hidden jealousy, only pure disgust, when he described his brother as a damned whore-buck.

Thus the connection between the brothers had come to an end without formal notification. It had not been confirmed with great exclamations that "you'll damn well never see me again, you idiot!" Postcards arrived on important birthdays, but not at Christmas, and certainly not at Easter. The temperature became established a little above zero through postcards on important birthdays. Nothing would have prevented them from speaking of the weather, had they happened to meet on the tramcar. Gustav was hurt, but liked it best the way it was, and Elfride gossiped across the hall that "my brother-in-law has grown uppety." Then a few years later their father died and they met at the grave. Again they pretended to be brothers and saw each other at long intervals. In a way Erling was interested in his brother, who on his side enjoyed a vague comfort in the thought he had been right on all points, and only due to sluggish law-enforcement was Erling still at liberty.

He stepped into the room where Gustav was sitting in a chair smoking his pipe, a rough laborer's hand on each armrest. He remained sitting and said between his teeth, "Well, you did find your way here again. You manage to put on worse togs each time I see you—it's a wonder where you get the money. You seem well fed too. Well, some people have their sources."

He blew a smoke cloud with a whinnying sigh from deep in his stomach: "Let's have some coffee then, since it's Sunday. I've hurt my foot. A stone rolled over it day before yesterday."

Erling thought, thank heaven, at last an accident has happened.

"But it wasn't caused from blasting!" said Gustav, triumphantly, as if reading his brother's thoughts. "Some man was fooling around with a stone on top of the hill, the fathead, and let it roll down on my foot where I was sitting with my pants down."

Erling quickly turned away to look out the window; his brother was no humorist. "Could just as easily have hit me in the head, or the knee, or in the ass," complained Gustav. "Or broken my back. But at least we have insurance which a working person deserves."

That hit home, thought Erling, and dared turn and ask if it hurt.

Gustav only grunted.

"I guess now you too get compensation?" he asked, presently. "Any-body gets it these days, and it's a hell of an injustice that people who don't work now get their compensation too. Make an out and out profit if a stone happens to roll over them. It was different when I was young."

He forgot that Erling was almost as old as he. It was odd with the age-difference between brothers; when Gustav became ninety he would still consider his eighty-eight-year-old brother a pup; and even then, mused Erling, I will not have lost my feeling that Gustav is my big brother.

Erling recalled the time when he had received the message to go underground and had had to leave the house immediately. Something didn't work out right that time, and he had found himself on the street without knowing where to go. For several reasons he had been unable to use a telephone, and he had thought of Gustav. But that recourse too had been barred: early in the occupation Gustav had gone to work for the Germans. A worker not familiar to Erling had one day stopped him on the street and asked if it was correct that Gustav Vik was his brother, and then the story had come out: the resistance people had gone to Gustav and berated him, but he had only been furious. What kind of a country was this if they tried to prevent an honest man from taking a job that suited him? He had—probably for the only time in his life—men-tioned his brother Erling's name for no reason: It was pig-heads like him who started such notions; they should stop interfering with decent workers.

Erling had replied he could do nothing with his brother, who was stubborn and never gave in once he had taken a stand. It would be futile to threaten him: Gustav would rather be skinned alive than change his mind. (It is in the family, thought Erling, surprised at discovering a character trait he had in common with his brother.) Nor would reason-ing or explanations have any effect on Gustav; he had the strength of the rhinoceros, and its mixture of stupidity and blind courage. He was the only person Erling knew whose eyes became bloodshot when fury seized him—*seized* him and tortured him until he howled in his insanity. Did his brother belong to *Nasjonal Samling?* No, Erling was sure he didn't. He had his temperance lodge and his union. (Of course Gustav *must* be a temperance adherent of the most militant sort, it struck Erling, for with his temperament he must harbor a deep fear of liquor.) But, said Erling, Gustav might apply for membership in *Nasjonal Samling* if someone told him he couldn't—for this, to be a free man in a free country, was his foremost thought.

Nothing had happened to Gustav after the war was over; probably he was one of the many they never found time for, because there were simply too many.

Erling had been quite aware of what would have happened to him had he gone to Gustav that time when he had to go underground during the war. First a triumph over the gullible brother who never had listened to the older, but knew where he was when needed. Then the rest would come as a spring flood: about people who never had done a day's work in their life, mixing in things not concerning them, until they must come creeping and pleading, imagining decent folk would set themselves up against police and law. "Don't try here! No one must say that I harbor criminals and useless fools who never have worked at anything decent! To prison with them, that's *my* opinion!"

The following day he would have told all about it to his gang while they were eating their lunch, eyeing each one of them with his pig-eyes under the bushy brows. At last he would have been able to speak out. All good reasons to disown his brother would have disappeared. He would have started with something like this: "After all, there is justice in the world."

Justice had now fallen on a man who had never been willing to work. Now he was caught in a trap he had long escaped. After all, these Germans might have something, if they only could pick up Quisling also, that lazy son of a bitch! Yes, he was the son of a clergyman! And keep their fingers out of the unions, or the devil take them!

Erling knew that it would have been one of the greatest days in Gustav's life. If Gustav hadn't been against the clergymen, who in his opinion had invented God as an excuse to be lazy, and if he had known the words, he might have quoted: The mills of God grind slowly but exceeding fine.

• Yo-ho-ho, Seaman Jansson—

At the time, during the Occupation, when Erling had been warned to go underground immediately, and felt he could not seek out Gustav, he had remembered his kind Uncle Oddvar, Oddvar with the moon-face, his father's youngest brother. According to Gustav, it was this uncle's as well as his grandfather's example Erling had followed when he took to drinking and grew too lazy to work. Yet, Gustav had been fairly gracious toward his Uncle Oddvar, who expressed few opinions, except for this one: You're right, sure as hell! He admitted *all* were right, since they so eagerly wished to be. Sure as hell, you're right! When Gustav scolded him for being a drunkard, Uncle Oddvar at once admitted the truth. Oddvar was rather listless by now, but in his younger days he had worn an elegantly turned-up mustache and patent leather shoes. Now his mustache hung gray and tired and drooped over his mouth, but he was lucky in that Ingfrid kept him company when drinking. Then they sat warm and red-faced and smiled at each other, and Oddvar said things were well with him, and he said often that sure as hell they were. In the morning he rose alone, brewed coffee, and fried pork, of which he was especially fond, went to his job in a factory, where he moved a lever with a handle back and forth. Erling had a few times tried to get Uncle Oddvar to tell him what was behind the lever, but without success. It is even possible that Uncle Oddvar did not know what he was doing, or what its purpose was. It is also possible that his mind was a clouded mirror that would catch only the simplest nouns, like table, chair, wife, liquor, cat, and these would make him smile or look sullen. There was a great silence in Uncle Oddvar's brain, definitely no banging of doors. Regardless of what was said he would always agree: sure as hell it was so. His face had by now lost some of its roundness, the color of his eyes had faded, he was bloated and bald. He and Ingfrid had grown to look very much alike. They never mentioned their children, but it was scarcely because they thought about them enough to wish to hide anything. Actually, they had forgotten them. There had been three, a boy named Nils, and two girls. Erling could not remember the names of the girls and felt uncomfortable when he thought of his cousins. They had been only half-grown when they left their parents, like animals breaking away from their origin, and became street-walkers in the neighborhood—entering an underworld lower than the one occupied by Ingfrid and Oddvar.

He had felt it would be all right to look up Oddvar. Erling was in the habit of calling on him two or three times a year, with a bottle. But how to get hold of a bottle *now?* He had some money, but not the current coupon of his liquor card. He thought of getting some on the black market, but knew of no outlet in Uncle Oddvar's direction. Well, he must come empty-handed, and hope at least Ingfrid was at home.

Oddvar and Ingfrid lived in a district that had superseded a torn-down slum. There had been much criticism about this experiment in moving people into small neat apartments with bathrooms, after they had lived all their lives in slums. It was said they cared not at all to live in such a manner. The same criticism had been heard in cities abroad, and Erling had an uneasy feeling that there was some truth in the statement. The comparatively new buildings already had the stamp of slums about them, and inside, the apartments were already damaged to an extent which it was hard to believe; bathtubs were not used for their intended purpose, but as containers for coal, wood, bicycles, refuse. After a few years it appeared the criticism had been misplaced, for the tenants were happy with their new accommodations, and had at last learned to live in them.

As Erling stood outside the damaged door (what in the world had they done to it?) he could hear gramophone music from inside. He rang several times, but short and cautious ringings, or Ingfrid or whoever was inside might take it as Gestapo-signals. The record played down and then it started all over again—"Yo-ho-ho, Seaman Jansson . . ." Erling rang again and now he could hear someone move in the entrance hall. The door opened and "Seaman Jansson" roared out onto the landing.

Erling was startled. His uncle looked terrible, standing there in his shirt and pants, the suspenders hanging down behind. He was unshaved and bloated, his eyes swollen. He must have wept much and long. He sobbed, "So kind of you to come," with a mouth that had turned into an irregular hole.

Good and drunk but also sick, thought Erling, as he stepped inside. "Is something wrong, Uncle Oddvar?"

He had to shout to make himself heard above the gramophone in the room.

Oddvar started to cry again. Erling walked ahead, but stopped short as he discovered a human form under a sheet on a board that had been placed on saw-horses. The beds stood empty, even the mattresses were gone. Beside the corpse stood a table with the gramophone, as well as a bottle and a cup. On the other side of the table was a lost-looking easy chair.

Erling stopped the gramophone: "Is Aunt Ingfrid dead?"

The old man nodded and cried. He held his hands before his eyes like a small child and sobbed, "She sure as hell is." Then he shuffled over to the gramophone and started it again. "And they want me at the old people's home."

Erling attempted to stop the gramophone once more, but Uncle Oddvar pushed his arm aside and sat down in the easy chair, crying. Good Lord, thought Erling, why can't they let him stay here to die. To take the liquor away from the old man will only hasten the process, and this is his home after all.

While the worn record screamed "Yo-ho-ho and Yokohama!" Erling learned that Ingfrid had died during the night—"and both of us will be fetched at five o'clock." Erling went to the kitchen and rinsed out a cup. He filled it and drank the wretched wartime liquor. On the floor stood an unopened bottle; he didn't feel he was robbing Uncle Oddvar, for he could not manage more before five o'clock, and these would be his last drinks—on this earth.

It was impossible to stop the gramophone but Erling insisted on opening a window. This was not easy. They were not in the habit of letting out the warmth. When he managed to open it to the raw autumn air he breathed easier. He suddenly felt hungry and fetched butter and bread from the kitchen. "Please eat, Erling, if you are hungry—it was so kind of you to come, but please, shut the window!"

Erling closed the one nearest to Uncle Oddvar and walked over to the one at the other end of the room, where he devoured the bread; he had not eaten since the morning of the day before. In recent weeks he had been constantly on the move. Now he had plenty of time to stand here at an open window and eat. He would have time on his hands from now on, not the least if he were picked up, for then there would be a great chance that he might meet eternity. How could wars be so boring!

He drank liquor as he ate his bread and managed to get some food into Uncle Oddvar also. "Otherwise you'll be too drunk when they come with the hearse," he said, and that was an argument Uncle Oddvar understood.

The gramophone bellowed about "your Stina and a dram and yo-ho-ho!" Erling closed the window as he could hear in the distance the revolting, hated tramping of boots. The steps were approaching. The group started to sing as they passed, those strained, stupid words in march time, like a chorus to accompany their own hanging. "Ohei! Ohiv!"

When they had passed he opened the window again. He had closed it lest they become suspicious and get it into their heads that "Seaman Jansson" was an insult to the Wehrmacht, that it was a national song or a Jewish hymn, or—worst of all—that people might be enjoying themselves. He listened to the dying sound of boot-tramping and the hoarse parody of singing, helped along by the screeching "Yo-ho-ho, Seaman Jansson!"

Fog in a dead street. A dead aunt on a board. A drunken uncle in a chair. Odor of wartime liquor, perspiration, dust, garbage, food, and corpses. There were two corpses, he now noticed. In the bottom of a cage lay a dead parakeet; it must have lain there some time, for it was caved-in and flat in death. The mixture of smells recalled something to him. What? Yes, now it floated up like a dirty sack through various associations and became a winter night spent in an empty freight car which apparently had been used for shipping rags or bones or something equally nauseating. He had got a cramp in his stomach from the cold for he wore neither overcoat nor underwear. There was a draft from the sliding door, but the howling blizzard outside was worse. They had been two in the car; they never laid eyes on each other; the other one had climbed on later, and they had growled to each other as animals in the dark, but each one had kept to his corner and no words had been exchanged. No match had been struck, so the other one mustn't have had any either.

Toward morning Erling had left, afraid to go to sleep as he didn't relish the idea of a trumpet of doom for an alarm clock. The comrade had growled angrily after him, perhaps something about closing the door. Erling pushed the heavy, ironshod door shut with such a bang he could hear the echo from across the pier. Then he stumbled on a pile of coal and hurt himself. This made him so furious he started to bombard the door with the heaviest pieces he could find. The man in the car yelled bloody murder, but Erling kept on hurling coal until some men came running in the dark and demanded what in hell was the matter. And war was something like that; life turned into a dull idiocy in the course of a single night, some incomprehensible trouble in the pitch dark round an empty freight car. He fumbled his way from the place and observed from a safe distance some lanterns and the door being pushed open; that troublemaker in there did not manage to make them accept his dubious explanation.

Erling remembered the box of checkers he had put into his pocket when he left his apartment. Had his last thought on leaving really been that he might play checkers in Sweden? "Uncle Oddvar," he said, presently, "would you like to play a game of checkers? You be Germany and I'll be Norway—no, I had better be Luxembourg, then I'm not entirely responsible for Norway in case I lose."

He pulled the box from his pocket and poured the pieces in a pile on the table. He knew that Ingfrid and Oddvar in their harmonious marriage had played checkers every evening until they got too drunk.

Oddvar looked dully at the pieces. His mouth resembled still more the hole of a cadaver someone had poked a stick into. Tears and snot clung to his mustache. But he was willing to play, and became almost cheerful. "Sure as hell!" he said, and filled his cup with liquor. "Seaman Jansson" had once more played to an end, and Oddvar rushed up to move the needle to the beginning of the record before he wound the gramophone with a trembling hand. "Yo-ho-ho!"

Erling had been so sure of winning from the completely drunk old man that he made a few careless moves before he realized that Uncle

Oddvar played like a thinking automaton. An old combination of checkers and drinking gave him the upper hand against one who had practiced these sports separately. It was necessary for Erling to win, he grew as tense as the hunter scenting game. Oddvar poured liquor down his throat and attended to "Seaman Jansson" as well. He laughed, pleased with himself: "No, my boy, sure as hell I'll show Ingfrid I can beat you before they carry her out!"

Erling felt that sure as hell that was a thought—yo-ho-ho—and groggily he weighed for or against, but decided he must stick with Luxembourg. Before they resumed they tossed their heads back and shouted lustily in chorus, "A drink in Yokohama, and a drink in—"

They cleared their brains and played a while. Then Erling discovered he would be beaten if his uncle made a certain move. And the bastard did it. In the same moment Oddvar lost interest.

Erling gathered up the pieces and put the box back in his pocket. Not entirely beaten, he thought; I only played for Luxembourg. He looked at the old drunkard who had forgotten the whole thing. "I staked something on this game," he said, aloud and dejected. "No, I don't like it at all; I shouldn't have played against Uncle Oddvar."

"Skol!" yelled his uncle. He had again filled his cup and raised it awkwardly in the direction of Ingfrid, who lay quite still on her board. For a moment Erling was convinced she had stirred a little, breathed out and adjusted her position.

Uncle Oddvar was now sleeping noisily in his chair, but gradually his head sank down in complete insensibility. Erling went to the kitchen and washed his head and face. Then he looked in the mirror and admonished himself to be cautious.

He would leave before five, he knew where he could go at that hour in the dark city, but mustn't arrive too late. He looked from his uncle to the shape under the sheet, and from it to the bottle. He left enough for a generous last drink for his uncle—if he hadn't already had his last. After the war Gustav had told him that Uncle Oddvar had lived almost a year in the old people's home, but had "wailed like a baby" because he was denied liquor. There had been triumph in Gustav's voice when he said, "Too bad about the old pig, but they did get him straightened out at last!"

• On the dot, the first of each month for thirty-six years

Erling sat with his coffee and the cake and looked at Gustav, who never seemed to manage an end to the story he had begun, about a hat that had been stolen from him. An exceedingly poor story about an old hat, but Erling listened dutifully to his big brother. He couldn't help recalling something he had seen in a zoo; there a sturdy male tiger had walked back and forth, back and forth, behind the solid bars. In the corner of the same cage a small terrier rested with her nose over the edge of her basket, her eyes following the tiger and the people watching outside. Erling wondered about this little bitch in the tiger cage. Just then the tiger was fed through an opening in the bars, and approached his meat. It seemed the dog had only been waiting for this impudence: it rushed to the middle of the floor and barked—woof, woof, woof! The tiger moved away, watching the angry little bitch, who had been given her own meal in a small dish. Each time the tiger tried to approach his food, the little bitch raised her back hair and started her woof, woof, woof! And the tiger withdrew in respect.

When the bitch had licked her dish clean, and taken her time at it, she barked a last woof, woof, at the tiger and lay down in her basket. The tiger cautiously approached his meat, and stopped dead when a drowsy woof! came from the basket. At last the terrier must have felt she had inspired sufficient respect; she went to sleep and let the tiger eat in peace.

Erling had asked the keeper what it was all about. It turned out the tiger had had an unhappy childhood; its mother didn't like it. Then they had given it to the terrier when her pups were weaned. The tiger had received a firm upbringing from its adopted mother, and since a tiger can't see itself, he wasn't aware he had grown so big. He remembered having received punishment and was careful. The bitch on her side had seen the tiger grow so slowly she hadn't noticed it, and remained sure in her belief it was easy to master a tiger.

Gustav started from the beginning with the hat. It had hung on a nail in the shed. "I know where I hang my hat. No, it wasn't a new hat, but it was *my* hat, and then—"

There was the choice of thirteen possible hat-thieves. Gustav had his own suspicions. "So one day I told him, cool as a cucumber, that is three weeks ago, yes, a Saturday, then I said, cool—"

The repulsive taste of his sister-in-law's cake and the wishy-washy coffee filled Erling with nausea. He caught himself longing for Uncle Oddvar and "Yo-ho-ho, seaman Jansson!"

"It's a nasty thing to have happen in one's place of work," said Gustav. "I told him coolly and decently about this business with my hat, but you should have seen that devil! He put his fist to my nose and told me to shut up about that 'lice-box.' That's exactly what he said, but I controlled myself. Well, I only told him to be a little more careful when speaking of lice, for when it comes to lice—"

"Was he the one who stole your hat?"

"Was *he* the one? Who else?"

No, Erling dared not say who else it might have been.

"Things have gone too far," said Gustav, and looked reproachfully at Erling, "if one no longer can hang one's own hat on a nail, but it is the same with so much nowadays."

Erling had no doubt what was meant by "so much." There was one who would suffer one day because he had failed to heed the advice of an older, wiser brother.

Elfride tripped nervously about, looking for something to put in order, or a speck of dust that might be moved, but she found nothing. "If I had known you were coming," she said, and pulled out a chair and pushed it back again, "then I would have had things in order."

"Erling must take it as it is," said Gustav.

Elfride stopped looking for disorder. "Now they've raised the rent," she said. "Everything gets so expensive one can't live."

"Yes," interrupted Gustav, "those who work are the ones to suffer."

Erling accepted the implication in silence.

"For thirty-six years now," said Gustav, and held his pipe in his outstretched hand, "for thirty-six years now I've paid the rent on the dot the first of each month. Thirty-six years. That makes four hundred and thirty-eight times precisely the first of each month, if it hasn't been a holiday, for then I've paid on the previous day. Thirty-six years the same apartment, the same landlord. He lives on the floor below us."

"That isn't bad," said Erling. "That's more than I've done."

It grew silent, and Gustav darkened; such a remark coming from an older brother would have been good for Erling. Instead, he made light of his own shame. Indeed, there was no doubt about the wantonness of his younger brother.

Elfride was straightening a curtain and said, nervously, surprised at her own daring, "Well, I guess you don't pay regular rent, Erling, or—"

Gustav wasn't looking at him either now and tried innocently to look at nothing. Oh well, thought Erling, that was what Elfride was aiming at when she spoke of the rent, but Gustav had not immediately grasped the diplomacy of Elfride: it was the house in Lier that bothered them again. Was Erling the owner, or wasn't he? It was a little pin-cushion to needle them.

"Well," he said, and looked out through the window. "It always costs something, wherever you live. Have you never thought of moving somewhere else?"

The question pierced Gustav like an awl. "Are you crazy? Why in hell should we move? There are enough of that sort, who can't stay in one place."

Now he was seriously angry, and Elfride's features turned somber; Gustav was so temperamental and now they wouldn't find out if Erling owned the house this time either. She herself had hoped he was a property owner, but when she expressed this thought to Gustav, he had said, in that case Erling must have stolen the money to buy it, and sooner or later things would go wrong for him. Elfride was disappointed; she wanted so to be able to say, "My brother-in-law owns his own villa!"

As so often before, Erling had a feeling he was reading two books open before him. He really liked Elfride. She puttered about, fairly satisfied, in her own microscopic world, and cared for and honored her capable husband. "My husband, bless him, doesn't drink. He always stays home evenings. Surely, I have nothing to complain about. It would have been so nice if our son hadn't gone to America. This I think about so often. Especially at Christmas. Oh Lord, how angry Gustav was that time. 'Don't imagine I will pay the ticket!' he said, but Fredrik said he wasn't asking him. Now he's married and all, and to an American woman, and he has a steady job, and children they have, four of them, and she works, too, and they have a house, and a garden with some pear trees. He drives a truck, but Gustav says perhaps he hasn't paid for it, and it's hard to keep up the payments, says Gustav, for it always turns out bad when people get too big for their britches, he says, and buy trucks when they don't have the money. But I feel the Lord gives His blessings too."

When Elfride had company and Gustav wasn't present, she always assumed a pious attitude, even to Erling whom she in many ways found dubious. He cared little about Gustav's and Elfride's suspicions. Neither of them could fly very far on the wings of fantasy. The worst they could imagine was that he undoubtedly went around speaking ill of honest folk. He had an illegitimate child, and that of course was bad, but it could be explained as a mishap; the worst was that he talked about this daughter of his as if she were as good as any child. Why did he have to mention her at all? In a way he was stealing secrets from his brothers and sisters, brothers-in-law and sisters-in-law: one couldn't whisper about something he himself spread openly. The same with his divorce, only much worse. They pretended they hadn't heard about it and would ask him to bear their greetings to his wife. About the life he led they knew nothing, and would never have understood anything had he tried to tell them, at least, they would not have taken it seriously. *That* gullible they were not.

• *Millennia's yoke on our shoulders laid*

Erling looked about in the room so familiar to him, and knew what Elfride would say as soon as he had left: "I don't like the way he looks at everything." Her eyes were on guard, awake, and went from him nervously to each object he happened to glance at. Was something wrong? Wasn't it good enough? Wasn't it with them as with other people? Was there after all some dust on the lamp-shade? He more felt than saw her trembling fingers move an ash tray to hide a minute speck he wouldn't have noticed without her aid.

He felt sorry for her, but he was also disturbedly conscious of the actual distance of many generations and thousands of miles that separated them, as well as him and his brother. If he gave Elfride a friendly pat on the hand she would become greatly confused, and Gustav would so lose his self-possession that anything might happen. The expression, "There is an abyss between here and there," is often only empty words, but at this moment he *saw* the gulf that separated him from Elfride and his brother, a cleft it would be futile to try to bridge. It was a depth moreover that separated two worlds. Suddenly it came over him how meaningless it had been in his youth to seek friendship and understanding from people like Gustav and Elfride—that is, with his own people, parents, brothers and sisters, everybody he had known until the age of twenty. He had torn himself to pieces to be one of them, but the abyss had been there before he was born. It struck him how many years had been wasted in a fight that was lost from the very first day. His desire had been to belong where he belonged.

Then he stopped himself: the years hadn't been wasted. It was hypothetical thinking, of the worst kind—and no one could say what his life would have been minus his vanity and his humiliating fight to become accepted in the family circle that had no use for him. He had not wanted to believe this; he must have been uncommonly unrealistic in youth, more than usually blind and deaf to what every person, every tree, every stone told him: We will have nothing to do with you; you are too stupid, too ugly; we can't bear the sight of you.

Then he had tried to make himself believe it was in his imagination, self-deceit, but he now realized it couldn't have been. He had been one *unable to adjust himself*—one expresses it as a failure-disease, a congenital shortcoming that must be cured; treatments are administered, and the victim treats himself as well, for the illness must be cured, one must adjust oneself and become like the others. They believe that deviation is abnormal. There has never been the slightest doubt in their minds that I am abnormal and must be cured. No one doubted it, not a single soul, until I found my way into that other circle where my abnormality was normal, and where Gustav and Elfride would have succumbed because no one could possibly have accepted them there.

Elfride kept fingering a newspaper. One shouldn't read newspapers when entertaining callers. But she couldn't help it. Erling watched her handle the newspaper like a cautious animal stealing from one special haunt to another among the columns until she finally reached her goal: the obituaries. She folded the paper, casually, looked indifferent, and lowered the neatly folded sheet while participating in the conversation. Then her eyes were caught in the announcements, and she forgot both Gustav and Erling. "Oh, Lord!" she exclaimed, suddenly, "here is someone dead by the name of Kaparbus! What strange names people have in the obituaries."

"Well," said Erling, "he must have had the same name while alive also."

He wished he hadn't said it, but now he had, and Gustav was already there to the defense: "Erling must always contradict."

In a way he was right. He had always wanted to contradict them. He should long ago have realized the futility of contradicting them. He should have seen and heard enough already at the age of twelve to understand that he was stupid when he had a thought of his own. And indeed, it was true that the most peculiar names did turn up in obituaries. Elfride was right; he had never forgotten the obituary of the Countess de Turd, and others equally silly—as if the dead had been thrown into an attic to dry until they were put in the paper. Elfride was right; one would never have encountered Mr. Kaparbus except in his obituary.

Being in a tolerant mood, mightn't Erling as well admit he was wrong—but dared he say so *aloud*? Dared he take the risk that Gustav would think he was making fun of Elfride? Gustav, so suspicious in every nerve, how would he react to an admission from his depraved brother? Erling decided to let the subject drop. During the last quarter of an hour it had become eminently clear to him that Elfride and Gustav never would see him again. Something had disentangled itself. He wasn't up to investigating what just now, but this was his last visit to any one of his relatives, and he could now see them in a friendlier light since this was the last time. He interrupted his thoughts, for he wished to hear something about Uncle Oddvar before he left this house forever: "Tell me, Gustav, what happened to Uncle Oddvar's children—his son and two daughters, our cousins?"

"Nothing but trouble. Nils has been dead many years now, but I guess you have had better things to do than to ask news about your relations. He got his head bashed in by some other drunk who mistook him for someone else and killed him instead of another drunk. Nils was in jail a few times, some burglary they tried to pin on him; well, I guess he is in another kind of jail where he is now. The girls started walking the streets before they were half grown. Then the authorities got after them, for moral reasons, and they landed in two different institutions; maybe they felt they had to keep them apart. When they were let out they went to work in some factory. To appear decent, at least. The authorities don't go after those street girls if they work, and there is something to that. Both were heavy drinkers. I heard they were married later, but I don't know where they live. They must be in their fifties, I reckon, if they haven't drunk themselves to death. Nils would have been sixty by now." Gustav went on without interruption, "So you looked in on Uncle Oddvar the day Ingfrid died?"

It wasn't mentioned but hung heavily in the atmosphere that Erling had failed to show up at Ingfrid's funeral. Erling didn't feel like explaining that he had been forced to leave for Sweden just then. Since it was his last visit with Gustav he thought there would be no use hearing once more how much and what good food there must have been in Sweden, but hadn't he been forced to work for it when he wasn't known in that place? He thought over his possible admission to Gustav, the one Gustav never would hear now; it would have sounded something like: I understand you, Gustav, better than you think. It wasn't for nothing we had all our experiences together when we grew up. Deep down I feel the way you do, when you talk of work, and what you mean by work. For a few years I managed to make people believe I had work, and wrote only evenings and Sundays. I used to lie, for three or four years, first and foremost because I had to deal with people of your sort, or people of other sorts but thinking exactly as you do. It wasn't right that a man only sat and wrote, something I soon learned. They bothered my wife, they bothered me, they put all sorts of pressure on us in matters that didn't concern them. One person was plainly ornery to me—he got me fired from a local paper so I wouldn't get big-headed and think I could earn a living from—well, from sitting and writing. As I say, people we didn't care for (and you were one among them), neighbors, casual acquaintances, every son of a bitch anywhere. Don't forget I was very young and terribly insecure and frightened. No one would have lent me a five-kroner bill because I was too proud to work. I might also tell you that some of my workdays have been longer than any of yours, even though it only is to sit on a chair and write and such.

That was one side. The other was that I too came from all the misery we had at Rjukan. The misery of me and you and the others—our unhappy parents, and the senile grandfather without any hands you and I had to take care of. We learned to work. To work the way you still think of work. To work—it meant to take hold with your hands and earn your daily bread in the sweat of your brow. *And this I have got away from just as little as you.* To the very last I have felt a secret shame that I don't daily appear in the factory or at the road gang and earn my pay and save my conscience.

We are labor boys, you and I, we will never be anything else, and now we won't see each other any more. We were endowed with quite different heads, and you had got it into yours that I as the younger must ape you in everything. That was rather stupid of you. But our concept as to what ought to occupy an honest person is fundamentally exactly identical—emotionally I'm with you, Gustav, but my mind has long ago said no. Yet I respect you perhaps much more than your pebble-filled skull has demanded as your right that I should do. Only, you made it hellishly difficult for me to show it. That's the way I see it now, and I want to tell you before I leave that in one respect your mind and mine have failed—when, endlessly many years ago, we started our competition to see which of us was the more stubbornly stupid. That was an idea of rare idiocy. And God help me—how furious you would be if you ever realized that I am responsible in no small degree for your reputation as a blasting-boss. Living up to this reputuation has been your own effort, and it pleases me that you never have let your little brother down. But this I'll never tell you. Because I have never hated you enough to see you choked from your own bile. And I am proud to have an experienced blasting-boss for a brother. A little of the reflected glory falls on the younger and lazy one.

• A sixtieth birthday
calls for a luxury telegram

Erling kept watching Elfride, who liked to talk about going to meetings.
He sensed that it gave her a warm feeling to think of good meetings.
There were so many nice notices in the paper about meetings, she had
said. His thoughts went to youth and loneliness when he looked at the
sixty-year-old woman. The notice as a substitute for a substitute. But
Gustav wasn't interested, Elfride might say in a vague, faded protest that
didn't even touch her consciousness, and so she had to be satisfied with
the temperance lodge. And those meetings were not so bad. She hinted,
however, that Gustav undoubtedly believed in God deepest down.

Erling felt this must be very deep down. Gustav had once and for all
stated that the ministers had invented Our Lord to have an income.
Ministers and teachers and office help and people like Erling had only in
mind to be lazy.

Gustav had a fearsome memory of every word he himself had uttered,
and stuck to it. Ministers and "their ilk" should be driven to work with
the rod, to learn something of life. In this social arrangement Our Lord
had become homeless, and finally had entirely disappeared, but Gustav
had never had any use for him anyway. People should work and meet
their obligations. All else was nonsense, invented for ease, reading,
writing, and laziness. This did not exclude an occasional fight with Our
Lord, in the same way Gustav let engineers and contractors know what
he thought of them; it was not compliments he wasted on such gentlemen.

A conversation with Gustav and Elfride was like participating in a
child's game. All utterances were planned with a definite goal in mind.
Many moves might be made without apparent result, as in a game. The
pay-off was information obtained in a devious manner. Direct questions
were against the rules. If they caught something they looked at each
other with what they thought were innocent faces.

It was the bitter experience of centuries, refreshed with painful
memories from early childhood: You mustn't expose yourself, you
mustn't ask—if you don't want your nose twisted. Don't give any
information, don't let anyone trick you into letting the cat out of the bag,
for then they'll only wait for the right moment to crush you. And never
ask questions about anything!

Again Erling looked about in the room. The air was saturated with years of pipe smoke. The furniture gave one the creeps, but it belonged to people who liked it. A highly polished dinosaur of a cupboard reached all the way to the ceiling. This was Elfride's dear companion when Gustav was out blasting mountains. If Gustav should ever put some dynamite under the cupboard, Erling felt he might regain his faith in humanity. He quickly pulled out his handkerchief and simulated a sneeze, as he recalled the degradation that had befallen the cupboard some thirty years ago. Uncle Oddvar had happened to need lodging for the night, and Gustav had given him permission to sleep on the sofa, since he was sober. But after Elfride and Gustav had gone to sleep, Oddvar pulled out his bottle and got going. The following morning Elfride discovered some fluid had been sprayed against the cupboard, for which Oddvar could give no decent explanation. Elfride felt insulted, Gustav was furious, but Oddvar never became angry; he suggested that perhaps someone had spilled something there the previous day. Elfride was beside herself at the insinuation that she would have squirted water against the elegant cupboard so that it ran down over the mirror. And poor Uncle Oddvar was driven from the house. He was demure as he later told Erling the story: "I did not squirt water about," he said. "But I had such a peculiar dream: I was walking from Christiania to Kalsas, to participate in a pissing-contest to see who could send a squirt across that little hamlet, and I received the first prize."

For the third or fourth time now Elfride brought up Gustav's sixtieth birthday, and Gustav listened in silence to her description of honors shown him. Erling recognized Gustav's pride in having reached sixty before Erling. It was as if he too had taken a first prize, but it was fairly certain that no one at the festivities had mistaken the cupboard for the toilet. Three extremely fine speeches had been delivered in Gustav's behalf, and a deputation had presented flowers and a silver chalice from the temperance lodge. Erling admired the chalice but did not voice his opinion that it was not sterling; he refrained from taking the risk of making his brother the blasting-boss a drunkard in his old age.

"Well, at least you sent a letter," said Elfride, half turned away.

Erling became sincerely sad; only in that moment did he realize his mistake. That he hadn't shown up in person was as it should have been, he believed; he hadn't been invited—even though he well knew they had counted on his coming to the last moment. Because this was a sixtieth birthday. And in a way they had left it to him whether he wanted to insult them by not coming, although Gustav would have taken it ill had he turned up. Indeed, Erling had thought of coming but had hesitated at encountering a whole temperance lodge and all the speech-making and all the listening. Everybody was sure he would only have ruined things through his presence, this famous brother who poked fun at people and drank like a fish. They would all have looked him over, casually as it were, and then agreed that thank heaven, he wasn't drunk, although he must have had something the way he looked.

No, the mistake had been the letter which ought to have been a *luxury telegram*. All the luxury telegrams were stacked, accusingly, on the top shelf of the cupboard. Well, well, so he had strayed that far. He had struggled with a friendly letter, a whole page long to make it especially good—and had long ago forgotten that a sixtieth birthday calls for a luxury telegram. Perhaps his failure to send one had some connection with a feeling of being ridiculous putting his name on such a multicolored stupidity. It was lucky at any rate that he had sent a letter, rather than an ordinary telegram, which would have been interpreted as an intentional insult. A full page letter wasn't the worst that could have happened.

Gustav sucked his pipe and ignored Erling completely, as he said to Elfride, comfortingly, "Well, we have talked that over, and I don't think any of our guests expected my brother to show any common decency."

• *The clock*

Erling had a strange feeling; he had got rid of his brother this Sunday, and now he felt compassion for him, but he was careful not to show it. His eyes fell on the beautiful wall-clock Gustav had picked up at an auction long ago. He felt he ought to take that clock with him; then there would be nothing to interfere with the taste of this warehouse-room.

"You're looking at the clock," said Elfride. "You must think it isn't much to have hanging on the wall, and we have in mind getting a new one."

Erling asked casually what they would do with the old one.

"It cost twenty-five kroner more than thirty years ago," said Gustav. "I don't think we ever will get that back."

"I need such a clock for my place in Lier," said Erling. "How much do you want for it? But I must take it with me, or it'll be too much trouble."

The hell of it is, he thought, they'll discuss for ten years whether I cheated them.

The clock itself seemed to protest; at least it could be heard unreasonably loud in the deep silence. Erling knew they must talk over such an important decision, and he went to the bathroom. When he came back he made no further reference to the clock. He talked of one thing and another but found no response until some ten minutes later Elfride approached the subject again: "Don't you have any clock in the place you live?"

"Well, I've managed with an alarm clock."

"Doesn't the time drag—living alone like that?"

Apparently she wanted to talk about that for a moment. Pick up one piece after another while selling the clock.

"Oh no! I like living alone!"

"Have you any help?"

"No, I prefer being alone."

He knew she was fishing for information about wife and children. Perhaps something else too, but that would be difficult.

Her voice trembled a little. "Don't you ever have callers?"

"Never."

Elfride was stuck in her ruts, it seemed, and Gustav said, "So you want to buy yourself a clock. How much do you offer?"

"I never make an offer. You tell me what you want, then we'll see. After all, you are the one to know something about the clock."

Gustav coughed and said a few nice words about the clock; there was nothing wrong with it.

"It's getting late; I have to meet someone in town in half an hour."

It became remarkably silent, thought Erling, and at the same moment he knew he had led Elfride and Gustav on the wrong track. They sat silent, like cautious animals, and wondered whom he was to meet; they waited for the name and the place.

They looked irresolutely about, and their eyes met conspiringly.

"Are you to meet someone?" asked Gustav, his eyes on the kitchen door.

Erling pretended not to hear. He had been outside this circle the better part of a human life, and they knew literally nothing about him any more, yet now they had taken up the thread as if left off from yesterday. How much of it was the old control, fear of not being taken into confidence, being left outside? To what degree would some old insult flare up into anger after he had left?

He went to the hall and put on his overcoat. "Well," he said, "I must be on my way."

"You must at least make an offer," said Gustav, and nodded toward the clock.

Erling shook his head.

"Let's say twenty-five, then—that's a good buy!"

"Too much!" said Erling, and walked over to telephone for a taxi; he put a coin on the table.

His first thought had been to pay Gustav the twenty-five kroner without a word, but he knew his brother. Gustav wouldn't feel the sneer in the act; he would put the money in his pocket and hold Erling as stupid as ever. That wouldn't have mattered. Something else decided him: it wouldn't be long, perhaps not even a minute, before Gustav would think he had been cheated, if Erling paid without objection; the clock must be worth much more, his brother had cheated him, something that would weigh heavily against him. Erling had haggled for Gustav's own sake.

"There is a tramcar," said Elfride, uncomfortable about the coin at the telephone she didn't want to return, uncomfortable about the expensive taxi, uncomfortable about the clock, and the cheap tramcar.

"Twenty kroner then," said Gustav, for it bothered him to see an expensive taxi ticking away down at the curb. Why couldn't Erling just as well have paid twenty-five and taken the tram?

Erling put the twenty kroner on the table and asked for a paper to wrap the clock. He fetched a stool from the kitchen and stepped up on it to lift down the clock. As soon as he touched it, Elfride began to sob. He let go and turned to look at her. "My clock, my clock, and it's hung there all these years!"

He looked at Gustav who had clamped his teeth together on the pipe and was holding on to the chair with both hands, staring first at the clock, now hanging askew on the wall, then at Elfride, and turning ash pale. What was the matter with him? Was it the clock or Elfride?

Erling stepped down from the stool and picked up his money. "I won't take your clock, Elfride, but I would like to tell you something: I don't think this clock is worth much, but you will never get another one like it, and it is the most beautiful piece of furniture you have in your home."

"Do you *mean* that, Erling?"

"It would be a shame and a crime to sell it. I have seldom seen such a beautiful clock. I had meant to give it back to you if you regretted selling it."

As he stood in the door and said good-by he noticed Gustav in his chair. It must have been both the clock *and* Elfride. He had never dreamt to see Gustav like that, and better not let on he had seen anything. He ran down the steps to the taxi. A heavy snow was falling. "To the Continental!" he said to the driver.

He turned about and looked at the old tenement house until it vanished in the blizzard.

• *All roads lead to Golgotha*

Early in February Erling came back to Venhaug. It was bitterly cold and the snow lay crusty in the forest. The pines were white with hoarfrost. He felt his tension ease as he sat in his usual chair before the fire and related news from Oslo, where he had spent a week.

Something that had come over him on the train only now had let go its grip. He was telling Felicia and Jan about it. He had gone into the diner where they knew him well enough not to stare when he ordered a bottle of strong wine for himself alone. He had a sandwich and was reading the Book of Esther in his English Pocket Bible. He had to use a magnifying glass now to read the fine print in the small vest-pocket Bible. He had been so pleased when he had found it once in England, for he was tired of loud wisecracks from simpletons when he sat in a bar with his glass of beer, reading Holy Writ. Now he had a copy he could hide in the palm of his hand. It was later that the need for a magnifying glass developed, and recently people had regarded him with an air of superiority, after beginning by snickering at the sight of something unexpected. One generally travelled avenue to agnosticism is not to read anything our ancestors thought or believed in. To be a free-thinker—that was apparently the aim Henry Ford expressed so well in his now famous words that history was only nonsense.

Once he had been visited by a couple who talked only about literature. Something had made Erling mention Kingo.* They had asked if he wasn't a religious writer. At the time Erling hadn't noticed the sarcastic implication—not against himself, against Kingo. He had taken Kingo down from the shelf and read from the Spiritual Chorals, Second Part:

> Oh Fleshly desire
> Which many with mortal lips have kissed,
> Your kindled tinder, your fiery sparks
> Have led many a one to eternal doom,
> Your cup seems honey but the draught is evil,
> Vanity,
> Vanity.
>
> Farewell, then farewell,
> You no longer shall entice my soul,

* Thomas Kingo, Danish clergyman and baroque poet (1634–1703).

Wretched world, good-by,
I bury you in the grave of forgetfulness,
I long to end my sorrow and need
    In Abraham's bosom,
    In Abraham's bosom.

There shall my years
Begin anew in eternity's sweet spring,
There shall not be day, nor sun, nor dawn,
No moon be full or new,
For Jesus is the sun whose rays shall comfort all
    In Abraham's bosom,
    In Abraham's bosom.

My riches and gold
Will always be abundant there,
No thief will steal from me,
Sophistry will not move me,
My riches are free of earthly vice,
    In Abraham's bosom,
    In Abraham's bosom.

Honor I shall have
From the throne where Jesus sits,
The crown will be given me with glory shining,
The blood of the Lamb has gilded all,
I'll gain it, e'en though Satan objects,
    In Abraham's bosom,
    In Abraham's bosom.

In grace I shall shine
Amongst holy angels,
Jealous eyes no more to see,
God's face will smile upon me
And I shall mock at jealous death,
    In Abraham's bosom,
    In Abraham's bosom.

Erling had stopped there and looked up at his two listeners. For the first time he had met eyes expressing actual incredulity. Both sat perplexed, disoriented, their cheeks flushed, and looked uncomfortable in their easy chairs.

And he had discovered they were angry. The reaction had been the same as if he had recited a versified edition of the Kinsey Report at a prayer meeting. They were not equal to the situation but kept looking in the corners and under the furniture before they regained their power of speech and said, "Is *that* supposed to be anything to recite?" There was no sarcasm, not even accusation, only injury, confusion, surprise.

"Do you know," said Erling, "it was suddenly clear to me, they felt I had disgraced myself, they felt ashamed of me, that was all; I hadn't come up to their standard, I didn't fulfill their expectations, I had degraded myself. When they had gathered their wits I could see they felt like holding their noses.

"But this time in the dining car on the train I was reading the Book of Esther, and not aloud. By the way, I don't understand why the Book of Esther is in the Bible, but I'm glad it has been preserved together with much else that has nothing to do with Christianity's early history; if the Old Testament had been gathered together in the seventeenth century, it might have included some of Shakespeare's plays that are lost to us."

Erling sat pondering; even though what he had read on the train had nothing to do with the European religion, yet the story was in the Bible, and indirectly it had made him again think of his old theory that Christianity's brutal myth had been too much for people; they had turned it upside-down and made grace and salvation into a pea soup.

Felicia shattered his farfetched vision, saying, "You look like Jan when you think."

Erling looked at Jan. Back in the corner stood a large copper kettle; Felicia had bought it a few years ago and put it there: "Now everyone must put all rubbish in that cauldron and not throw it on my floor!"

Jan had interrupted his eternal pacing back and forth; slowly he stooped down, picked up the copper kettle and inspected it closely, as if he had never seen it before. "Come here, Jan," said Felicia. "Erling is going to tell us what he is thinking about."

Jan put the kettle in its place and asked, "Is it something worth listening to?"

"It's the whole meaning of Christianity, Jan," said Erling.

"That I would like to hear," said Jan, and approached with reluctance. In the middle of the floor he stopped and looked back. "That copper kettle," he said, "it's one of those the soldiers used to cook in. When the tinning wore out, the whole regiment died. Not a bad way of waging a war. I was thinking about the same thing last fall, I guess it was in September but we still had full summer—but what I was going to say—they had fired an atom rocket in Nevada, and then they had to pray it would explode (which it did) when they discovered it was headed home again. Truly a clever rocket. Who was it that said he would win or die in his kettle?"

He sank down in a chair. "What about that Christianity business?"

Erling said, "I can repeat word for word what I was thinking when Felicia interrupted: that Christianity's brutal myth, which it actually was, became too much for people immediately it was conceived. That is why they turned it upside-down and made salvation and grace into a pea soup. That about salvation and grace, Jan, has been twisted and maimed. Jesus meant it seriously, I'm sure. Try to imagine yourself nailed to a cross, and how much has been made of it. Naturally something lies behind it all. Moreover the myth is thousands of years older than the form in which it has come down to us. Jesus repeated it and wanted to give it its old meaning. He thought we would discover reality by facing it, not hiding it. By facing the truth that all of us—each and every one of us—must one day be nailed to a cross. Find peace and salvation in all of us dragging a cross to Golgotha, with hammer and nails in our pocket— and the comfort is not to be despised that a Simon from Cyrene will aid a little along the road, a one who knows the day will come when he himself might need help."

"I can't say," admitted Jan, "that I have formulated very clearly to myself what you are saying, but if the message from the cross was not *Hither come all*—then I don't know what it was. I consider it a suspicious thing that we daily are urged not to understand something of the whole, and for that very reason accept it. It is much too cheap to be accepted. Even if there is a great gap between God and a human being, it needn't altogether resemble the distance between the chief doctor and the patient in an insane asylum."

Jan resumed his floor-pacing. Erling said, at last, "I got entirely away from what I wanted to say, and it wasn't so remarkable at that. To tell the truth, I forgot it the minute I was back in my chair here in front of the fire and felt secure again. It must have been nerves. Something horrible happened on the train, but I don't really know what it was. I sat there with my Bible and the magnifying glass and read about Queen Esther, her wonderful purification before she was to be brought in and taken by the king, and all that which once was serious and then turned into great comedy. Time often works strangely and well. Holberg has become humorous even when he meant to be serious, and Swift's fury over social conditions has become a children's book. I. P. Jacobsen has for half a century been a confirmation gift, and books that made tears stream three hundred and fifty years ago now require great effort of the philologists to comprehend.

"While reading about Queen Esther and Mordecai and Haman and the all-powerful king, I looked about in the diner a few times and my mood grew worse each time. I couldn't understand it. I was comfortable and ought to feel well. I had had dinner, I had my bottle of wine, a courteous waiter, and Queen Esther, and I was on my way to Venhaug. What more could a person wish?

"After a while I happened to notice a lady, a few tables from me and with her back to me; she paid her check, poked about in her handbag, and left the car. She didn't turn around, and I didn't know who she was or whom she reminded me of. She had come in after I did and she must have seen me. I noticed how she was dressed and looked for her as I left the dining car, but even though I went through the whole train I didn't see her. There might have been some reason for this, but I watched at every station and she didn't leave the train, as far as I could see—unless at Kongsberg where a great many passengers left the train, and many people were at the station.

"The strange part is that it definitely was that woman who had caused my bad humor. At first I did not connect my feeling with her, it was only when she rose to leave the diner. There was something familiar about her back, and all her motions. She was a person I had no desire to meet. I might express it still more strongly: there was something evil about her, or she reminded me of someone who is evil, without my being able to understand who it might be. There was something eery in the air as if she was thinking of me and wishing me all kinds of calamities. I know of no one who could hate me so intensely. No, don't laugh, you know how I am about such matters at times—but who could the woman be?"

Jan had stopped his walking to listen. "I am willing to take it seriously," he said, "if you promise not to be naïve in another matter. It is actually comical of you to say you can't imagine any woman who might hate you so intensely; you must be lying to yourself so that you can sleep nights. But it isn't my business to enumerate all of them, besides the daughters and the mothers of those involved. You have made one great mistake in your life; it might have got someone on your neck whom you have forgotten by now."

"What mistake?"

"That you once were as anonymous as a protozoan, but had girls in those days as well. Most of them you have forgotten, which doesn't help matters. Now they are sour women. And most sour on you. Well, we might overlook that—there's enough of the others. What do you think of—"

Jan started to walk again. He finished his sentence with his back to the others: "What do you think, for example, of the one with that fairy-tale name—wasn't her name Gulnare or something?"

Erling looked at Jan but did not reply.

"I have a better one than that," said Felicia, accusingly. "You came from your idiotic carousing in Oslo. Sitting on the train you were trembling with delirium. Why aren't you like Jan—he is not a drunkard so he doesn't see any dastardly female backs in the diner between Drammen and Kongsberg. You have never in your life seen the lady you speak of and anyway she was probably on her way to make an impression on a rich aunt who lives in Kongsberg and has hemorrhoids and keeps porcelain dogs on the bureau. Still more probable—you had some bat in a hotel in Oslo and then you thought the woman's back reminded you of her."

No more was said about the matter, for at that moment Julie came in with some flowers she had picked in Felicia's greenhouse. She handed the key to Felicia, laid the pungently fragrant chrysanthemums down among the coffee cups, and in passing planted a kiss on Erling's forehead. She brought with her a wave of winter cold.

Felicia patted her on the hand. Erling looked at his daughter. It was like looking himself in the eyes; he had the joy of having a daughter, and none of the inconveniences.

• "With sorrow I lay down, from tears was salt my mouth—"

The whole evening Felicia had fought to hide her feeling of depression. She had succeeded well. Erling had called from Oslo in the forenoon and Julie had answered. He had asked if it suited them that he come, he would just manage to catch the train. Julie told Felicia a little later as she returned from her greenhouse. Julie had wondered why Felicia had not shown happiness at the news.

A wave of hatred toward Tor Anderssen had risen in Felicia when she heard Erling was expected, a feeling she had not thought she would ever waste on the gardener. She had just allowed him to stand half an hour in the bitter cold and peek into the land that was not his promised one. First she felt paralyzed with a bitterness of having made herself unworthy, but then her hate for Tor Anderssen emerged, he who had ruined the waiting for her lover. *Why couldn't Erling live at Venhaug!* She knew that then Tor Anderssen would always find a closed ventilator, that devil would be cast out.

She knew this quite definitely but made no attempt to explain to herself how it was that she could supplant her longing for Erling by playing with a peeker. She knew that only two men had had her in their power; the first was Erling, whom she had succumbed to in absolute contradiction of anything she could have imagined herself doing before she met him. Chaste Felicia had been seduced by Erling Vik, a sexual tramp. In old-fashioned and poor taste she had let it happen. The second time, my will was broken by Tor Anderssen. I am seduced by no less than two men, the last one Tor Anderssen—with a wall between us. Why? I think it happened because then I could get all men through that stupid one—on the other side of the wall. In that greenhouse warmth I have been steamed in the whole male-world's lust. I have lived in an intense fever which I would begrudge no other woman, while my thoughts have run: Today he'll bring his gun and shoot me through the ventilator. More than once I've been on the verge of screaming: Aim at my head, you with your reputation of never missing! But perhaps he *would* miss, and maim me, with the ventilator between us, perhaps it's just what he would like to do. I have thought often I would so like to be shot with all men at the trigger, not by a single man, as it would be if Erling or Jan fired.

No one except Erling could liquidate and replace the peeker. She started in her chair as she thought of the word: *liquidate.* When Erling wasn't at Venhaug, she had orgies with a demon in a demonic game, but for her there was only this one demon. She had succumbed to Tor Anderssen's way of making love. If he should leave, or die, there would be no more fascination in this any longer. Then, to her, the set-up would only be *stupid.* Why was Erling the antidote? Was it the raw streak he showed in making love, which she grudgingly admitted she liked? And was it perhaps because—though it seldom happened any more—he could explode like a sort of mountain troll and lose consciousness when he culminated. She recalled her horror the first time this had happened in Stockholm and she thought she was lying with a corpse.

Today again she had followed her impulse toward this wolf-like, empty creature Tor Anderssen, succumbed like an animal dragged forth for fertilization, she thought in fury. But there must have been a fist in his stomach too when Jan knocked on the door today and came in.

Tor Anderssen was stupid. Not because he was a peeker, a peeker whose dreams had been fulfilled beyond the expectation of any peeker—

he was stupid through and through. When one said a person was limited, one must mean his world had shriveled up. She had liked to have a limited person standing out there. It was the impersonal male sex that stood and peeked at the ventilator, as excited and as impersonal as a packed movie house—and as impotent and passively debased. The stupid man at the ventilator represented the whole world's maleness, with a brain the size of a dried-up walnut kernel, the male-world's collective phallus placed the way the men themselves had managed it—helpless and suffering at a stone wall with a peek-hole, helpless and scared, with weak desires relieved through sadistic dreams. That time in humanity's dawn, which Erling so well described, when some being, with the power of a nuclear bomb's mushroom-cloud, rose from the animal world and forever laid the beast behind him, then the love-call went out to the new being's *eyes,* and a person lived in the lust of the eyes, even when alone in the dark. Humans had been given a precious gift, neither deserved nor undeserved since nothing under the sun was either. They managed their gift poorly, like all their gifts. They made such a mess of it that the joy of hearing a call with the eyes was degraded to peeking—peek or be peeked at, naturally accompanied by a moral code that allowed all to speak of it in condemnatory words, because it must be aired. The transfer of sexual evaluation to the eyes had perhaps been the first germ of free will, which grew stronger as the individual was liberated from definite mating seasons. A will could raise itself above the mating-force. Individuals even appeared who could go without, something never before seen or imagined. *They* managed to get a great part of humanity to adhere to their idea, not because anyone outside the narrow circle of real ascetics actually wished to go without, they only thought it was a good idea to deny it to others, while they themselves always found some solution. It was as if all humanity landed in a sordid compromise. Some might get permission if they had a license. If they took a trip it was practical to bring along the mating license, which showed what partner might be used.

Felicia wished she had broken off the game long ago, or rather, never started it; but she had been tempted beyond endurance, and it was Erling's fault. When she reflected upon her dependence as a vice, her thoughts went to Erling's dependence on the bottle. For rather long periods she managed to keep the ventilator shut when she was in the greenhouse; but, not unlike the alcoholic, she found her way back, and did it with self-deception. And like the drinker she had compounded strange reasons. When, during the periods she called "weaning," she discovered that it also aroused her to know that that beast was closed out and suffered his agony, then she might as well let him peek. Her skin became red and warm when she knew that he stood degraded at a closed ventilator, and it must be more humane to relieve him. She felt a vague lust when Tor Anderssen, cheated and made a fool of, stole away behind the spruce trees, his mustache drooping—she must investigate whether it was false, as she was sure it must be, his stubble appeared so sparse and scraggly when he was pale.

Then today it had happened that Jan came and knocked. He did this very seldom and it had never before happened while she gave a séance to Tor Anderssen. She had gone to open for him at once, there was nothing else to do, nor did she mind. Jan had only stayed a few moments, it was something he wanted to ask her. When he was through talking he had stuck one on his hands into her silvery hair-halo and gently pushed her back and forth. She had stood with her arms dangling, looking on the ground, as he swayed her body. Then she had closed her eyes and thought: now in this moment that mountain troll out there must be bursting. Jan smelled of oil, he was attending to the farm machinery today. He took hold of her, and she felt his rough hands in the small of her back as he pulled her toward him and kissed her hard and long before he left. It was lucky he hadn't gone farther, she could have done nothing but let it happen.

Felicia did not get over her shame and depression until she had been with Erling for a couple of hours, and she lay down to sleep where she was. She had also felt something else. Was it sorrow, despair? She did not know. Before she settled down to sleep, she said, "One night recently it came over me that since I don't recall my mother's face, it must be because she is one who never will die, and has her face with her wherever she is."

Afterwards it struck Erling she must have had a premonition.

About what?

She had wanted to confide, surrender for once. When she awakened about three o'clock and was hesitating about going out in the intense cold, she thought about it again but felt it smelled too much of admission and confession—and what would he think and *not* say? He would have helped her over it, but she begrudged it him. And she was so afraid that if she brought it up she would be unable to refrain from saying that he could help her. And that she would regret. Erling must move to Venhaug for his own sake, not for hers; this she had once and for all fastened her mind on and would not change.

She did not manage to dampen either her stubborn pride or her worry over what Erling might think and *not* say.

Nor did she follow her impulse to seek help with Jan. The course of events could have been changed, but was not changed. To one walking in fog beside an abyss, not much is required for a change in direction. Nothing was done, and Felicia fell.

• *"I had been told as a tiny maid—"*

Sunday morning Felicia, Julie, Jan, and Erling had been visiting in the living room, while the children as usual were noisy outside. They seemed to be enjoying a skiing race. Felicia went to attend to something, and when she returned she was dressed for a walk, in ski pants, sweater, boots, but nothing on her head. The pale sun fell across the floor. "How nice you look!" said Julie.

Felicia smiled pleasantly. "That's always nice to hear, especially from a girl. I'm going to fetch the mail—I'm curious about a letter for me."

Only seldom did they fetch the mail on Sundays; Felicia felt they should not disturb the postmaster then. Now Julie asked if she couldn't go instead, or at least keep company. Felicia hesitated a moment. "No," she said, "this is one of those days I want to walk alone. You stay here and keep the men company."

No one thought about it then, but many were to ponder those words later. They hardly expressed anything except a person's desire to be by herself for a short while, and this was nothing unusual with Felicia. Yet, for months those words would be quoted, searched, analyzed.

"It's going to snow again," said Felicia.

Jan looked out. "It seems so. The sun shines only through a little hole. Well, it is snowing already. That's sad for the fruit saplings. It looks like a lot of snow—the whole world has turned gray. Well, now the sun is gone."

Felicia thought she would have coffee before she left; she sat down and poured herself a cup. Erling was stretched out in his chair, nursing a drink beside him. "Felicia, I've often wondered how you, a society girl, with such polished speech, could marry a horrible farmer with a rustic accent."

"I'll tell you why. The accent suits Jan well. The minute I laid eyes on Jan I knew how he would talk, and I must say I grew warm when he started caterwauling; I felt so embarrassed for him."

Jan chuckled.

"I consider his accent something especially Jan-ish," said Felicia. "A sort of personal beacon for women in distress. I don't like to hear a country accent from anybody else; it should be Jan's private tribal call; it should be reserved for *him* only. We would never have had any children if he hadn't seduced me with his accent. I almost laughed myself to death, and that's good for the offspring. And that time he was quick as lightning. At any other time I wouldn't compare him with lightning; nobody can take his time the way Jan does. No matter what might happen Jan would begin to build up again and would give himself plenty of time for it."

"Well, I'm gifted with that sort of patience," said Jan.

Erling thought of Jan's relationship with the girl called Vigdis: Jan had drawn the logical conclusions from his experience with her, and had built something that stood up better. Like an architect, he had seen mistakes in the old building and not repeated them. He had not repeated the jealousy.

Jan and Felicia exchanged glances. Erling moved his eyes to Julie. How strange, he thought, when Julie uses her hands, especially when she reaches out to pick up something, she acts like a left-handed person. She uses her right hand as sparingly and awkwardly as if she might be; it reminded him of a baby flexing its little arms without having control of them. Julie used her right hand as others use their left. He was always conscious of it. But only now it dawned on him what had taken place; she had gone through her own torture. Why hadn't he ever thought of that before?

"Julie," he said, "were you left-handed as a child?"

She looked at him, hesitated a moment before she realized what he had asked. She blushed suddenly as she almost whispered, "Yes."

"You get that from me," he said, and looked away from her. "They forced me, too, to use my right."

At last Erling felt he had discovered a clue—the first. The nice hand and the *ugly one.*

He had stuttered as a child. He knew that the left-handed stutters in his indecision. Julie had stuttered a little even when she came to Venhaug. Like him she hadn't been quite sure of the difference between left and right, choked with that crushing: No! not *that one! That one—or?*

Now there was some understanding that one could not overcome left-handedness, only transfer it to something else. But was it known that a *schizophrenia* resulted when a child hesitated as to which hand was which? It was well known that there were people so strongly split that the one ego wasn't aware of the other—had it been established that such people were born left-handed and had grown up with a demand to switch their two brain-halves?

He was interrupted, for Felicia was ready to leave.

They were to remember her as she now, for a few seconds, stood in the doorway, half on the veranda where the snow whirled against the windows. At home around Venhaug she went bare-headed in all weathers. The last they saw of her was her happy, wise look, her hair like a silver helmet, the brown, shiny sport boots, the tight blue pants, her living body, her breasts proudly expanding the sweater.

They heard her call out something in the yard. Later, at the investigation, it came out she had called to the children, saying as she had said in the doorway that she would be back in three-quarters of an hour. As she left the yard she met Tor Anderssen and asked him to confer with Jan about some seeds. The gardener had come in just as Felicia had left. They were to be pressed hard on that point. How long after, had he come in? Perhaps five minutes, Jan had replied. Julie thought it was only a couple of minutes, after they had heard Felicia call to the children. In any case not many minutes, Erling replied. The result was that all three could say not ten minutes had elapsed. It also came out that the children had seen both Felicia and the gardener, and the latter starting on his way to the house and entering. Nor was there any motive. He had been offered coffee and a drink, and none of the four—the gardener, Julie, Erling, or Jan—had left the room until they started to wonder what had become of Felicia.

By then she was dead. Their thoughts remained on the picture of her as she had stood in the door, her hand lifted, ready to leave—a picture burned in like an etching.

• The promise

No one had heard or seen her after she had passed the greenhouses, no one from Venhaug. People living at the place who were away because it was Sunday could so definitely account for their activities and had such undeniable alibis that no one among them could be suspected. Everything ended with a furrow in the snow, a few spots of blood in the furrow, and bubbling water in a black hole in the snow that covered the frozen Numedal River.

The one she had met had perhaps known she would come, and had perhaps been familiar with the hole in the stream. That was all.

Toward morning, shortly before six, Julie and Erling were sitting in the dark in the living room. They heard steps upstairs and listened. It must be Jan emerging from his room. They heard him switch on the lights as he approached. Suddenly Julie and Erling too sat in the strong light. Jan walked into the room without seeing them. He had a bottle in his hand and put it beside the chair where he slumped down. He looked up at the enlarged photographs of Harald and Bjørn whom the Germans had murdered. Julie and Erling could not see his face. A few times he drank from the bottle. After perhaps a quarter of an hour he rose and kicked over the bottle; with the sound of a faintly purling brook the contents emptied on the floor, spreading an odor of cognac through the room. Then Jan said, in a low, clear voice: "She avenged you."

Returning to his room he switched off the lights, one after another. The house was again dark. Erling reached over and turned on the reading lamp. He looked at Julie, who clung to him, one arm firmly round his neck. Her face was distorted from weeping. From the corner of the house the man with the police dog looked at them, expressionless. Erling turned off the light again and mumbled to Julie, "Jan promised them he would avenge her. That means he is going to live."

Julie sobbed. "What about you, then, Erling?"

"I don't know."

• What had the forest and the river seen

They had read so many plausible solutions—all equally implausible—that their thoughts and speculations had become more firmly focused on her last walk, and what the forest and the river might have witnessed.

Day after day they had experienced the wish that arises when something of this sort happens: What could the forest and the river have told?

Erling had felt it strongly one day as he again stood where it must have happened. Something was struggling to give voice: Now, *now*.

Nothing came, nothing assumed articulation. He looked at the trees as he slowly walked back to Venhaug. The trees could not utter the words they wished, they could not manage to say it. What had the birds in the winter forest seen, what had the squirrel seen, the wild mink?

He sat staring at Jan's hands; they had always in some inexplicable way seemed a little helpless. His work-paws reminded one both of an ape's and of a child's hands; yet these sturdy paws were the hands of a strong and sensitive man.

It had always been as if the weather over Venhaug followed Jan wherever he was. Erling thought, illogically and bereft of common sense, one could in the atmosphere around Jan sense that generations of the Venhaug family for centuries had here looked at the forest and the Numedal River and the skies above them.

"He feels the same as I, Felicia, and will never be rid of it. He sees the Werewolf at the river when you were pushed under the ice and the current carried you away, he sees him turn and twist your body, under the river's ice-floor, but perhaps you will land at Erlingvik and wait for us there."

Three weeks had passed. Jan and Erling were sitting at the low table in front of the fire. Jan was rather preoccupied and read the paper Erling had handed him; he thought this would cut short Jan's floor-pacing today by at least a few hundred yards.

Jan had turned gray but his features no longer seemed so tense. He will survive, thought Erling.

It was the first time Erling had observed the truth that tragedy can make people gray-haired, even if not in the reputed single night. He couldn't take his eyes off Jan's gray hair, not even now, as Jan with a tired gesture put the paper aside, apparently wanting to say something.

Newspapers can't afford to consider the family, except through whining sentimentality, to the honor of entirely different people. At Venhaug all this had gone by unnoticed. They had all the information first-hand and were not in need of detailed descriptions. Possibilities not apparent to them were of no value—and the tragedy was greater than the wish to see it solved. But sometimes they read a piece based on factual knowledge:

"Many consider the mystery in this case has deepened with the murder of Torvald Ørje," the paper reported, "but isn't this on the contrary a ray of light? This paper has from the beginning maintained that the cause of the tragedy at Venhaug must be sought somewhere during the war years 1940–45. Since the turn matters now have taken we are more than ever persuaded that such is the case. On the other hand it appears the police will learn no more from the three persons with a possible key to the double mystery.

"It is clear as daylight Felicia Venhaug was not murdered by anyone living at Venhaug or visiting there. Nor by some tramp. They are always easy to apprehend, especially in this cold weather. Nothing indicates robbery as the motive, nor sexual attack. As far as is known a jealousy-murder is also out of the question."

Jealousy-murder out also? both Erling and Jan had thought as they read the article. They were not so sure.

"This last possibility has for special reasons been thoroughly investigated, but the person or persons who might come under suspicion (from the point of view of the man in the street) were cleared immediately."

The man in the street, eh? thought Erling and Jan.

"It is difficult to imagine any other motive than revenge. We wish to point out that no shadow falls on the memory of the dead one because those who perhaps know the answer remain silent. They were close to Felicia Venhaug, and perhaps there is something from the war years they don't wish to touch upon. Perhaps, mentally speaking as it were, they have receded to the illegality of the war years. It should, however, be pointed out that no one has the right to withhold information that might lead to a solution of no less than two murders now in peacetime. But if certain people keep silent, and if there is no proof that they know more than they have already divulged, then the investigation must start where the train of events once had its beginning. This would mean an investigation into the wartime activities of the late Felicia Ormsund, Jan Venhaug, and the gardener at Venhaug, as well as Erling Vik—more precisely, their activities from the time the two brothers Ormsund lost their lives until Felicia Ormsund escaped to Sweden. Some incidents in those days might lead us to the two murders now in 1958.

"When Felicia Venhaug was killed and thrown into the Numedal River—there has never been any doubt this was what happened—all leads came to an end. The great snowfall took care of this. Excluding the children, the last person to see her was the gardener at Venhaug, Tor Anderssen, and he entered the house only a few minutes later. The alibis of the three men are impeccable. This is true also of Julie Vik, who knew she was named in Felicia Venhaug's will. All people on the place confirm each other's statements. It has been ascertained where each one was at the critical moment, at least within a few minutes, and no one even approached the road Felicia Venhaug took. A police officer went on skis in a circle around the estate before the snow had obliterated possible tracks. There was no sign of tracks in the forest.

"It has been impossible to ascertain how many might be involved in the murder, but the authorities lean to the opinion only one person was the murderer. Even with two involved, it has been estimated, the dastardly crime would have taken at least half an hour; in that case one or more of the estate people would have been away for at least an hour, if they had been involved.

"There has been a search for motive among the people on the estate, but all assumptions come to naught, since none of them could have perpetrated the deed. We are offered a sort of collective alibi, covering everybody. Too good an alibi, it has been said. At least three people on the estate have long ago proved themselves capable of obtaining alibis when needed. There is something in this—yet, in the long run their false alibis during the war did not hold, and they had to flee headlong to Sweden. We must exclude the childish notion that fourteen persons, among them children, would have engaged in a conspiracy against the mistress of the estate, especially since she was well liked by all. When one hears insinuations that the police officer who was first notified is a friend of the three men and might have delayed investigations, as he had been involved with Jan Venhaug during the war, in liquidations, and wished to protect old war-comrades—then too much nonsense enters in, and must be stopped. A respected, capable police officer heading fourteen other false witnesses is more than we can accept.

"In view of the said police officer's knowledge from the war years, he was indeed more qualified than anyone to get to the truth. His first task was to ascertain where each person had been at the critical hour, at the same time keeping his eyes open for other suspects. We know he interrogated Jan Venhaug, Erling Vik, and Tor Anderssen, as to their connections during the war, as well as who Felicia Venhaug's friends and enemies had been in those days. He was seeking a revenge-motive behind a seemingly senseless murder. In this connection he learned of Erling Vik's recent encounter with Torvald Ørje, the notorious 'Chief of Police' in Os during the war. It is possible the authorities acted a little too quickly in arresting Ørje. The traitors got water for their mill when his alibi also proved to be watertight. Again cries were raised about 'those poor, persecuted ones who long ago have paid for their sins.' It is no news that the police after every crime first look up known criminals. Now there can be little doubt that Torvald Ørje was involved in some way, if we are not throwing all common sense overboard, and it might have been to his advantage if we, here in this country, had something called 'protective custody' where he could have been kept.

"Torvald Ørje was found murdered in a one-room apartment at Maridalsvei, and this intensified the mystery, according to the reports. To us it would rather seem a clue to the solution of the murder at Venhaug. But then came the fatal misinterpretation of Erling Vik's activities, and with it probably some clues were lost.

"Before the tragedy Erling Vik had stated that he thought Ørje capable of anything, except murder. Tor Anderssen did not state his opinions. Like Jan Venhaug he must have had his suspicions. That Ørje was capable of being accessory to almost any crime, no one seems to doubt.

"Did Ørje know who killed Mrs. Venhaug? Was he himself behind the murder? Was he a victim of his old and new crimes because someone must have realized he was not to be trusted, and would squeal when the authorities finally got him?

"The suspicion of Erling Vik was pure bad luck for the further investigation, according to the police. When Ørje was found murdered during the night, the news broke first over the radio, in the morning, and it was played up greatly in the afternoon papers. The possible connection with the Venhaug murder was not minimized. This caused one woman to report to the police that she had seen Erling Vik the previous evening at Skøyen, far from the Ørje apartment yet close enough to raise suspicions. The lady in question insisted he acted mysteriously, as if trying to avoid being seen. When this came out, others also came forth who had seen him in the vicinity. All of us might have business in different places, but when it comes to Erling Vik, the old saw has a special meaning: 'No one knows where the hare runs.' Indeed, his specialty is to turn up in places least expected. And now there is a new episode to his saga—the wonderful roundabout journey to get from Oslo to Lier unseen. Arriving home, he was arrested because a final witness had appeared who insisted on having seen him outside Ørje's apartment house the night of Ørje's murder.

"It does not take much acumen to figure out how all this came to pass, according to the police. Due to the possible connection, the murder of Torvald Ørje caused a great sensation. In such cases the police are always swamped with information, and witnesses eager to identify the murderer.

"After the arrest the various witnesses were again interrogated, especially the lady from Skøyen, who insisted she knew Erling Vik personally and must therefore be considered rather reliable. She insisted it was he. The police admitted she was speaking in good faith but was probably mistaken. The other witnesses offered pure fabrications.

"Consequently when Erling Vik arrived at the Oslo police station from Lier, he was immediately informed that he was free, and the police offered to drive him home again, if he wished. The fact is, it had become quite irrelevant and a purely private matter wherever Erling Vik was the night he was seen so many places, because it was twenty-four hours after the murder had taken place—at least. So the post-mortem showed. And for that time Erling Vik had an incontestable alibi; he had been at Venhaug.

"Thus today he is above suspicion in the murder of Torvald Ørje. However, it is not clear that he is thus out of the Ørje affair and altogether blameless if other avenues of investigation were dropped by the police, owing to the 'fertile imagination of certain individuals.' Possibly the police themselves could have used more fertile imaginations on that occasion. It is true only one of the witnesses still dares insist she saw Erling Vik in Oslo the evening after Ørje's murder. But doesn't the police department also consist of human beings who perhaps felt a little cheated, and as a consequence treated the witnesses a little roughly on the second go-round? Roughly, in the sense that perhaps during the renewed interrogation they might have said: 'Listen now, Torvald Ørje wasn't killed the evening you assume you saw Erling Vik in the city, and Vik himself says he wasn't here, and moreover, we have no charge against him.' Isn't it probable that witnesses under such circumstances are liable to become less sure of themselves, indeed, downright embarrassed, and disappointed, because there was no case, regardless of whether they had seen Mr. Vik or not? What stand would they have taken if their assumption had been correct as to the night when Ørje was killed? And what stand would the police then have taken with the witnesses? Instead of poking fun at them, wouldn't they have tried to gain more information?

"Now the police seemed to see the case this way: *If* he had been at Skøyen that evening, *if* he had been at Maridalsvei, and *if* he had been in all the other places, so what? Was that anybody's business? And *if* he didn't want to be seen by the lady at Skøyen, so what? Perhaps he didn't like the lady, and so what? Or perhaps he wanted to visit someone at Skøyen, so what? After twelve o'clock? Well, so what? Things do happen in the best of families after twelve o'clock, without being of the least interest to the police. And when he now says he was at home and all is nonsense, so what? If it weren't the right of an individual to lie, how would we all manage?

"These obvious observations no one would have made if it actually had been the murder-night when he was seen, and in court the district attorney would have considered these useless statements by the witnesses as extremely important, even perhaps strong enough to convict the suspect.

"But—all this information has now come to the knowledge of the police; then why not pursue that line? All this about Erling Vik's right to move about as he pleases and where he pleases is of course correct. But it is also true that he is a close friend of the Venhaug family and was a guest with them when the mistress of the house was killed. It is as true as before that the police through him became aware of Torvald Ørje. It is also true that one of the witnesses maintains that she saw him outside the apartment on Maridalsvei. And another witness who knows him well insists he was in Oslo.

"The police have failed to investigate why Erling Vik—if he *was* in Oslo—failed for the first time in many years to use the opportunity to call on old friends. A suspicion remains that his visit had something to do with what happened at Venhaug, and with Ørje. Did Erling Vik wish to get some admission from this man? It was announced that the door was unlocked when the body was found. It might also have been unlocked when some other person came there and tried it. Now it is said Erling Vik had no reasonable cause to deny his presence in Oslo, if he actually was there. How does one know that? If he came to that apartment in Maridalsvei and saw Ørje dead on the floor, he had good reasons to get away and keep out of the sight of all who knew him. He did not know that Torvald Ørje had been dead for a whole twenty-four hours, and that he without fear could go to the police. He was no friend of Torvald Ørje, he must count on being arrested. Erling Vik may have had heavily weighing reasons not to report to the police.

"And what might Erling Vik possibly have wanted from Torvald Ørje? *Did he perhaps come for a purpose which the murderer had feared someone would appear for? Did Erling Vik come twenty-four hours too late to force Torvald Ørje to divulge the murderer of Mrs. Venhaug? Doesn't it seem unavoidably obvious that Torvald Ørje and Felicia Venhaug suffered death from the same hand?*

"Erling Vik knew whom he had to face—a man who once had started a conspiracy to take his life, and whom he not long ago had chased from his house. This man knew that Erling Vik had close ties at Venhaug, and had a daughter living there. It is not unlikely that Torvald Ørje knew people who hated Erling Vik and the Venhaug people as much as he, and could tell them how all that Venhaug group could be stricken through one single individual. Sad to say, it is possible Erling Vik himself might have given Ørje that thought; he had demanded that the stolen paintings be sent to Venhaug."

How many were conceivable? Quite a few, but it is not the rule in Norway that hate leads to murder. Strangely enough, most were women, and Erling's thoughts touched upon the one closest in a geographical sense and therefore first to raise his suspicion—Vigdis in Kongsberg, Jan's friend of his youth. As so often before, he soon had a full dozen names but shook his head. It didn't quite check with any one of them. There was no lack of hate, but they were too stupid. The silent, clueless planning aimed higher than any one of them could conceive. "I believe you are checkmate, Monsieur Poirot," he thought, and smiled gloomily.

Among the stacks of letters that flooded headquarters was also an anonymous letter about his collision at the Bristol with Gulnare, now Mrs. Kortsen, but the letter-writer had been unable to identify the lady. Nor did the waiter recall the incident. Jan wasn't asked, and Erling only shrugged his shoulders: "Pure nonsense. Some woman I didn't know; I believe she had been drinking." Nor had the police expected anything.

He could not get away from the fact that there was something to what the paper had said—"not unlikely Torvald Ørje knew people who hated Erling Vik and the Venhaug people as much as—"

There could be many of those. Only yesterday he had heard a rumor that Mrs. Kortsen presided over a sort of traitor salon, and that Torvald Ørje had moved among that crowd.

But something was missing. Erling had seized on the fact that Felicia herself had mentioned the one who might take her life—but not the *name* of the woman she hated.

It need not be someone Erling knew by name. Of these he recalled only four. The first was Sissel Haraldstad. She was a widow when Felicia met her, now sixty-two years of age, and had not remarried. She lived a quiet life in an apartment on Arbien Street, where she gave music lessons, mostly to have some occupation. She was in good circumstances, had a grown daughter and a few grandchildren. Felicia's aversion had long ago turned into self-reproach, but he wasn't quite sure. That Sissel Haraldstad now, so much later, would have done away with Felicia did not seem plausible. Erling had never seen her, all his information had come from Felicia who never could forget her.

Number two was Cecilie Skog. During the past years she had changed her name many times, but recently she had taken back the name of her first husband and called herself Mrs. Skog. Probably without his permission. Cecilie was a few years older than himself, sixty-one he thought, although she looked older; she had not been one to preserve herself. Her last husband she had shot with a rifle in 1946, at Lysaker, and had escaped by saying she shot in self-defense. And the neighbors had testified they had heard a terrible brawl from the house before the shot was fired. People who knew her could not help but smile when they heard Cecilie Skog had needed a rifle to defend herself, but Cecilie had displayed a black eye, and there had been no witnesses in the room. The Cecilie Erling had known unfortunately developed a great taste for cognac, but had been sober the day she had seen him at Skøyen, which she reported to the police the following day. They couldn't endure the sight of each other, and were uncomfortable when moving in the same circles. Felicia herself had not seen her since about 1939. It had not surprised Erling that Cecilie could shoot her husband in a fury fired with the right amount of cognac, but he could not picture her as a calculating murderess.

Then there was Viktoria Hagen. She hated Felicia to such an extent that she never could control herself when her name was mentioned.

The fourth was Margrete, Julie's mother, who had got the child with Erling that Felicia herself had wanted, and who never stopped reminding them of her existence through vague hints of blackmail now and then.

Erling arrived at the conclusion it could be none of them. But who was she, then, the woman Felicia never had called by name?

"Listen, Jan," said Erling, "I think I have a possible theory about what happened when Torvald Ørje was killed. I imagine when that little Goebbels was in the news recently, the wounds might have been reopened in some one of our boys from those days; one who like you and me had forgotten about Ørje, forgotten that he was one of the many who never had to pay the piper as we had then expected. This boy of ours, he had forgotten, and was forgotten himself, but like Torvald Ørje he wanted to remind us of his existence. I can picture him so clearly among the many now totally obscure—a man of average looks, an average Norwegian who didn't react too strongly to foreign boot-tramps in the streets at night, an average guy who sluggishly and at long last gets good and mad. He has heard they are picking on the king, both in the papers and in their broken Norwegian. Actually, he had never thought much about the king, but had in his slow manner attended to his own business. Now he gets it into his head that our king—what in heck have those people to do with *him?* He is *our* king, and this is Norway. What in hell are they doing in our country?

"And as surely and as slowly as always, he gradually approaches the heart of the matter. Perhaps his father was arrested or killed for one reason or another, and he grows ever more restless. But one day there is peace again, and he goes back to planting cabbage which he likes best of all. The years pass by, but one day something awakens him again; he reads in the papers that the little Goebbels from Os is active again. That man? Is he free? And our average guy, this serious and slow man, goes one day to this apartment house at Maridalsvei. Someone opens the door when he rings, as people do nowadays when they no longer expect Gestapo-calls, and a man of average appearance recognizes the one who opens, and bangs in his skull with a two-inch pipe about a foot long."

Jan's eyes had taken on something of their old, wondering naïveté. He said, "I didn't read in the paper that he had left any such tool lying around."

"Neither would I have."

Jan looked vacantly at him for a moment before he rose and resumed pacing the floor. Presently he asked, "Do you think the police will dig any more into your—your possible visit to Oslo, now that the paper tells them what to do?"

"My dear Jan—of course they thought so right along; to put it mildly, they assumed I had been in Oslo when so many had seen me."

He looked about, tired. "There has been so much, Jan, and you know my thoughts are on something else. But I told them I would give them some information if they would treat it with discretion when they found it was useless. They agreed after some stalling. I told them it was correct that the lady had seen me at Skøyen, but all the rest was nonsense. Of course they had to ask if I hadn't been to Maridalsvei as well, but I said no, I don't know anyone there. I didn't wish to say more than necessary, and my visit to Oslo they would have discovered sooner or later—and perhaps read more into it if I hadn't told them myself. Then they asked me to look through some reports; it was only gossip and nonsense, and they felt the same, but they had to keep everything for the record. Then there was that woman who had seen me at Skøyen. For some reason they wanted to assure her she was right; I said I didn't care as long as she didn't shoot me. They thought this was quite funny, but one of them suddenly thought of something and said, very seriously, 'Is it correct that you two are deep enemies?' I admitted nothing worth recording."

He rose and started walking the floor also, the two of them making the figure 8 in their wandering. "It must be annoying to the police," continued Erling, "that they are made out to be more stupid every day through the newspapers. It must be something peculiar with those police-reporters, perhaps reading too many detective stories. Some sort of wish-fulfillment to be a Sherlock Holmes and not waste their time on incompetent policemen. The papers offer advice and clues to the police, and tell them what they should do, which has been done already long ago, unless it's pure nonsense."

Jan said, tonelessly, "I hated so to stir things up any more. After this here with us, and Torvald Ørje—after I got you off—"

He waited a moment and continued, "I had to strike, or know that someone did. Once Ørje had—well—perished—then I wanted nothing further. One day it'll all come out. Let it take its time. I believe such a person himself might feel there is something unfulfilled in the whole matter until the secret comes out. He might confide, make a slip of the tongue. Save something that shouldn't be saved. Drink too much one day. Confide to a diary and leave it on a table. The wish to confess is there all the time. I agree with the journalist—it is something from the war years."

He stood still for a moment, looking at the pictures of Harald and Bjørn. "It is so strange to look back at it now. They tell us to forget, now that they have paid for their crimes. Who has paid? Thousands of Norwegians at Sachsenhausen did pay. The others? A few were beheaded, and the small sinners paid fines or served short prison sentences. Otherwise, as far as I know, not a single one has paid, not even according to law. All of them were let off. Yet, we must listen to this untrue, sentimental talk, that they have expiated their crimes. People who have not expiated their crimes, and never will, are now screaming in the newspapers and elsewhere, but the ones who came back from Sachsenhausen, their health broken—"

Jan stopped. He looked through the window at Julie, who was spreading grain for the hens which she had let out on the only bare spot in front of the chicken house. "We'll have more eggs again tomorrow now that the hens are let out," he said. "Fresh air, exercise, lust for life, an occasional green blade—Julie has good chicken sense." He looked at Erling. "I mean of course that she understands chickens."

Yes, Erling had understood what he meant.

"Felicia had it too," Jan added, as if apprehensive lest he elevate someone at the expense of Felicia.

There is something good about farmers, thought Erling, when they are top quality.

Jan turned and looked at Erling. "What about you, now—are you going to move to Venhaug?" he asked.

They looked at each other for perhaps half a minute. Then Erling replied, with an attempt to use his natural voice, "Do you think I should sell my house in Lier then?"

Jan spoke up quickly. "Oh, no! I've thought about that. If you otherwise think as I, that is. It's a remarkable house, solid as a fortress, and you like it. I don't see why we couldn't move it here. I think you would feel more at home in it—but you stay at Old Venhaug if you wish."

"It would cost a lot of money to tear down my house, move it, and raise it here again."

"That I have figured out. You can sell it to me for what it costs to move it and put it where you want it. And keep the right to live in it."

"You want to make a pensioner out of me?"

There was no sting in his voice, only bitter self-irony.

No more was said about it. Jan turned and looked again at Julie and the chickens.

Erling also turned and resumed his walk. He thought of Felicia and the birds.

Jan approached Erling. Julie was no longer there to look at. "It is like having something in the head that must be operated on," he said. "I've been thinking and thinking this over until my head wants to burst."

"You mean the letter Felicia said she was curious about?" asked Erling. "I know they pressed you hard to make you think of something. What was it? You never told me."

"There was no letter she could have been interested in—indeed, there was no letter for her at all. Nor during the following days. No more letters ever came for her."

"I bring it up because I forgot to tell you the Oslo police also asked that question. They asked me in detail and several times if it was like her to say something without any particular meaning—as people often do—make a statement in the air. I said I thought not. I said that when Felicia Venhaug said she expected a letter and was curious about it, then it was so, and she would have explained later. Both in Kongsberg and in Oslo they considered this quite important—that she was curious about a letter even though she didn't like to disturb the postmaster on a Sunday."

Jan said, in a strangely dry and formal tone of voice, "Of course they must think the same as we—that some message had come from someone who wanted her to take that road and hoped she would be alone. Or knew she would be alone."

After some moments Jan added, "She had secrets only when she wished to surprise us and bring us joy."

They walked around each other in their figure 8, and Erling did not reply, for a person must have time to calm his voice.

"Yes," said Jan, "she was very happy when she left. There was no secret she would have kept from us with that letter—that damned letter—"

They continued to walk round each other in that ingenious figure 8.

"It would have been a secret only until she returned," said Jan, and seemed quite calm now. "She would never have hinted if it didn't concern us. On the contrary—she wanted to raise our expectations about something."

They walked a long time, studiously keeping their paces. Jan seemed to have forgotten what he had in mind.

"What else, Jan?"

"Well, I'm thinking of some sort of personal description; the one who fooled her must have been terribly jealous and sly. So jealous of Felicia that she personified black evil. A person with no life worth while of her own who therefore must take it from someone else. And stupid this person must have been, for only stupidity uses slyness."

Yes, Erling was familiar with stupidity turning sly. He could picture to himself Evil in person approaching through the trees. He felt a chill at his hair-roots at the thought of what Felicia had seen.

Jan continued. "When I realized this fully I recalled Torvald Ørje. He was sly. But I felt that the one who killed her was not just a cheap personification of Slyness. I can't sleep nights. I see this impersonal Sly as something emerging from the forest, following her along the road, while the snowfall grew heavier and we sat here in comfort and knew nothing. I remember I was thinking I could hear her steps crackle against the ice—"

Jan grew silent again. His voice had been normal, as if he only were talking about the weather. He stopped and faced Erling. "Just look at what the principle of evil has wrought at Venhaug! If you have observed the children you must have noticed. There is something that can't bear for people to be happy. Something that in the name of morality crushes happiness. For this is the deed of an intense moralist."

It must have been planned, thought Erling. There could be no doubt about that.

He recalled how the detective at the police station had shown him the cork which a dog had found, and said with a grimace. "This is all we have!" and tossed the meaningless object back into the drawer. "If it had been *you* who were lost," said the detective, "then we could have followed that clue—that someone had treated you to home-brew." Or a rag with something else in it? Erling had wondered. "We found the bottle also, and the cork fits, and it was indeed home-brew. Yes, we thought of a rag with something also. We have gone through everything in the minutest detail—even your meaningless journey through Oslo. We have nothing of value, only that last sentence she uttered, about a *letter*. Surely, this must be the most anonymous letter in the history of criminology."

Jan resumed: "It was done by someone who envied her her goodness. A creature who hated the very name of goodness the way a churl hates. Someone crushed her to get peace, but will never have it now. It was done by sly and wounded jealousy itself. A creature intent on carrying out God's judgment. And here is my conclusion, what I know must have happened: This sly, subhuman being knew a trap could be set for Felicia through her expectation of some joy she could bring back, probably for the children."

"Who was it, Jan?"

"I don't know who it was. And I'm not sure it's something that can be traced back to the war years—even though that's probable. It needn't be *only* so. Deep down it is something much older; it was done by someone fighting for a principle—sly stupidity's hatred for everything it doesn't understand, which therefore must be rooted out. I don't know whom the Werewolf used for his tool, but something tells me it was a woman who lay in wait for Felicia."

Erling had sat down. He agreed with Jan. He didn't wish to say why, couldn't say why. He felt confused and unsure. It was this way: yesterday morning as he sat on the edge of the bed, getting into his clothes after another bout with nightmares, his eyes happened to fall on a crumpled piece of paper on the floor between the table and the bed. He had noticed it a few times before; now he picked it up. It was folded several times and crumpled before being thrown away. He smoothed it out and read its contents.

Then he sat and looked vacantly before him. He knew at once how the paper had got there; the last time Felicia had been to Old Venhaug, she had felt for something on the bedside table and had happened to sweep off her open handbag. He recalled her annoyed exclamation as she leaned out of the bed and gathered in the contents of the bag from the floor; she had overlooked the small piece of paper; as was usual, they did not have on the electric light, only a small candle which left the floor under the table in deep shadow.

On the paper was written in Felicia's sure and clear script: *If I could kill her with black magic I wouldn't hesitate.*

He had read it several times before he burned the paper. He realized only too well what he might start; he might as well put a match to a gasoline tank. That *he* should be the one to bring this dark message from Felicia—so to speak, from his own bed.

Things will always turn up to make one work against the police, he thought. People who have not encountered tragedy can hardly understand it in advance; they take for granted we must give the police all the information we can. Such must seldom be the case.

Jan stopped in front of him and asked, "That woman you saw in the train dining car and couldn't locate later—you said she might have left the train at Kongsberg?"

It surprised Erling that he had entirely forgotten that experience, but that was the way it was, he told himself; many experiences that make great impressions can get completely lost in forgetfulness, especially if they lack obvious meaning or cannot be fitted into a pattern. Only slowly did it dawn on him—oh, yes, the back of a woman, a woman who literally *looked* at him through her back, while he sat in the dining car and read the Book of Esther.

But Erling was worn out, and he knew how tired Jan was. He thought of Julie and the children who had lost their Felicia; the older daughter was in the hospital with hysterical spasms. And he thought of what he himself had almost done to Torvald Ørje, done in his thoughts, lived through in every detail with many variations, a deed he ruthlessly would have perpetrated—if someone else had not already been there. Someone else who perhaps also had brought a two-inch pipe of suitable length, but who scarcely had a pig-snare with him as well, to make sure. Indeed strange. When Torvald Ørje in 1942 had sent people to murder Erling, the Gestapo also had been on the way. Two had been on the way also when Ørje's turn came.

Jan was standing in front of him waiting for an answer.

"Yes, I remember now," said Erling. "Well, you know I get those feelings for no reason at all. It was probably as Felicia said—I might have drunk more than I should while in Oslo."

Again he pictured to himself that sinister something he had visualized—not at all a man of ordinary appearance, as the saying goes. Who could it have been? He felt himself in the midst of a sinister something, and he had caused it. With both hands he would have taken the pipe, arched his back like a butcher ready to hit an ox in the head. The victim would have felt something was wrong, would have turned half about; he would have hit Torvald Ørje on the top of that dog-head, and heard a crunching sound—and the agony he had heard then, in a call from far away, the ringing call of the gladiators: We who are about to die, greet you, Caesar!

That too had happened differently. He had, in the stranger's shape, or inside him, waited for Torvald Ørje in the street, and they had walked up the steps together. "I never can use a belt for my trousers the way you do," Erling said. Torvald Ørje replied that a belt was more convenient, and rather handy if one wanted to hang oneself. Erling had taken his eyes off the belt. Well, he had replied, nothing like being prepared. They had walked along the upper hall to the door. Ørje unlocked it. "I'll go in first and turn on the lights," he said. Erling pulled the snare from his pocket and unrolled it, as the Messenger from Venhaug followed Torvald Ørje inside—

In that moment realization came over him; he bent forward in his chair, panting: the Messenger from Venhaug—the gardener, who had taken the car to "drive a bit"—five hours! Old habits are difficult to change: Tor Anderssen Haukas from Venhaug had been to Oslo and murdered Torvald Ørje.

"What is the matter with you?" asked Jan.

"I had a terrible cramp in my stomach."

"Better go to a doctor; one must be careful in such matters," said the matter-of-fact Jan.

· When Gustav got in the newspaper

Erling received a letter from Elfride. She pleaded with him not to tell Gustav she had written, almost as desperately as she asked him to pray to God. Elfride was not a letter-writer, but he understood it was most of all an appeal not to burden them with more unhappiness. The letter was spotted with tears. "If you only had some permanent place to live," it came at last, "and some steady work, then we would not be exposed to so much evil."

The happenings at Venhaug had struck them like an earthquake. Earlier, they must have had their speculations, but they had never heard of Venhaug, and all they now read seemed to them as from some land or some place one might see at the movies but never quite believe existed. Erling realized how much it must have aged Gustav when, on top of everything, he too "got into the paper," in the very headlines: *Erling Vik's Brother Believes Him Capable of Almost Anything.* Well, yes, Gustav had talked to a man who asked one thing and another. Nothing but talk. And Gustav had said nothing, except what rightly and truly was the case, that Erling—well . . . . Yet, the headlines announced it like the end of the world. There are ways and ways of saying a thing, and he *had* talked, but—

During the following night the mountain-blaster came close to praying to God. Pray God that his brother actually was the murderer, so that

Gustav's words would prove truthful. But thank heaven he was too stubborn to turn to Our Lord, for they had soon been informed by the radio that the police had let Erling go. The police chief must be stupid. The only comfort to Gustav was that he hadn't made himself ridiculous before Our Lord, by praying for something he would not have been granted; now on the day of judgment he could meet his maker with a proud look.

Gustav and Elfride understood only that they had been shamed in the paper, regardless of whether Erling was guilty or not. Nils, Uncle Oddvar's son, had been in the paper when he was killed in a drunken brawl. Erling had been in the paper many times without being shamed, but others had been in his stead. That should have been enough. Now Gustav too had been in the paper, exactly like murderers and authors and drunkards and whore-bucks. It was insufferable, and Gustav had only told the man—

Gustav had gritted his teeth. If Erling ever dared knock on his door again—

Elfride cried when alone; there *must* be something good in Erling. She could remember, now that she really thought about it, that he had never insulted her, and never tried to act uppety with her or hurt her. She had been able to confide in him that she liked to go to meetings; they had talked about it at length, and she had seen no sneer on his face, however crazy he otherwise might be.

Her hands trembled at the thought that she too had once been in the paper, and she herself had caused it. If Gustav ever knew—but that was as far as she dared think such a horrible thought. Oh, when she had read the Question and Answer column all these years, how she would have liked to participate. It was like a cozy family circle, so warm, they asked if anyone remembered the beautiful song about Mother, the one that started so and so, and always someone came up with it, and Elfride cut out such songs and kept them.

She had fought with herself many months, almost a year, and then she had written. A few fearsome days had followed, almost two weeks, while she suffered and lost weight; they didn't pay any attention to her letter, she should have known.

One day it was printed. She would never forget that day. She was one of them. It was like having a hundred brothers and sisters. She would die if it ever came out it was she; they might not then count her as one of them.

And they would discover that after all she was not attending meetings. They would see her as she was. She must never let them know she had stolen into their circle, with a contribution. Her cheeks flushing she would feel under the sheets and pillow cases in the drawer: she must read it once more. (How many times had she read it!) It was two years now since she had written in the paper, the same as Erling:

WHY SO LATE?

It is now usual with meetings 8 o'clock in the evening. Don't believe people who have to get up early in the morning can go out so late. And not at 7:30 either. The time should not be later than 7 o'clock.

Something else while I write. Please put up boxes for suggestions outside the meeting halls. How often have I carried home my suggestion because my courage failed.

Greetings from one who also goes to meetings.

Elfride hid her relic again. Through a veil of tears she read the announcements: *Society for the Lonely,* cozy meeting for women. And there was *Hebron,* missionary party tonight. *South American Missionary Society,* no, America wasn't quite up her alley, and she had always supposed before that they were baptized and confirmed in America. Hope Fredrik wasn't married to a heathen. No, she remembered he had written about baptism, praise the Lord. The Society for the Lonely, cozy meeting for women, how lovely it sounded; but she wasn't alone and might not be admitted. She couldn't lie outright at the door. Fearfully she could picture Gustav: first astonished if she told him she wanted to go out, and what a fury a moment later! One read in the paper about people who said they were taking a walk. Erling might say, "I think I'll take a short walk by myself." On the other hand, his wife had left him and he needn't tell anybody he was taking a short walk, he only went. It must feel funny to be so footloose. She wondered if it was really legal, when a person wasn't a widower or something.

Elfride dried her eyes and spotted a match on the floor. Well, who would have thought—! How lucky she herself had spotted it. Not that Gustav would, he never saw anything. But suppose anyone had come, she thought with a shudder, as she carried the used match out to the kitchen where her polished garbage can stood behind its flowery curtain in the corner. With some hesitation she placed the match in the can, went back to the room again to try the radio, but there couldn't be anything this time of day to put one in good humor and help one shed a few tears over one's dissolute brother-in-law. Elfride dreamed him young and kind again; then he could have lived with them and had his steady work, and they would have found a girl worthy of him. Instead, it had turned into a frightening world they had better stay away from—all those distant, horrible goings-on that now almost lurked at her door, divorces and such, and terrible murders, much worse than two drunkards fighting and killing each other, and she shivered in horror at the thought of that woman from an estate named Venhaug, with an un-Christian name, a regular Babylonian harlot, the preacher had said, according to a neighbor's wife.

Elfride sat down and cried again; she managed anyway, without the music.

• A black hole in the ice on the Numedal River

None of them had wished to voice apprehension when Felicia stayed away so long. It was Jan who gave way first and called the post office. Erling could hear she hadn't been there, and he dropped his cigarette on the floor. Jan looked helplessly into the air as he put down the receiver, awkwardly.

Julie offered to run over to Aunt Gustava. Felicia must be there, of course she must (but why send someone for her then). They saw her run down the road as a person does when the ground is slippery, making unexpected jumps, gliding along, sometimes suddenly colliding with the trees. But Jan was fearful of evil, and all were apprehensive. Almost an hour and a half had passed, and there seemed no explanation except an accident. Jan ran out and started the car; he had just put on the chains. He drove off alone, the same road Julie had taken. The old snow on the road was packed and slippery and now covered with new-fallen snow. Now and again the wheels spun in the slush, while the snow kept falling with increasing thickness. It was calm but the vision was clear only fifteen to twenty paces ahead.

Someone came running from Aunt Gustava's cottage; he saw it was Julie and waited for her.

Felicia had not called on Aunt Gustava, Julie panted through the open car window, but stopped when she received no answer. Jan sat looking at his hands; he had turned pale.

"Jump in," he said, presently, and when she sat beside him he turned the car about. He drove like a crazy man the mile back to the house. He switched off the motor and rushed with hat and overcoat inside to the telephone. There was only a constable in the Kongsberg police station, so he called the home of Chief of Police Rud. They were old acquaintances and had gone through school together. He explained the situation and said in a controlled voice that an accident must have happened. Could Rud take the car and come at once? Could he bring a dog and some men?

Rud tried to say something about Felicia being sure to turn up soon and explain all very simply.

"Listen!" said Jan, sharply. "You know Felicia; she would never dream of scaring us this way. It isn't like Felicia, and you know it. This is not her doing, whatever it is."

He turned with the receiver at his ear and when he saw that only Erling was in the room, he continued in the same frozen voice, "You know as well as I there is little hope of finding her alive."

He and Erling started down the road to meet the chief's car and perhaps discover some clue. The snow kept falling and a wind was coming up. They skidded on the slippery surface under the snow. They could see no tracks leading into the forest on either side, and if there had been any they would surely have been deep enough to show through the fresh snow. Shortly before they reached Aunt Gustava's road they met the police car, which came with a speed that was insane in the poor visibility and the treacherous road condition. It slowed down and stopped in a cloud of snow. Rud jumped out with a police dog on a leash.

"Anything new?"

"No."

"This weather," said Rud, but didn't bother to finish the sentence. He was given what little information they had. Then he instructed the sergeant at the wheel to follow them toward the post office. They walked ahead with the dog who sniffed the snow and pulled at the leash. It stopped and looked up at Rud. "Well, what is it, Samson?"

The dog said definitely nothing, and they continued their walk.

Quite suddenly Samson left the road and wanted to take off into the forest on the right. He whined and trembled as he poked his nose into the snow and came up with an ordinary bottle-cork. Rud took it and smelled it. "Thrown away recently," he said. "Look, it's quite dry." He smelled it some more.

They all had the same thought: someone had drunk a pick-me-up here. But that person must have emptied the bottle also. As far as that was concerned, anyone might have had a cork in his pocket and thrown it away.

"It doesn't smell of alcohol," said Rud.

The dog was wild to get farther into the forest, he scratched and ran hither and yon as far as the leash would permit.

Rud ordered him to keep quiet. He was inspecting what all three now saw, and he called to his sergeant.

There was a deep furrow in the snow, half a yard to a yard wide. It seemed someone had tried to obliterate it at the edges. It led as far as they could see into the forest, rather indistinct under the falling snow, but not to be mistaken. Rud felt with his hands in the snow. "The old snow is broken," he said. "This indentation has been made after the snow started to fall, I'm sure."

It became difficult to handle the dog. They followed the furrow at the side of the excited animal. Samson sniffed eagerly in one place and scratched up something from the snow, snorting with excitement.

All saw simultaneously the little clump of bloody snow. Erling felt his whole body revolt, and in the same moment Jan tumbled over like a falling tree.

"Take care of him, Erling," said Rud. He was almost as hoarse as the frenzied Samson. "Come with me!" he called to the sergeant.

They struggled on, stumbled and groaned. The ground was hopelessly cut up down here near the river. Jan had regained consciousness. He and Erling stumbled after the others. Neither one of them attempted to say anything. They caught up with the other two men who stood in the snow a few yards from the edge of the river and looked into a black hole in the ice, where the current boiled and clucked. The furrow led to it.

Stricken, Jan and Erling sat down in the snow a few paces away. The dog sniffed and sniffed toward the hole.

The wind was increasing. In the whirling snow they were as isolated from the rest of the world as in a diving bell. Rud took the cork from his pocket and looked at it glumly. Erling sat staring at the hole. Jan sat with his head lowered and his bare hands stuck into the snow. He had lost his hat and the snow gathered in his hair.

The policemen approached them with the dog. Rud tried to control his voice: "Have you had any dealings with that collaborator crowd since the war?"

Jan did not move and did not reply. Then he raised his head a little, his eyes happened to catch the hole, and he looked down again; his head seemed to hang loose. Erling replied, thickly, "Jan gave some boys work shortly after the war, when things were hard for them. Some boys that had gone astray only. He was on good terms with them. I myself have seen a few collaborators, quite obviously, but have spoken to only one, who came to call on me early in August, last year; I threw him out. It was that Torvald Ørje, the one we used to call little Goebbels, the one they made chief of police at Os."

• A messenger from Venhaug

Two weeks had passed since Felicia disappeared. Erling shuffled about in his room at Old Venhaug. Dusk was falling and, as was his custom when not working, he lit a candle; his sight had grown weaker during the last years; he needed strong light when he worked but couldn't stand it for long. Thus he made short interruptions from time to time when he lighted a candle and sat in the dark. After the tragedy with Felicia he had managed with a candle or the dark. The thought of work seemed as distant to him as the memory of a legend; one that was as difficult to interpret as the fragments of a lost religion on a papyrus scroll. All values had sunk to bottom prices or nothing. He did not listen to the newscasts, read no newspapers. All his mail remained unopened; he threw it into an old bag to escape the sight of it. Was it sorrow? How answer when the question means nothing? He left the bottle untouched. He managed to eat a little, but food had no taste; yet, it was easier to eat than be plagued by Julie or Aunt Gustava. He thought that such must life be for robots, for one couldn't make souls for them synthetically. Without the necessary soul—or ghost, as he thought of it—they could not love, hate, enjoy, or detest anything. He was sure our first parents never comprehended what suddenly got into Our Lord. I have lost my ghost and must have become what is known as a materialistic person, completely neutralized and without higher interests. I don't care if I get back my ghost, it may wander about as a ghost wishes. It will be its own problem to get back home again. Stay away, ghost of mine! I don't wish to have any dealings with thoughts or *geist*. You can find yourself a home in someone who doesn't have a soul, then we'll see what happens. Get yourself right into John Foster Dulles. Only, keep away from *me*, I've had enough of such. Move into the Archbishop of Canterbury and promise to stay there. Or still better, if he has room for a human soul, move into my brother Gustav. Then Elfride might be allowed to attend prayer meetings and feel at home. Oh, to remain without one's ghost, insensible. But my ghost will find its way home, never fear, just as sick people get their ghosts back and start yelling the moment the anesthetic wears off.

Outside it was still light enough to see. He recognized Tor Anderssen in the yard. He must not have much of a soul, not wishing to be called Haukas. Hope my ghost gets into him and stays there.

Tor Anderssen started to busy himself with the car. Why did he bother? To look at all that dirty snow? Why bother? There came Jan down the veranda steps. Why did he bother?

Jan stopped and said something to Tor Anderssen, who replied something. Why bother to talk about anything? Just as well stop.

He sat down on his bed. There it occurred to him that he had also stopped smoking.

He turned his hands this way and that, studying them. Actually repulsive instruments, hands. All the silliness one had done with them, whether it was to wave after a train which, thank heaven, was leaving, or to feel about in girls' clothing, or to hit people without making them worse or better, or to pick one's nose, or raise the flag on the king's birthday. There was no end to the many uses one had made of one's hands, like helping a horse get on solid ground when it had fallen into a swamp; it repaid him with a kick, and he discovered suddenly that it was a horse with good sense.

Someone was coming up the stairs. Erling looked apathetically at the door. There was a knock and he said yes. It was Jan.

It seemed unnatural, and both felt equally uncomfortable. Jan had never been inside this room in his own house since Erling had occupied it. Something must of necessity shape up between them; they saw her so actually alive that both for a moment must lower their eyes.

Outside the car started. Erling had risen and taken a few steps. He looked out at the dusky yard.

"Tor Anderssen is going out with the car, I see," he said.

"Yes, he wanted to take a little ride."

They spoke low but their voices filled the room, creating a hundred whispering replies. The fluttering light threw deep, living shadows on their faces. Erling thought of the shadows on Felicia's mature body as she used to walk across the floor. Jan sat down, finding a chair with his body as it were, the way one sits down in a doctor's office and knows one is being observed, that the diagnosis to a certain degree already is being made. Or at the police station, it struck him, where they also make diagnoses and can be wrong.

"Erling," said Jan, and breathed heavily. "There is something I want to ask of you."

Erling felt the murmur of the silence; he pictured himself as a Lilliputian sitting and listening at the mouth of a conch shell. Jan had never asked anything of him. Well, small matters. To buy a coil of rope in Oslo, or stop by the saddle-maker and order a belly-band. Last time it was a dozen copper nails with octagonal heads. What did Jan want him to do?

He would do anything, or nothing; it was equally indifferent to him. "Just tell me, Jan."

But he discovered he was becoming curious and thought: Could my ghost be on its way home?

Both of them at the same time became aware of the clock's ticking. Jan sat quite still, one hand on each knee, and looked at Erling.

"It is nothing you can promise in advance," said Jan. "It lies entirely outside of the ordinary."

"Just tell me straight out."

Jan raised one hand and rubbed his forehead. "I want you to go to Oslo and kill Torvald Ørje."

Now it was Erling's turn to rub his forehead. Well, he thought. Go to Oslo and kill Torvald Ørje. That is a definite order. The ticket doesn't cost much, I can easily manage that. Roundtrip. No—won't need return ticket. Very cheap.

The clock ticked and ticked and wouldn't stop, it had become so remarkably persistent, his alarm clock. Erling didn't know for how long it was the only sound he heard. The reply came without his knowing if he had thought what he should say: "Of course I will."

Well, that would be the end. Just as well. Perhaps Jan had forgotten that peace had come several years ago and that it would be a little more difficult. Now there were no police to help him hide—at least not in the same way. No Sweden to slink away to and undisturbed await better days. Certain private activities had, plainly speaking, been taken over by the authorities. Perhaps Jan had forgotten there would be no chance of hiding in a hospital bed under a false name and with false entry-date, no chance of getting an injection to keep one from talking too convincingly in delirium, no chance of changing sex and lying in the women's ward after abortion, as Øystein Myhre had done.

But just as well. He had no lust for life the way it had turned out; it was monotonous, colorless, valueless. He might as well commit suicide, which of course he would do, as soon as he had managed things as Jan asked him. A long-drawn-out, widely publicized trial, and life imprisonment, was not a culminating experience he would relish. Suicide wasn't in his line either, but it wasn't *so* abhorrent.

It was a great sacrifice Jan asked of him and he writhed under it, but he felt he would manage to face it, if Jan didn't change his mind.

He had not heard the clock for a long while. Now it broke through again.

"I believe she wants it done," he had heard from far away.

How long ago?

Now he replied, "You know Felicia is gone forever. There is nothing she wants."

"You know quite well what I mean," said Jan, in the same tired voice. "You know what she did when they had murdered her two brothers, and therefore you must know what she would have expected from us now—if she were able to expect anything. I want *them*—you know who—to gain nothing from having silenced her."

Jan wet his lips. "She would have demanded it of you, could she have stepped through that door at this minute."

They felt she was in the room.

Erling looked at Jan and smiled. "You have had my answer, Jan. If you consider it must be done, it will be done. It is not *that* I am talking about, but I would like to understand the whole matter a little more clearly. By the way, it sounded remarkably beautiful, what you said now, that she would have demanded it of me. Why of *me?*"

"Of course she would demand it of you—she couldn't fail to see the risk of apprehension. Well, matters being the way they are, her children are mine, and I am the one capable of running a farm, like it or not. She always said her children must inherit it in good condition."

Erling looked down and thought further on behalf of Jan: He is fifteen years younger besides and clings to life more than I, and perhaps this makes him somewhat less perspicacious. Besides, he will soon marry the only one who can take Felicia's place, the only replacement the children will accept, and he himself can manage. Yet, that you should know me so little, Jan. You too. If we didn't think that our work has had, and will have, a certain value, what use would there have been in living? Call it prejudice if you wish, but I *hadn't thought of myself dying as a criminal.* You can sit there, Jan, and demand that I throw everything to the dogs. Just a petty bourgeois prejudice, I might have said twenty-five years ago. But I see it this way now, that it is not only my life you demand; that is unimportant the way things are now. But that just you, the one of all men I would have liked to understand me, demand my reputation also. It would be impossible to save it, after all the legends that already have grown up. The searchlight will once and for all concentrate on all extraneous matters. But the symbolism will hit home: I was one to fight windmills, one perhaps never seriously dreaming of anything but this single point: how to disarm stupidity, isolate it and put it on display in some circus, drive it from power in the land, and then let it live on its own natural plane. Isn't it a joke of the greatest magnitude that my best friend throws me into my grave with my fingers round the throat of an unworthy thrall?

Just then Erling remembered Felicia's eyes which had turned ice-cold that time when she said, "How dared one of those unhanged ones call on *you!*"

Erling kept pondering. Jan was waiting, silent.

Probably Jan knows the line of my thoughts—even though I suspect him incapable of grasping what is really essential to me, and just how critically I view the rest. Jan is peculiar. Once a realist always a realist. Erling was a little confused at meeting so much common-sense calculation in a man who for the present was rather far removed from normality (sending me to Oslo to kill a man!). He could see how logical Jan Venhaug had been and was to the end. Here he had in clear words said: Felicia had two men, and she would not like to see herself unrevenged, but if it goes wrong, then *you* are the more expendable one.

It could be seen from that angle. And Jan knew very well what he was doing, by saying it here at Old Venhaug, in Erling and Felicia's room. It must be said to all that lay in the atmosphere here, so that she herself was almost a witness, when after all these years for the first and only time she was discussed by her men. She must be a witness also to the implication that if anything went wrong, Jan had no part in the blame; he would deny it point-blank and remain at Venhaug with the children —and Julie.

Erling had not for a moment intended to withdraw his promise, not even as he tried to think matters through after his answer had been given. Now something happened to him that lay beyond all reasoning: Jan's commission had pulled him out of his vacuum and placed him in the midst of life again, now when it was decided that he probably would have to leave it. The pressure on his brain had eased. It was no longer true that Felicia was gone and dead. He stood on the floor and felt it now; sorrow rose up like thunderclouds, his soul had returned home. Erling Vik must live! this stormed up potently within him and therefore he could pay the price Jan Venhaug demanded.

"Jan," he said, "you must be counting on me doing it because the chances of escape are so minimal?"

"No! You're crazy!" exclaimed Jan, in surprise. "Of course you'll manage. That's to say, when it's *you*. You will get away; since it's you. I, I would have no luck now, in these new times. With you it's something —something particular. And something with you and Oslo."

He sounded so confident Erling could have laughed.

"There are many reasons why it must be you. Unlike me you are not afraid of the dark. And then you are so impractical in many ways."

"Impractical?"

"Well, I mean—suppose I did it and were caught, then you would start some nonsense that it was your idea. And what would happen to the children? I am much wiser. *If* it goes wrong for you—but it won't—I would be much more practical since I couldn't help you anyway."

Erling could hear Felicia's laughter as it rang out in the good old days at Venhaug: Jan, oh, Jan, you precious Jan!

"Now it is my turn to give instructions," said Erling, and gathered his thoughts. "You have nothing more to say or ask. We must use old experiences now—you must not know more than absolutely necessary. My instructions to you are these: I go back with you and get a bottle of cognac. I bring it with me here and wish to be alone until I show up tomorrow. You remark casually this evening, or tomorrow, that I intend to go to Lier. Sometime in the afternoon I'll call for a taxi. That's all. There is much we could talk about, in case we never see each other again, but you'll manage all that, and much better without my aid. You are so practical, you know.

"There are also a few questions I would like to ask. First, do you realize you'll never see me again if anything goes wrong—afterwards?"

Jan nodded.

"Secondly—why just that stupid ass? And why anyone for that matter? I have never before this evening doubted that you are normal— within certain limits, that is. In principle it is of no consequence to me what you answer, but before I set out on an expedition of this kind, I would like to know—"

"It's simply that blood-revenge must strike that family."

Jan could see that Erling failed to understand and that his thoughts went off in another direction. "I mean," he added, "that revenge must strike that family or that *species,* if you wish. I never experience revelations, and perhaps I've thought too much about this matter, but we have to do here with one of that *species.* Since we don't know which one, lightning must strike among them. I don't think it will hit far from home. And not one of that brood will be in doubt that lightning has struck from Venhaug. You'll escape. They can't start any trouble, they can't do a thing, they'll just have to suffer the only reply they under-stand. Not to a single one of them will there be—and certainly never has been either—something called—" he contorted his lips, "—a Venhaug mystery."

Erling made his plans in the evening. Now that he wished to live, nothing must go wrong. He knew before he parted from Jan that tonight he would sin against the Holy Ghost—forcibly open the spring of inspiration, utilize it for a murder. He would brutally commit this sin for

Felicia and all at Venhaug. The bottle—well, he would empty it when the Holy Ghost had given him information. He intended to commit sacrilege against the Spirit and use it as advisor for a murder.

It was a sunrise from the Garden of Eden when he rowed into Erlingvik and pulled up the boat on the shore. He stood long and beheld his kingdom before he walked over to the three tall white birches against the mountainside. He did not look up at the wall on the other side where they were sitting, watching him; he did not wish to do so before he reached the slab between the birches. He did not bend over the slab, he felt he must first have permission. Perhaps after all she did not wish it. He looked up. Felicia sat with her feet pulled under her as he so often had seen her do; she wore a blue dress with lace at the neck and a broad belt round her narrow waist. He was rather surprised at seeing the dress, she had not worn it since he returned from Las Palmas. Steingrim held one of her hands, he was leaning forward a little the better to see Erling. They did not move. He looked at them and waited. They were very solemn, but a great peace lay on their faces. The closed severity was gone from Steingrim's face, it appeared rather boy-like curious—what errand might Erling have?

He stooped down and raised the slab on edge before he looked at them again. They sat as before. Then Felicia would not forbid it, and he took the golden hammer he had found at life's dawn in the rat-hole at home, but had not known it was gold until the family moved to Rjukan. Carefully he brushed off some dirt from the shining hammer and when he again looked up at Felicia, a faint warmth was already at work in his blood, soon to turn into an intoxication. She must hurry now and give a sign if she was against it, but she only watched him with her big, deep eyes. Steingrim did the same. Erling could see no motion except in Felicia's hair, when a breath of wind fluttered it. Well, it must be so, he thought, and the tears came—he knew it, knew it once and for all, that the dead and the living are equally dead to each other. To the dead one, all are dead. One could thank the deity for at least that much. He knocked on the mountain wall with his gold hammer and called aloud; then a white, crackling light streamed over him. It rushed like floods of wild horses over the broad fields, he ran from dungeon to dungeon and loosened all the ropes of dreams, hit the law's watch-dog in the head at the door, and opened the sluice gates to the springs of life; he blasted his mind to pieces, some of which floated away down the streams, while other pieces escaped like dark birds to rank heaths where they were more at home. He raised a new heaven and a new earth, but in the new-created world were also Felicia and Steingrim, this he could see as he pushed out the boat and the smoke lifted from over Erlingvik.

About two o'clock in the morning he was standing on the floor, swaying like a conductor calling for order and attention before he slowly raises the baton. All eyes in his consciousness were waiting for the sign.

He had risen from the dark well into which Felicia's disappearance had pushed him; he was not undamaged, but he was whole; dark moments undoubtedly lay ahead, but he would live. Now it only remained to get it over with, this that he must do in Oslo tomorrow, or, if necessary, to wait there until he could strike. He felt as if everything was already done, only one detail remained.

He opened the bottle Jan had given him and sat down to drink. It was twelve days since he had tasted liquor and he needed it now. The poison rose quickly to his head. He had a recollection about something black he had seen during the night, some slinking, formless shadow over the snow. He remembered what it was. That damned Haukas who considered it elegant to be called Anderssen had returned with the car. At that hour the moon had been high, now it was low. Shadows from this long-legged, long-armed, long-backed creature, actually a beast who confused people by wearing clothing and who for some reason walked on two legs, it was his shadow he had seen slinking over the dirty, moon-green snow. People like Tor Anderssen should be forbidden a shadow. He leaned back in his chair and recited, pathetically:

I the Fool sit here alone,
Like God within His heaven.
The clock ticks unflaggingly:
Lonely, alone, alone, lonely.

The bottle is empty and I am drunk,
The woman you gave me
Someone took from me.
Lonely, alone, alone, lonely.

At dusk the following day they were standing on the veranda, waiting for the taxi. Julie had been seized with weeping and had gone inside.

"I noticed you take along everything," said Jan.

"Well, for all eventualities."

"You take along everything," repeated Jan. "Everything, even the thing you might be just as well without—in an eventuality."

Erling did not reply. He felt for the thing he had in his pocket.

"It looks as if you had in mind to stay away, Erling—*however it turns out.*"

Something was wrong with Erling; he could find no words.

Jan looked down at the floor. "It's my doing," he said, indistinctly. "I ask you to return. Julie—"

Erling was low today. He would rather everything was left open and that Jan would refrain from appealing to his conscience. It was nothing to hold up to the light. He turned aside and said, slurringly, "It is not certain I can decide that myself."

"You know you will decide it yourself, Erling. And I know I only plague you the way matters stand. I only wanted to say I feel like a beggar. I am your son-in-law. It's my hopeless fear of the dark that brought it about before—before it ought to have happened perhaps, but Felicia—I believe she'd have understood."

Erling took him by the shoulder. "Shut up, Jan! Felicia understands."

"Julie has saved me, Erling. My mind—"

The taxi was approaching down the road; the headlights hit the barn.

Erling felt better, and of course he knew that he never could tear himself loose and that he did not wish it either—but some door must be left open. Well, he didn't know. Jan was a strange person. This was like the time the Germans were in the country. Then Jan was very young, but had automatically become a leader at the first moment. Not one to give orders and forget, but one who always got his way, and no one had been the loser. Erling had not been Jan's man during the war, had not even known him, and had consequently not encountered Felicia. He had heard about her through Steingrim who was a contact man for several groups.

Jan held on to Erling's sleeve and followed him down the steps. No, he had not been Jan's man, yet he felt as if he always had been, as if he remembered from before how Jan Venhaug would send a man out into the night. Before he closed the taxi door he called, unnaturally loud, "See you soon, Jan!"

• *The collector*

Julie, thin and pale, stood working at the kitchen table. Aunt Gustava had been given a comfortable chair and sat in a corner with her cogitations. She had voiced a few stray thoughts about her depraved son, and her husband who hadn't had sense enough to die like decent people.

She had also made a few statements about the farmer who no longer permitted her to live in her own cottage and had threatened her with the old people's home. Well, now at last she was secure in the pensioner's cottage at Venhaug, because at all times there had lived decent people on that farm. "Where good people walk, there God has His road."

With this sentence Aunt Gustava encompassed Bjørnson, God, and Venhaug, but Julie did not react.

"Imagine! He filled my cottage with chickens! Ruined my kitchen drawers, used them all for the hens to lay eggs! There's no law and order in this country any longer! Chicken-shit all over! What a fool! But such are men."

She looked askance at Julie, who didn't seem to listen.

"No, don't ever trust men," sighed Aunt Gustava.

No reaction was apparent and she started again. "Trust them one cannot. They're up to one trick or another. They're a different breed. Look only at your father—nothing to that man from beginning to end, but at least he has the decency to keep an old pensioner woman company at times. No one else does that. And helps me drink my cider. But that gardener, Tor—"

No reply.

Aunt Gustava sighed as only one of her proportions might. "They are peculiar," she said. "Like my husband. It took time before we got together, I'll tell you. I didn't want him—he was such a fool. And then to fly up in the top of a tree while his wife was busy washing windows."

She stopped and looked with wide-open eyes at Julie, who was kneading dough. Then she looked back in the corner for a moment, before she resumed. "I didn't have much of underwear, no, I didn't, nothing I could afford to lose—"

Julie gave Aunt Gustava a tired look. Was the old woman getting confused in her head?

Aunt Gustava caught the sign of life, and continued. "Imagine that stupid fool—he stole my pants!"

Julie rested her hands on the edge of the kneading trough and looked at Aunt Gustava. "What are you jabbering about?"

"My fiance, of course. He stole my underwear. And he got a shameful death, too. It couldn't be anyone else, you see. And so I told him—"

Aunt Gustava described how she had taken her husband-to-be by the neck and held him until he confessed the whole pitiful business.

Julie kept watching Aunt Gustava until the old waman was through with the tale.

"I've read about such things," said Julie, with effort.

But Aunt Gustava had discerned something in her voice. She looked out through the window and said, "There he is now, at the car, that Tor Anderssen."

Julie glanced through the window, too. "I thought you were talking about Tor Anderssen a moment ago. I don't believe I really heard what you said."

"Ah, just stupid men in general. Where is he off to now?"

"To Kongsberg."

"Well, I guess we won't see him for a few hours then. He must fill himself with beer, too, I guess."

Julie looked down into the trough. She picked up a knife and slowly scraped the sticky dough from her hands. Then she crossed the floor to wash them.

"Aren't you going to finish?" asked Aunt Gustava, her eyes on the dough trough.

Julie was standing in the middle of the kitchen and looked at her. They heard the car leave. Julie had turned still paler. Her voice trembled. "Let's have it, Aunt Gustava! Is *that* what you mean?"

"Well, as you said—perhaps I'm only jabbering."

They could no longer hear the car. Julie said, "Would there be any use in me taking a look?"

Now their eyes met, the young and the ancient ones. Aunt Gustava could suddenly keep absolutely silent.

Julie pulled out a drawer and picked up a big bunch of keys. Her hands trembled. She looked again at Aunt Gustava, who sighed mightily and said, "Oh, these men—"

Julie put the keys in her apron pocket and went out.

Aunt Gustava remained sitting in her chair, looking down on her stomach. She knew nothing, but she knew what she knew. She knew men were a damned nuisance. They got notions. One must keep one's eyes on them, then everything was clear as daylight. Stupid they were also. Hadn't she herself been sitting in this very corner telling the police a thing or two? And what had they done? They only said please answer their questions and forget about the rest.

Sometimes things might be wrong with girls too. Only look at Julie. She was a fine girl, as far as Aunt Gustava knew, but she had been shamelessly hasty to secure house and home for herself; and her father was a little off. And so was her mother, one might say. And she had been in the kind of homes where they send depraved parents' children. And Erling and Felicia. And Tor Anderssen, that drooler—

All this added up to a plain sum in mathematics, to Aunt Gustava's

common-sense mind. Julie was one, the gardener two, Erling three. One
of them had stolen from Felicia. And sometimes picked up other objects,
to make it less apparent. She found no others to put on her list; it must
be one of them. Now Julie had been sorted out, and Aunt Gustava
allowed herself the human weakness to discount her whilom drinking
companion. There remained only the gardener. The murderer was more
difficult. It could not have been any one of them. Well, well, my dear
Lord, you must know my husband never touched my pants, well, I
mean, not when they were hanging on the line. But do look at my good
intention, and anyway, he had his notions at times.

She waddled in to the living room, where through the window she
could see the chimney and part of the roof on the gardener's house. Aunt
Gustava looked at the clock and sat down at the window. Half an hour
must have passed when a black, nasty smoke rose from the chimney.
Aunt Gustava studied the smoke as if it might tell her something, and it
did: the thief was Tor Anderssen.

Smoke was still pouring forth when Julie appeared among the bushes
and, almost exhausted it seemed, approached Venhaug. In one hand she
carried a table napkin or a piece of cloth with something in it. She went
into the kitchen, put her burden in a cupboard, and banged the door
shut. The contents of the cloth had clattered.

Aunt Gustava had regained her chair before Julie returned but did not
hide the fact that she had been watching. "What was it you burned,
Julie?"

Trembling and hoarse, Julie replied, "I only took—only pieces of
jewelry and such. The rest I put in the fireplace and poured kerosene
over it."

"I thought as much."

"How did you get on to it, Aunt Gustava?"

"Ah, well, you see, men—they get their notions."

"And the other—?"

Julie's voice broke. "That other, Aunt Gustava—you who are so
wise?"

"No, Julie, that other, that's something I don't think we'll ever know
now. That poor devil is gone. But you see, the police, they're so eager to
put their claws into someone, and now they can at least cage up a
gardener—"

"You keep quiet about this, Aunt Gustava!"

"Well, I thought as much. There's already been enough nonsense
about Felicia and if they get to know about this as well—"

Julie raised her hand as if ready to strike. "Stop it, Aunt Gustava!"

Aunt Gustava quickly dried her eyes with the back of her hand. "It's a peculiar thing, my little girl. To get to be as old as I, I mean. Then the most peculiar things can happen which one never sees, yet one has seen them anyway, Julie, and you must never trust men, of whatever kind they may be, that I want to tell you, for they have their notions. One must hold them by the ears, and keep an eye on each finger, and never pay the slightest attention to what they say."

She added, pathetically, "They will 'fall by their own counsels.'"

The rest of a cold beef roast stood within reach on the kitchen counter. Aunt Gustava pulled it toward her and looked for something with which to slice it. Julie handed her the bread knife. "Help yourself, Aunt Gustava!"

Aunt Gustava cut herself a fairly good-sized slice. "I must always have something to chew on before dinner," she said, "to deaden the painful appetite a little. Otherwise I'll eat too much and grow too fat."

She cut herself one more appetite-deadener and said, with her jaws full of meat, "I don't suppose they thought I knew anything about that thievery, eh? But Aunt Gustava knows when to listen well. They must have thought it was you, my little girl?"

At last the tears came. Julie brushed them away and said, "I suppose they did. Like you."

"No, not I," said Aunt Gustava calmly, and chewed on. "But men are terrible in that way. Now you'll see the gardener take off this evening, and then we'll have one less of them."

• The lightning struck from Venhaug

Jan asked, "You haven't by any chance let slip anything about that drive Tor Anderssen took the evening before *you* left?"

"The possible connection did not occur to me until so late," said Erling, "that it seemed quite unimportant to mention it. Once I thought of it, I have hesitated even to speak to you about it."

"I think it must be so. It somehow fits the man. I'm not so sure he was out for revenge—I don't know of course, I don't even know that he did it. It could be that his dark mind thought up some other valid reason to go out and kill. Perhaps he thought we were at war again; you strike, I strike. He was sorry when peace came to the country. By the way, did that journalist hit the nail on the head when he speculated about a second visitor at Torvald Ørje's apartment the evening after the murder?"

"Right on the button. As if he had been there himself."

"What did it look like? I mean, was there anything to give one a definite clue?"

"No. It was really a strange situation. And equally strange that for a few seconds I wondered if it had been done by a man or a woman. I couldn't come to any conclusion, haven't now either. There is a lot of talk about male and female methods, you know, but I don't take much store in them. Some time ago I was with a cartoonist and his wife. They showed me a drawing done by a woman. I happened to make some remark about female lines. I shouldn't have. They pulled out a stack of drawings and wanted me to tell which ones were drawn by women and which ones by men. I dared not even try to guess. Once a book of mine came out under a female pseudonym. The reviewers swallowed it hook, line, and sinker, and discovered the influence of other women writers.

"When it comes to murder, one can find examples that fit any preconceived idea as to the behavior of fragile womanhood. But this is pure romanticism. I have never in my life met a woman who was fragile. If you read various foreign papers you constantly see reports of female criminals, and every time it's pointed out as a rarity, even though practically an identical report was in the paper the day before. It's an axiom that 'fragile' women use poison, and men a sledge hammer; we _wish_ to believe it is so, and it _must_ be so, but equally often the case is just the reverse; but without changing our conviction concerning the mild woman who gently kills us with strychnine, while the brutal man uses an ax, plowshare, or empty bottle. You know the saying about a drunken woman being such a sight, and there is something to it, but if there is a difference in the behavior between the sexes in such a situation, then I believe the man takes the prize. It is madonna-worship that is rampant again; a woman must not shout or drink, this she must let the man do alone; she must be a blue flower in the field to be eaten by the first bull-calf passing by. It's also an axiom that if a woman falls she falls much lower than the man. Can you tell me how she could manage _that?_ The answer is simply that you feel insulted when she stinks of sewer to a degree you can't sleep with her. But she too might have a sense of smell and object to men who carry on and smell like old drunkards. Those who insist a woman's degradation is so much worse than a man's will always as a last and deciding argument ask you what you would say if you saw your mother or sister like that. If such an argument means anything at all, it must be that the mother or the sister has nerves of steel wire and wouldn't at all object to seeing her male counterpart in a corresponding state of degradation. Where then is the mild fragility and the woman to be protected?

"The method used with Torvald Ørje at Maridalsvei, in my opinion, points as much to a woman as to a man, even though the papers might profit more by making it out a woman. It was not a pill in a cup of tea, which either might have figured out. It was a crushed head which also either one could have perpetrated. It ought to be obvious that it is a situation a murderer is able to create which decides how the murder is accomplished. When it comes to hitting hard, well, not even this is a male specialty; not even when a doctor states that the blow has been delivered with a force indicating a man; doctors seem to forget there are small men and big women."

"Did you look for anything? Did you investigate anything?"

"No, all I could do was to disappear and not touch anything at all And I don't suppose you think I had been drinking? You must have read in the papers what I did. I couldn't have described it more in detail myself."

"Was everything you observed mentioned in the papers?"

"In some ways not. When I read that only one blow had been delivered, with some blunt instrument, I felt as if walking against a red light. I began to suspect some trap but couldn't figure out what. Because it did not agree with what I had seen. Then came the post mortem report, which repeated the same thing. You know, if someone had shown me that head at an interrogation and asked how it came to look like that, I would have said it must have been crushed by a pile-driver. I must say it pleases me you have a new gardener."

Jan turned away, as he said, "Tor Anderssen has strengthened his alibi, even though he needn't. After this, no one would suspect him of Felicia's murder."

"It has bothered me since I began to think of Tor Anderssen," said Erling. "I'm unable to understand how the police have missed getting on his track. When they made so much noise about my journey to Oslo, one might think they would have inquired who else was away from Venhaug."

"I guess you weren't aware of it, but if it is Tor Anderssen, he knew what he was doing: everyone here went to some party in Kongsberg, except Julie, Aunt Gustava, and you and me. I don't think he would trust us exactly either, but he must have known the servants inadvertently could have said something. So he waited until that evening. Don't you see?—actually he could feel pretty safe if he avoided being seen in Oslo. No one here was suspected of anything, and no one would be, because the police, the papers, all were immediately led on the wrong track with their theory of a murderer's having been killed by a fellow criminal. *You* happened to be mixed up in it because you had been seen in Oslo. The police didn't think you fitted into the picture. Nor anyone else here at Venhaug. Why would they ever suspect revenge?"

"But Julie and Aunt Gustava?" asked Erling. He felt confused; had Jan wanted to protect him?

"I had to tell Julie not to mention anything about Tor Anderssen taking the car that evening. It was of no consequence, I told her, but the police would start poking in it and something else might turn up. I don't know how much she swallowed of that explanation. I'll explain the rest to her some other time."

"She must have seen through you. Was she frightened?"

"I can't say. She thought for a moment, and her reply was a little unusual. She told me when she first came to Venhaug, after she had been here only a couple of months, she stopped talking about anything here."

Erling had nothing to say.

"As far as Aunt Gustava is concerned, she had definitely drawn her conclusions. She won't say a word; she'll carry it to her grave."

"If there is room enough," said Erling, dubiously.

Jan let the joke pass and said, "Aunt Gustava is a most remarkable phenomenon. I have known her always. She is among my earliest memories. She is like my parents—they also could not tolerate anything being blown up into a sensation. Only people with empty lives pursue such. Aunt Gustava is curious, but she never carries tales. It might look bad for almost anyone around here if she did. Her policy has been to hoard what she hears. In a way, she has earned her bread by her silence. But in this case something else enters in; I guess you know she has Julie to thank that she wasn't sent to the old people's home, but instead has her own cottage here where she can enjoy her cider and eat all she can cram in. I might almost go so far as to say: a secret is best preserved when given to Aunt Gustava's keeping. I believe she is thinking Tor Anderssen has met his obligations, in a sense. She doesn't doubt that he killed Torvald Ørje. But you may be sure she'll keep it to herself. I sometimes picture Aunt Gustava sitting alone in her cottage, stretching one of her ears and talking into it like a funnel, confiding in herself."

There was something Erling wished to ask, but felt it was difficult. At last he let it out, "Tell me, Jan, what do you think of this other business with Tor Anderssen?"

Jan strode across the floor and came to a stop in front of the liquor cabinet. He took out two glasses, put them on the table, and filled them with cognac. When they had emptied them and Jan had poured another one for Erling, he fetched a cigar and lit it. Erling stuck to his cigarettes.

Jan said, "What do I think? I prefer to discount his pathological collection mania; only a sort of weakness in a lost man. A collecting nature, as you call it. I've read about fetishism and such and recall some from my adolescent days. Something that has remained with him. Julie wants us to forget it.

"But if it was the matter of Felicia's murder you have in mind, then I want to tell you that in spite of all attempts to find something else, I have not for one moment had any doubts, and do not have any now. I cannot put my finger on any individual, but I know the riff-raff who are behind this misery that has struck us."

"Now it has become Julie with the Birds," he interrupted himself, and sat for a long moment watching the smoke from the cigar in his hand.

"*They* have no doubt," he continued calmly, "that we know who sent the Werewolf after Felicia. A little while ago you were stirred up about male or female methods, but the more I think through this, I can't get away from the belief that a woman was mixed up in it. She wanted to strike everyone here, but Felicia above all, for she knew that that would hit us the worst. I know quite a few who might wish us evil, but only one or two I could suspect of this. But it could also be some avenger we don't know."

He pondered a while. "A man would first think of killing the one he considers the male head of the business he has in mind. But we don't know what business is involved, or which one among us could be considered the head. I believe it was a woman.

"In any case, we do know the group or groups that have fostered the Werewolf that struck here. And it was intended that we should understand. As much as I have been able to, I have tried to learn if Felicia had been enticed to bring along money; in that case it must have been cash she had lying around, but I never knew her to have big sums. Julie says the same. She had written no check. Thus it was not robbery, not even camouflaged robbery. It looks to me like a token act, a sort of calling card.

"Therefore *they* could never doubt that if someone struck back, the strike would come from Venhaug. They would have thought so under any circumstances, so I'm glad they're right. And how do I like it that it happened to be Tor Anderssen? Fine! It seems fitting that the Werewolf in person came from Venhaug."

• Eros and the deathwatch beetle

Erling walked over the black slate flagstones and saw through the white birches the contours of Old Venhaug, which was now his home. There I will sit and look at the pensioner's cottage, where Aunt Gustava will sit and look at Old Venhaug. He smiled. I'll sit many a good day yet and share a mug of cider with Aunt Gustava. Was it really ordained in the stars that she would be the last one? Life has indeed brought me plenty of one thing and another, and finally it has brought me Aunt Gustava.

In a few days it would be May. Today was the first evening of Spring after a long winter. From the top of one of the birches a blackbird was still singing in the twilight. Julie and Jan had gone to bed an hour ago; he himself had remained sitting in the living room, looking at the portrait of Felicia which now had been placed between the enlarged photographs of her brothers. Jan, unlike Erling, could not be alone. He found no peace after the sun had set. Jan himself thought this feeling would now soon abate; it was already lessening, he had said to Erling when they were alone for a moment, "and as long as Julie is with me nothing can happen to *her.*"

Erling did not share in his fear. The one to suffer most in the dark now was that unknown one, and that person was gone with the wind, as Aunt Gustava put it. Erling had discussed it with her only once. She had been quite sharp where Tor Anderssen was concerned. But Aunt Gustava could not be lured into any insinuations, even if she had speculated in some definite direction. She voiced the opinion that it must have been a man, for men got all kinds of notions in their heads, and now he was gone, and it hadn't been God's will, what that fool had done, even stupid men could understand that much, and if they thought it was God's will, then they were only trying to invent ideas about Our Lord, and they would all "fall by their own counsels."

Aunt Gustava herself had no intention of falling by her own counsels, as she now approached ninety, and had pressed Erling to promise her a wheel chair "when my knees go real mean." Aunt Gustava's disintegration had begun slowly, from below, but it had taken more than twelve years to reach the knees. Erling looked tranquilly forward to the day when he would be wheeling Aunt Gustava about Venhaug in an elegantly chromed chair, and had promised to wheel her right up to the graveside in it. This had raised her ire and she had prophesied that "fire would destroy the blasphemer's house." He could never quite figure out if she was wiser than most or a little feeble-minded, but either way he liked Aunt Gustava. Between meals he often came and gave her food through the window of her cottage.

Erling was not so sure that Julie and Jan had started their conjugal life on an especially good foundation, but he said nothing about the matter, and he himself had always voiced the opinion that no love resembled an earlier one, and each new one must be measured by its own standards. He himself had sought women when he was afraid, but had not simultaneously sent his father-in-law to commit murder. That Julie's devotion to Jan must lead her to where she now was, had been completely obvious, but there was something about Jan he didn't understand. He himself could not dream of having anything to do with a woman for a long time to come, perhaps never. He had loved many, and one girl he had loved had died suddenly from eating poisonous mushrooms. It had taken two years before the dead one stopped coming between him and other women.

Yet, always everything happened *differently*. It would not be a corpse to interfere this time—a dead one, but not a corpse. What interfered now was not one single object, but everything that was Felicia. It was a black, clucking hole in the Numedal River and the Werewolf that caught her there. It was almost becoming a habit of his to walk every evening to the place where the hole had been and look for a moment down the stream where she had disappeared. She would never be found now, and this seemed to him fitting. But among the many visions and memories and moods there was one tie that held him completely, and he felt that that tie would never break—it was a prayer, a tender call he heard: Always it was you, my Erling; I was the born one-man's-woman and always it was you. But you crushed it for me, you put your heel on my dream, you, my Erling, who must act the son of the limping village tailor, long after he was dead in your heart. But behind a soiled and defiled dream I remained faithful to you every hour from the moment I met you until the Werewolf took me, I, Felicia, who never wished to have anyone but my Erling.

She had bequeathed him a crushed dream, she would not wish him to meet other women, it was high time he became faithful to her, she had wanted it that way—Felicia, the woman who became too strong for him and refused to bear him a child. Now she had him and so it must remain. He could never go to another woman after having seen that black hole. She whispered to him from somewhere out there in the early spring night, from the forest down in the Numedal valley. She sent him a message through the words Queen Gunhild gave Hrut Herjolvsson to take along on the journey when he wished to leave her, but there was no longer a curse in the words after a thousand years had passed:

Had I so great power over you as I believe, then I put this burden on you that you will never carry your desire to fulfillment with the woman you expect to find in Iceland.

Let it be so, Felicia, until we meet in Erlingvik.

He stopped between the tall birches and listened to the blackbird. He smiled wanly to himself. Jan Venhaug was fifteen years younger than he, and must have a different view in many matters. What have you actually thought, Jan, of the threads that were spun, up to the night you lay down to sleep with my daughter and made me the old pensioner on your estate?

Now he could see clearly, without irritation, that fate had lavished on the tailor's son all he could wish. By long and devious ways he had been given all he had asked. There would be no complaint if the hammer one day should fall. He had been a puppet in the hands of unknown powers, a person who strangely enough had always felt humiliated and a little ridiculous because he had gained people's favor and people's hate, and during the last dozen years also people's envy.

And then? He recalled a late, mild and misty summer night when he and Felicia had walked over to Old Venhaug. She had held him by the fingers of one hand and pulled him, pretending that he was reluctant, and had recited:

> Ride, ride rouse,
> To the miller's house,
> Where nobody's home,
> But a rat and a mouse,
> And a little fellow-nick,
> Who says dicke-dick,
> Dukke-dick.

He entered Old Venhaug where nobody was at home, except a rat and a mouse and the deathwatch beetle in the wall, which said dicke-dick, dukke-dick.

• It happened in Felicia's time

The following morning Erling was standing at his window, watching a new workday begin at Venhaug. When he went to bed last evening he had wondered if he actually had any insuperable desire to awaken again. Now he couldn't understand it.

During the night he had slept well, for the first time in months, better even than in his good days. A bad dream had awakened him, but he had shaken it off and gone to sleep again. Now he remembered it clearly. Once when Erling had happened to mention Gulnare, Felicia had said that she would have liked to meet him when he was sixteen.

"How silly," he had replied, "you couldn't have endured the sight of me—besides, you weren't even born."

"I know," she had said, seriously, "but that has nothing to do with it, how old I was, or even if I didn't exist: my desire is equally great."

He knew she wanted all that was his. She could never reconcile herself to that first-love time she had been denied and never would know. Someone else had received it. Not she. She had loved him deeply. One time she had said she would have liked to be his twin sister so they could have held hands through life. He had never divulged anything to her about Gulnare and Mrs. Kortsen. Gulnare she had heard about, but surely not the connection with Mrs. Kortsen (he wasn't quite sure). He had been afraid of what he might read in her face had she ever learnt whom she *also* had struck that time when she avenged her brothers.

Once more he had thought through the situation which had created these enmities and sharpened them. Theoretically it was all meaningless, without roots in reality, to discuss the war-killings that were so absolutely in a class by themselves. It was completely senseless to call them political murders, which would have covered something quite different. The liquidations in Norway could not be compared to anything that had happened or been experienced before. They were a self-defense, thrust upon them during a gangster regime, and he had never heard anything other than that all the killers today were completely free from regret. He himself was. Those who shot informers and other traitors, had worked as soldiers in war. The means might take various forms against any enemy that flouted human rights and with hands dripping blood boasted and preached high-mindedness and nobleness. All came down to sober mathematics: that or that man will cost us so and so many lives if we don't take *his*. No one had shuddered crossing an informer's grave. There could never be any debate about this, not even when those who carried weapons declared to their accusers: You were not in my shoes, you sat at home, attended to the interests of the foreigners—or, you kept quiet as mice and had nothing to say until you attacked *us*—after the danger was passed. They had hid under the beds in those days when all suns were extinguished; now they abuse us because *we* did not follow a conscience they now say they had sixteen years ago.

Everything had been upside-down. Thousands had been sent from the country as slaves, other thousands had been driven into exile. How many thousands had been murdered? What redress had been given the one-time slaves? None. The official watchword during the war had been: no honor except for traitors; it seemed in these latter days about to become a reality. After thirteen years since Norway and Denmark regained their liberty, who was now the spokesman? Could anything be discerned except vapid, quarrelsome self-righteousness among those who sat at home chewing their nails at election time in Scandinavia? First it became un-dangerous to say which horse one would have backed if one had dared back any, then it became crafty to join the masses of people with a bad conscience, and the perhaps not quite so many who now showed quite clearly which side they had chosen in their hearts. For them no internment laws were written, and they were not black-listed by the overlords. Physically this would have been impossible.

He shed his bitter thoughts as he espied the new gardener walking between the greenhouses, smoking his morning pipe, a peace pipe. He pondered the phenomenon Tor Anderssen Haukas; one evening he had come to Jan and said he must leave at once, for there were ghosts at Venhaug.

Tor Anderssen was not the only one to discover this. It is human nature to hold on to a sensation as long as possible; therefore its life must be prolonged with ghosts. This invention of Tor Anderssen could have been painful to him if his alibi had been less definite.

The following morning Erling had been called in for a council of war. Julie had confessed to Jan. There they had sat, Julie, Jan, Aunt Gustava, and himself, without much being said, yet they had to make a decision.

Julie insisted that all be kept secret, and they let her have her will. Jan had not said a single word, but the other two knew he would agree with Julie. The police had gone into every detail about Tor Anderssen at the time of Felicia's murder and it was proved beyond doubt that he did not do it. Must they then let the police dig into all this other business? The police would undoubtedly be anxious to pursue this new lead, but all of them knew it would divulge nothing. "Aunt Gustava and I," said Julie, "would never have said a word about it, if it hadn't been that I can't live here at Venhaug as a thief. Felicia would have agreed about this. She would also have agreed that this Tor Anderssen business must not be spread through the national press, and perhaps even abroad."

"You're right!" interrupted Aunt Gustava. "I would have felt the same if it had been from my bureau drawer he—"

All ended up in a forced smile—Tor Anderssen was safe. Jan had intended to say right along, "Whatever Julie wants, and then, never another word about this."

"I only want to add this," said Aunt Gustava, "it's now clear why poor Felicia thought it was Julie. How could she imagine it was a man—but I tell you—"

Jan raised his hand, and they were denied information about the notions lurking in male heads.

The new gardener, enveloped in his smoke clouds, was walking toward his cottage. They had looked with disbelief at him when he came to Venhaug, for never had a description fitted so well as Felicia's of the old gardener at Slemdal. All was there, the white locks, the age, the friendly smile, the trustworthiness, the serenity. He had asked that the birds be left in Felicia's greenhouse.

"I feel I recognize him," Julie had said, "but the one Felicia knew must have been a hundred by now, so unfortunately it couldn't be him."

Erling was again thinking of his dream, which must have risen from what Felicia had said about wishing she had met him when he was sixteen. He had met her there in the yard, he had felt it must be she. She was very young. How old he himself was he could not understand, but in the dream he seemed to have passed through several age periods, not chronologically, but round and about in his ages. Felicia had asked why he never returned, but he did not understand what she meant, and did not wish her to discover she was not Felicia at all. She was Gulnare whom he dragged into the hay and raped. She hit and kicked, pleaded and cried, but could not escape. As far as he could remember it was the first time since puberty that, awake or in dreams, he had considered the encounter with woman as a deserved, cruel, lascivious, and sneering punishment. He had awakened in a cold perspiration, in time to keep from vomiting.

From where he was now standing he could see part of the roof of Felicia's greenhouse. Inside there, sitting on a chair feeding a fledgling, she had said to him, "I feel so strangely sure I will never be forgotten. In the neighborhood here they'll one day say: It happened in Felicia's time."

Your time, my time, our time, our forefathers' time. One said it without meaning anything in particular. Your days, my days, our fathers' days. Words once sated with meaning, sated with nostalgia. Felicia no longer shares time with me. She has used up her days.

She would be right. She would be remembered, but the memory is nothing to the dead who have no days and don't know they have been, don't know they existed once on the wave of time, don't know they showed their faces in time's gliding mirror. No one lives in his own saga. It is in your consciousness and mine they are a saga. One widens one's consciousness with one dearly loved, with one's dead child, or dead friend, they are nowhere else, they are obliterated from the picture. God's kingdom is within you, nowhere else.

She was married to Jan Venhaug, one of my forebears who took a woman from outside, after one of the great wars, they will relate. That was very long ago. It is told she brought many new customs to Venhaug. The old people said she went to the underground demons and never returned, but it has also been said that they pulled her down into the Numedal River.

What we see now is only the end, Erling said to himself. I will take up what went before. I will dig it all up and begin with the spring night of 1934, when she and I had our fate linked together so that in many ways it became one. Some day I will walk across the yard to New Venhaug, and tell Jan and my daughter Julie: "Look here," I will say. "I've been sitting at Old Venhaug and have written down all that happened in Felicia's time, about Norway in peace and Norway at war, as seen by Erling from Rjukan."

With this accomplished he might quit story-telling and move to another Venhaug; it is called Erlingvik, and there he will find Felicia.